SCARLET OAKS

AND THE

SERIAL

CALLER

A SCARLET OAKS NOVEL

MICHAELA JAMES

This book is a work of fiction. Names, characters, places, and incidents are products of the author's imagination or are used fictitiously. Any resemblance to actual events or locales or persons, living or dead, is entirely coincidental.

Copyright © 2017 by Michaela James
MichaelaJames.net
MichaelaJames.co.uk

All rights reserved, including the right to reproduce this book or portions thereof in any form whatsoever.

ISBN-13: 978-0-9828409-2-4

Published 2017 by LW Media Group Ltd
LWMediaCo.com
Printed in the United States of America

Cover image acknowledgments:
Spondylolithesis, iStock.com Contributor (upper front)
Denis Mishchenko, Dreamstime.com Contributor (lower front)
yevgeniy11, Shuttersstock.com Contributor (pig back)

Unfailingly supportive, fearlessly protective, unceasingly patient, and surpassing my Mr. Darcy fantasy daily.

This is for you, Doug. I love you.

Acknowledgments

A huge thank you to my wonderful friends, Michelle Farren, Mindy Flannagan, Lisa Carter and Eileen Clark, who read, critique and always support me.

PROLOGUE

If pressed and able, Miranda might admit what transpired that cold and foggy night wasn't wholly unexpected. After all, her quiet and unassuming husband was undoubtedly a sociopath.

Miranda's own frustrations may have clouded her ability to register his. Why, after months of barely a civil word between them, would he offer her a relaxing spa treatment?

Maybe she was less intuitive than she chose to believe. A sad revelation to experience at the moment your head is forced beneath freezing water.

Green hues swelled and undulated above her. Light from the Golden Gate Bridge alternately shimmered and twinkled atop the soft and tranquil waves. Miranda's lungs became agonizingly dense, screaming for some relief. A burning pain encompassed her rapidly constricting throat. Just when her body could take no more, comforting warmth enveloped her. Mother must have added hot water to the bathtub. Miranda relaxed into it, feeling nothing but absolute peace.

1

Happiness, like a tray of long stemmed, cut crystal wine glasses, held high aloft a sea of merrymakers … can be precarious.

The acne scarred young waiter, with hair the color of polished copper, had at that moment his own definition of happiness. Balance. In his case, the noun achieved the verb. An even distribution of weight enabling someone or something to remain upright and steady. If he managed to keep all the champagne glasses in a steady position, they wouldn't fall. Clearly, Mr. Voonburg, the headwaiter, didn't think his new charge looked nervous enough. Sidling up to the young man as he exited the kitchen, Voonburg reminded him each glass was worth sixty-nine dollars and seventy-five cents.

Joe Oaks, somewhat mesmerized by the shards of blue, yellow and red, playfully swimming above the young waiter's left shoulder, declined the offer of champagne. Turning to his daughter as the waiter moved on, he confided, "I didn't want to offset his balance."

For the last few months, frankly more like years, Joe had been offsetting or comparing the value of one thing with another.

Was anticipated happiness, more important than keeping his family intact? How many of his friends, if owning the truth, would admit they regretted their choice of life partner? Why should Joe seek to escape what so many of his peers endured?

Looking at his wife, Joe observed the familiar jewel adorned hand, placed upon her throat as she laughed. One of the men surrounding her and their two daughters must have said something amusing. If memory served, which it did all too well, a sequence of actions would now follow. A slight tilt of the head as the chin lifted, glossed lips separating, and heavily made up eyes, seductively narrowed.

Marilyn Oaks felt Joe's gaze upon her. Confused as to the reason, she gave him a brief, fake smile. Painfully aware her husband found her vacuous, she angled her back to him, effectively returning her attention to the young Policeman.

Distracted by thought, Joe's eyes skimmed but never focused on the bobbing heads belonging to the who's who of Aptos. Enticed from their million dollar homes to see and be seen, they celebrated Aptos Police Captain Murry, or Mick, as Joe knew him, receiving a Medal of Honor.

Unaware at the time, how the words would haunt him, Joe clearly remembered his parents' comments from almost two decades earlier. They'd met Marilyn a handful of times and subsequently heard his intention to marry her. "Joe, she is beautiful and full of fun. But do you share a respect and admiration? Will she challenge you, make you want to be a better man?"

Joe had, to his later shame, dismissed their advice as old-fashioned and out of touch.

In fairness to Marilyn, she was unchanged since their wedding day. Sadly, here lay the problem. Still beautiful and, if he'd had a glass of wine or three, still fun. But, that fun loving, stunning girl, never grew into a woman he could respect. His wife still had to be the center of attention, still needed to be the prettiest girl in the room.

Forced from these musings by the arrival of his son, Trent, Joe readied himself for an introduction. The young lady Trent appeared quite taken with was Lisa Nordeen. After a few minutes of polite small talk, Joe watched the couple disappear back into the crowd. Smiling to himself, Joe reflected on how his son was deeper than he'd been at the same age. Maybe if Joe had found beauty where others struggled to see it, he'd have a happy, fulfilling marriage today.

Many things in life are hard to plan. The day you leave your marriage is surely one of them.

Joe had waited until the children were older. When that day came, it changed to ... once the children were more settled. Then ... Marilyn needed to be less fragile ... perhaps after this next business trip. Add to this, a pesky conscience with reminders of duty and commitment and Joe felt the day might never come.

Right or wrong, the day did come. Bringing with it no real hope, albeit self-justification, of other alternatives.

Joe and Marilyn's daughter, Violet, had attended a rock concert in San Francisco, then... just never came home. A postcard arrived two weeks later, declaring she was having a blast traveling with the band and would return to Aptos when the fun ended.

Marilyn had been hysterical for days, her barrage of abuse beginning to take its toll on Joe.

In desperation, Joe had asked his mother, Rose, to drive up from San Francisco. It was a risky maneuver considering his wife and mother had never exactly been close. But he hoped an attempt at mediation might bring some calm and order to the Oaks' tempestuous home.

Rose was good, but she wasn't a magician.

Disappointingly, Trent was happy to throw fuel on the fire. Firmly in Marilyn's camp, he'd stated, "If Dad had been stricter with Violet, had not tolerated her 'hippy' behavior in high school, our family wouldn't have borne all this humiliation."

Ignoring this comment, Joe had looked over to his youngest, and at present, most sensible child. Scarlet sat quietly on the couch, some vampire inspired novel grasped between her slim fingers.

Coming to sit next to her, Joe quietly suggested, "That's either an unbelievably captivating book, or you're faking interest to escape your tumultuous surroundings."

Smiling up at him, Scarlet had responded, "When Trent makes comments like that, I'm reminded how living in a small town is akin to living in the nineteenth century. If there were a town newspaper – which of course, there isn't – Violet's first known shenanigan would have been front page news: *High school sophomore caught naked, smoking pot with three similarly dressed young men on Jackson's Dairy Farm."*

Having tuned out Marilyn's rantings and Trent's intermittent gibes, Joe and Scarlet's chuckling only ceased upon hearing Rose's voice.

"Marilyn, please," Scarlet's grandmother had urged, "the blame game doesn't get you anywhere; goodness knows you've been trying it for years now."

Scarlet bit her lip and waited for the implosion, which was sure to follow. And it did. But, Scarlet considered, there may have been a method to Gran's madness. Violet was forgotten, as was her Father's nomination for 'The most useless man in the world.' Now, it was all about Rose. How she'd always hated Marilyn, never supported her as a Mother, and spent countless hours trying to figure out ways to turn Joe against his wife.

After a brief pause, bone china collided with a stone kitchen floor.

"I've always hated these stupid teapots," Marilyn had screamed by way of explanation. "Heaven forbid, you could have given me something I actually needed," she continued, in short, shallow gasps.

All eyes were drawn to the remnants of exquisitely crafted teapots from Africa, Asia, and Europe. Gifts, carefully transported back, by Grandma Rose and Grandpa Herb, from travels abroad.

The scene was most certainly comedic. Silence filled the room while stoic family members stared intently at the broken china.

Then the tears and apologies began. Marilyn didn't really hate the teapots. She even used the one with the spout shaped like an elephant's trunk. Rose had hugged her, telling Marilyn she understood the stress she was under, that sometimes breaking things was the only remedy. No, she didn't think the teapots could be saved, but it was okay, and she should have given Marilyn something more practical.

That evening, over a Chinese takeaway, Trent had announced he was planning to propose to his longtime girlfriend, Lisa. Desperate for a diversion, the family had all, rather dishonestly, professed their excitement.

2

Joe had moved out of the Oaks' family home the following week. He'd failed to produce Violet or determine where she was. He'd failed to stop people in Aptos from whispering behind Marilyn's back and most importantly, he'd refused to shoulder all the blame. Because of these indisputable facts, Marilyn asked him to leave. Then, she appeared visibly shocked when he did just that.

Now years later, Scarlet felt there were still days Marilyn couldn't quite comprehend it having happened.

Scarlet had moved to the city upon obtaining her degree. Joe followed soon after. With his kids dispersed, there remained little reason to stay in Aptos.

Clasping a blanket around bent knees, Scarlet stared at the one photo she hadn't, as yet, torn into minuscule pieces. Max was smiling into the camera, Scarlet up at him. Photos capture a moment in time, but then it really is just a moment. If she'd gathered every picture, before destroying them, how many moments would there have been? Enough to class their relationship a happy one?

Despite regular visits to her Gran's, and now Father's, home, Scarlet had never introduced them to her boyfriend, Max. This reality had perplexed her often. Why wouldn't she introduce her live-in boyfriend to people whose opinion meant so much to her?

In hindsight, it had been a red flag. Hell, it was a row of them, waving madly in a brisk bay wind.

Scarlet was selective in what she chose to give back to Max after he left. Certainly, he could have his clothes, countless shoes, and five messenger bags. His departure was so hurried; all he'd taken was his laptop and a mountain of toiletries. It had been unpleasant, as most breakups surely are, but also quite odd. What started out as a simple debate, similar to many debates they'd shared, had turned into a full-blown rant. Max's voice had become loud and high, as he accused Scarlet of never respecting his job, or acknowledging how hard he worked. Did she have any idea what he and his colleagues went through on a daily basis? Perhaps it was time she dated a like-minded individual at the radio station. Allowing him, the suddenly put upon and tortured Max, freedom to find companionship and understanding from someone in his own intellectual field.

Scarlet had been, at the time, too stunned to be sufficiently offended. All she'd mentioned, while they ate their weekly sushi, were the long hours he was putting in, and how she wished they had more time together. She'd said the same thing over Spaghetti two weeks earlier, with only a nod and, "I know it, Babe," from Max.

Of course, during countless lonely nights that followed, Scarlet had plenty of time to guess the real reason for the outburst. The hours at work must indeed have grown longer when Max began seeing his Boss. Scarlet received this little eye opener courtesy of her good friend, Niles, who worked just three cubicles down from Max.

Scarlet proceeded to bend many ears. Mostly, the little pointy ones belonging to Niles. After a few weeks of venting, she forced herself to look inward.

Was she like her mother? Nice to look at, good fun, but beyond that, pretty shallow? She'd fought against those genes for as long as she could remember. She'd seen how hard it was for her Father to have an intelligent conversation with his wife; witnessed his exasperation at having to compliment and reassure her continually. Scarlet had gone to college, joined debate teams, and volunteered at the local soup kitchen. Her mother had pushed her and her sister, Violet, to compete in beauty contests as children. The minute Scarlet reached the age of understanding, she'd refused to partake. Working as a DJ for a radio station wasn't exactly utilizing her business degree, but Max had said he loved what she did. He'd been impressed by the level of multi-tasking and thinking on your feet, her job required.

Combined salaries had afforded them a beautiful home on Upper Terrace in San Francisco. Now, Max was living in a six-bedroom house on Pacific Avenue with his forty-seven-year-old girlfriend. This left Scarlet with two choices. Move out and find a place she could afford or... stop eating, never turn the heat on, end her social life, and never buy so much as a scarf, ever again.

Sitting on her couch in dated sweats, two pairs of socks, and one of her Gran's crochet shawls, Scarlet looked out over the city, to the bay. By standing to the far left of the window, she could see one tenth of the Golden Gate Bridge. Who needed food when you had a view like that?

Snuggled next to her, was something else she chose not to give to Max. Certainly, he'd originally wanted the little creature as badly as Scarlet had.

A friend of a friend had posted a photo on Facebook. It was a miniature pig, posing in front of a mirror wearing a pink tutu and tiara.

Scarlet and Max had fallen in love with the little animal, and the following twenty pictures they googled of pigs in unnatural scenarios, thereafter. Two weeks later, Max, after earning a particularly fat commission, surprised Scarlet with a micro pig. They named the new arrival, Prudence, delighted the neighbors by taking her on walks, and spent a small fortune on clothes and bling.

If Cynthia Reynolds at Trade Elite, or Trade Up, as Scarlet liked to call it, had been even remotely interested, Scarlet was sure she'd be sharing custody of Prudence. But, a woman like Cynthia was far too busy making millions and, Scarlet imagined with a cringe, bedding men half her age, to take care of an animal.

Amid contemplation of adding another sweatshirt, the doorbell rang. Prudence, making her usual squeals and snorts, ran to the door.

"Dammit Scar, it's cold in here!" Niles declared upon gaining entry and walking into the kitchen.

Routinely putting the kettle on, Scarlet responded, "If I keep my power bill low, I can afford my rent at the end of the month. I have a sweater you can wear."

Niles, shaking his head as he placed a grocery bag on the kitchen counter said, "Milk, tea, bread, cereal, and Oreos. All the staples a person needs to thrive and grow. Talking of growing," Niles added, "Is that pig not staying as little as the three-thousand-dollar price tag assured you it would?"

With mock horror, Scarlet whispered, "That pig is Prudence, and she's still tiny. Just a little bloated today, that's all. She's already upset she can't fit into my Louis Vuitton Neverfull purse, so be nice. I think it must have shrunk in the rain."

Niles ran a hand through his hair in frustration. "Firstly, if you sold that purse Max gave you, you could eat very nicely for a month. And secondly, Prudence *is* growing bigger. If anyone is going to be upset, it'll be that sleazy landlord of yours. He thinks you own a teacup poodle, remember?"

"I know I need to sell the purse," Scarlet volunteered, purposely skirting the issue of her pig. "Thank you for the groceries, Niles. It is quite possible I would starve without you."

Opening the tea box, he'd just bought, Niles replied, "I think the word is probable. How much longer can you last like this, Scar?"

"Well, I have a twofold plan!" Scarlet said, handing him a cable sweater she'd chosen to hold back from Max. "I'm ready to start dating again."

Niles pulled the thickly woven garment over his head. "You are?"

"Yes, I am," Scarlet voiced with assertiveness while grabbing the family size packet of Oreos and following Niles into the living room.

Niles placed two cups on the coffee table. "So how is this plan twofold?"

Nodding her head as she simultaneously stuffed a cookie in her mouth, Scarlet began, "You know my friend Mia?"

Niles removed Prudence's pillow from the couch. "Now that you've sold half your furniture, could this little lady perhaps sleep on the floor?"

Scarlet offered Prudence a look of sincere apology, and Niles continued, "Big boobs, short skirts, hooker earrings?"

"That's her," Scarlet replied, unphased. "Mia suggested I try that speed dating thing, where you have a little timer and attempt to get to know if a person is worth spending more time with."

Looking dubious, Niles said, "Go on."

"So," Scarlet began, warming to the subject, "I'm going to do my own version. I'm going to get on all those dating sites, probably with a fake name, then have lovely men take me out to dinner. That's why it's twofold – I can eat again!"

Niles raised his blonde eyebrows. "And when they all fall in love with you, because you know they will, what then?"

Smiling sweetly at her friend, Scarlet responded, "That's the beauty of my plan. Just three dates each. That way I don't have to, you know, give anything I don't want to. If they're kind enough to feed me, I'll amuse them with witty dialogue. I won't feel bad ending it after three dates because neither of us will have had time to form a serious attachment."

Stroking Prudence's round belly, Niles said, "It seems dangerous to me Scar. Why don't you want to date any of the guys I've got waiting in the wings for you? They're all financially set and chomping at the bit to take you out."

Scarlet pulled a face. "You mean Howard, who talks about how many crunches he does each morning and looks like he plucks his eyebrows? Or Peter, who you said was ideal for me? Niles, he has six cats and will only feed them fresh salmon from that seafood company on Mission Street."

Trying not to laugh, Niles responded, "I pluck my eyebrows and what's wrong with a man who takes care of his cats? Think how well he'd take care of you."

Standing, and taking Niles' now empty cup into the kitchen for a refill, Scarlet said over her shoulder, "I appreciate your help, Niles, but I'm looking for a man I can introduce to my Grandmother."

3

Holding her breath, Scarlet steered her MINI Cooper into the local gas station on what, judging by her gauge, could only be fumes.

Twenty minutes later with a latte, she couldn't afford, in hand, Scarlet walked into the lobby of Bay Radio. Bombarded with the usual questions and comments from the receptionist ... "What had she done with her hair? Was that a new purse?" And "Wow, her boots were rockin' it." Scarlet made her way up the steep, thinly carpeted, stairs.

Nodding at fellow DJs sitting in their glass-fronted studios, Scarlet, with a contented sigh, entered her own. Looking around the familiar little cave, she decided it was time to replace some of the posters. Not, *Bruno Mars* – he'd been super sweet at the meet and greet – the signed ones must stay.

After unceremoniously pulling down *Queen* and *Poison*, Scarlet began sorting out giveaways and checking levels. Drinking her customary three dainty sips of water, she hit the switch connecting her to thousands before chatting about the next four songs in a row.

Ignoring a large neon 'On Air' sign above the door, station manager, Brian, walked into her studio.

Casually concluding with, "You're listening to the Scarlet forty," Scarlet turned off the mic and looked expectantly at her boss.

Heavy lidded eyes looked everywhere, except at Scarlet. Brian began, "We've got to talk, Scarlet. It's just not working out with Harold."

Neither of these declarations made much sense to Scarlet. She wasn't Harold, and why did this issue concern her.

Dramatically flopping onto the guest stool, Brian shook his head. "The man clearly has a drinking problem. I'm sick and tired of him showing up late if he bothers to show up at all."

Scarlet attempted to give an expression of sympathy, then after an awkward silence said, "I'm afraid I hardly know the man. I don't think I'm the one to try and help him."

Giving a wry smile, Brian retorted, "Oh, I think the man is way beyond an intervention. Besides, I'm trying to run a friggin business here, Scarlet."

Still, at a loss as to why this involved her, Scarlet suffered through the silence and waited.

Standing up and finally looking at her, Brian concluded, "The only answer is for you to take over his show. You start Monday."

With that, Brian opened the heavy studio door and walking much faster than his large frame usually allowed, disappeared down the long hallway.

Staring out at the empty corridor, imagining maybe Brian would reappear saying, *fooled you, just kidding!* Scarlet sat, with an uneasy sense of disbelief swirling in her head.

Did Brian expect her to do the top forty and Harold's show? More money would be great, but she already spent seven hours at the station. What *was* Harold's show anyway? She'd only ever met the guy at Christmas parties and, admittedly, he was drunk at every one.

Scarlet looked at her board. One more song and she was live again. Deep breaths; keep calm. This was surely all a misunderstanding, and she just needed Brian to see reason. He wasn't known for seeing it, but there was always a first time.

That evening, holding Prudence a tad too tightly, Scarlet paced back and forth in her living room. Niles, having had little success in calming her down, wasn't quite ready to give up.

"Okay, let's go over what we think we know for sure…one more time," he urged.

Having a list of things to report seemed to calm Scarlet for the moment. Kissing Prudence's damp little snout and setting her on her Little Mermaid sleeping bag, she began, "He's fired Harold. Harold's show is a call-in show for men, using sports analogies to fix their problems. The show runs from seven until midnight. And I take that job, or have no job."

Niles swore under his breath for the fourth time that evening. "And no mention of why it has to be you? No mention of who'll be doing your top forty show? No concern over the fact you know nothing about sports?"

"I don't understand it," Scarlet replied in a high-pitched whine. "Do you think he's just hoping I'll quit?"

"It's possible," Niles replied rationally. "But it doesn't seem likely when your show receives such high ratings. He knows you're a hard working, reliable employee who sells air time. So why get rid of you?"

Shaking her head, eyes filling with tears, Scarlet responded, "I don't know. He must just hate me."

Standing up and taking Scarlet in his arms, Niles said, "He doesn't hate you. Something wacky must be forcing his hand. When we know what that is, we'll go from there. Why don't you come running with Tom and me tomorrow? He just got back from Delhi. Said he couldn't find anywhere to run there that wasn't chockablock. We'll swing by at eight and no, Prudence can't come – people will stare."

Scarlet agreed the endorphins would do her good. Prudence needed a slightly larger pair of running shorts anyway. Her silver spandex ones must have shrunk in the wash.

After seeing Niles out, Scarlet, depressed and exhausted, climbed into bed. Turning off the light she attempted to disable the thought – *life as she knew it was forever altered.*

4

Employing her Gran's just get on with it attitude, Scarlet was ready to go when Niles and Tom pulled up bright and early the next morning. Even without a pig on a leash, they turned a few heads. Tom was brown as a berry after a three-week assignment in India. His dark curls were perfectly coifed and his cologne so strong, Scarlet imagined, even in the expanse of the Golden Gate Park, he was invading people's sensory space.

Niles, bless him, wore his usual mismatch of colors. Red shorts, orange running shoes and a green and purple striped t-shirt.

Scarlet ran between the two men, a high ponytail swinging from side to side. Her ensemble of white shorts and t-shirt with electric blue running shoes almost balanced the trio out to a look of normalcy.

Forty-five minutes later, with drama and glamor perfectly intertwined, Tom pronounced he couldn't possibly run another step. After blaming it on all the Masala Chai and Naan he'd consumed, he proceeded to say their next run must start at the Ferry Building. "It was time," he continued, loud enough for every passerby to hear, "they started training for their first half marathon and that, of course, is where the route begins."

Although thankful for the diversion and happy to see Tom again, Scarlet chose to spend the remainder of her weekend in a more leisurely fashion. On Sunday evening, in an attempt to stay up as late as she could, she began watching the Downton Abbey DVD collection her Gran had given her the Christmas before last. Max had refused to watch period dramas so all the finery, history, and traditions, tightly covered in impossible to unwrap cellophane, still awaited her.

From what Scarlet had heard, Downton Abbey's Lady Mary was pretty racy by last century's standards. Apologizing for the spoiler, her Gran had divulged the following...Mary treated one of her sisters horribly, showed disdain for her mother's heritage, and had numerous men falling at her feet.

Yes – a little of Lady Mary's spit and fire was just what Scarlet needed right now. If it could keep her awake until one or two in the morning, even better. Not an easy task when she was used to going to bed around nine.

Thanks to Mary's Turkish Diplomat, not to mention the nerve of the Irish Chauffer, Scarlet and Prudence didn't wake up until ten on Monday morning. Trying not to dwell on the oddness of this new schedule, Scarlet brewed some tea and gave Prudence sow nuts. After the little pig had consumed her usual one-pound portion, she stood staring at the empty bowl.

"You're still hungry?" Scarlet enquired. "It must be this fall weather. I feel the same. Lay on the carbs!" Giving Prudence a second bowl, Scarlet, thanks to Niles, ate cereal and toast while doing a little research on her new job.

The reviews on Harold's show were mixed. Some complained he was an old hack who needed to retire. Other listeners said his sports analogies helped them tremendously with their relationship woes.

"How on earth," Scarlet asked Prudence, "could a reference to sports help a relationship problem?"

Thankfully, Scarlet's new studio was situated on the opposite side of the building, avoiding the doubtless pain of walking by her old one. There were still so many unanswered questions, but this was not the time to think of them. In half an hour she'd be on the air, helping troubled Bay Area sports enthusiasts with personal issues...well, hopefully helping them!

Making a mental note of all the work needed to make her new workplace feel like home, Scarlet checked the equipment and located the websites she'd perused earlier. After some dusting, removal of empty fast food containers and adjusting of the mic and stool, she was ready to go.

With comparable ease, Scarlet introduced herself to this new audience, gave major kudos to the Giants for their World Series win and discussed the upcoming games for the 49ers.

Then, proclaiming it to be a good baseball number, she began nine songs in a row. "That should give me enough time to have a few sports analogies ready to go," she said aloud, with not even a little pig to hear her.

Uncertain as to which scenario would have been worse, no callers at all or the reality of six on hold, Scarlet attempted to control her breathing.

The first two guys were seemingly curious about who she was and what had happened to Harrold. Scarlet assured them she wasn't new to radio, but this was certainly a different and exciting avenue for her. She voiced her belief Harrold had retired, then felt sad imagining him half passed out in front of, *Wheel of Fortune*.

The third caller wanted to talk about the 49ers chances against the Redskins. Scarlet, shaky on the subject, opened the window showing stats on the game. Luckily, Rod from Modesto, evidently wanted Scarlet to hear *his* thoughts on their chances.

The fourth caller said how unimpressed he was having a woman hosting a men's relationship show. Was Bay Radio so hard up they couldn't find a male DJ to fill this time slot? While offended, Scarlet inwardly agreed with him.

The fifth caller was her first *real* relationship problem. The way the man spoke about his wife was quite bizarre. But when Scarlet thought about it, bizarre was probably going to sum up this new job of hers.

The man introduced himself as Stewart, but Scarlet could call him Stew. He spoke very slowly and after stating something would add an unnecessary self-confirmation, as if you'd doubted his truthfulness. Stew confided, his wife belittled him constantly. The woman had done it since they married two years earlier. She'd pretended to like him and find him funny, but now she didn't want sex and was only interested in his paycheck.

Something about Stewart's voice made the hairs stand up on the back of Scarlet's neck. What kind of sports advice could she give him? Wanting him off the phone and off the air, she feverishly clicked on each of the websites she'd previously opened. Panic began to set in. Finding nothing even close to appropriate for the problem he put forth, Scarlet started mumbling how sorry she was for him. With sweat beads forming on her upper lip, she repeated her circuit through sports sites. Elation, when she saw a somewhat fitting analogy, lasted but a moment. As her shaking finger went to enlarge it, the window maddeningly disappeared. In a desperate attempt to recall what she'd just seen, Scarlet suggested, "Maybe it's time you sent her for a bath."

There was a long pause. Scarlet cringed imagining how many people were laughing at her right now.

"Do you mean showers?" Stewart finally offered.

The humiliation almost complete, Scarlet said, "Oh yes, of course, showers. I just like baths more…nothing like a deep, relaxing bath."

That was it – unmitigated humiliation. She wasn't talking to busy Moms who like pampering. This was a men's relationship show. Any man listening right now was sure to never listen again.

"You think a bath would work better?" the man enquired in his slow drawl.

Wishing he'd just go away and trying to keep her voice from quivering, Scarlet responded, "I do, yes."

After Stewart hung up, Scarlet braced herself for the sixth caller. Looking at the board, she saw the light had stopped flashing. "Astonishing," she muttered sarcastically.

Leaning back and allowing her body to un-tense, Scarlet looked at the clock. *Oh, joy, just three more hours to go.* Setting up another row of nine songs, she took a deep breath thinking, *Well, it can only get better.*

5

Once a month, Scarlet packed her pepper white MINI Cooper with eighty percent pig gear. Added to this were gifts for her nephews, something from the Bobbi Brown counter for her Mom and in the little room left, a change of clothes for herself.

After strapping Prudence into her luxury console car seat, designed for dogs, but also perfect for a pig, they were ready to go.

The one and half hour drive to Aptos was more than welcome after the stress of her first week on Mending Men. Beautiful fall weather enabled Scarlet to have the top down on the MINI. Prudence, wearing a sparkly pink visor and positioned so close to Scarlet she could almost be driving, evoked priceless looks when they stopped at traffic signals.

Forty minutes into the drive, the route diverted slightly to walk the Redwood Shores Bay Trail. Prudence's leather harness strained slightly across the chest as she trotted happily alongside her owner. Scarlet sighed at the thought of having to buy a larger one. Max had returned from work one evening, shortly after he'd surprised Scarlet with Prudence, arms laden with everything one could possibly need to take care of a micro pig. Now, with evidence Prudence was not staying tiny, her diva dressing days may have to end. Breathing in the smell of damp leaves beneath her feet, mixed with the signature red bark of enormous trees, Scarlet put future expenses out of her mind. With whispers of stubborn fog in the air, the two travelers got back on the road, just a short distance left until they reached Aptos. Scarlet felt invigorated by the walk but Prudence, after being one with nature, slept for the remainder of the drive.

The MINI mastered its last curve of the winding driveway, to reveal Scarlet's mother standing outside a familiar blue front door.

On tip-toed feet, Marilyn, right arm extended, drained a painted, steel watering can into a begonia-filled hanging basket.

'It's eleven AM," Marilyn pronounced. "I was so hoping you'd be here earlier. I do miss you, Scarlet."

Popping the trunk, Scarlet responded, "I'm sorry Mom, but you know my schedule is seven to midnight now."

As if Scarlet had said nothing at all, Marilyn continued, "If you don't leave my side I guess it will be okay." Sighing, she added, "But I'm sure you plan to call on your brother while you're here. How much time will that leave us? I only get to see you once a month as it is."

"I'll stay with you the whole time, Mom. I'll visit Trent and Violet on my next visit."

"Violet!" Marilyn repeated, looking astonished. "Why would you want to visit her when she's purposely distanced herself from all of us?"

Groaning inwardly, Scarlet unstrapped Prudence from her car seat, allowing the little pig to run free in Marilyn's ample front yard. Kissing her mother on the cheek, Scarlet finally answered, "Because she's the only sister I've got. I'm certain it's impossible to get access to her anyway. I'm all yours Mom, it's good to see you. What a gorgeous day."

Smiling, Marilyn said, "Sixty-eight degrees, per that cute new weatherman on channel thirty-nine. Did I tell you I saw him in Santa Cruz? He was sitting one table away from me with a very homely young woman. Isn't it odd he wasn't with someone glamorous?"

Scarlet, unloading the trunk, looked up, "Maybe it was his sister."

Watching Scarlet struggle into the house with pig paraphernalia, Marilyn said to her daughter's back,

"I hardly think that's likely. All three of my children are good looking, I can't imagine she was related to him."

Walking back out to the car for one more load, Scarlet tried, "Maybe she's adopted."

This idea seemed to satisfy Marilyn, leaving Scarlet to brace herself for their next mundane discussion.

It took place twenty minutes later, over a cup of green tea.

"I'm thinking about moving," Marilyn declared, looking around her living room, wistfully. "I saw a darling house for sale, overlooking the Sea Scape Golf Course. The deck is practically on the green. What do you say to your Mother living on a golf course?"

Scarlet procured a shortbread cookie. "Really? You would never play when Gran wanted a fourth for her charity events."

Marilyn pursed her lips. "Well, of course, I never wanted to do anything to help that old dragon. But, this isn't about Golf. This is about the men who play Golf."

Giving an expression which she hoped resembled interest, Scarlet said nothing.

Placing a hand on her ankle and subconsciously sliding it up to her knee, Marilyn continued, "Mrs. Snow, who owns the Pharmacy, said I still look like a girl. Can you imagine? What a sweet thing to say. Then Stan, who's mown our lawns forever, said he can't fathom how I'm still single." Giving a strange little smile, she went on, "Picture this my darling ... your mother sitting out on her deck drinking something fruity with an umbrella in it, and all those rich, charming men, walking by on the green. You and your sister will be bridesmaids of course...I'm thinking lilac just above the knee, with loose stems of white roses in your hair."

Wanting to scream, *you haven't bought the house or met the man yet*, Scarlet instead declared, "Prudence could be the ring bearer."

Hearing her Mother laugh and watching her run over to hug the little Pig, Scarlet knew it had been the right thing to say. After setting up a play area and litter box for Prudence, Scarlet joined her Mother in the back yard.

"Can you believe how much this rose bush has grown?" Marilyn asked, holding pruners in one hand and deadheads in the other.

Scarlet smiled. "Wasn't this started from your wedding rose?"

Lifting the dead flowers closer to Scarlet, Marilyn, voice raised, said, "This is what I am to your Father. Great to have around while I was full of color and life. Now that I'm old and shriveled, he just throws me on a heap." At this, she dramatically threw the dead roses into a rusting wheelbarrow.

Trying not to giggle at the theatrics, Scarlet responded, "Mom, you're not old, and you're still beautiful. What did you just tell me Mrs. Snow and Stan said."

Marilyn pushed her chin out. "That's true, and those aren't the only comments I've had either."

Scarlet linked her arm through Marilyn's. "I'm sure they aren't. How's the pond? Has that netting worked at keeping the pesky Herons away?"

Mother and daughter marveled at the number of Guppies filling the old pond. After scooping away some algae and tightening parts of the netting, Marilyn went inside to start their lunch. Now solitary, Scarlet took a reminiscent roam around her childhood yard.

How long had it been since she sat under the willow tree? It seemed so claustrophobic now, but with youth's imagination, it had been the land of Queen Philippa. Better known as Barbie, Philippa had ruled with an iron hand. Violet, being the older sister, spoke for the queen. Scarlet's seemingly less attractive Barbies were there to serve her.

Walking past the faded and peeling shed, Scarlet spotted her beloved swing. Not trusting the old wood with the weight and hips of a woman, she just stood and remembered the girl. For hours and hours, she would swing, and with every leg bend, every lift of her dark wavy hair came immense happiness.

What happened to that simple childhood joy? Scarlet mused, *where did it go, why did it go?* Ironic how adults seem to spend their life searching for a happiness children can find on a wooden swing.

Over a lunch of hummus, crackers, and smoked salmon, Marilyn brought up an often-contentious topic ... Violet. Opening a bottle of red wine, needed more than wanted because it pained her so much to talk about it, Marilyn began, "Yes, your sister's back in the area, but she might as well be a million miles away. This so-called commune is simply a bunch of hippies. They never wash and just go around having sex with each other all day long."

Marilyn paused to pull a face.

Scarlet reigned in a smile. "I thought it was a little farming community, where they live independently off the land."

Marilyn almost choked on her cracker. "Farming, my eye. I've seen them shopping in Aptos."

"You've seen Violet in Aptos?" Scarlet enquired.

Marilyn daintily patted a napkin to her mouth. "No, not Violet. But hippie types!" Taking a decent gulp of wine, she added, "And they were buying beer."

"Shocking!" Scarlet retorted, the sarcasm lost on her mother.

Marilyn leaned back in her chair. "Your brother says he will never speak to her again. You know his wife, Lisa, comes from a very religious family. He can't risk being associated with this sort of thing."

Treading carefully, because with Scarlet's mother there was only one right opinion and it was always hers, Scarlet suggested, "This really isn't that scandalous. For all we know they may be a nice group of people who simply choose to live off the grid."

Marilynn gave her daughter a *you're so naïve* look before asking, "Is it my imagination, or could my Granddaughter be getting a little chunky?"

Looking at the wine bottle, Scarlet understood why chunky sounded suspiciously like shunky. The bottle was empty, and Scarlet had only consumed half a glass.

"Mother," she began, "I realize I'm completely loopy in the way I treat this little pig, but I have to draw the line at you calling her granddaughter."

Marilyn giggled. "She may be the only one I get from you. When are you going to bring a nice young man home? I don't suppose you'll ever find one as good looking as Max again. You should have held on tighter to him."

Feeling the sting, but not wanting to let it show, Scarlet responded, "The tighter you hold, the harder they squirm."

With what Scarlet perceived to be a little wave of reality flowing over her mother, Marilyn said she was going to take a nap. Scarlet agreed it was a great idea and after she cleared away the lunch things, joined her mother and Prudence in the living room. There was plenty of room to spread out on the sectional sofa. A combination of warm afternoon sun coming through the large bay window and the gentle hum of a nearby lawnmower, allowed two women and a pig, to sleep contentedly for the rest of the afternoon.

In the early evening, Scarlet delighted Marilyn with a new mascara.

"You're so lucky living in the city with all the best of everything around you," Marilyn declared. "This place is so tiny, I'm lucky if I can find a decent shampoo."

Knowing this to be a great exaggeration, and knowing she couldn't afford it, Scarlet still offered, "You let me know if there's anything you need and I'll bring it to you."

Smiling, Marilyn walked to the large ornate mirror above the fireplace and began applying her new mascara.

"How do you feel about egg drop soup and the first season of *Twilight*?" Marilyn enquired while fluttering her newly lacquered eyelashes in the mirror.

"I can't imagine one without the other," Scarlet replied with a grin.

Hours of Vampires and Werewolves made for a late night, and despite the nap, Scarlet slept well surrounded by her childhood toys and boy band posters.

The next morning was spent patiently listening to more of her mother's imagined theories about Violet's new home.

"You know no man will ever want her now," Marilyn said as they picked up fallen apples from the pink lady tree. Gratefully accepting a bag to take home, Scarlet said,

"I'm not sure Violet ever wanted to marry anyway."

"All pretty young women say that when they've got men chasing them all over town," Marilyn responded knowingly. "What do you think happens when those young women start to age?" Not needing an answer, Marilyn continued, "The men start sniffing around the younger women, and where does that leave you?"

"Out in the cold, I guess," Scarlet answered with a frown.

"You bet it does," Marilyn said, eyes narrowed. "You better get a ring on your finger while you can."

Consuming one last cup of tea, and hearing how a good daughter would visit more than once a month, Scarlet said her goodbyes before strapping Prudence into her car seat.

Feeling a little emotionally drained as she maneuvered down the windy drive, Scarlet decided once a month was just fine.

6

Going against the sometimes it's better not to know rule, Scarlet stopped by the radio station the following morning.

"Forgot my charger," she dishonestly informed the receptionist with an exaggerated look of dismay.

Turning in the opposite direction of her proclaimed destination, Scarlet stealthily crept down the long corridor and up to the window edge of her old studio.

Fighting against a scream forcing its way up her windpipe, Scarlet turned and ran into the nearest restroom. Looking at herself in the mirror, she waited until the expression staring back at her resembled one she recognized, then headed back downstairs.

"Did you find it?" the receptionist asked.

"What?" a startled Scarlet, replied.

"Your phone charger, silly," Tara responded, smiling sympathetically as if Scarlet were a little senile.

"Oh, yes," Scarlet lied, patting her purse. "The red and black stripes in your hair look great," she offered, pulling on the heavy glass door.

The young receptionist said something about adding one more color, but Scarlet was already halfway out the building. Despite her original comment, she was in no mood for hair talk.

"This is Niles," filled her vehicle before she'd even pulled out of the station's car park.

"Niles, I need you," Scarlet gushed. "Can you get away?"

"Sure, you want to meet for noodles?" came a voice sounding unfazed by the urgency in Scarlet's.

"Yes please," she replied, relieved she could share her news so quickly. "I'm coming up to Broadway. Can you do China Town?"

"Getting in the elevator now," Niles responded. "You want to say Pacific Avenue?"

"Perfect," Scarlet confirmed. "I'll get a table."

Clicking the button on her steering wheel to end the call, she breathed deeply, then felt a flood of guilt.

If Max had been right, being a stockbroker was more stressful than many knew. Niles could be juggling a million problems right now, and yet here she was, cutting to the front of the line with hers.

Feeling almost calm when Niles strode into the restaurant, Scarlet began, "Before I tell you about my latest issue, I want to say how grateful I am for your friendship."

Niles was about to say something, but Scarlet put her hand over his, asking, "Do I listen enough?"

"Yes Scar, you do," Niles said with a smile.

Letting go of his hand as the waiter brought them tea, Scarlet persisted, "Truly Niles? Please tell me if this friendship is ever too one-sided."

Niles laughed as he lifted the small clay teapot. "Your life is more interesting. And besides, after hearing about your problems I always feel better about my own."

Giving a sardonic smile, Scarlet said, "Happy to help."

They were interrupted again by the arrival of two steaming bowls of wonton noodle soup.

Content to let the dish cool a little, Niles asked, "What's up? You don't usually call me in the middle of the day."

Sighing, Scarlet replied, "Normally I would be on the air right now, playing Top Forty hits and loving my job."

Niles gave a sympathetic nod. "Right, this new gig starts at seven PM, that does suck."

Scarlet hastily swallowed a noodle. "My body clock is completely out of whack. A couple of times last week I almost nodded off during the music bed. But wait 'til you hear the worst of it."

Deducing his voice wouldn't be needed for a while, Niles began wielding chopsticks.

"Did I ever tell you about Candy?" Scarlet enquired. When Niles shook his head, she elaborated, "Her real name is Veronica. She does the traffic." Scarlet pulled a face. "It's imperative to have an on-air name like Candy when you do traffic."

Wiping a drop of noodle juice from his chin, Niles asked, "Why don't you have a radio name?"

Scarlet gave a wry smile. "I'm sure people think I do."

Niles nodded. "Good point." Pushing his bowl to the side, he suggested, "I'm sensing you're not overly fond of this Candy slash Veronica person."

Scarlet narrowed her eyes. "The girl's tops are so low cut that during our last strategy meeting, one of her boobs actually plopped out onto the conference table."

Trying not to laugh, as Scarlet clearly wasn't in the laughing mood, Niles asked, "Was she suitably mortified? What did she do?"

"Are you kidding? Scarlet responded. "She just gave her irritatingly-high giggle, and scooped it back in."

Niles refilled the small handle-less cups. "We're not just upset about her unruly bosoms though are we?"

Deflating slightly, Scarlet leaned back in her chair. "Niles, they gave her my Top Forty show. All she's ever done is traffic, and now she's hosting one of the top-rated slots in the Bay Area."

Looking intently at Scarlet, Niles said, "That is seriously messed up. What are they thinking?"

Thanking the waiter as he cleared her bowl away, Scarlet said, "That's just it…Brian doesn't think. He just does, then everyone has to scramble around trying to make his crazy decision work."

Niles grimaced. "Remind me again why he's station manager?"

"Because his mother-in-law owns Bay Radio. She's super wealthy…even by San Fran standards."

"Let me guess," Niles said, rubbing his hands together. "She's so wealthy, she cares nothing about the running or the profit-making of the station."

Scarlet sighed. "It's all one can presume."

Walking back out into the bustle and noise of China Town, Scarlet thanked Niles for lunch and, more importantly, his time.

Hugging her and saying he'd be by later in the week with provisions, Niles returned to his job, leaving Scarlet to head home and ready for hers.

Spirits were lifted slightly, first by the warm welcome from Prudence and then by three messages on the dating site.

Gary, a civil rights lawyer, and windsurfing enthusiast was, 'looking for quiet dinners with great conversation.'

Pete, a high school English teacher, loves to hike and ski. 'His ideal date is a stroll through Golden Gate Park, ending in a picnic prepared by his own fair hands.'

Allen, a photographer, professed 'his perfect evening is seeing a great play, then discussing it over a bottle of wine with a beautiful soul.'

Chuckling at their posed headshots and flowery declarations, Scarlet decided Gary would get a response. The other two sounded far too light in the food category.

Two hours later, settling in for the start of week two on the new job, Scarlet reminded herself men weren't that different from women. They too needed help understanding the other sex and making their relationships work. But why she wondered, must a sports analogy be involved. Were they that shallow? Was it truly the best way to fix their problems? After clicking on every sports analogy she could find, Scarlet routinely adjusted her mic, deciding maybe it was better not to know.

7

The station had dealt her an unfair hand, but Scarlet was determined to make it work. The curious callers were still alive and well. One man questioned whether Harold had been fired. Two more callers jumped on this bandwagon saying they'd heard him slur his words many times. Scarlet stayed neutral, doing her best to change the subject.

The last man of the night was her first repeat caller. Flooded with mixed emotions, Scarlet listened to him say, "This is Stewart, but you can call me Stew."

"Yes, I recognize your voice, Stew," Scarlet said, inwardly cringing at the memory. "How are you tonight?" she asked while clicking the mouse to wake up her computer.

"I'm calling to thank you for your help," Stewart said.

"You are?" Scarlet replied, sounding a little too surprised.

In his painfully slow speaking voice, Stewart reported, "I put my wife in a deep bath, just like you said. Yes, I did."

Reliving the humiliation of saying bath instead of shower, Scarlet replied, "That's great Stew, and things are going well for the two of you now?"

Following a long pause, Stewart said, "I'm much happier now. She doesn't belittle me anymore. No, she doesn't."

Feeling elation at this small victory, Scarlet said, "That's wonderful news, Stew. Thanks so much for calling in and letting us know how well you're doing. Please stay in touch."

Starting the song bed off with *Led Zeppelin's Stairway to Heaven,* Scarlet sat back in her chair. Perhaps she'd been too quick to poo-poo the whole sports can fix you concept.

In a continued attempt to feel more at home in her new studio, Scarlet set about putting up some of her favorite posters. There was always room for Amy Winehouse...rest in peace. *Red Hot Chili Peppers* were still rocking. Yes, maybe James Blunt was a little six years ago, but what girl hadn't had an incredible make-out session to, *You're beautiful.*

Feeling she may never be at home with her new hours, Scarlet, at just after midnight, darted to her car. Noticing the outside temperature of fifty-five degrees on the large round Tachometer, Scarlet instinctively rubbed her hands together. While turning up the heat, something caught her eye. There were, what appeared to be, wildflowers under one of her windshield wipers. Reluctantly, getting back out of the car, she lifted the wiper and removed the flowers. If it had been one or two, Scarlet would have assumed the wind had blown them there. But, this good-sized bunch, carefully positioned, certainly had human intervention. Keeping one, she threw the others into nearby bushes. Consumed with thoughts of who'd left them, she made the ten-minute drive home.

Having not used her real name on the dating site, she doubted it could be from any of the men who'd responded yesterday. Niles would have left food. Maybe they were from Max. Shaking her head, she reasoned, *Max, picking wildflowers ... never in a million years.*

Leaving the mysterious flower in the car, Scarlet put it out of her mind, affording her and Prudence a relaxing hour of mind-numbing late night television.

****

"Tom has some exciting news for you!" Niles announced, with what Scarlet knew to be forced enthusiasm, from her doorstep the following morning.

Tom and his cologne walked in a few seconds later. "Wake up beautiful, I have your favorite coffee."

Bleary eyed, Scarlet shuffled into the living room. "Guys, it's not even eight yet!"

"Sorry, Scar," Niles replied. "Tom's just so excited to tell you his latest scheme. You know he gets a little antsy when he's not on assignment."

"It is not a scheme!" Tom retorted, looking affronted. Viewing Scarlet through narrowed eyes, Tom continued, "Niles tells me you've joined one of those ghastly dating sites."

Taking a sip of her Caramel Brule Latte, Scarlet said, "This is delicious, thank you." Waving a finger in the air, she added, "But, did he also tell you how it's twofold?"

"He did," Tom replied condescendingly. "But I have a better idea…I'm going to throw you a party, full of the most eligible men in the Bay Area."

Scarlet gave Niles a furtive, *help me* look.

Stroking Prudence's soft underbelly, Niles gave an apologetic shrug of his shoulders. "Tom has a very innovative way of letting you know whom to spend time chatting with, versus who just gets a, so lovely to see you."

Shifting forwards, until he was on the very edge of the couch, Tom began, "I work with engineers who put their lives on hold to fundamentally change this world of over seven billion people. Their compassion and their knowledge of sanitation is life-saving for underdeveloped countries. We don't stay in five-star hotels when we …"

"Tom," Niles interrupted, "can we get to how this pertains to Scar?"

Tom blushed. "They're rich, too."

Niles, realizing he'd thrown his partner off track, picked up the original conversation. "Tom's idea is to introduce you to some of these engineers. The only snag being, he hasn't known many of them long enough to determine their sexual orientation."

"I know I should know," Tom admitted, throwing his arms in the air. "It's just we work so damn hard. At the end of the day, we go to our hotel rooms and crash. When we're done, we fly home."

With a half grimace, half smile, Niles reported, "Tom was up most of the night, figuring out a way for you to know who is who, or should I say, who they like." Standing up, Niles concluded, "I'm going to feed this pig before she gnaws my arm off. I'll let Tom explain his ingenious evites."

"So," Tom began animatedly, "the engineers I know for a fact are straight, received evites saying all men must wear a tie. The ones I think are straight, but wouldn't put my life on it, received evites saying to wear a striped shirt. My gay friends, I've asked to wear a bow tie. All gay men own at least one bow tie."

Coming back into the living room, Niles said, "Tom felt we had to ask some of our gay friends. Firstly, to help fill the room, but also to make you feel a little more at ease. Kind of nice knowing, not every man you meet wants to ravage you."

When both men regarded her eagerly, eyebrows raised and idiotic grins on their faces, all Scarlet could say was, "Thank you so much! I can't wait."

Tom, in a sympathetic tone, said, "We're here to help…Max dealt you an unfair hand."

8

Be kind, for everyone you meet is fighting a hard battle. It wasn't until Scarlet reached her late teens, that she discovered Plato had said this over twenty-three hundred years before her Gran.

"I do understand, Dave," Scarlet soothed. She and the Bay Area had been listening to him rant for the last fifteen minutes.

"So what if I forget to unstack the dishwasher," Dave continued. "Is that a crime? Yes, I like to watch the 49ers on Sundays. What man doesn't, right? But you know what she does, Scarlet? I bet you can guess what she does."

Sighing inwardly, Scarlet replied, "I'm not sure I can, Dave."

Speaking in a slightly quieter tone, as if his wife were in the next room, Dave elaborated, "She holds out on me, Scarlet. I have needs. What man doesn't, right? Can you guess how long she makes me wait?"

"I couldn't hazard a guess, Dave," Scarlet forced herself to reply.

"Three weeks!" he responded, in almost a whisper.

Unable to ignore the flashing light signaling four callers on hold, Scarlet said, "I think you and your wife need to huddle, Dave. It's evident you need some sort of a compromise. If you could maybe just watch the last half of the game. And perhaps your wife could be clearer about what chores are yours to get done on a daily basis. There's a good chance these issues could be resolved."

Dave's subsequent tirade made it clear, suggesting a man only watch the last half of a football game was akin to women only watching the part of Titanic where the ship sinks.

Scarlet voiced apologetically, "Wish I could have helped more, Dave, please stay in touch." Thankfully, the next caller was Rod from Modesto, asking her thoughts on the 49ers' chances against the New York Giants. Feeling smug, Scarlet rattled off some facts. She'd done her homework, knowing Rod would call sometime this week. He allowed her a minute, it might have even been a minute and a half, then entertained the Bay Area for a good twenty minutes with his predicted stats on the upcoming game.

Two calls had dropped and fearing she was seconds away from losing the one remaining, Scarlet interrupted with, "You're so knowledgeable; it's great to get your input every week, Rod."

Basically, hanging up on him, she flicked the switch, saying, "Thank you for calling Mending Men. This is Scarlet, how can I help?"

"I used to listen to you do the Top Forty," the man began.

Feeling nostalgic at the mere mention, Scarlet replied, "Thank you so much. I'm happy you found my new program. Who am I talking with?"

"I'd rather not give my name," came a gravelly reply.

Thrown for a moment, Scarlet took a breath. "What can I help you with tonight?"

"How many other people are with you at the station right now?" came the man's response.

His tone, coupled with the question, had Scarlet's heart rate increasing by what felt like tenfold. "We always have security here," she lied. "And I have colleagues working in the adjacent studio."

"Is that right?" the man asked sarcastically. "I think you only have your P.I.B. and who knows if they're even still there."

Attempting to stay calm, Scarlet said, "I'm sorry caller, but if you don't have a relationship problem, it's time for our nine in a row."

"I didn't say …." The man began, but Scarlet cut him off, playing, *Chasing Cars, by Snow Patrol.*

Barreling out of her studio, Scarlet shouted, "Sylvia!" Deducing she was not close by, Scarlet ran down the corridor still calling the girl's name. Shaking and panting, Scarlet stopped at the top of the stairs, fumbled with her phone, and dialed Niles. Breathlessly giving him a synopsis of the scary man's call, she took the steep stairs two at a time, before practically falling into the lobby. After screaming Sylvia's name again, the sought-after girl finally appeared.

"What on earth is all the hullaballoo about?" Sylvia asked in a tone that suggested the art of speaking was exhausting to her.

Seeing another person, who wasn't wielding an axe, allowed relief to outweigh Scarlet's anger.

"Sylvia," Scarlet gulped for air, "where were you?"

"In my uncle's office," the girl replied as if that were a perfectly reasonable place for her to be.

Having calmed down a little, Scarlet noticed Sylvia's state of undress. Her denim shirt was untucked and half-unbuttoned. She had no shoes and more lipstick on her chin and cheeks than on her lips.

Anger now fought a battle with fear as to who was in charge. What surfaced was something in between. "Aren't you the P.I.B tonight, Sylvia?"

"Yes," Sylvia replied, her eyes focused towards the ceiling.

Scarlet sucked in a deep breath. "Then why weren't you in the control room on the studio floor?"

Looking over her shoulder into the station manager's, and conveniently her uncle's, office, Sylvia retorted, "Everything was working fine, so I took a break."

Anger definitely winning the battle now, Scarlet said through gritted teeth, "I would really appreciate you, at least, being on the same floor as me. If you need a break, please let me know where that break will be taking place."

Still looking bored, the girl turned towards her Uncle's office. "Okay," she said, dragging out the second syllable much longer than necessary.

Seeing car headlights appear on the opposite side of the station's glass doors, Scarlet ran to unlock them. Hugging Niles tightly, she thanked him for getting to her so quickly. Firmly gripping his hand, Scarlet led him upstairs to her studio. Concluding a healthy amount of venting and a little laughter at Niles' comments on her poster choices, she decompressed. Half an hour later, Niles watched Scarlet close shop for the night. Descending the staircase, they found Sylvia, seemingly eating the face off a man an inch shorter than herself.

"See you tomorrow night," Sylvia called as Scarlet and Niles left the station. Not trusting herself to speak, Scarlet raised her arm in response.

Shaking his head, Niles spat, "See you tomorrow night my ass. You're getting her fired first thing in the morning."

Curling her lip, Scarlet said, "That won't happen...she's connected."

Niles, jaw set, responded, "I swear this place is run by the friggin mafia."

9

"She's it? She's your entire backup in that whole forsaken building? Just you and her, all night long?"

Two hands around her large mug of hot chocolate, Scarlet replied, "You know how tight Brian is with that sort of thing. If it doesn't *show*, he's not prepared to pay."

Stroking Prudence's head a little too roughly, Niles said, "So this Sylvia girl is the P.I.B? Remind me again what that is."

Putting her mug on the coffee table, Scarlet leaned forward. "That's just it Niles, people who don't work in the business wouldn't know what a P.I.B is. How did that caller know? P.I.B stands for Person In Building. Their job is to make sure all the stations keep running; dead air is suicide for radio."

Watching Prudence escape from his firm hand, Niles asked, "So how is that little tart connected?"

Scarlet gave a wry smile. "She's Brian's niece. Apparently, she can't keep a job so, surprise, we get her!"

Getting up to heat more milk Niles said, "This is insane, Scar. How can you ever feel secure in that building again?"

Following Niles into the kitchen, Scarlet replied, "I knew it was only the two of us, but until tonight I hadn't given it much thought. She's certainly not allowed to have a *friend* there with her."

Niles poured warm milk into their large mugs. "Tell me exactly what that caller said. You were understandably rattled earlier."

Adding a generous spoonful of Ghirardelli's sweet ground chocolate mix, Scarlet took a breath. "He said he remembered me from my Top Forty show. I was all happy about that for a moment. Then, he asked how many other people were at the station with me. He knew I was lying about having security and tried to make me question whether Sylvia was even there. It's not like he said he was going to come and kill me or anything, but it still freaked me out. I shouldn't have let it."

Taking both their mugs, Niles retorted, "You should damn well let it, Scarlet."

Raising her eyebrows at, *Scarlet,* only used by Niles when he was displeased with her, she said, "Niles, I've been in this business a few years now. You've heard all the stories. Radio personalities, for whatever reason, attract the loons. It's all part of the job."

Taking an initial tentative sip of his hot chocolate, Niles smiled in remembrance. "Like that guy who put your photo on a T-shirt and wore it to all your remotes."

Scarlet began giggling uncontrollably, leaving Niles to continue, "Or the guy who painted a big sign, marry me, Scarlet, and held it five feet away when you did the Farmer's Market remotes."

Her giggling now under control, Scarlet said, "He was quite cute actually."

Trying to sound serious, Niles replied, "Yes, and so was the massive python he had hanging around his neck."

The giggling returned, and Scarlet admitted, "I'd forgotten about the snake!"

"But Scar," Niles said in a sobering tone, "a crazy T-shirt guy or reptile dude is one thing, but when someone goes out of their way to make you feel unsafe…"

Nodding her head slowly, Scarlet said, "I agree. Maybe now that I'm in the night market I've acquired a whole new breed of loons."

"Sounds an awful lot like acceptance to me," Niles said reproachfully.

Scarlet ran a hand through her shoulder length dark hair. "Short of hiring my own personal bodyguard, there's not much I can do but accept it."

Looking up from a glance at his watch, Niles said, "You've got to sit down with that idiot Brian. I don't care how unreasonable he is; you have to try. I've got to get...I'll call you."

Following Niles to the door, Scarlet said, "I'm having lunch with my friend, Janet, tomorrow. She's the DJ for Bay Radio's country station and always in the know. I'm going to get the scoop from her first, then go into Brian's office knowing the gossip...I mean facts," Scarlet concluded with a grin.

****

Accompanied by the clarity morning often brings, Scarlet wondered if she'd overreacted to the caller. But, the fact of the matter was, she didn't like working at night, and it just wasn't fair. Okay, maybe she wouldn't use that verbiage with Brian, but she *was* going to ask him why. Why, after years of great ratings, he unilaterally moved her to a men's relationship show? Allowing Candy, with zero experience, to sashay into an established and thriving market.

Janet looked glamorous in a turquoise tunic-style top and skinny jeans. Engulfing Scarlet in a perfume filled, jewelry jangling hug, Janet then flashed overly bleached teeth at the waiter.

A man with narrow hips in tight black pants hurriedly made his way to their table. Janet, teeth still displayed said, "This is Armando. He makes the best cucumber-cilantro margaritas in the world." Winking at the handsome waiter, she added, "We'll take two and keep them coming."

Armando lifted his arm with the flair of a bull fighter. "I shall return ladies!"

Despite the margarita tasting refreshing and delicious, Scarlet took tiny, infrequent sips, mindful of why Harold had been fired.

"Thanks so much for taking the time to visit with me."

Downing her margarita in three swift gulps, Janet replied,

"Oh sweetness, it's my pleasure. I miss seeing you at the station. What time do you come in now?"

"Seven PM," Scarlet groaned.

"Ouch!" Janet replied, waving her empty glass in Armando's direction.

Seconds later, Scarlet imagined he had them made and ready, Armando appeared with two more drinks. Thanking him, Scarlet professed she'd barely made a dent in her first. Feeling like an amateur, she explained the need to be in charge of her senses for Mending Men that evening.

Janet gave a low throaty chuckle. "Darling girl, I'm at a remote in two hours. A new Western Bar's opening at the Wharf. They're paying yours truly to talk it up a little." Raising her glass in the air, she continued, "This, just makes me talk a bit more."

About the time Scarlet was wondering if they were actually going to eat anything, Janet waved Armando over again asking, "What do you recommend for us today?"

With what Scarlet would bet was more of an accent than he truly possessed, Armando suggested they have the panko crusted fried avocado wedges, on a flour taco shell with charred tomato sauce crème.

"Sold!" Janet declared, loud enough to catch the attention of nearby tables.

Scarlet was fascinated. Apparently, it wasn't only men who felt they could order for you. The avocado dish did sound delicious; she just hoped it was a decent size and not one of those little artistic numbers.

Breaking into Scarlet's thoughts, Janet asked, "Okay, what do you want to know about Candy?"

Leaning back in her chair; finally feeling as if they could have a real conversation, Scarlet began, "What I would love to know is, how she landed the Top Forty show when she has no programming experience and no longevity at Bay Radio."

Janet gave a dramatic sigh. "That's easy my sweet friend. She's sleeping with Brian."

Scarlet wasn't a good enough liar to look shocked. Of course, this scenario had occurred to her many times in the last ten days. But, despite knowing the power of sex, she'd hoped it couldn't be true. To acknowledge it, was to admit she had no security in her chosen career whatsoever. That no matter how hard you work or how much success you acquire, some trollop could appear on the scene and steal it out from under you.

"The word is," Janet added conspiratorially, "Candy threatened to tell Brian's wife about the affair if he didn't give her a show."

Suddenly needing to gulp instead of sip her drink, Scarlet suggested, "And I was the sacrificial lamb; the antelope with a gammy leg."

The topic was paused to thank Armando as the food arrived. It was in Scarlet's opinion, disappointingly small.

Janet began cutting her avocado into tiny pieces. "You're too nice…too easy going. He's terrified of me and do you think he'd dare move Simon away from his beloved Jazz station. Candy had no interest in Tony's oldies or Pat's holy rollers, so yes, it was down to you."

Fork, halfway to mouth, Janet speculated, "I'm sure his wife must be aware he can't keep it zipped up, wouldn't you think? Surprising really that Candy's threat held water."

Swallowing a scrumptious mouthful, Scarlet said, "It's one thing to suspect, but to have it pushed in your face is altogether different. No doubt, his long-suffering wife has found a way of coping. Brian's, no doubt, aware Candy could push the poor woman over the edge."

Regarding Scarlet with what appeared to be drink-induced awe, Janet said, "I bet you're right."

Small talk and laughter filled the rest of their time until Janet's boyfriend came to drive her to the Wharf.

Walking to her car, Scarlet processed what she knew. Even if, or she should say when the affair ended, Candy would still have the leverage to keep Scarlet's show. Pathetic as the wages were at Bay

Radio, they still paid more than other stations in the city. She'd better get used to hosting Mending Men because goodness knows she didn't have a backup plan.

10

Head held high, Scarlet walked from her car to the station's front doors. In one hand, she held a powerful flashlight and in the other, a man's sock with a large bar of soap in it.

Upon returning home from her luncheon with Janet, Scarlet had found Tom deadheading roses in her front yard while Niles looked on in apparent bewilderment.

Thanking Tom, she and Niles had left him to it.

"Please tell me he's got another assignment soon," Scarlet jokingly whispered, looking back at the avid gardener.

Hands over his eyes, Niles groaned, "No word of one yet."

Joining them in the house minutes later, a large bag over his shoulder, Tom said, "Niles told me about your creepy caller. I'm very concerned Scarlet. I have a couple of things here I want you to use."

Digging into an oversized tote, Tom produced a large and cumbersome looking flashlight, one gray woolen sock and an enormous rectangular bar of soap.

"This," he said dramatically holding up the flashlight, "is used by the Military and Law Enforcement. It is not a weapon," he added with a wink. "It merely enables you to see in the dark while walking from your car to the radio station. This," he went on, as if the garment needed explanation, "is a man's sock. And this is simply a bar of soap."

Niles, Scarlet, and Prudence stayed silent, captivated by Tom's bag of tricks.

Destined to be on QVC, Tom continued, "When you place this bar of soap inside a sock, you have a very effective means of defending yourself. But... It is not a weapon." Again, this was followed by an exaggerated wink.

Trying not to giggle, as Tom was clearly taking this very seriously, Scarlet pictured herself telling a police officer she simply had a fetish for men's socks and never knew if she might get dirty.

Putting the items back in the bag and giving it to Scarlet, Tom concluded, "If anyone approaches you, swing and whack, swing and whack. You could do some serious damage with these things. Certainly enough to allow you time for an escape."

Scarlet thanked Tom with sincerity, asking if he was sure he could spare such a nice flashlight.

Smiling, he assured her he could spare anything to keep her safe.

Now, five hours later, she marched confidently into the radio station, surreptitiously stuffing the sock-covered soap into her coat pocket.

With heightened self-awareness, she ascended the staircase to her studio. Switching the light then waking up her equipment, Scarlet deposited her coat and bag before going in search of the elusive Sylvia.

Not finding the girl in either of the two places she should be, Scarlet, came to the conclusion that either she had not put her point across forcefully enough, or Sylvia just didn't give a damn.

Only minutes to spare before she was live on, Mending Men, Scarlet found the P.I.B. in Janet's studio. Noisily smacking gum, Sylvia walked long purple fingernails atop a row of CDs. Having to stand in front of the girl to catch her attention, Scarlet motioned for Sylvia to remove her headphones.

Trying to keep her patience, when Sylvia gave her a *why are you bothering me* look, Scarlet asked if she could please stay in or near the control room tonight.

Sylvia nodded, put her headphones back on and continued rifling through Janet's CD collection.

Running back down the long corridor, Scarlet barely managed to catch her breath before saying, "Thank you for calling Mending Men, this is Scarlet, how can I help?"

"Do you have brothers, Miss Scarlet?" A deep male voiced asked.

Feeling a little gun shy at immediately being asked a question, Scarlet replied, "I have one brother." Then added, "Who am I chatting with tonight?"

"This is Henry from Bernal Heights."

Regaining her composure, Scarlet asked, "What can I help you with this evening, Henry?"

"I know it's the oldest saying in the book," the man said, "but my wife really doesn't understand me."

Thankful this was radio and not television, Scarlet raised her eyebrows. Then, fighting to suppress a smile which experience had taught her could be heard in your voice, enquired,

"Why do you feel that way, Henry?"

"Well, there's a reason I ask about you having brothers or not Miss Scarlet. I feel without that childhood interaction girls grow into women who have no clue about how us lesser mortals tick."

Trying to predict where the conversation was going, and a suitable sports analogy, Scarlet bought time by stating the obvious, "Your wife doesn't have any brothers?"

"No," said the caller, "and she went to an all-girls school and university."

Genuinely interested, Scarlet said, "I could see that being tricky. You're correct, growing up with a brother takes away some of the mystery."

"Exactly," Henry agreed in his baritone brogue. "We met at a dance, she was so damn cute and oh my Lord was she boy crazy. It was as if I were some rare forbidden fruit she was finally allowed to sample. I didn't complain; I was young and reveled in the attention."

Opening her preselected websites on the computer, but unsure if she'd need them, Scarlet asked, "How long have you been married, Henry?"

"Twenty years," he replied promptly.

Wanting to say, that's a lifetime when you're unhappy, Scarlet instead said, "A good amount of time. Have you always felt this disconnect?"

Yikes, Scarlet thought. *I'm beginning to sound like a bad psychiatrist!*

Thankfully unperturbed by the question, Henry said, "Certainly for the lion's share of it. We tried counseling a couple of times but with little success. She refuses to take part in anything I do or anything I'm interested in. I play softball, and I begged her to try it. I love listening to Jazz; there are so many great jazz joints in this city. No interest. Her idea of a good time is watching soaps, going to scrapbooking parties, and getting her nails done."

Scarlet had been about to ask if he'd tried getting involved in things his spouse liked to do. But, if the list he'd given her of his wife's interests was accurate, the poor man had few options.

"Gosh Henry ..." Scarlet began.

"It's okay, Miss Scarlet," Henry interrupted. "I don't need a sports metaphor, as good as they are."

Oh, that thin line between politeness and dishonesty, Scarlet mused.

"It just feels good to talk to you about it. Would it be alright if I called again?" he asked.

"I hope you do, Henry," Scarlet replied warmly.

Saying she would play, *Let it Be,* by the Beatles, Scarlet concluded the call before emitting a contented sigh.

Next in line was Barry from Daly City. He'd called three times last week, and Scarlet felt he was making up problems just to talk on the show. It wouldn't have been so bad if the problems weren't completely ridiculous. *Why were waitresses so friendly to you and then refuse to go on a date? And then, why shouldn't a man buy a bride in a catalog?* Such bizarre open-ended questions left Scarlet speechless and with nowhere to go, other than an equally ridiculous sports analogy in response.

Welcoming Barry back to the show, Scarlet wondered how many times they could play this out.

"I think there should be bars where only single women can go," he said. Before Scarlet could get a word in, Barry added, "That way us guys can go in there and know we're going to score. Plus, we won't get beaten up by some chick's boyfriend."

Finding an analogy, Scarlet figured was closer than he deserved, she said, "You can't expect to knock it out of the park every time you step up to the plate. Thanks for calling Mending Men, Barry." She ended the call without saying stay in touch, though she knew, invited or not, he would.

Beginning her nine in a row with, *Wind of Change,* by *the Scorpions*, Scarlet decided to head to the cafeteria for some below average vending machine hot chocolate. Walking to the end of a corridor and finding a dead end, she was reminded she'd maybe made this trip twice since starting at the station. In the good old days of hosting a hugely popular show, she'd had drinks brought to her by engineers, board ops, and sales staff.

Encouraged by what sounded uncannily like the whirring of a vending machine, Scarlet rounded one more corner. About to turn into the impersonal room with a flickering overhead light, she halted upon hearing laughter.

Holding her breath, Scarlet peeked around the open door. A pry bar in one hand and a hammer in the other, a short, stocky man casually worked on breaking into the soda machine. Sylvia stood at his side, giggling.

Trying not to release the gasp traveling up her throat, Scarlet slowly turned and walked, be it faster than normal, down the long corridor until it turned into another. Now she began a half run, half walk until she reached her studio.

Taking deep breaths, Scarlet reached for her soap in a sock. Clasping it tightly to her chest, she pondered whether safe and normal were luxuries of the past.

11

Anxiety was still rearing its unwanted head, but day-by-day Scarlet felt a little more at ease in her new position. The weekend having taken the slow train, eventually arrived. Friday night socializing was now a distant pleasant memory, with San Francisco nightlife ending around the same time as Mending Men. Weekends began when she and Prudence opened their eyes on Saturday.

This happened a little earlier than expected, as Scarlet had forgotten to pull her drapes closed the night before. It was an unusually bright fall morning, rays of sunlight highlighting the need to clean her room. A layer of fine dust covered her shabby chic vanity and three-drawer accent chest. Long thin cobwebs formed a delicate bridge from a black resin ballerina lamp to her very pink ballerina jewelry holder.

For a girl who'd never enjoyed ballet, Scarlet had a surprising number of objects and collectibles inspired by the dance. Fifteen years after its release, Scarlet's Mother had seen, *Breakfast at Tiffany's*. Although only twelve years old at the time, the movie made an impact. Decades later, and after watching Audrey Hepburn star in over twenty-five films, Marilyn enrolled her daughters in ballet. Violet was five and Scarlet, three. Many girls their age took dance lessons; there was nothing out of the ordinary about that. What was rather unusual was the frequency of the lessons. Four times a week, the little girls were squeezed into tights and tutus and deposited in an old church hall for an hour. Not until Violet ran off between the third and fourth of the five basic ballet positions had the question been asked, was this amount of instruction fair on such young girls.

Violet had been found, two blocks away in a comic store. Scarlet, vaguely remembered the police bringing her home and her mother's prolonged crying. Violet never suffered through another lesson, but Scarlet still attended once a week.

Many years of arguments and resentment stemmed from that day. Didn't Scarlet's father understand ballet had helped shape Audrey Hepburn into the incredible woman she was? Did he think that kind of posture came from volleyball or track? Was he aware, Audrey spent many years at a professional ballet conservatory?

As for Violet, Marilyn never forgave her for telling the police she hated ballet, and her mom made her do it. Marilyn informed anyone who'd listen, how the Police had treated her like some kind of criminal. Was it a crime to want your daughters to emulate the poise and grace of Audrey Hepburn?

Scarlet, to appease her mother, continued with her ballet lessons until she was thirteen. At least once a month, Marilyn would buy Scarlet a dance themed gift. Ninety percent of them ended up in Scarlet's closet. The reason was twofold. She felt bad about getting gifts when her siblings didn't and said gifts were on the gaudy side.

A decade later, some pink and taffeta remained and was cherished. Vowing to give the bedroom a thorough clean after breakfast, Scarlet checked her calendar.

Plenty of time before her first meal, err date, with Gary. Debating whether to pull the drapes and try for more sleep or get up now and enjoy a full day, Scarlet decided on the latter.

****

Breathing in fresh, crisp air, Scarlet parked her car feet away from a narrow path leading down to China Beach. Spreading a blue fleece blanket on the sand, she sat, knees up under her chin, looking out onto the Pacific Ocean. The Golden Gate always took her breath away, even with the top of its towers hidden amongst rain leaden clouds. In the distance, a cargo ship moved effortlessly towards the wharf. Its massive steel bow causing subtle ripples, which seconds later morphed into powerful white foam hitting the glistening sand.

Squinting against welcome sunlight, Scarlet tried to decipher which of the two, almost naked, men she was here to see.

Determining it to be the one who'd just submerged his entire body in the freezing water, Scarlet patiently waited. Surely, she thought with a shiver, it couldn't be too long until he returned to dry land.

Scarlet stood as the man, hastily drying his body with a towel that appeared inadequate, walked towards her.

Shaking water from his ear in a rather dog-like fashion, Joe said, "Your Gran told you my secret."

Scarlet smiled at her father. "I think it's great. She said you try for three times a week."

Nodding his head but looking off towards the parking lot, Joe said, "Let me run to the car and grab my sweats. Is that a thermos I spy in your basket?"

Smiling and concurring it was, Scarlet watched her father clap cold hands together before running to his vehicle.

Minutes later, father and daughter, steaming mugs of hot chocolate in hands, sat together on the blanket. With only an odd screech from overhead seagulls, the pair, while soaking in the beauty around them, were content to say nothing.

At length, Joe broke the silence, "Have you seen your mother lately?"

Scarlet pushed her mug down into the sand. "Last weekend. She's talking about moving onto the golf course."

Joe sighed. "I'd heard that. Believe it or not, Marilyn calls your Gran every now and then." With a smile, he added, "I think usually after a few glasses of wine."

Joe turned his head towards Scarlet. "You know I tried my very best?"

Scarlet placed a sand covered hand over her father's. "I do. I was there."

Swallowing hard, Joe continued, "Your Mother accuses me of having a stereotypical midlife crisis, and she's the undeserving victim. I can honestly say the timing had nothing to do with my age. But ... she may be right about the crisis part."

Scarlet paled. "You're okay, aren't you?"

Turning an empty mug in his hands, Joe said, "I'm fifty-seven years old and living with my mother. My son won't talk to me, and my oldest girl is living on a commune with no means of communication." Taking in his daughter's look of concern, Joe hastily added, "It's all fixable. Your old Dad's fine."

Unscrewing the thermos for more hot chocolate, Scarlet suggested, "It hasn't been that long. You and Gran are great roommates. When you're ready, you'll get your own place. Besides, that house is big enough you could go for days without bumping into each other. As for Trent, ever since he married Lisa he's adopted this holier than thou attitude. None of us can please him, so why bother trying? Violet, well she's Violet. I'm going to barge my way in there one of these days if you want to join me."

Laughing and thanking Scarlet for the refill, Joe said, "My job has reached the level of stress only handled well by a younger man. For the last five years, I feel as if I've been there on borrowed time as it is. I've made some smart suggestions and proposals, but I feel like a fraud. Every day I wonder if they're going to realize they promoted the wrong man and acknowledge I'm not good enough for the job or the salary."

Shaking her head, Scarlet confessed, "I had no idea you were going through this."

Patting her knee, Joe said, "I'm glad, and I hope you don't mind me offloading with you now. I'm thankful you and I have always had an honest relationship."

"Me, too," Scarlet responded with a smile. "So, what are you going to do?"

Joe brushed sand off the blue blanket. "There's a lot of back and forth right now about growth in the industry. Many believe we should focus on economic growth over the expansion of domestic airports. I have a feeling there's going to be some reshuffling going on. This could be the perfect opportunity to put my name up for a different, less stressful, position."

Draining her mug, Scarlet urged, "Do it, Dad. Sooner rather than later."

Joe pulled a face. "There's one rather large snag."

Scarlet waited expectantly. Closing his eyes for a moment, Joe said, "Alimony."

Putting the pieces together, Scarlet said, "Less stress means less money which means less alimony for Mom."

Resignedly nodding his head, Joe said, "But enough of that. Do you have time to come by the house?"

Scarlet checked her phone. "Yes, let's go."

Laughing, Joe watched Scarlet unceremoniously stuff the blanket inside the basket. With comparative delicacy, he placed the thermos and cups on top.

En route, following her dad's Honda Accord, Scarlet noticed a flower lodged next to her gear stick. Momentarily confused, she remembered it was retained from the bunch left on her windshield.

Fifteen minutes later, she pulled into the rose lined driveway of her Gran's home. Securing the handbrake, Scarlet grabbed the almost unrecognizable flower.

"I have no idea," Joe said after his daughter held it forth for inspection. "But I bet your Gran will know, withered petals or not."

Hugs and kisses were exchanged before Rose carefully examined the dried flower.

"I'm pretty sure it's a Franciscan Wallflower," she said. Walking into the sunroom located at the rear of the house, she added, "They have four petals, usually cream colored and arranged in a cross shape."

Studying the flower intently, she asked, "Where did you say you found it?"

"It was on my car when I finished work the other night," Scarlet explained. "Placed under my windshield wiper."

"Odd," Rose muttered. "I'm going to get my wildflower book from the library. How about you two rustle up some lunch."

Cutting thick slices of granary bread while her father retrieved cold meats and salad from the French door refrigerator, Scarlet continued with their earlier conversation, "If you're making less money, Mom *has* to get less alimony. Would it not be enough for her to live on?"

Placing turkey, ham, and roast beef on a platter, Joe replied, "Define, enough to live on."

Stopping mid-saw through the loaf, Scarlet said, "I see."

Pouring boiling water into a large bone china teapot, Joe continued, "The house is paid off, as is her two-year-old BMW. After she pays health and car insurance, utilities, food, and general living expenses, she'd still be left with around three thousand every month."

Adding sliced bread to the tray, Scarlet asked, "You're not talking now, but with the lesser paying job?"

Joe, eyebrows raised, nodded in the affirmative.

Placing fine bone china mugs on a tray, Scarlet declared, "That's more than fair. I'm sure Mom will be okay with it."

Joe shook his head. "I broached it to her last night. She said she wouldn't take a penny less than what was agreed to in our divorce settlement."

Retrieving knives and forks from the cutlery drawer with more force than required, Scarlet retorted,

"We're just going to have to make her see reason."

Joe removed the cutlery from Scarlet's tightly clenched fists. "Unfortunately, probably not. She can claim I'm willfully underemployed. Because she hasn't worked since we married, it's my burden to support her in the style she's accustomed to for the next decade."

Muttering about the unfairness of it all, Scarlet followed her father into the sunroom.

As Joe placed the tray on the large round, glass-topped wicker table, Rose said, "By the look on your faces and the grinding of teeth, I'm guessing you were discussing Alimony."

Father and daughter solemnly nodded their heads.

Looking up from her book, Rose said, "It's a modern form of slavery, no ifs ands or buts about it."

Accepting a cup of tea from her granddaughter, Rose looked back down at a small pastel colored illustration. "It's definitely a Franciscan Wallflower. I confess the timing has sent a little chill up my spine."

Hastily swallowing her gulp of rooibos tea, Scarlet asked, "Why?"

Returning her cup to the table, Rose replied, "Because just this morning on the local news, they were talking about a woman's body found washed up near the base of the Golden Gate."

Having been so close to said location just an hour earlier, Scarlet and her father exchanged looks of horror.

"Was it a suicide?" Joe enquired.

Rose stared at the dried and withered flower now lodged in the spine of her open book. "No, it was murder. The woman's mouth had been duct taped. When the layers of tape were removed, they found it had been crammed full of wildflowers."

Not needing to ask, but doing it anyway, Scarlet said, "Franciscan Wallflowers?"

Seeing her granddaughter's face drain of color, Rose quickly said, "Just a silly coincidence. They're probably everywhere right now."

Acting as if that statement fixed the whole matter, Rose changed the subject and soon had Scarlet and Joe in peals of laughter. Had they heard about the time Scarlet's nephews lifted their mother's skirt above her waist? The young boys deduced it was the quickest way to end her long discussions with the minister after church.

Not long after the laughter had died down, Scarlet reluctantly left the relaxing company of her father and Gran. Wishing she felt more enthusiasm for it, she headed home to dress for her date.

12

Deciding it must be a positive sign she looked good with little effort taken, Scarlet drove to North Beach. Needing to stop for gas on the corner of Seventeenth and Van Ness, she arrived at Cristofano's ten minutes late. Scarlet spotted her date before she even walked through the door. The small windows were beginning to fog, but there at a corner table just one foot away from an animatedly chatting couple, sat Gary. Confident he couldn't see her out on the street, Scarlet stole a moment to assess him. Nice features, dark blond short hair, and hard to tell as he was sitting, but he looked to match the six feet he'd claimed to be on the site.

Trying to look more self-assured than she felt, Scarlet walked into the small Italian restaurant and right up to his table. The poor man looked positively panicked as she shook his hand and took her seat.

"I'm so sorry I'm late," Scarlet began, "I had to stop for gas and, of course, hadn't allowed myself time to do it."

Starting to feel less and less at ease with his lack of conversation, Scarlet did what came naturally when nervous. She began talking faster and faster and with only half her words being relevant or even making sense.

Finally resorting to staring at her menu, she was relieved when the waitress appeared at her side.

"Would you mind telling me your specials?" Scarlet asked.

"What the hell are you doing?" the stern-faced waitress asked Gary in answer.

Scarlet's date stammered, "Darling, I swear I've never seen this lady before. She just sat down and started talking to me."

Certain she'd turned a deeper red than the tablecloth, Scarlet asked in a slow, shaky voice, "You're not Gary, are you?"

"No, he's not Gary," the woman who clearly wasn't the waitress snapped. "He's *my* fiancé." With hands on her hips and looking daggers at Scarlet, she added, "Do you make a habit of sitting down next to men you don't know? Could I have my chair back if it's not too much trouble?"

Face burning, Scarlet hurried, head down, out of the restaurant. Vaguely aware of passing a man at the entrance, Scarlet, captivated by her shoes, marched on. Nearing the car, she heard a voice call behind her, "Miss Reynolds, is that you?"

Taking three more steps before remembering Reynolds was the last name she'd used on the site, Scarlet, turned to face the voice, "Gary?"

"I'm terribly sorry," he gushed. "I was called into a teleconference. It happens more weekends than I can tell you. I drove like a maniac but still almost missed you. I don't blame you for not wanting to wait any longer. Can you forgive me?"

Like the poor man in the restaurant and like his photo on the dating site, the real Gary had blond hair and an aquiline nose. He looked maybe a little under six feet tall, with broad shoulders.

Scarlet's mortified side wanted to say, hello and goodbye. Go straight home and sit on the couch eating chocolate and feeling sorry for herself. Her slightly more grown up side argued, mortified or not, she was here now, wearing makeup, and looking better than she had in months. Besides, she was all out of chocolate.

"There's nothing to forgive, Gary. But would you mind if we went somewhere else? I've already managed to outstay my welcome at Cristofano's."

Gary gave a somewhat confused smile. "There are plenty of other good restaurants around here. Let's grab the first empty table we find."

Liking him already, Scarlet agreed. The newly acquainted couple walked and chatted until they discovered that table.

Happily sipping her red wine, Scarlet listened while Gary passionately talked about being a civil rights lawyer. His field was constitutional law, and he was fortunate enough, at the age of thirty, to be a senior associate with Ridel, Ames, and Deemer.

Over barbecued oysters, Scarlet told him a little about her radio career. Gary appeared to find it more exciting than she did, with plentiful and intelligent questions on the subject.

Mid-way through Crab Louie and an Aperol cocktail, Gary confessed of his obsession for windsurfing. Any minute of the day he wasn't working was spent at Chrissy Field. "Unfortunately," he added with a downturned mouth, "the thrills typically only last from May until August. Come September, I'm a little lost and craving the ocean."

Working his way through a generous portion of Tiramisu, Gary listened as Scarlet, daintily eating Lemon Ricotta Granita, recounted stories of growing up in the small town of Aptos. Her dinner companion admitted his fascination for the locale, having grown up in the bustling city of Brooklyn.

"East Coast," Scarlet said for lack of anything less redundant to say.

Smiling, Gary suggested, "You're surprised because I don't have the accent."

Nodding, she suffered through a slight brain freeze from her desert, before agreeing, "Not even a trace."

Gary relaxed into his seat.

"I have a little luck with voices. I can change how I sound on a dime. It comes in pretty handy I can tell you." Leaning in conspiratorially, he elaborated, "When negotiating, I've found Texans, Southerners, etc., will listen with a more open mind if they suspect you're from their neck of the woods."

Scarlet smiled politely. "You'll be a partner before you know it."

Lifting his cocktail glass, Gary said, "From your lips."

Ten minutes later, while sipping their cappuccinos, Gary returned to his favorite subject, the ocean.

"I'm planning a trip to La Jolla," he stated enthusiastically. "Have you ever snorkeled?"

Unbidden, Scarlet remembered her trip to Hawaii with Max. "I have."

Nodding with apparent approval, Gary paused before saying, "How would you feel about swimming with Leopard Sharks?"

Feeling suddenly awkward as to whether this was a rhetorical question or an invitation, Scarlet said, "Swimming with ... and sharks, are three words which I believe, shouldn't be said consecutively."

Gary, eyes wide, held his hands up defensively. "The water's so warm you don't even need a wetsuit. Plus, you only need to be five feet deep to see a ton of them. You should think about coming with me."

Experiencing a mixture of amazement and horror, Scarlet struggled to find her voice.

Seemingly assuming her look of astonishment stemmed from the shark comment, Gary added, "Leopard sharks are harmless to humans."

The evening ended pleasantly with Gary walking Scarlet back to her car. Leaving each other with the agreement they'd be in touch, Scarlet began the fifteen-minute drive home to her soft bed and equally soft pig.

Five minutes from Upper Terrace, her phone rang. Seeing it was Niles, she answered with Bluetooth.

"How on earth did you know I just said goodbye to my first date in forever?"

"Scar, much as I love you," Niles said. "I do have my own life. I'd forgotten you had a date tonight."

Feeling suitably put down, Scarlet enquired, "Oh, then to what do I owe the honor of this call?"

"Well, I sort of lied about having my own life," Niles mumbled. "Tom and I have spent the entire day planning your coming out party."

"Coming Out!" Scarlet repeated in mock horror.

"Didn't you say your great grandmother was British?" Niles reasoned as if the two things obviously went together.

"Yeah," Scarlet replied, wondering where this admission would lead to.

"Debutante," Niles explained, "is French for a female beginner. To come out means the young lady, having reached the age of maturity, is ready to be presented to society."

Scarlet wasn't sure which was funnier, the thought of her being the innocent young deb or Niles and Tom's friends being considered society.

Chuckling, Scarlet stopped at a four way, beside a bright street light. Niles' voice continued to fill the car. Amidst complaining how Tom was refusing him any input on the evites artwork, Scarlet blurted,

"Oh no. Please no."

"It's okay, Scar. We're not actually calling it a coming out party on the invitation."

Her breathing labored, Scarlet continued, "I don't believe it. Niles, it can't be."

"It was just a joke Scar. I don't know why you're so upset about it. I know Tom gets carried away with details but ..."

"The flowers," Scarlet interjected.

"What flowers?" Niles asked, now aware their wires were crossed.

Hearing his friend stammer something about water and murder, Niles asked, "Where are you?"

"I'm a minute from home," Scarlet croaked.

"We'll be right there," Niles said before abruptly ending the call.

Thankfully, due to the fact, her friends lived two minutes away on Palo Alto, they arrived mere seconds after Scarlet.

Niles made a brief examination of the MINI's interior as Tom helped Scarlet from the driver's seat.

Hand shaking, Scarlet pointed to the bunch of flowers under her windshield wiper.

"This is what terrified you?" asked an incredulous Niles.

"These are just wild flowers," Tom added in his best soothing tone. "Nothing to be upset about." Grabbing Scarlet's purse, Tom kept his arm around her until they reached the sanctity of her couch.

Niles, having removed the offending flowers from Scarlet's car, followed close behind. "What is it with these flowers, Scar?" he asked.

Scarlet, sitting white and stoic replied, "They're a sign. A sign that I'm going to be murdered."

13

Strangely, once Scarlet had voiced her fears, she immediately felt better. While telling the guys about the flowers and their significance, countless cups of tea had been produced, and Tom made an impromptu trip to the market for chocolate.

Finding coverage of the woman's murder online, Niles and Tom had admitted the Franciscan Wallflowers were unnerving, but they still believed, just a coincidence.

The article said the woman had been dead at least seven days. The coroner's report confirmed the victim's arms and legs had been bound. Multiple layers of duct tape covered the woman's mouth - which had been forcefully crammed with wildflowers. The bruises on her neck were conducive with being held under water until she drowned.

Three friends gave a collective shiver before Tom said, "See, in the next paragraph, it says how these wildflowers are very common around the bay. Plus, you were parked in the North Beach area, which is full of Italian restaurants. Which means lots of Italian men."

Trying not to giggle at the assumption, Niles and Scarlet waited for an explanation of Tom's logic.

Raising hands in the air, Tom continued, "Italian men are very romantic. One of them probably saw you exit your car and thought, Mama Mia – I'm leaving that girl some flowers."

Scarlet was tempted to ask Tom what planet or era he was from. But, thankful for his attempt to make her feel at ease and so grateful for his friendship, she instead said, "Yes, that could be."

Niles, knowing Scarlet was not buying this theory, gave one of his own. "There are a ton of MINI Coopers in this city. What are the odds those flowers found their way onto the wrong car? It *was* dark."

Scarlet felt the vice around her heart loosen. "I'm just overreacting because of the news story. You're both right. Those flowers are everywhere and mean nothing."

"That's the spirit!" Tom enthused.

Walking into the kitchen to start another round of tea, Niles enquired, "So how was your date?"

Finally, relaxing into her velvet Chesterfield couch, Scarlet replied, "It was okay."

Niles returned with a tray. "Just okay?"

Frowning, Scarlet explained, "I couldn't really pinpoint what made it just okay, except there was nothing fun or wacky about him."

Tom laughed. "Just wait 'til our party if it's fun and wacky you're looking for."

"He fed you well, I hope," Niles joked.

Scarlet giggled. "He did, and he was very nice. He's smart, good-looking and polite. There was just something a little off, almost like he was playing a part."

Offering her an Oreo, Tom suggested, "He was probably just nervous."

Scarlet then proceeded to tell her friends about the mortifying start to her evening.

"Was it really necessary for the fiancé to be quite so vile?" Tom asked, giving Scarlet a sympathetic look.

"Clearly highly jealous and incapable of seeing humor in the situation," Niles contributed. Shaking the teapot to hurry the brewing process, he added, "As for the real Gary playing a part, aren't we all a little guilty of that on a first date?"

Nodding, Scarlet said, "True. He also sort of asked me to go scuba diving with him, which I found a little premature."

Niles raised his eyebrows. "I warned you about going on those sites. Lots of lonely, desperate people, not to mention serial..." Catching himself, he redirected, "I think you're going to meet some wonderful guys at this party Tom's throwing you."

Narrowing her eyes at Niles, Scarlet responded, "I know lots of happily married couples who met on *these sites!*"

Niles conceded, "I agree with Tom, he was probably just nervous."

Tom looked out from under dark lashes. "And mesmerized by that smoky look you gave your eyes this evening."

Scarlet gave a coy smile. "Thanks, Tom. I watched a YouTube video on how to get the movie star look."

Stating it was way past the witching hour and they must make a move, Niles stood. Stretching, he asked, "Why is that pig naked?"

Smiling despite herself, Scarlet said, "Shh, you'll make her self-conscious. I must have shrunk all her clothes in the wash, nothing fits her any more."

Unsuccessfully hiding furtive glances, Tom and Niles covered by saying they now knew what to get Prudence for Christmas. The two men left Scarlet with sincere assurances she had nothing to worry about. Except … what dress to wear for the party next weekend.

Letting that wardrobe dilemma fill her mind, Scarlet fell into bed, smoky eyes and all.

Sunday was spent cleaning her bedroom, then messing it up again when she threw half her closet onto the floor. Burying poor Prudence under a mound of clothes, Scarlet scooped her up, complaining to the little pig she hated her entire wardrobe.

Prudence's expression showed heartfelt sympathy, prompting Scarlet to feel guilty that her faithful companion had no clothes at all.

An 'aha' moment followed seconds later. Excited energy had Scarlet running to the kitchen for scissors. She then eased Rose's old sewing machine down from the highest shelf in her closet.

By ten pm, Prudence had three new outfits and Scarlet, fewer clothes to take to goodwill.

Significantly rejuvenated, Scarlet strode into work the next evening, ready to tackle the week ahead. She and Prudence had embraced the glorious autumn day by taking a walk through the Golden Gate Park. Prudence's new outfit had drawn many an eye, and Scarlet felt refreshed with each delicious crunch of foliage beneath her boots.

Looking for suitable party attire had led to her sorting through more than just clothes. She'd found some photos, candles, and sentimental knick-knacks for her studio. With the top forty show, she'd had too many people filing in and out, for her to feel comfortable having personal items on display. Now alone and at night, Scarlet felt the nostalgia was warranted. After strategic placing, she gave the cavernous room an appraising look. Almost there, she decided. Just a few string lights and it would feel all hers.

Levels were adjusted, sports' pages opened, and then all Scarlet needed was a little positive self-talk, and she was ready to turn on the mic.

The first caller was Rod from Modesto. Scarlet, smugly, opened her thermos and poured a mug of hot chocolate. Instead of his usual prediction of future games, Rod began ranting about the 49ers loss to the Seahawks. Scarlet let him instruct the Bay Area on how the game should have been played, and then skillfully cut him off. She was, thankfully, getting better at doing that.

Two more men called to weigh in on the 49ers, Hawks game. The first was in Rod's camp and the other utterly furious at the last two callers' lack of understanding. Relieved her three callers had no desire for her input or advice, Scarlet welcomed her fourth caller to the show.

"This is Barry from Daly City," he began.

Scarlet inwardly grimaced. "Welcome back to Mending Men, Barry. How can I help?"

"Why do women wear low-cut tops, then get upset when you look at their boobs?" he enquired.

Cringing, Scarlet said, "Well …"

Barry interrupted her, "There's a woman who works at the same place as me. She looks at me, and I look back at her. When I'm getting a soda, she always seems to be there at the vending machine too. I've paid for her drink a few times, and she seemed pleased. This morning, I bought her a Reece's peanut butter cup and then I asked her out. She said no. She didn't say she was washing her hair or nothing, she just said no."

Finally, able to get a word in, Scarlet said, "Don't let it get you down, Barry. You put yourself out there, and it didn't work out for you this time. It doesn't mean you shouldn't try again. Sometimes you hit singles, sometimes doubles, then every once in a while, you may be able to hit a home run."

Cutting him off, almost as expertly as she had Rod from Modesto, Scarlet finished with, "Here's *Crimson and Clover* by, Joan Jett and the Blackhearts for you. Take care, Barry."

Scarlet had one more open call time after the nine songs in a row. She'd started the evening with so much gusto, but now as the hours rolled on she was feeling the results of a busy and stressful weekend.

Keeping one eye on the clock and the other on the phone line, she groaned when a call came in two minutes before cut off time.

Scarlet immediately relaxed when the caller introduced himself as Stewart, but you can call me Stew. He was a little creepy sounding, but beggars couldn't be choosers. This man, she had actually helped. He'd even called back to tell her as much. More importantly, he told the whole Bay Area.

"You remember how you helped me with my wife, yes you do," he voiced slowly.

"I do," Scarlet replied. "You called to tell us things are so much better now."

"Not anymore. I have a problem with another woman now, yes I do."

Closing her eyes, Scarlet tried to fully understand his meaning and moreover where to go with his statement. "Um, this other woman, is she part of you and your wife's life?"

"She wants to be part of my life, yes she does," Stew replied. "But she's no better than my wife. She keeps talking and doesn't know when to shut up."

Going off the man instantly, Scarlet attempted to stay focused. "If you and these women were all part of a team, how would you find a way to work together?"

"Do you think I should do the bath thing you suggested for my wife?" Stew asked.

Feeling relief that she'd soon have him off the line, Scarlet replied, "It did work well with your wife; didn't it Stew? Why wouldn't it work for this other lady too?"

"I'll do it. Yes, I will," Stewart said at a marginally faster pace.

"Wonderful!" Scarlet said. "Let's get some more great music going, starting with *Rocket Man* by Elton John. Thanks for calling Mending Men."

Tired but with a feeling of accomplishment, Scarlet walked to her car at the end of the evening. She didn't carry a sock, a bar of soap or a flashlight. She wasn't even worried about finding flowers on her car.

She hadn't seen her P.I.B. all evening and had no idea if Sylvia and her criminal boyfriend had even been in the building.

"I'm not afraid," she shouted out to the empty parking lot. Strange times demand slightly strange behavior she told herself and felt much better for it.

14

Tie straight, stripes who knows, bowtie other team. Scarlet repeated this over and over in her head while standing in her closet regretting the decision to give half her clothes away. Only herself, Tom and Niles were in on the 'let's find Scarlet a boyfriend' theme. The other party guests had been informed it was a casual get together before the busy Thanksgiving and Christmas season.

Scarlet reasoned the dress should reflect not too much effort made.

"Less is more," she informed Prudence while scanning her rack of clothes. Half an hour later, hot and sweaty after trying on countless outfits, Scarlet settled on a little black number. She'd found it on the clearance rack at Nordstrom and, like many bargains in her closet, had never worn it. Though not intentional, she'd certainly lost enough weight to do the dress justice. The bodice was fitted with a sheer chiffon overlay gathering at a dropped waist. The short slinky skirt was just visible under corded lace. After viewing the dress from all angles in her full-length mirror, Scarlet deduced it was certainly less is more, but maybe not in the way she'd intended. Far too pleased with her reflection to wear something else, she instead went for subtle shoes, jewelry, and makeup.

Nerves strongly in play, she made the very short drive to Niles and Tom's Tudor mansion on Palo Alto. A line of taxis hummed in unison on their steep drive. Feeling grateful, Scarlet clicked the remote Niles had pressed in her hand the previous day and steered her MINI into their garage.

She made her way back up to the large wood paneled front door, surreptitiously pulling at her skirt a couple of times before joining the huddle of guests in the entrance hall. Tom spotted her immediately and taking Scarlet's arm, led her into one of their many reception rooms.

Adele was playing in the background, letting everyone know she'd find someone new. Scarlet felt herself relax as the sounds of clinking glasses and laughter filled the house. Then she saw Niles. He was as red in the face as she'd been earlier changing clothes. Registering his exaggerated eye movement to the right, Scarlet untangled herself from an oblivious Tom and followed Niles into the kitchen.

In pantomime style, Niles began to show Scarlet the dumb waiter. Through a grimace of a smile, he asked her, "Do you notice anything odd about our guests this evening?"

Pressing the elevator type button, Scarlet exclaimed, "I love these things." Then mimicking Nile's tone, added, "Apart from the ties and stripes."

Taking Scarlet's hand and leading her into the butler's pantry, an uncharacteristically rattled Niles said, "You, Scar, are the one and only female among some eighty men."

"There you are," Tom said from the pantry entrance. "What on earth are you doing in here when I've got so many people waiting to meet Scarlet?"

"I'm simply alerting her to the freaky reality of you not inviting a single woman to this party," Niles retorted through clenched teeth.

Waving a hand in the air, Tom said, "I didn't want her to have any competition."

"Look at her!" Niles replied loud enough for a couple of passing men to glance in on the odd grouping. Scarlet pulled at her dress hem one more time as Niles elaborated, "She wouldn't have had any competition. But now," he sighed dramatically, "we may as well sell raffle tickets to win her for the night."

Taking a large gulp of his silver oak wine, Tom mumbled, "I'm sorry guys, I guess I didn't think that part through. I got so caught up in the dress code and hors d'oeuvres. Scarlet, you have to try the antipasto kabobs," he finished with a sheepish grin.

Scarlet affectionately patted Tom's cheek. "I will and don't worry about the guest list. Maybe no one will even notice."

Niles muttered something under his breath that sounded like, *yeah right.* He then followed Tom and Scarlet into the throws of single, but sexual orientation in question, men.

Nerves now heightened, though she'd never let on to Niles and Tom, Scarlet once again repeated the dress code. *Tie straight, stripes maybe, bowtie other team.* Catching a bemused look from a handsome red-haired man, she realized although emitting no sound, her mouth had been moving.

Tom, who was supposed to be introducing her to his guests, had disappeared the second they entered the great room. Niles was over at the bar pouring himself a large glass of something. The red-haired man started walking towards her, wearing ... a striped shirt!

Ten minutes later, Scarlet knew Boris was an engineer with World Health Organization or WHO as he called it thereafter. He clearly lived and breathed his work. Scarlet was enjoying the conversation when over Boris' right shoulder she saw Niles, waving something resembling a tie in the air. Managing to cover the large room in three strides, he appeared at Boris' side.

"Scar, I'm sorry to interrupt, but Tom needs a female perspective on his Grand Marnier Soufflé. He's panicked it hasn't risen enough."

Smiling and offering her apologies to Boris, Scarlet found herself back in the butler's pantry with Tom and Niles.

Holding a navy-blue silk bowtie towards Scarlet, Niles said with all seriousness, "This belongs to Boris. The handsome red-haired man you've just wasted valuable time talking to."

Marveling at how unglued her generally calm and steady friend had become this evening, Scarlet said, "I did not waste time. He's very interesting, and I was enjoying his company."

Taking her hand and patting it, Tom said, "You don't need to sell us on how interesting gay men are Scarlet. Of course, his company is enjoyable, but that's not what this evening is about is it?"

Before Scarlet could come up with a suitable response, Tom continued, "I'm going to turn the heat down, so no one else removes articles of clothing. Until then, only talk to men with regular ties."

Wishing she were at home on the couch with Prudence, Scarlet reminded herself, lunatics or not, Niles and Tom had gone to a lot of trouble and expense for her. So, with a nod and a smile, she let Tom lead her to the library where he explained, he'd overheard sports type conversation.

Sure enough, five men wearing regular ties sat in Georgian style leather chairs, discussing the 49ers' chances in the upcoming game against the Oakland Raiders.

Feeling that, at the very least, she'd learn some valuable insights for her show, Scarlet pushed back the urge to retreat from the library as Tom announced her to the room.

Not surprisingly, all five men found it amusing when Tom explained the nature of Scarlet's job. It also appeared to break the ice somewhat, and they included her in their discussion. When there was little else to be said about Kaepernicks' skills, the conversation turned to the merits and pitfalls of being stockbrokers.

Just as Scarlet was devising a plan of escape, she heard a name which greatly peaked her interest. The man with the Kirk Douglas chin asked the man with no chin if he'd heard about Max and Cynthia. Of course, just her bad luck, only moments before this question, the man with piercing blue eyes and designer stubble strayed from the herd to give Scarlet his undivided attention.

Thankfully, his voice was low and melodic, and by leaning forward in her chair, Scarlet managed to get the gist of the other men's conversation. Max and Cynthia were no longer together, and Cynthia wasn't pleased.

"Only if you're not busy, of course."

Despite having tuned out designer stubble guy, Scarlet heard herself respond, "No, I'm not busy."

Head spinning, Scarlet tried to focus on the male to her right.

The man smiled. "Wonderful. I'll pick you up at two."

Frantically thinking of a way to find out his name and where they were going, Scarlet was furtherly distracted by the arrival of Niles.

"Scar and anyone else who's interested," Niles said to the room, "Tom is about to play a tune he's been practicing all week." Pulling a face with the last three words, Niles was rewarded with raucous laughter.

The occupants of the library adjourned to the drawing room, where laughter was replaced with admiration for Tom's talent.

Sitting straight as a board at his baby Grand, Tom played Bridge over troubled water, followed by Your Song. Coffee and soufflé were served, and guests began to sit more than stand.

Huddled together in a window seat, Scarlet explained her predicament to Niles.

Niles pulled his chin in. "Smart choice, Scar. James is a nice guy with David Bowie good looks. Two o'clock," he added, biting his lip. "Where would he be taking you at two o'clock?"

Grabbing one of his hands in her two, Scarlet said excitedly, "I'm not sure we'll need to worry about it, Niles. I don't think I'll be going anywhere with him."

Bemused, Niles reasoned, "But he's a …."

"I think Max is coming back to me. He's left, Cynthia!" Scarlet interjected.

All the color appeared to drain from Niles' face. "What are you talking about Scar?"

"Your stockbroker friends in the library," Scarlet said by way of explanation. "That's why I didn't hear a word David Bowie said. They were talking about Max leaving Cynthia and how displeased she was with his departure."

Niles, in a barely audible voice, responded, "Max got married, Scar. To a model from LA. He lives in Venice Beach now."

Instantaneously, Scarlet became aware of how much alcohol she'd consumed. A rotund, balding man sang while Tom's nimble fingers glided across the keys. Certain the wine had begun curdling with the soufflé she'd devoured, Scarlet managed to thank Niles for a lovely evening. Oblivious to the cold and rain, she began walking home. Moments later, a coat was placed around her shoulders and an umbrella held over her head. Neither Tom nor Niles said a word as they walked either side of her.

15

Refusing to believe Scarlet would rather be alone, Niles and Tom spent the best part of Sunday plying her with tea and chocolate. Tom had even made a trip to Ghirardelli Square, fought his way through tourists and returned with a decadent hot fudge sundae.

"How long have you known?" Scarlet asked Niles as he walked into her living room with a fresh pot of tea.

"A while," he admitted. "The guys you overheard in the library have just returned from our sister company in Hong Kong. It's old news to everyone else."

"Why didn't you tell me?"

Sitting, Niles put his head back. Staring up at the ornate ceiling he replied, "Because it wasn't the right time. I wanted to wait until you were a little stronger."

"And that never happened!" Scarlet interjected with a smile.

"It did," he said patting her thigh. "But then I had to ask myself, what was to be gained in telling you."

From his place on the floor with Prudence, Tom enquired, "Would you really have taken him back?"

"Well, I ..." Scarlet paused and thought for a moment. "It's just we never actually fell out. In hindsight, I guess he fell out of love with me. But the way it ended that night was so bizarre. Then to learn he'd moved in with a woman twice his age. To be honest, I think I chose to believe he was going through some temporary insanity and it wouldn't last. He'd come back, begging for my forgiveness and we'd work it out and be stronger than ever."

Tom and Niles exchanged a sideways glance that said, *damn, she's more messed up than we'd imagined.*

Draining her cup, Scarlet continued, "It appears Cynthia *was* a period of insanity for Max, but when he came to his senses he still didn't want me."

No appropriate words from her friends were forthcoming, leaving a thoughtful silence hanging in the air.

"Oh looky, looky!" Tom exclaimed, changing the room's mood in an instant. Niles and Scarlet looked down to see a glow from Tom's laptop illuminating his and Prudence's face.

When his friends made no effort to get up from the couch, Tom slowly unfolded his body into a vertical position, before squeezing himself between them.

Hitting the enter button to reawaken his computer, Tom said, "Guess who?"

Closing his eyes, Niles said, "Really, Tom. Really?"

Crestfallen, Tom began to close his laptop.

"No!" Scarlet rushed. "I want to see what Mrs. Max Devin looks like. I want to move on. I want to stop being so pathetic."

Color slowly returned to Tom's face as he began scrolling through the images of Max's new wife. With each new picture, he mimicked her facial expressions. Encouraged by Scarlet and Niles' laughter, he stood, moved to the opposite side of the room, and attempted to recreate one of her poses. Head and shoulders awkwardly leaning against the wall, he thrust the rest of his body up and out, his arms dangling down and feet in ballet points.

Amid howls of laughter, Niles said, "Perfect, except you weren't showing enough anguish."

Standing, Scarlet said, "I'm seriously about to pee! I'll be right back."

She returned to find Niles and Tom in the kitchen, searching in vain for some real food. Hanging up with the local Chinese takeout,

Niles said, "If I'd known Max was looking for a lean body with not a curve on it, Tom and I could have hooked him up a long time ago."

Scarlet smiled warmly at her friends. "Honestly guys, I'm okay. I admit it came as a bit of a shock last night, but my keep it real side knew it was over. This is good closure for me. Besides …" she added, "I'm very grateful to Max. I met two incredibly wonderful men through him."

Tom beamed, leaving Niles to say, "Do you remember that first night? You were in here. Your hair was a fright, no makeup on, and you were desperately trying to find something to feed us."

"Oh yes, I remember," Scarlet responded dramatically. "Max comes home from work with, surprise, four colleagues in tow. No warning phone call, nothing."

"What a douche!" Tom volunteered, shaking his head.

Niles placed his hand on Tom's arm. "That's not the best of it. I saw Scar was panicked and tried to lend a hand. Fortunately, she had buttermilk biscuits and sharp cheddar cheese in the fridge. We found some garlic powder in the recesses of her pantry and voila, garlic cheddar biscuits were born." Smiling in remembrance of his resourcefulness, Niles paused long enough for Scarlet to elaborate.

"So here we are producing these little miracles and having so much fun in the process, because yes, we did have wine. Mid giggles and garlic powder, in walks Max, demanding to know what we're laughing about."

Tom's look of horror was comically paired with the ringing of the doorbell and Prudence's subsequent squeals. Eagerly exchanging cash for hot and delicious smelling Chinese food, they returned to the comfort of Scarlet's living room.

Tom, barely allowing them time to sit down, enquired, "Then what happened?"

Scarlet, mouth crammed full of noodles, let Niles reply.

"Scar and I were dumbstruck. If it hadn't been for the thunderous look on Max's face, we'd have assumed he was kidding. Scar tried explaining to him how I'd saved the day with my three-ingredient appetizer. But Max didn't even let her finish before accusing *me* of hitting on his girlfriend."

Tom let out a scarily Prudence-like squeal. "He didn't?"

"Oh yes he did," Niles said while perusing the selection of entrees.

"How have we neglected to tell Tom this story?" Scarlet, twirling more noodles around her plastic fork, enquired.

Niles procured an egg roll. "Probably because between the three of us, there are plenty of current dramas to be discussed."

Tom, eyebrows raised nodded his agreement. "So how did you manage to become such great friends?"

Giving a piece of his egg roll to an attentive Prudence, Niles replied,

"I left after his outburst. Didn't even take a garlic cheddar biscuit with me. Scar walked me out, apologizing as if she were in any way responsible. I gave her my card and said call me if you ever need a friend. Scar, of course, knew my orientation, but her dumb ass boyfriend who'd worked with me for years had no idea."

"I called Niles the very next day," Scarlet said with a big smile.

Tom leaned back into the couch cushions, a hand resting on his full stomach. "Niles tells me you're going to give Rocket Man a try."

The rest of the evening was spent with Scarlet, Niles, and Tom trying to outdo each other with clever David Bowie song references. A great deal of laughter ensued. So much, in fact, no one heard the late-night delivery deposited on Scarlet's doorstep.

16

"I didn't know you had the paper delivered," Tom exclaimed, clicking the remote to start their car.

"Delivered!" Niles repeated, "Scar doesn't even read the paper."

"Does anyone anymore?" Scarlet enquired, looking down at the foreign object.

Niles bent down to retrieve the paper. "Hang on a minute. This wasn't here when we arrived. Even presuming it was deposited on the wrong doorstep, I'm pretty sure papers aren't delivered at night."

Frowning, Scarlet suggested, "Maybe the takeout guy dropped it."

Deciding this was a dilemma to be fixed, Tom switched off the car. "That doesn't seem very likely."

Catching a look of concern on her friend's faces, Scarlet gave a half laugh.

"Guys, it's just a paper." She took the offending object from Niles. "With old news. This is dated yesterday; they're talking about the upcoming game." Stepping into the house, Scarlet threw it towards the couch and missed. "You two gave up your entire Sunday for me, now go home. And thanks for bringing my car," she called out as the men folded themselves into Niles' Nissan Leaf.

Scarlet awoke the next morning with a renewed feeling of determination. She was going to have the best call-in show in the Bay Area. Max was just a distant memory and ... how were Prudence's clothes shrinking when this particular outfit hadn't been washed yet?

As Scarlet stared at her – not so little anymore – pig, Prudence looked right back as if to say, *What?*

"*You* are beautiful!" Scarlet proclaimed, scooping up Prudence and cuddling her all the way to the kitchen.

Pouring them each a bowl of muesli and promising her pig she'd pick up more sow nuts on her way to work, Scarlet walked into the living room and placed Prudence's bowl on a plastic mat. Noticing the much talked about paper on the floor, she picked it up. While crunching, in unison with Prudence, on granola and flax, Scarlet read the headlines.

Two topics on the front page piqued her interest. The first being the upcoming 49ers game with the Oakland Raiders. She knew the outcome, but it wouldn't hurt to read some of the sports terminologies. The other article was on the hunt for a Bay Area woman who'd been missing for two days. This caught Scarlet's eye because two days didn't seem long enough to panic. Turning to page six, she began to read more. The first paragraph talked about the woman's job as a visiting angel. Scarlet assessed this to mean she visited seniors in their homes and helped where needed. The second paragraph went into depth about the Angel Organization, how they'd been active in the Bay Area for over twenty years and the scope of services they provided.

The third paragraph explained the perceived need to panic after just two days. One of the seniors the missing woman, named Velma Ordman, visited on a twice-weekly basis was mother to a person of interest in a recent Bay Area murder.

The fourth and last paragraph sent a chill through Scarlet, despite warm midday sun streaming in through her living room window. It recapped the horrific incident of a woman being drowned in the shallow waters of the bay. The victim's mouth had been stuffed with local wildflowers and repeatedly secured with duct tape.

Scarlet threw the paper aside. Taking deep breaths, she attempted to push aside the unwelcome memory of those exact flowers being deposited twice on her windshield.

Reaching for her cell phone with a slightly shaking hand, Scarlet pressed a preset number before hearing,

"You must be psychic! Your father and I were just talking about you. We're hoping you'll join us for Thanksgiving next week."

"Oh my goodness, that is next week, isn't it?" Scarlet conceded.

"I'm going all out this year," Rose said with a chuckle. "I'm constructing a Turducken! It's a chicken in a duck in a turkey."

"Wow, Gran," Scarlet exclaimed. "Don't you normally do some veggie inspired type dish?"

With more laughter, Rose continued, "I do, but I have a man in the house this year. He wouldn't be too amused with all my lentils and quinoa, so I thought why not go all out and stuff some birds into each other."

The visual of her Gran's slender and frail fingers pushing a chicken into a duck enabled Scarlet to almost forgot the reason for her call. "Gran, you didn't happen to leave a newspaper on my porch last night, did you?"

"Why no dear," Rose replied. "Why would I do that?"

"Well, it's only that last time I saw you, we chatted about those wildflowers I found under my wipers. You'd read that article about the murdered woman."

"I remember," Rose responded, all the laughter now gone. "You're referring to the article in yesterday's paper. The missing woman who the police believe may have a connection to the elderly lady's son."

Neither one wanting to bring up the word, Franciscan Wildflower, the conversation hastily returned to chickens, ducks, and all things Thanksgiving.

17

Struggling to shake off her morbid thoughts, Scarlet re-read stats on the 49ers' loss to the Raiders and predictions for the upcoming game against the Seahawks.

She'd arrived at the radio station an hour earlier than normal. All part of her new day, new me philosophy. If only she could stop those damn wildflowers from popping into her head every five minutes.

Almost jumping out of her skin, Scarlet looked up to see the knuckles, having just rapped on her studio window, belonged to Sylvia the P.I.B.

Motioning for her to come in, Scarlet observed the girl's eyes to be red and swollen.

Despite suspecting she may regret it, Scarlet asked, "Is everything okay?"

Shaking her head, Sylvia pushed herself up onto the guest stool. When it became evident the source of the girl's misery was Scarlet's to determine, she enquired, "Do you want to talk about it?"

Over a loud sniff, Sylvia began, "He was just using me. He never liked me. It was all lies to get into the station."

Checking there was enough time before going live, Scarlet asked, "Are you talking about the guy I saw you with a couple of times?"

Nodding, Sylvia said, "He liked you, though. Said you were his next girl."

Not wanting Sylvia to see the look of horror on her face, Scarlet looked down at her hands. "Young men tend to show off Sylvia. I wouldn't put too much stock in what he said."

"Stock?" Sylvia repeated crinkling her nose.

Feeling like an old fuddy-duddy, Scarlet rephrased, "Don't believe half the crap that comes out of their mouths."

Smiling for the first time since entering Scarlet's studio, Sylvia said, "I'm sorry I wasn't around like I shoulda been."

Softening to the girl, Scarlet responded, "It's okay. I probably overreacted that evening 'cos I got a little spooked."

Sylvia, reaching for a Kleenex, mumbled, "He did a lot of bad stuff."

"Like breaking into the vending machine?" Scarlet suggested.

Looking sufficiently embarrassed, Sylvia nodded. "He stole from all the studios, too. Except yours," she added quickly.

Struggling to maintain an aura of calm, Scarlet asked, "Because I'm here late at night?"

"No, he was here way later than you." Her face coloring, Sylvia continued, "He said he had other plans for you."

Feeling quite ill suddenly, Scarlet enquired, "Did he mention what those plans were?"

Sylvia looked down at her feet. "I think he wanted to scare you."

Knowing she had to appear relatively unphased, or Sylvia may clam up, Scarlet casually asked,

"Did he call my show that night?"

Still looking at her shoes, Sylvia nodded her head slowly.

Her voice, unnaturally high, Scarlet said, "So scaring me was just something to do, just for kicks kind of thing?"

"I guess," Sylvia replied. Then, seemingly noticing the change in Scarlet's composure, added, "But he's gone now. The idiot's back in San Diego."

With a million questions and the need to throw something or shake a certain someone, Scarlet instead viewed the person sitting across from her. Feverishly picking at already chipped nail polish, Sylvia kept her head down. Imagining the young girl was lonely and somewhat broken, Scarlet heard herself suggest she return later to share a hot chocolate.

Revealing a lovely smile, Sylvia said she'd be waiting, just down the hall, for the next break.

Two of the three callers on hold wanted to vent about the 49ers' loss to the Raiders. The third caller was a young man named Justin from Brentwood. He'd just moved to San Francisco and felt terrified at the thought of talking to city girls. His grandmother had cautioned him they were fast and loose. What did that even mean? he'd asked. Scarlet did her best to explain the old expression, without offending Bay Area women or Justin's grandmother.

Flipping the switch to start nine songs in a row, Scarlet leaned back and allowed herself a moment to digest her earlier conversation with Sylvia. A moment was all she got. A plastic cup in each hand, Sylvia gave the unspoken universal sign for, *please open the door*.

Intermittently checking her board, Scarlet listened. Only an occasional nod of encouragement was required while Sylvia narrated a life seemingly on a fast track to disaster.

When the fifth song began to play, Sylvia reached the part where, *Mr. I like to scare women*, made his entrance. Scarlet wondered if it were her life story, how many songs it would take before Max arrived on the scene. Mentally shaking herself with the reminder of starting a new chapter, she focused on words candidly spoken by her new studio companion.

Sylvia had met Andree in a club on Utah Street. Scarlet doubted Andree was his real name. He looked more like a Lenny or a Vince to her. Sylvia recounted Andree appeared more interested in her friend at first. But when her friend was chatted up by another dude and Andree and Sylvia had a chance to talk, he seemed super interested in her.

Trying to speed the details up a little, Scarlet asked, "Did you talk about your grandmother owning this station and your uncle managing it?"

Sylvia nodded. "He was desperate to see it. Once he did, he wanted to spend all our time here. I kept asking him to take me to a movie or dinner, but he wouldn't."

"What did he steal from the studios?" Scarlet asked.

Shrugging her shoulders, Sylvia replied, "Just the shit they give away at Remotes."

Scarlet glanced at the console. "Like CD's and t-shirts."

Sylvia nervously chewed on her lower lip. "He said he could flog the CDs. Sometimes there was cash in the desk drawers, and he'd take that. He even stole Janet's hand lotion. He said he'd give it to his mom for Christmas. Isn't that so weird?" she added pulling a face.

Scarlet wanted to scream, *it's way past weird,* but instead, in her continued attempt to speak like Sylvia, said, "That's pretty messed up."

One song left on the bed before she was live again and thankfully it was *Purple Rain*, a nice long one.

"You two seemed pretty into each other." Scarlet, remembering the face sucking, suggested.

"Like that was so weird too," Sylvia began as she took the last gulp of hot chocolate. "He said I was too immature and didn't have plans like he did. He said he'd wasted his time on a kid when he shoulda been with a woman." Opening her mouth wide for added effect, Sylvia concluded, "He was only two years older than me."

Prince sang, *but you can't seem to make up your mind,* and knowing the song well enough Scarlet said, "Less than a minute and I'm live."

Offering moderately sincere sympathy for the breakup, Scarlet watched Sylvia, head low, shoulders sagging, quietly exit the studio.

Sighing, Scarlet moved her mic into position. "Thank you for calling Mending Men, this is Scarlet, how can I help?"

Settling back in her stool she listened to Adam from Oakland's outrage at hearing the two 49er fans whine about losing to the Raiders. "Outplayed," he said three times with increasing degrees of loudness.

"Plain and simple," was said twice but the second time, again, with increased volume. When he turned his outrage to the type of people who support the 49ers, Scarlet happily cut him off.

Her last caller was Rod from Modesto. Scarlet was surprised he hadn't called in earlier. Typically, he liked to be the first to enlighten her listeners on how the game should have been played. Tonight, despite being a little humbler, he chose to point out some serious errors the Raiders had made. Scarlet felt this was redundant as they'd won by eleven points, but what did she know.

Feeling emotionally spent on the drive home, Scarlet had a little trouble keeping up her new day, greatness ahead, state of mind.

18

Scarlet felt as if the fog weaving its way through the cables of the Golden Gate Bridge was also snaking its way into her place of work. The minute she stepped through the double glass doors, she felt panicked and disorientated. Ascending the steep stairs to her studio, Scarlet now likened to walking the green mile. But worst of all, every time the light on her console signaled a caller on hold, she broke out into a cold sweat.

With a vice-like grip on her hot chocolate, Scarlet marveled how debilitating fear was. One good thing *had* come out of the Andree scare. Sylvia and Scarlet were now friends. *Would they have been under different circumstances,* Scarlet pondered, *maybe not.* But here, thrown together in this dark and musky building night after night, stories were told and dreams shared.

"What are your plans for Thanksgiving?" Scarlet asked, handing Sylvia her own thermos of hot chocolate.

Raising her eyebrows dramatically, Sylvia answered, "Grandma's house, if Mom doesn't back out at the last minute."

"Why would she back out?"

"Because..." Sylvia paused for effect, "last year Grandma drank too much and said some pretty nasty stuff."

Smiling despite herself, Scarlet asked, "What kind of stuff?"

Mid-pour of hot chocolate, Sylvia explained, "Mom is on husband number four. Grandma warned her with the last two exes and the dufus she's with now, to get a prenup. If she didn't Grandma would leave her nothing. Mom was furious she brought it up last Thanksgiving in front of the dufus, a.k.a. Travis. Dufus, who was almost fall-down drunk at this point, said he wasn't with Mom for her money. Uncle Brian started laughing, and then Mom accused him of running this radio station into the ground. Grandma said my mom and aunt were both a disappointment to her. Over the top of Mom's shouting and my aunt's crying, Grandma says she's going to cut them off and leave everything to Uncle Eric."

Wide-eyed, Scarlet enquired, "What does your Uncle Eric do?"

"I think he assembles stuff," Sylvia replied, looking thoughtful. "He's always been Grandma's favorite."

Scarlet formed a mental picture of the soap opera type scene. "Has this caused a rift between the three children?"

Sylvia shook her head. "No, Mom and Aunty Sue are crazy about Uncle Eric. Uncle Brian loves him too."

Seeing Scarlet's slightly bemused expression, Sylvia added, "Uncle Eric has down syndrome."

Acquiring, be it grudgingly, a new respect for Brian, Scarlet said, "That's a lovely detail I wasn't aware of. I have to ask ...*Did* your Mom get Travis, a.k.a. dufus, to sign a prenup?"

Laughing as she topped up her hot chocolate, Sylvia replied, "Hell no. That woman has no self-esteem. She'll march any loser down the aisle as soon as look at him."

Frowning, Scarlet looked at her new friend, waiting for the irony to hit. That blow never came and feeling it was too early in their relationship to point out harsh realities, Scarlet enquired,

"Do I even need to ask how you get along with dufus?"

Sylvia curled her lip. "My brother and I call him three trick Travis. Trick one is before he's had a drink. He's all fidgety and irritated by everything we say or do. Trick two is after his first or second drink. He's suddenly interested in us and talks to us like we're real people. Then trick three is after his third, always the third, drink. It's weird, but his face even looks different. He asks us if we know who our father is. When we ignore him, he says he didn't think so, how could we if our Mother doesn't."

Wishing she hadn't brought up such a painful subject, Scarlet changed the topic. "I didn't know you had a brother. Is he younger or older than you?"

"Story Sam!" Sylvia exclaimed with a huge smile, saving Scarlet enquiring how they got along. "He's four years older than me."

"Story Sam," Scarlet repeated quizzically,

"Just Sam to everyone but me," Sylvia explained. "I've called him Story Sam since I was three years old. I get confused which dude it started with, but I think it was our first Dad. He used to hit our Mom something awful. When Sam could, he would take me to a different part of the house. He couldn't always 'cos I think we lived in a motel room for a while. Sam would tell a story to take my mind off the violence. If we were stuck in one room, he'd make me focus on him while he spoke so I wouldn't see our Mom getting hit. The story was about a family of mice who were looking for their perfect home. All the mice had names and personalities. He would describe what each one of them was wearing and what musical instrument they played. This same story carried on for years and years, through all Mom's husbands and the abuse. Whenever it began, whether it was yelling, breaking shit or worse, I would say *Story Sam,* and he'd begin. These mice traveled everywhere. Always having adventures and stuff."

Suddenly aware there were a couple of tears rolling down her cheeks, Scarlet checked the console.

"Sylvia!" she almost shrieked, "look at the time."

Opening her mouth in a silent gasp, Sylvia gave a small smile and left the studio.

"I've been on hold for ten minutes," came the familiar voice of Rod from Modesto.

Four hours later, setting her equipment to sleep mode, Scarlet looked up as Sylvia entered the studio.

"I'm going to miss you," Scarlet stated.

With a turned down mouth, Sylvia said, "Not as much as I'll miss you. I still have to be here, whether anyone's on the air or not. You do realize I'll be all alone in this dump until you get back."

Having forgotten a P.I.B.'s role, Scarlet felt a mixture of worry and guilt flood over her.

"Sylvia, you can't be here alone. Not after all that weirdness with Andree."

"He's in San Diego," Sylvia replied, waving her right hand in the air.

Scarlet doubted that to be true. "What about Story Sam. Could he hang here with you?"

"I guess," Sylvia mumbled distractedly while rooting around in her large, but still crammed to the brim purse.

"Sylvia, humor me here," Scarlet urged.

Holding her lip balm in the air as if she'd just found Willy Wonka's golden ticket, Sylvia replied,

"Geez, Oaks. I may as well have been here alone when Harold was doing your show."

Scarlet took a moment to savor the affection she felt for her new friend. From the military style name choice, keep it real attitude and multicolored hair, Sylvia had become one of her favorite people.

"Alright!" Sylvia conceded after Scarlet stared her down for a few seconds. "He gets back from college today. I'll ask him as soon as he's settled."

19

Standing to the far left of her picture window, Scarlet felt some semblance of normalcy returning. Clear blue sky engulfed the Golden Gate. Likewise, the fog she felt she'd been heaving her body through was dissipating too. Maybe Andree *was* in San Diego. Besides, Scarlet had decided he was nothing more than a petty thief who spouted scary threats to impress young women.

Due to this deduction, she'd chosen not to tell Niles and Tom about Andree. Her own needed questions as to how the caller knew about a P.I.B. had been answered. He'd obviously known enough, was close enough, to really scare Scarlet. But ... he'd been showing off for Sylvia. Long nights and honest declarations left Scarlet in little doubt as to Sylvia's resolve on making better choices. Andree would never be a part of either girl's life again. Besides, Niles and Tom worried enough about her already.

As if on cue, the bell rang. A stunning view, Scarlet mused as she unlocked the door, was as time-consuming as a favorite television show.

"Sorry guys," she exclaimed seeing Tom and Niles take in her state of undress. "I lost track of time this morning, but I'll be ready in a jiff."

"No worries, we've got time," Niles said reassuringly. "We'll make some tea while you cha.... Oh, my word."

Halfway down the corridor, Scarlet turned, "What?"

"That pig is huge!" Niles declared. Tom, hand over his mouth, volunteered no comment.

"By *that pig*, I presume you mean Prudence?" Scarlet asked indignantly. "And yes, Prudence has had a little growth spurt recently."

A short snort of laughter came out from behind Tom's hand. Niles' mouth moved, but no words came out.

Both men, lowering their heads, hastily made their way into the kitchen.

Lifting her chin, Scarlet addressed her pet, "Ignore those rude boys, my love. You are the most beautiful pig in the world."

Making a little squeal sound, as she always did when Scarlet spoke directly to her, Prudence followed her staunchest supporter into the bedroom.

Fifteen minutes later, dressed in skinny jeans, a black t-shirt, and her cherry red Doc Martens, Scarlet found Niles and Tom, tea in hand, sitting at her breakfast bar. Kissing them each on the cheek, she said,

"Happy Thanksgiving!"

"Happy Thanksgiving to you too, sweetheart," Tom said, standing to give her a hug.

Niles had bent down to make amends with Prudence. But in doing so, struggled with his vow to desist with the rude remarks. Prudence had reappeared from Scarlet's bedroom wrapped in some sort of shawl. The garment, tied in the center of the animal's back, boasted sequins, beads, and tassels. Poor Prudence now resembled a spooky little fortuneteller.

Aware of the hilarity of this outfit, Scarlet willed herself not to laugh.

Niles stood up straight. "Yes, Happy Thanksgiving to you and Madam Prudence."

The trio said their goodbyes to the little clairvoyant then began the journey to St. Christopher's Dining Hall.

Remembering why she never wore perfume around Tom, Scarlet cracked her window as 'Oud Wood' scented anyone within six feet of him.

Moments after finishing their friendly debate of whether they'd exceed last year's four thousand, six hundred pounds of turkey served, Tom steered around a corner to reveal hundreds of people in line, blocks away from the church.

Four hours later, exhausted but happy, the three volunteers relaxed on Scarlet's couch and exchanged stories. Niles had overseen yams and now, sweaty and sticky, stated if his Great Aunt Beatrice dared to produce one at their Thanksgiving celebration he would have to get up and leave. Tom admitted that, for the third year straight, he'd been bullied by Amanda and her receding hairline. Smiling at her uncommonly disheveled friend, Scarlet informed him the poor woman just had a high forehead.

Raising his dark eyebrows, Tom retorted, "Whatever she's got going on with all that exposed head, I don't like her."

Taking in the shocked expressions, Tom explained, "Well honestly, mashed potatoes should have a bit of texture to them. If she had her way, I'd be pouring them onto the plates from a jug."

"And you, Scar?" Niles enquired when the laughter died down.

"Oh, the usual bottom pinching and marriage proposals," Scarlet said with a smile.

"And what about the men, any trouble from them?" Tom asked, laughing raucously at his own joke.

Vowing to help at St. Christopher's more than twice a year, Niles, Tom, and Scarlet all walked to her front door. Wishing them a wonderful Thanksgiving dinner with no yams and suitably chunky mashed potatoes, Scarlet hugged the men in turn.

"Have fun in Aptos," they called in unison before making the short drive home.

Bypassing the kitchen for the shower, despite the urging of her rumbling stomach, Scarlet transformed herself from table server to dinner guest. Looking at Prudence and agreeing with Niles that all she needed was a crystal ball, Scarlet decided the pig would go au natural tonight. Luckily, Gran had a pellet stove which kept the dining room toasty warm.

Not sure if it was a reality, or because she felt ravenous, Scarlet smelled chicken in a duck in a turkey from the base of her Gran's steep drive. Or was it a duck in a chicken in a turkey? Smugly thinking she'd soon find out, Scarlet lifted Prudence from her car seat and carried her to the door.

Complimenting Gran's new hairdo as she entered the large foyer, Scarlet put Prudence on the floor and kissed Rose's cheek.

Patting tight curls, Rose said, "It'll be okay once it settles a bit, but for now I have the generic little old lady perm."

Smiling, Scarlet enquired, "Where's Dad?"

"Right here!" came a voice to her left. A hard-backed book in hand, Joe walked out of the library and hugged his youngest child.

With an exaggerated frown, Scarlet asked, "Why aren't you two sweating and covered in flour?"

Chuckling, Rose took Scarlet's arm and led her into the kitchen. "I assure you we were, but that bird creation takes four hours to cook. The sweating is done my dear, heat and time does the rest."

As Rose proudly displayed her efforts baking in the oven, Joe asked, "Red or white girls?"

Following exclamations of wonder and delight at the browning monstrosity, Scarlet replied, "Red for me, please Dad."

"I think I'll wait for dinner." Rose said, retrieving a large gravy boat from the pullout shelf to the right of the six-burner stovetop.

All hands were on deck for the next thirty minutes. The result was turducken and sides presented on Rose's San Mateo Double Pedestal Dining Table.

Having saved her appetite all day, and exerted herself with waiting countless tables, Scarlet was the first to reach for the trimmings.

"I'm going to say what I believe we're all thinking," Rose began. "I know family members are missing, but I felt your Dad was a bit fragile this year."

Joe forced a look of mock fragility. "I persuaded your Gran not to invite Uncle Cecil. Do you remember how inappropriate and hurtful he was last Thanksgiving?"

Grimacing with remembrance and watching as her father sliced through the boneless turducken, Scarlet responded,

"Something about a caveman?"

Joe deposited generous portions of meat onto three plates. "That was one of his tirades; you may have missed a couple of earlier ones while you were at St. Christopher's."

Thinking back a year, as she served her grandmother and father trimmings she'd already made a dent in, Scarlet said, "Wasn't it something about acting like the cavemen did? Practicality untainted by emotion or some such nonsense."

"Well remembered," Rose said, placing a cream-colored linen napkin on her lap. "He said cavemen chose wives who were young and fit. That good looks equaled a healthy woman who'd produce likewise children."

Smiling at Joe, as he filled her wine glass, Rose continued, "As you know, Elsa's struggled with her weight. And bless her, Anna does too. They just need to look at food, and it's on their hips."

Joe topped up Scarlet's drink. "Your Aunt Elsa can cope with his nasty comments. Shouldn't have to, but has done for years. But your cousin Anna, the poor girl was naturally mortified. She's at a tricky age anyway, what is she Mom, seventeen?"

Rose, with a mouth full of food, nodded her agreement.

"Unforgivable!" Scarlet said, remembering her cousin's look of embarrassment and subsequent refusal of Rose's, impossible to resist, English trifle dessert.

"The ugliness I believe you missed," Joe continued while helping himself to more mashed potatoes, "began when your Aunt Harriet and Uncle Kevin arrived. Cecil, Elsa, and Anna had been here for maybe fifteen minutes. Anna had lost herself in your Gran's library as she loves to do. Josh and Ben bounded in behind their parents, and Cecil makes this big show of what strapping, healthy young men they are. Then he gushes to Harriet about how it wasn't hard to see where they got their good looks and lean bodies from."

"I certainly remember, the minute I walked in the door, feeling you could cut the tension with a knife," Scarlet said. "Gran this dinner is beyond delicious, you've outdone yourself."

Thanking her granddaughter and saying she would have to humbly concur, Rose continued telling Joe's story.

"I think you know, don't you dear, that your Aunt Elsa had two miscarriages. One before Anna was born and one about three years after. Well, they were both boys, and Cecil has made no secret of his disappointment in not having sons."

Scarlet closed her eyes, imagining her aunt's pain at this loss compounded by constant blame from her idiot husband.

Rose looked at her son. "Do you remember how our love grew for Kevin that day?"

Grinning, Joe said, "Did it ever." Placing a hand on Scarlet's arm he explained, "After Cecil's insipid comments to Harriet, Kevin looked straight at him, well not straight at, as Cecil's almost a foot shorter. Kevin says, loud enough for Anna to hear in the library, *Actually Cecil, the boys take after my side of the family. Clearly, they get their height from me. Short men tend to have short sons.*"

"Your father and I were so relieved to have someone stand up to him," Rose interjected. "You know Elsa forbade us from doing that years ago."

Crunching into her last snap pea, Scarlet asked, "Why does she allow him to belittle her?"

Rose watched Joe clear away the dinner plates. "I can only liken it to that little frog. Your Uncle Cecil hasn't always been vile. These insults and criticisms have increased slowly, but steadily, over the years. Your aunt, just like that little frog, has had the temperature of the water turned up so gradually she didn't feel the heat and jump out."

Sighing, Scarlet asked, "So what can we do?"

Both women looked at Joe as he reentered the dining room, holding a large pecan pie. "Your aunt needs to feel the boiling water around her and want to exit the pot, we, unfortunately, can't do it for her."

A shadow of sadness falling over her lovely features, Rose suggested, "I say we take this desert into the living room and get really comfortable."

No argument was made to this suggestion, and Scarlet made tea to accompany the pie.

"I trust no more wildflowers have blown onto your car lately have they, my dear?" Rose asked as Scarlet entered the living room, struggling slightly with the weight of her grandmother's large Wedgewood teapot.

Carefully setting the tray down on the low coffee table, Scarlet responded to what she believed to be, forced nonchalance from her grandmother.

"Why do you ask, Gran?"

"Have you?" Joe interjected in a rush. Clearly, her father was not as skilled at this pretense of casual inquiry.

Setting the milk jug back on the tray, Scarlet perched on the edge of the chaise and shook her head.

Observing Rose momentarily close her eyes and her father appearing to physically decompress, Scarlet, asked, "Did they find another body?"

"You remember the missing woman?" Rose enquired.

At Scarlet's nod of confirmation, Rose continued, "They found her body this morning. In the same area and with the same ..."

Rose paused, appearing to have difficulty finding the words.

"The same flowers stuffed in her mouth," Scarlet volunteered emotionlessly.

A great effort, by Rose and Joe, proceeded in minimalizing the fact identical flowers had appeared on Scarlet's car twice in the last month. Wildflowers were called wild for a reason. They were native to this area. The wind coming off the bay could easily carry them around. Scarlet almost laughed out loud when her father and grandmother began debating the possibility Scarlet's wipers were damaged and frayed. It was very likely the case and, therefore, made them highly susceptible to picking up debris and wildflowers in the air.

But, despite their efforts to portray a unified belief in mere coincidence, there was no mistaking the look of worry on their faces.

Aware most of their Thanksgiving celebration had been filled with sadness and morbidity, Rose suggested watching one of Scarlet's favorite movies while digging into a box of See's candy. Because apparently, they hadn't eaten enough.

20

"How long will you be in Aptos?" Joe asked his daughter over coffee the following morning.

"I took Monday and Tuesday off, but I think I'll just stay tonight and tomorrow, then drive back on Sunday."

"Perfect!" Rose said, shifting her attention from the electric juicer to Scarlet. "That gives you time to get organized before you head back to work. Talking of work…" she continued, "your father and I were saying how fun it would be if we drove you." Before Scarlet had a chance to respond, Rose rushed, "Then we could pick you up and share a hot chocolate afterward. You do love your hot chocolate."

Feeling her granddaughter's scrutinizing gaze, Rose focused once again on cutting through large navel oranges.

With a wave of love and gratitude, Scarlet smiled at Rose. "Honestly Gran, there's no need. Besides, Tom has loaned me some weapons that aren't weapons, for my short walk from the car."

Still laughing, an hour later, from the demonstration of how to correctly swing a soap-filled sock, Rose and Joe waved goodbye as Prudence and Scarlet began their trip to Aptos.

Ending a journey filled with more thought than focus, Scarlet pulled into the winding drive. Wishing Prudence could carry something and mentally devising a cart for her to pull, Scarlet struggled up to the front door.

Soon settled and drinking blueberry mojitos in the backyard, Scarlet attempted to not stare at her mother.

Apparently, she must have failed. Marilyn stated, "I've had a little filler in my lips."

Wanting to say... *a little? You look like Bart Simpson!* Scarlet instead responded with, "I have a MAC lipstick for you."

Smiling, as much as her swollen lips would allow, Marilyn exclaimed, "Oh you darling girl, that's what all the models are wearing."

Over dinner, Marilyn shared slideshows of the four homes she was contemplating buying.

Remembering the conversation
she'd had with her father about the constraints of alimony, Scarlet was lukewarm on three homes and overly enthusiastic on the fourth.

"Really, you like the single story?" Marilyn questioned, eyebrows raised. "I'm not sure there's enough room for Rodney and Hayden to run around."

"Don't you tend to go to their place, though?" Scarlet reasoned.

"Well..." Marilyn began, coloring as if caught in a lie, "I think Lisa's easing up on her rules a little."

"Oh, is she allowing them to see your African Bumi Woman sculpture now?" Scarlet enquired.

Taking a bread roll from the basket, Marilyn replied, "Well, it is a little odd, those women took all the time to wear fifty bead necklaces but couldn't manage to cover their breasts. I think Lisa just got tired of the boys giggling about it. Besides..." she added buttering her roll, "that's yours if you'd like it. I don't want anything Rose gave me spoiling my new home."

Sighing inwardly, Scarlet changed the subject.

"Are we going to get all caught up with Bella and Edward tonight?"

Marilyn clapped her hands together softly, "Oh yes, time for *New Moon* and everything vampire."

Scarlet insisted on taking care of the dishes, then joined her mother and Prudence on the couch for the second season of their *Twilight* addiction.

The following morning, cringing slightly as Marilyn applied her new lipstick, Scarlet asked, "How long do they ... stay so full?"

"This particular filler should last about three months," Marilyn explained, standing back and admiring her reflection in the kitchen mirror. Smiling at herself, she then proceeded to remove the mirror from the wall.

Before Scarlet could ask why, Marilyn enlisted her help in removing all the mirrors, except for the ones in the bathrooms and bedrooms. Observing the look of confusion on her daughter's face, Marilyn, hesitantly confessed it was necessary for Lisa's comfort.

Removing the Retro Baroque mirror from the hall and almost crumbling under its weight, Scarlet asked,

"Lisa's comfort?"

Opening the hall closet door and depositing the two mirrors, Marilyn attempted to clarify, "You know Lisa has become quite involved in this new church."

Scarlet, confused, responded with a slow, "Yeah."

Marilyn, having glanced at the Grandfather clock, exclaimed, "Oh my, they'll be here in half an hour. I'll talk as we de-mirror."

Exasperated and irritated, Scarlet asked, "How many more rooms have them?"

"All of them," Marilyn said unabashedly.

Four hands were needed to remove the Florentine Gilt Antique mirror from above the fireplace. Scarlet dared not ask how they'd ever manage to re-hang them properly.

With deep, shallow breaths, Marilyn began, "This new Pastor, or whatever they call him, believes it's a sin to look at your reflection too often. He's fine with mirrors in rooms where you groom and dress but anywhere else, he says, is just feeding your vanity."

"Perhaps we should just go to Trent and Lisa's house?" Scarlet volunteered.

"I know this is such a pain," Marilyn agreed. "But I was there for Thanksgiving two days ago. If only you could have been with us."

Having expected this yearly complaint from her mother hours ago, Scarlet said, "I'm sorry Mom, but you know how important it is for me to keep my commitment to St. Christopher's."

Marilyn sighed dramatically, "I guess I do. But really, couldn't they set the food up in more of a buffet style? Then people could help themselves and daughters could be with mothers who truly need them."

For lack of anything else to say, Scarlet apologized again while continuing to labor for Lisa's comfort.

When the doorbell rang, Marilyn made a last-minute dash to hide her *Vogue* and *Cosmopolitan* magazines, leaving Scarlet to invite her brother, sister-in-law, and two nephews inside.

Rodney and Hayden made a beeline for Prudence after a fleeting hello to their grandmother and aunt. Trent, once known as the best-looking boy in high school, admittedly it was a small high school, hugged his sister with a now decidedly portly frame.

Lisa was unchanged since Scarlet's last visit with her. She wore her blond hair in a ponytail and not a trace of makeup. Navy cotton pants, allowing room for growth, were matched with embroidered stars strewn across a white cotton shirt. Tan, open toed flat sandals completed the ensemble.

Finding the boys petting a rather shocked looking Prudence in the living room, Scarlet asked them the obligatory questions expected of an aunt.

Rodney was now six years old and loved anything to do with Science. Looking at his Mother, he asked, "Can I show Aunt Scarlet my Pop Bottle Science kit?"

"In a little while, yes," Lisa replied looking at Scarlet rather than Rodney. "Trent and I believe," she continued, "anything allowing children to be hands on and using their imaginations is time well spent."

Nodding gravely, Trent said, "Plus, this kit was written by four-time award winning, Bill Nye the Science Guy."

"We used to love his show," Scarlet exclaimed, smiling and turning towards her youngest nephew.

Hayden informed her he'd just turned five last week. Scarlet, feeling mortified she'd forgotten his birthday, silently vowed to remedy that fact before leaving Aptos. Hayden then proceeded to list off all his presents, and some were so good they got mentioned twice. His favorite toys right now were Legos.

"Again..." Lisa interrupted her youngest child, "Legos are perfect for fine motor skills and creative thinking."

Watching the boys resume their affections on Prudence, Scarlet professed to Trent and Lisa how grown up and polite they were. Receiving complete agreement from her brother and sister-in-law, Scarlet began to ask what she could get her nephews to eat and drink. This simple inquiry earned Scarlet a warning look from Marilyn.

Stopping mid-sentence, Scarlet waited for someone else to say something.

Lisa was happy to oblige, "Trent, be a dear and get the boys' snacks from the car."

Smiling smugly as her husband jumped up, Lisa explained, "Trent and I believe it's beneficial for the boys to consume food free of colorings, additives, and preservatives."

Mentally and verbally agreeing, Scarlet was subsequently disappointed when Lisa added,

"We'd also prefer them not to see the commercial packaging. Trent and I believe how the food is served is as important as the food itself."

Catching the core of this statement as he walked back in the room, Trent declared, "All these food containers are made from bamboo, sugar cane, and corn."

At a loss for words, Scarlet looked at the collection in her brother's arms and smiled.

Watching as he placed the unique assortment on his mother's coffee table, Scarlet, almost holding her breath, asked Trent and Lisa if she could get them a cup of tea.

To Scarlet's relief, this appeared to be allowed. Marilyn followed her daughter into the kitchen and whispered,

"Sorry, I forgot to warn you about the food rules. I tried to find the right food, went to every health store in the area, but Lisa always managed to find something in the list of ingredients that was taboo."

With a new understanding of why Marilyn needed her around at Thanksgiving so badly, Scarlet gave her mother a wink, "I'll learn as I go."

The afternoon went relatively smoothly, the boys being a great distraction. Rodney built a volcano, which he then proudly erupted. Hayden meticulously built an impressive Lego Tower. When little legs needed to be stretched, the boys fought over who held the leash for Prudence's walk up and down the street.

A couple of times Trent tried to bring up the subject of their father. How weak it was of him to give up on his marriage and run away to the city like a teenager. Scarlet wouldn't bite, instead using her Mending Men talk show skills to redirect the conversation.

After a short discussion regarding his job and where he felt it was heading, Trent looked towards his Mother, "Did you tell her about Violet?"

Suddenly fascinated by the length of her nails, Marilyn shook her head.

"What's wrong with Violet?" Scarlet asked, feeling panic rise inside her.

Lisa let out a snort like scoffing sound and Marilyn coughed nervously.

Sitting up a little straighter on his mother's couch, Trent began, "Well that's a leading question, isn't it? There hasn't been much right with her since the eighth grade."

Knowing her patience couldn't hold out too much longer, Scarlet asked, "Is she hurt, unwell?"

Raising his eyebrows, Trent said, "No, nothing like that. She's just humiliated herself and, more importantly, us, once again."

Marilyn put her hand on Scarlet's knee. "Your sister has *apparently*," she paused to look pointedly at Trent, "featured in an adult movie."

"What?" Scarlet responded, struggling to comprehend the statement.

Closing his eyes as if he were suddenly exasperated, Trent said, "Mom, there's no apparently. It's a fact."

Rubbing hands nervously up and down the length of her thighs, Marilyn replied, "I don't know about that Trent. I'm not sure I trust your source."

"Who's your source?" Scarlet interjected, marveling at how this conversation possibly could, but was, becoming even stranger.

Trent cleared his throat. "As you know I work for the police force."

Desperately trying to reign in any telling expression on her face, Scarlet said, "You maintain their phone system."

Enough! she'd politely oohed and aahed for hours while Trent and Lisa talked about the exceptional talents their children possessed. She'd even bitten her tongue when Trent made derogatory comments about their father. She couldn't sit here for another minute pretending the Emperor was wearing clothes.

Silence descended upon them until Marilyn suggested, "Well, a police force isn't too strong without a reliable phone line."

Lisa, eyes narrowed, stared at Scarlet. "Remind us what it is you do? From what I've heard, it's talking about sports with a bunch of losers."

Scarlet exhaled slowly. "Guys, I didn't intend to start a verbal slinging match here. I'd just like to keep it real and not, perhaps falsely, accuse our sister of ..." choking over the words, she ended with, "making a poor career choice."

At this, Trent and Lisa started loudly talking over one another. Between them, Scarlet was called a fool, delusional, naïve, and ridiculous.

Seemingly appeased after voicing these insults, Trent continued in a calm voice, "Do you remember that old warehouse on Juniper Street?"

Scarlet nodded slowly, hating the direction this conversation was taking.

Trent's voice took on a serious news reporter's tone. "Residents of the Yew Tree Motel reported seeing lights and hearing music, despite the fact it's been vacant for years now. The police were called to the scene and low and behold, interrupted the production of a porn movie."

Receiving a violent nudge to his arm from Lisa, Trent colored as his wife reminded him, through gritted teeth, "We don't say that word in front of the children."

"Right, sorry," Trent said, the reporter inflection now gone. Looking over to his sons who were happily and obliviously playing with Legos, he rephrased, "The police found, right here in our little town, a bunch of low life degenerates making an adult movie."

"And one of the policemen recognized Violet?" Scarlet said, hoping to remove a little wind from her brother's self-righteous sails.

Giving his sister a look that said maybe you're not as dumb as I imagined, Trent continued, "I don't know if you remember Pete from my year?"

Frowning, Scarlet enquired, "Pete Rudelski?"

In a desperate attempt to lighten the mood, Marilyn said, "Of course, she remembers Pete. He had the biggest crush on Scarlet in high school. I'll never forget him coming over on Saturday mornings all summer long, offering to mow our lawn." Stroking Scarlet's long dark hair, Marilyn added, "Do you remember how you'd refuse to come out of your room until he'd gone?"

Scarlet pulled a face. "Yes, but Dad would always engage him in those long conversations."

"Well, he's happily married now." Lisa cut in, clearly not enjoying this little trip down memory lane.

Raising his voice, evidently feeling it necessary to keep his sister's and mother's attention, Trent picked up where he'd left off. "Pete, very tactfully informed me our sister, Violet, was one of the ..." lifting his hands, Trent made air quotes, "actors in this movie."

"Did he actually see Violet being filmed?" Scarlet asked casually.

Trent pushed his chin out defensively. "No, and because of that fact, he let her go with a warning. But, of course, she was involved, why else would she be there?"

Scarlet could think of a few reasons but decided they'd be wasted on this audience.

Standing, she offered everyone a drink in the hope it would prompt a recognition of the time. Her scheme worked. Lisa said the boys had a very strict schedule so as not to interfere with their body clock. Scarlet eagerly helped the boys pack away their Legos and Science experiments. Prudence was hugged fondly by the children, and all the adults dishonestly claimed to have had a lovely time.

Both feeling emotionally exhausted, Marilyn and Scarlet agreed more vampires and werewolves, accompanied by tea and lots of chocolate were required for the remainder of the day.

The next morning, Scarlet woke before her Mother. Whole grain waffles topped with blueberries and cream greeted Marilyn when she entered the kitchen.

Smiling in appreciation, Marilyn sat at her breakfast bar. "I'm sorry about yesterday. I know how difficult your brother and Lisa can be. It's just ..." Marilyn stopped talking and using the paper napkin next to her plate, wiped at her eyes.

Scarlet placed a hand on her mother's arm. "You have no reason to apologize. Try those," she added, motioning to the plate of waffles, "before they get too cold."

Marilyn dutifully ate her waffles while Scarlet brewed a fresh pot of coffee. Handing the steaming cup to her mother, she saw fresh tears threatening to spill from Marilyn's eyes.

"It's just…" Marilyn sniffed, "Trent and Lisa live right here in town. Rodney and Hayden are my only grandchildren, and Trent is very sympathetic towards my sadness over your father."

Scarlet could think of more accurate words than sympathetic, but this wasn't the time.

"I understand," Scarlet soothed. "Do you really believe Violet is involved with this adult movie thing?"

Marilyn shrugged her shoulders, the tears beginning to travel down her cheeks. "I would usually ask your father what to think. He's so good in these situations. He'd always help me see things clearly."

Tears of her own threatening, Scarlet quickly busied herself with clearing away the breakfast dishes.

"Would you do something for me?" Marilyn asked in a soft voice.

Scarlet turned to face her mother, "Name it."

"Would you watch the movie for me?"

Scarlet bit her lip. "Gosh Mom, the third season? I thought we'd save that for next time."

Wringing her hands, Marilyn replied, "No, not *Twilight*. I mean the adult movie Trent was talking about."

Knowing all the color had drained from her face, Scarlet asked, "You want *me* to watch a porn movie my own sister may be in?"

With a note of desperation in her voice, Marilyn said, "I *have* to know. One way or the other, I have to know."

This point could certainly be argued. The family had all but written poor Violet off. What difference did one more shenanigan make?

"Didn't Trent seem pretty sure she was involved?" Scarlet reasoned.

Marilyn placed her hands out, palms upward. "Trent *wants* to believe she was involved."

Suppressing the desire to ask her mother to analyze that statement for a moment, Scarlet instead voiced, "We don't even know what the movie's called."

Pursing her very full lips together, Marilyn walked into the entrance hall and opened a desk drawer.

Holding up an index card, she read aloud, "The Love Farm."

At a complete loss for words, Scarlet stared at her mother.

"It wasn't too hard to find out," Marilyn said tapping the card against an open hand. "You can just imagine the talk around town once they were discovered. When I overheard the name, I wrote it down so I wouldn't forget."

Typing the movie title into her iPhone, Scarlet said in a flat monotone, "Okay Mom, I'll let you know."

Putting the card back, Marilyn proclaimed, "You are such a lovely daughter. Besides, you young people watch this sort of thing all the time."

Eyebrows raised, Scarlet said, "I assure you we don't."

In heightened spirits, Marilyn got back onto the subject of her prospective new home until the time came for Scarlet and Prudence's departure.

21

"She wants you to do what?" Niles exclaimed amid Tom attempting to quell snorts of laughter.

"My Mother believes this type of viewing is commonplace for us twenty-somethings," Scarlet replied with a wide grin.

Niles placed fingertips against his temples. "Now let me get this straight. Tom and I will actually be watching this high-grade movie while you're hiding behind a throw pillow?"

Attempting to look solemn, Scarlet nodded her head.

Responding to his raised eyebrows, she explained, "I can't watch my own sister do this, this stuff."

No longer laughing but still breathing heavily under the weight of holding Prudence, Tom said, "Of course, we'll do it. What else would we be doing on a Wednesday evening?" Turning to Niles, he added, "We'll need to DVR American Idol."

"Thank you so much," Scarlet gushed.

Niles furrowed his brow playfully. "I haven't been home yet. I'll change into sweats, set the DVR for that ridiculously addictive show, and then we'll be ready for our evening's entertainment."

"Perfect!" Scarlet agreed. "I'll have pasta in pesto sauce ready to go."

As promised, Scarlet had cereal bowls generously laden with cheese topped pesto pasta waiting when the two men returned.

In the middle of scrolling through the internet, Tom paused and looking upward as if the soon-to-be-mentioned man were dead, whispered, "Thank you, Max, for leaving the smart TV."

Equipping her friends with the most recent photos available of her sister, Scarlet busied herself in the kitchen. She simultaneously smiled and cringed as intermixed sounds of horror and laughter traveled the short distance from the living room.

At the very moment, Tom screamed, "That's her!" fast, and unnecessarily hard raps were delivered to Scarlet's front door. Almost scalding herself with boiling water from the kettle, Scarlet took a second to decide which outburst should receive her immediate attention. Reasoning it should probably be the door, she looked through the peephole and saw two shiny police badges staring right back at her.

Feeling instantly guilty, heart racing and hands shaking, Scarlet opened the door.

"Ms. Oaks?" one of the two men asked.

Scarlet slowly nodded her head.

"I'm Detective Smyth, and this is my partner, Detective Williams. Would you mind if we came in and asked you a few questions?"

Finally finding her voice, Scarlet stammered, "I don't normally ... I never ... it's just that my sister, well my Mother asked me ..."

A voice behind her said, "Scar, it's not illegal to watch a porn movie."

Lifting his chin slightly, Detective Williams volunteered, "Providing the actors are of legal age, it isn't."

Nodding at the men who had now appeared behind Scarlet, the two detectives introduced themselves once more.

Sensing Scarlet had lost the use of her limbs and vocal cords, Niles invited the detectives into her living room.

Tom went into the kitchen to finish making the tea Scarlet had started. Niles sat next to Scarlet on the couch, his arm protectively around her shoulders.

Lifting his suit pants up at the knee, Detective Smyth sat on the ottoman opposite Scarlet and Niles. Detective Williams, misjudging the height of Scarlet's red velvet high back accent chair, almost fell to the floor.

Apologizing for the lack of furniture and then feeling silly for doing so, Scarlet held her breath, terrified to learn the reason for this visit.

"We're investigating the murders of Miranda Steele and Velma Ordman, Ms. Oaks," Detective Smyth began. "We think you may be able to help us."

Niles' vice-like grip on her shoulders relaxed, as did Scarlet's temporary paralysis. Ever since her sister, Violet, had chosen to live life on the wild side, Scarlet and the rest of the family had feared they'd be hearing about her on the ten o'clock news.

Thanking Tom for the tea and waiting as the detectives did the same, Scarlet said, "I think there must be some mistake. I don't even recognize those names."

"We're aware of that, Ms. Oaks," Detective Williams, scooting forward in his low chair, replied. "It's your call-in show we have some interest in."

Tempted to say, *I'm happy to hear it interests someone*, Scarlet inwardly acknowledged nerves were making her silly and attempted to focus.

"Mending Men?" she asked, still sure there was some mistake.

Retrieving a small notebook from his pocket, Detective Williams flipped back a couple of pages. Then, head down, read, "On Monday, November seventeenth, you received a call from a man by the name of Stewart."

Seeing Scarlet was struggling to remember, Detective Smyth said, "It was your first day on the new job, Ms. Oaks."

Staring back at the handsome black man, Scarlet narrowed her eyes in thought. "He said I could call him Stew."

At this, the detectives gave each other a sidelong glance.

F*eeling as if she'd passed the first question on a test*, Scarlet *an*xiously waited for more.

But surprisingly, no more came. What did come was an instruction and a warning.

Detective Smyth stood and placed his half-empty teacup on the coffee table. "He's our primary person of interest at this time."

Detective Williams stayed seated while writing, Scarlet couldn't imagine what, in his little pad.

"Do you record your callers, Ms. Oaks?" Detective Williams asked as he pocketed his notepad.

Looking at Niles, who appeared as bewildered as she, Scarlet shook her head.

Standing to join his partner, Detective Williams continued, "We'd like you to record all your callers from now on. We'll need to know if or when Stewart calls your show again."

Handing her his card, Detective Smyth said, "Please be on high alert and take extreme caution in your day to day business. We believe Stewart Steele may be the first serial killer the Bay Area's seen in some forty plus years."

"Hang on a minute!" Tom almost shouted as Detective Williams handed Scarlet his card. "Is that all you're going to tell the poor girl? Record and beware."

Both Detectives turned to look at Tom who stood sentinel in the archway leading to the entrance hall.

"We don't have any concrete evidence, thus far," Detective Williams replied calmly.

"You say he may be a serial killer, Is Scarlet's life in danger?" Niles enquired from his place on the couch.

Detective Smyth gave a subtle, but still evident, sigh. Repeating the little lift at the knee of his suit pants, he resumed a seating position on the black leather ottoman.

Looking directly at Niles, he said, "From the evidence we have and his psychological background, we don't believe he intends to harm Ms. Oaks."

"Shouldn't she have some sort of protection, just in case?" Niles beseeched.

"Sir," Detective Williams began. "If we believed..."

"Oh no!" Scarlet interjected.

All eyes turned to her. In barely more than a whisper, she continued, "The wildflowers on my car. The first time could have been a mistake, but it happened twice with the same flowers."

Retrieving his notebook, Detective Williams asked, "Do you remember what type of wildflower, Ms. Oaks?"

Unable to form the words, Niles said for her, "Franciscan Wildflowers."

Detective Williams, returned, with more realization of its low proximity, to the high back velvet chair. "You are aware I presume, of the connection that flower has to the two murder victims."

"Yes, my Grandmother read me the article from the paper," Scarlet responded in a small voice.

Shifting himself towards the couch edge, Niles suggested with some force, "It could just be a coincidence, though. That particular wildflower is very common to this area."

"In our line of work, we don't believe in coincidences," Detective Smyth said while retrieving a similar sized notebook to his partners.

Niles, biting his lower lip, marveled at how Policemen voiced these proclamations with a straight face.

Detective Smyth, pen poised, said, "This new information is cause for concern Ms. Oaks. Arrangements will be made to have you under twenty-four-hour surveillance. But rest assured you will never know we're there."

"I'm going to be watched, and I won't be able to see who's watching me?" Scarlet asked with a note of hysteria in her voice.

Blue eyes softening slightly, Williams explained, "We understand it's an intrusion Ms. Oaks, but *it is* most likely Stewart left those flowers on your car."

Deep in the recesses of her psyche, Scarlet had known this to be a reality. Hearing it from strange men with shiny shoes and badges was another thing.

The next hour was spent wracking her brain for dates, times, and locations of finding the flowers. She, Niles, and Tom then had to part with professional and personal details until, finally, the detectives took their leave.

With a necessary lowering of his head, Detective Smyth walked through the arched doorway. "We'll return tomorrow with a photo of our suspect."

Forcing out a thank you when she wanted to scream, *I don't want to see it,* Scarlet closed the front door on the departing detectives.

"I don't care what those men said," Tom whispered, observing Niles head for the kitchen. "Those flowers *could* just be a coincidence."

Fiddling with the neckline of Prudence's homemade dress, Scarlet admitted, "I didn't tell them everything."

What and *why* came back to her in stereo.

The, *what* was from Niles, returning to the living room with three teacups entangled through his fingers. The, *why,* was a gentler inquiry from Tom, who now occupied the blond-haired Detective's seat.

Niles carefully placed the cups on the table in front of Scarlet, then pulled a packet of Oreos from his sweat pants pocket.

"Was it relevant to the case?" Niles asked with feigned casualness.

Scarlet absentmindedly pulled an Oreo apart and began licking at the cream center. "No not really… well maybe."

"Scar …" Niles encouraged.

Moving Prudence from her lap and reaching for a teacup, Scarlet explained, "I'm supposed to give advice to these men using sports analogies. You know I'm no sports expert. Plus …" she added with a slight whine in her voice, "It was my first night on the show."

"Totally understandable," Tom soothed, sliding to his knees and reaching for a couple of cookies.

"Absolutely," Niles agreed.

From behind a teacup, held possessively in both hands, Scarlet took a deep breath. "I think he killed those women because of the advice I gave him."

22

    Peaks and valleys of optimism and despair flowed into the wee hours. Niles, having the last word and hoping it was one of reason, coaxed an exhausted Scarlet and her, clearly pained to be up so late, pig into bed.

    Hours later, in the throes of a startlingly real nightmare, Scarlet awoke to Prudence's high-pitched squeals. Taking a minute to absorb the reality of being at home rather than a studio filled with Mending Men listeners, Scarlet stumbled out of bed. Bleary-eyed, she watched Prudence, charade style, tell her there was someone at the front door.

    Having assumed it to be Niles and Tom, Scarlet was met with a mirrored look of surprise from an attractive, ebony skinned detective. Now fully awake, Scarlet embarrassingly assessed Smyth's surprise didn't derive from whom he saw, but more what he saw.

    Mumbling an invitation to enter, she stole a glance in the hall mirror. Masses of dark hair were practically standing on end, no doubt from the amount of times she'd run her hands through it in frustration. Her eyes were panda like from not removing yesterday's eye makeup, and she was wearing a nightshirt she'd had since she was a teenager.

    Self-consciously aware of how the length was only appropriate for her former thirteen-year-old self, Scarlet stood behind her antique wooden coat rack.

    Detective Smyth lowered his head to view Scarlet's face, now nestled between a fake fur collar and a navy-blue scarf. Pulling at a strand of wool, which had attached itself to her decidedly clumpy mascara, Scarlet asked the detective to make himself comfortable while she changed.

Attempting to conceal a smile, Detective Smyth nodded and moved into the living room.

Crossing paths with Prudence in the corridor, Scarlet entered the sanctity of her bedroom. Wishing, not for the first time, she were one of those organized women who hung their clothes in a closet, she scrambled for something to wear.

Laundry bound items were kicked aside before Scarlet finally settled on skinny jeans and an old faded sweatshirt Max hadn't deemed worthy of taking.

While gargling with baking soda mouthwash, she dipped a q-tip into moisturizer and expertly wiped it under both eyes. The morning panda look wasn't new to Scarlet.

Throwing clothes from floor to bed, in search of her flip flops, she gave up and settled for slippers.

Finding Detective Smyth studying a framed photograph of Mother Teresa, hanging alone and glorious above the fireplace, Scarlet informed him, "My grandmother met her in India in nineteen ninety-five."

The Detective turned to face her. "That must have been just a couple of years before she died."

Impressed, Scarlet said, "Yes, she died in nineteen ninety-seven."

Revealing even white teeth, the Detective looked down at Scarlet's feet. "Ballet and Winnie the Pooh characters."

Following his gaze to her slippers, Scarlet said, "I'm not sure Eeyore ever did ballet."

Smyth laughed, "No, I don't believe he did. I was referring to your nightshirt."

Feeling her face color, Scarlet blurted, "Would you like tea or coffee?"

"I noticed you and your friends drink tea, how about we stick with that?" the detective replied rubbing his large hands together.

"Tea it is," Scarlet mumbled, rushing to the kitchen.

Detective Smyth followed her. "I want to apologize if we were a tad abrupt last night, Ms. Oaks. Sometimes our ultimate goal takes precedence over our humaneness."

A cup in each hand, Scarlet turned from the sink and took note of his face, despite having seen it for hours the night before. Flawless skin was pulled taught across round cheekbones. A full mouth sat beneath a perfectly formed nose, and dark eyes appeared to penetrate whatever they observed.

Busying herself with the electric kettle, Scarlet said, "You were fine. I'm sorry I was so scattered."

Receiving no argument to this statement, she continued in a small voice, "My life's been a little topsy-turvy lately."

"I'm sorry to hear it," Smyth replied with a frown. "I can tell you, judging by the amount of time that's passed since Mr. Steele made contact, that it's highly unlikely you'll be bothered by him again."

Scarlet momentarily closed her eyes. "Thank God."

The detective moved a couple of steps towards her. "Highly unlikely, but not impossible, Ms. Oaks."

Biting her lower lip, Scarlet turned her back to him and poured the now boiled water into a teapot.

"I do need to show you his photograph," Smyth continued to Scarlet's back.

Placing one of Rose's hand-knitted cozies over the pot, Scarlet kept her hands firmly around its multicolored warmth. "Yes, of course."

Observing Scarlet's unaltered stance, Smyth asked, "Could we sit down perhaps?"

Robotically organizing cups on a tray, Scarlet led the way into her living room.

"Do you mind?" the detective asked, motioning to the spot next to Scarlet on the couch.

Shaking her head, Scarlet watched the signature pull at the knees of his pants, then felt suddenly small as he lowered himself down next to her.

Reaching into an inside pocket of his navy-blue blazer, Detective Smyth produced a folded piece of white paper. Carefully bringing the document to its original legal size, he smoothed it out atop the coffee table.

The image resembled an enlarged driver's license photograph. Stew wasn't what Scarlet had expected, but then she hadn't given his appearance any thought. There was no fork-tail, no horns or fangs. This suspected serial killer had reddish blond thinning hair and pale blue watery eyes drooping at the outer edges. The skin around his jawline and neck was loose and wrinkled.

"This photo is a couple of years old," Smyth said, refolding the paper and returning it to his inside breast pocket. "He could have less hair and perhaps gained or lost weight in those years." Picking up his cup, Smyth enquired, "Do you recognize the face?"

Scarlet shook her head. "No, but he does look very average. I could have seen him and not remembered."

"Yes, serial killers do tend to look like your average Joe living down the street," Smyth responded.

Prudence let out a loud snort as if doubting the credibility of Smyth's pronouncement.

A slight frown forming across his broad forehead, Detective Smyth asked, "What type of pig is she?"

Scarlet pulled a face. "If you look at the sales receipt, she's a micro pig. But, if you look at the wardrobe she's grown out of and the amount she's eating, then she's ..."

Pausing for a minute and letting her head fall back onto the sofa cushions, Scarlet voiced for the first time, what until this very moment she'd been afraid to admit, "Going to be really, really big!"

Detective Smyth leaned forward to pat Prudence's soft head, "Or perhaps she's just a slightly larger breed of micro pig and is very close to her full weight potential."

Feeling a new and sudden warmth for the man, Scarlet said, "I do hope you're right or I'll be in all kinds of trouble with the landlord."

Draining his teacup and standing, Detective Smyth joked, "You'll need to buy a farm."

Wondering if he knew more about her sister, Violet, than she did, Scarlet gave a half-smile and nodded.

Smyth glanced at his oversized stainless steel watch. "Surveillance is in place and operational. You just go about your regular daily routine and leave the rest to us."

Feeling as if nothing would ever be normal again, Scarlet, seeing him to the door, thanked him for his time. An invitation of more sleep posed to Prudence, received no argument as the pair snuggled back into bed.

23

Scarlet felt some sort of filing system was required to sort through the various emotions bombarding her person.

First and foremost, was she going to be killed? Sanctioned or not, the three conversations she'd had with Stew kept replaying in her head. His speech *had* been eerily slow but that aside he'd come across as ... well... just grateful.

Then there was the matter of what she'd said to Stew. Surely he hadn't misconstrued bath to mean drown a poor woman in the shallow waters of the bay? Was Scarlet insane to imagine it was, in any way shape or form, her fault for misquoting the sports analogy? Admittedly, her closest friends, Niles and Tom, had insisted her mere contemplation of this scenario was, if they were honest, certifiable behavior.

Then there was Andree. Was it sane to worry about him? Scarlet reminded herself he was nothing more than a spineless, petty thief. Yes, this one she'd file in the back under, *no need to worry, took his creepy self off to San Diego.*

Right behind Stew, she'd need to file her older sister and what to tell their Mother. The last mention of Violet was Tom screaming, *that's her,* accompanied by Police rapping at the front door. The movie was all but forgotten after the detective's arrival.

Deciding it was high time to get up, Scarlet gently nudged Prudence to her own side of the bed. Taking the three-step journey to open her bamboo shades, Scarlet, with the remembrance of a surveillance team, rapidly ducked down, and hastily closed them again.

Prudence awoke to the sound of running water in a cast iron claw foot tub. Trotting in and giving her owner a *rather you than me* expression, the little pig sat nearby as Scarlet lowered her body into the steaming water. Wincing from the heat for a couple of seconds, Scarlet reached up to the pedestal sink and pressed the voicemail button on her phone.

Message after message echoed around her black and white tiled bathroom. Two from her Gran stating how much she'd love to see the Mending Men studio and how could Scarlet possibly deny an old woman's simple request. One from her father, who laid out a schedule of rides to and from the radio station that were entirely for his benefit as he had business in that part of town. Three messages were from Niles and Tom. Niles was attempting to talk but kept getting drowned out by Tom shouting things like *we need to see you today,* and *it's imperative we chat with you today* in the background.

The last two messages were from James and Gary. James, happy to be back on American soil, was looking forward to seeing her again and would be by at two p.m. on Saturday as agreed. Gary said he enjoyed their first date and would she consent to a second one.

The bathroom finally silent, Scarlet realized the water was almost cold, and she hadn't even glanced at a bar of soap. Hurriedly washing, she grabbed a towel and shivered her way back into the bedroom.

If clean clothes were the goal, Scarlet had few options. However, she was pleasantly surprised at the end result of black tights, tall black riding boots, and a floral sleeveless summer dress over a long sleeved black t-shirt. Hurriedly putting on a load of laundry and feeding Prudence, Scarlet drove up the hill to Niles and Tom's home.

Greeting Scarlet with great enthusiasm, they led her through their large house to the enclosed patio.

Continually talking over each other and effectively saying the same things, Niles and Tom appeared to be eliciting Scarlet's help. The final words blurted out with emotional energy were how they barely coped and would she, in all essence, save their lives on a daily basis.

"What on earth are you two babbling about?" Scarlet asked, as the men finally sat in the comfortingly warm and bright room.

Tom, evidently baffled she hadn't understood their heartfelt plea, offered her a plate of scones.

With a sidelong glance at his partner, Niles explained, "We really need you here with us, full time. I'm getting busier and busier at Trade Elite, and as you know, Tom gets very little notice before he's off to some third world country."

Tom handed her a cup of tea. "Exactly! Off I go, poor Niles is all alone, and everything's in chaos around here. Please say you'll quit your job at the station, move in here, and work as our personal assistant."

Scarlet leaned back on the cushioned wicker sofa. "So, when Tom is away working overseas and you," she added, looking at Niles, "are putting in a ten-hour day, trading stocks, I'm needed here to ...?" Trailing off, she raised her eyebrows in question.

Tom began rearranging the remaining scones. Niles, after momentarily sticking his chin out in defiance, appeared to physically deflate. "Scar, we're worried about you."

"Make that terrified for you," Tom interjected.

Leaning in towards the men, who sat poised on the edges of rattan chairs, Scarlet said,

"I am so lucky to have friends like you. And believe me, I'm very grateful for what you're trying to do here. But ... I've decided while being super careful, not to let Stewart change how I live my life."

"Scar, that's very brave and all," Niles said, refilling her teacup, "but the man has killed two women already. Then ..." he added raising his voice, "bragged about it by leaving you those damn wildflowers."

"You said you spoke to him three times on the show?" Tom asked for clarification.

Nodding her head slowly, Scarlet exhaled. "Yes. He called on my first day. As I told you, I was so flustered about giving sports minded advice, I said bath instead of shower. He called and thanked me about a week later. Then, maybe two weeks after that, he said he was having an issue with another woman."

"May I please just say again, for the record," Tom said with his hands in the air, "you saying bath instead of shower has nothing, *nothing,* to do with these murders."

Giving Tom an appreciative smile, Scarlet said, "I'm sure you're right."

Niles waved his empty teacup in the air. "And if you *had* told those two detectives about it, I guarantee they wouldn't even have written it down in their silly little notebooks."

Reaching over and grabbing a perfectly formed scone, Tom said, "What is it with the pen and paper? Are those guys living in the last century or what?"

Scarlet began giggling. "Can you believe the timing of their visit?" Eyes wide, she added, "Oh good heavens, I keep forgetting to ask you about my sister."

Niles gave a sympathetic smile. "Hardly surprising. Well, dear Scar, we have good news there."

Putting her teacup on the coffee table, Scarlet, placing her hands together, looked expectantly at Niles.

"Violet was wearing short shorts and a ..." making some peculiar hand movements around his chest area, Niles concluded, "top."

Over a mouthful of scone, Tom said, "Like Elly May from the Beverly Hillbillies."

Niles pulled a face. "What? Elly May wore jeans and a buttoned up long sleeved shirt. She was a tomboy who loved critters."

Curling his top lip, Tom said defensively, "Forgive me, I only watched maybe two reruns."

Looking at Tom and tapping his hand on his thigh, Niles said, "The Dukes of Hazard, remember the girl with the shorts."

"Guys!" Scarlet interjected impatiently, "was my sister decent?"

With matching sheepish grins, Niles and Tom nodded their heads.

"But you were only ten minutes into the movie," Scarlet said with a slight scowl.

Without a trace of embarrassment, Tom informed her, "We finished it when we got home."

At Scarlet's raised eyebrows, Niles explained, "We had to find out what happened to the young newlywed who'd fallen from her horse, lost her memory, and wandered onto this farm of love."

Head in hands, Scarlet chuckled. "Thank you both so much for doing that for me. I'll have some good news to tell Mom, and I'll worry a little less about my sister."

Right forefinger pressing gently against his lower lip, Tom confirmed, "She was in maybe three scenes, always, be it scantily, dressed."

Draining her cup, Scarlet declared, "I have to get into that compound, or whatever it is, and see her. It's been too long; she may need me."

"But it's a farm of love," Niles argued in mock horror.

"Yes," Tom said in a theatrically deep voice. "The husband had to come and rescue his young bride and remind her of his existence." Putting a hand to the side of his mouth, he added, "Although he was a little late."

Niles stifled a laugh. "But he ended up loving the farm and staying there forever, with all those very friendly people."

Once the three friends had regained their composure, Scarlet concluded the farm discussion by saying, "Well then, you two must be my chaperones to this commune place that *isn't* a farm of love." With a grimace, she added, "I don't think."

Niles smiled broadly, "We'd love to meet Violet."

Tom, still flushed with laughter suggested, "Our lives would be so dull without you, Scarlet."

Silently wishing for a little dull, Scarlet sat back and let the two men reiterate their need for her to move in with them. It appeared, despite having a housekeeper, cook, and gardener, Tom and Niles could, suddenly, barely make it through the day without Scarlet's help.

Scarlet scrunched up her small nose. "I know this new gig at Bay Radio may not be the right fit for me. And ... I know things are creepy right now, but I have faith it will all turn out okay in the end. As for my safety, I'm being watched around the clock and who's to say they don't catch this freak in the next couple of days."

Conceding this to be a possibility, Niles and Tom walked Scarlet to her car.

After informing them of her upcoming date with James, Niles enquired, "Still no idea where he's taking you?"

Scarlet frowned. "No. Do you think I should just call him and admit I wasn't listening when he told me?"

Mid-nod, Niles stopped as Tom exclaimed, "Goodness no! Men like you to hang on their every word. That would not be a good start to this relationship. Just wear jeans and a cute top, and you'll be fine."

"Belt and heels?" Scarlet asked in all seriousness.

Without hesitation, Tom replied, "Yes to the belt, no to the heels."

24

"Hawaii!" Scarlet repeated as she sat drinking hot chocolate with her new young friend.

"Friggin' crazy, huh?" Sylvia said with a smile.

Checking how much time she had left before going live, Scarlet asked, "How long's the trip, you lucky girl?"

Sylvia stretched her back. "A week. I'll be back to work on the thirtieth. Mom just blurted it out on Thanksgiving. I think it's what got her through the day, to be honest."

"As bad as ever?" Scarlet asked tentatively.

Shuffling silver bangles up and down her lower arm, Sylvia replied, "The good news is Grandma wasn't drunk this year. She still said some shit, but it wasn't as nasty as when she's had a few. I guess Uncle Brian is, *dipping his wick,* as Mom calls it, where he shouldn't be." Pulling a face, Sylvia added, "Nothing new there, but somehow Grandma found out about it and isn't pleased."

Suspecting the dipping recipient may be Veronica, or Candy as she called herself on air, Scarlet, not knowing for sure, stayed silent.

Although curious to hear more, Scarlet clicked her mouse, saying, "Sylvia, I'm live in three."

The young girl picked up her thermos. "I'll be back."

Hitting the record button, Scarlet voiced her new signature, "Thank you for calling Mending Men, this is Scarlet, how can I help?"

Groaning inwardly when the caller announced himself as Barry, Scarlet patiently listened.

"Expensive shoes!" Barry began.

Taken aback at a statement instead of a question, Scarlet waited. It paid off, moments later he continued, "That's all a man needs to get laid in this city."

Sadly, it didn't pay off a second time. Barry apparently needed a response to this one. Following an uncomfortable silence, Scarlet managed, "Is that right, Barry?"

"Damn straight it is. My friend Dean from the Gym clued me in. He said chicks always look at your shoes. If they see the real deal, they assume you've got serious bucks in the bank and give it up real easy."

Disliking the man more with each call, Scarlet responded, "I think you're playing hardball here, Barry. If the shoes are intended to mislead the women, then you're not an honest player. Plus, why would you want to be with someone whose interest in you relies purely on what she believes your financial status to be?"

Barry gave an unmistakable snort. "You don't get it 'cos you're a chick. Chicks can get laid anytime they like. That's why it should be a man doing this show. A man would understand the problem and be impressed with my solution."

Scarlet closed her eyes for a second. "I'm sorry I couldn't help with this one, Barry. Thank you for calling Mending Men."

Prevented from screaming out loud by the other calls on hold, Scarlet took a deep breath and braced herself for the next onslaught.

"Hello Miss Scarlet, this is Henry from Bernal Heights," the deep voice began.

Sighing with relief, Scarlet remembered this man to be her one and only, now she knew Stew was psychotic, pleasant caller.

"First of all," Henry continued, "much as I respected your predecessor, I think having a lady on this show is much more valuable." With a throaty laugh, he concluded, "You can let us dumb guys in on the female perspective."

"Thank you so much, Henry," Scarlet gushed. Wanting to hug the man, she continued, "I think you have an excellent point there, proving you are most certainly not a dumb guy."

Politely thanking her, Henry explained the reason for his call. "I'm not sure if you remember, Miss Scarlet, how my wife and I have little in common. Forgive me, how could you remember with all the calls you get."

Wanting to say how could I forget you, but feeling as if the gushing had gone on long enough, Scarlet instead said, "I think I remember she liked to scrapbook and have her nails done."

"That's exactly right," Henry said. "Now she's joined a book club which, initially, I was pleased about. I love to read, and even though the club is just for her lady friends, I thought maybe I could also read the book allowing the two of us to discuss it."

Nodding, despite the fact no one could see her, Scarlet said, "Sounds good to me Henry, but you said initially."

In a more dispirited tone, Henry continued, "Well, last night it was her turn to host. There are eight women. I know maybe two of them from her scrapbooking club. I kept out of the way as instructed, but when I heard raucous laughter, I became a little curious."

Imagining Henry must be confident his wife and her friends didn't even know the radio dial for Mending Men, Scarlet said, "Understandable."

"I've finished the book," Henry explained. "It's incredibly somber. I can't remember a funny line in it."

"Keep in mind, Henry," Scarlet interjected, "these book clubs are as much about getting together and enjoying friendships, as they are about the actual book."

"Agreed, Miss Scarlet, but my eavesdropping revealed a group of women who find their husbands ridiculous. I couldn't repeat the things they said about them. It was shocking to hear how little respect they have for their spouses."

Scarlet took a moment to process this information. "Obviously, I don't know your wife or her friends. I have no idea how they feel about their husbands. But, I can guess there was a fair bit of exaggerating and maybe even a little showing off going on in that room."

"Why on earth would they want to show off how embarrassing and revolting they find their husbands?" Henry enquired.

"Consider this…" Scarlet began as she relaxed her back into the high stool, painfully aware she'd maintained a tense posture since Barry's call. "These women may feel undervalued, belittled, even bullied by their husbands. Here, at this little book club surrounded by friends, they feel liberated and no doubt safe enough to share their feelings."

A longer than comfortable pause ensued. "Damn, Miss Scarlet, you have an excellent point there. I rest my case. You are perfect for this show. Thank you for listening and for your sound female perspective."

Feeling elated, Scarlet thanked him for calling and asked him to stay in touch.

Observing there were no more callers on hold, probably due to the length of Henry's call, Scarlet set the song bed off with *Dire Straits' Money for nothing*.

"Someone's happy!" came a voice from the door.

"I think I just helped someone," Scarlet said with straightened posture.

"Good for you," Sylvia said with a playful scowl.

Checking she had eight more songs followed by four commercials lined up, Scarlet focused her attention on the young girl. "So, tell me more about your Thanksgiving."

Laughing as she scooted her stool towards Scarlet, Sylvia responded, "Your life must be pretty dull, Oaks, if you're so interested in mine."

Knowing Sylvia nor anyone else at the station for that matter knew about Stew, Scarlet just smiled.

"Would this be a good time to give you a little bad news?" Sylvia asked.

Scarlet, eyes wide, nodded.

With a grimace, Sylvia went on, "Uncle Brian's not finding a replacement for me. I know you're still spooked about Andree and honestly Oaks if you want me to not go, I won't."

Suffering through a fleeting moment of panic, Scarlet reassured her friend, "Not go to Hawaii, are you crazy? I'm not spooked by Andree anymore." Receiving another scowl from Sylvia, Scarlet reiterated, "Honestly I'm not." Scarlet wondered what Sylvia would think if she knew Andree was small potatoes compared with the real threat looming over her. "I have a couple of very good friends who live just up the hill from my home. They'll hang with me for sure."

Eyes narrowed, Sylvia asked, "You're certain?"

"Well, I wouldn't blame you if you *wanted* to stay," Scarlet teased. "I mean you'll be missing mid-fifties versus eighty degrees in Hawaii."

Smiling broadly, Sylvia said, "I can't wait. We're going to the Kohala coast of the big island. Sam and I are going to leave poor Mom with the dufus and be gone all day exploring and shit."

Scarlet closed the open sites on her computer. "I'm sure your Mom can handle him. You and Sam deserve some time alone. Hand me your thermos, it's time for us to go home."

25

Scarlet faithfully recorded each caller, but Friday arrived and with it, no sign of Stewart.

The surveillance on her was, admittedly, undetectable. Rose and Joe, on the other hand, were not.

Initially, Scarlet had walked up to their car ready to be upset. They'd not listened when she assured them all was fine. But, after hearing her father and grandmother come up with bizarre reasons for finding them in the Bay Radio parking lot, her resolve weakened. She likened the pair to a bad, but sweet and kind, comedy duo.

Now, each night, she'd wave, and they'd wave back. Scarlet would then climb into her cold car and chuckle as Abbot and Costello followed closely behind. Only when she'd opened her front door, put the light on and given a thumbs up sign, would the Honda accord make its way home.

"Happy Friday, Prudence," Scarlet announced, before apologizing to the pig for the rather frigid house temperature.

Devouring two bowls of cornflakes with warm milk and lots of sugar, Scarlet and Prudence huddled together in bed, almost smothered by every blanket Scarlet owned.

Just when she'd found a position where every part of her body felt covered and warm, the phone rang.

Guilt washing over fatigue, Scarlet remembered she'd forgotten to call Niles and Tom. Since news of San Francisco's suspected serial killer, it had become a nightly ritual. Reaching for her cell phone with the arm that wasn't under Prudence's round belly, Scarlet hit the talk button. "Sorry Niles, I'm home and in bed with a pig."

"They were by way of a thank you," the slow voice began, "I just wanted to thank you, yes I did."

Jolting upright, Scarlet's skull hit the headboard as Prudence let out a loud disgruntled snort. Frantically looking around her dark bedroom, Scarlet asked, "How did you get this number?"

"You helped me with my problems. Women like flowers, yes they do."

Scarlet's heart thumped at a speed she wouldn't have believed possible. Her hands were trembling so badly she needed them both to hold the phone. Wobbling limbs somehow got her upright and over to the bedroom door. With her left hand, she turned the light switch on and off in quick succession.

In as steady a voice as she could muster she said, "But, why did … I mean you…."

"I'm much happier now, yes I am," the eerily slow voice interrupted her.

Three loud thumps came at the front door. Prudence let out a high-pitched squeal, and the phone jumped from Scarlet's shaky hands.

Running to the door and turning on every light switch as she went, Scarlet heard the men, before looking through the peephole.

An unknown male voice asked, "Ms. Oaks, are you okay? This is Sergeant Harraway and Sergeant Collins."

Leaning against the door, but not opening it, Scarlet replied, "I think I'm okay."

As one of the men appeared to call for assistance, the other enquired, "Do you need medical attention, Ms. Oaks?"

A lump in her throat and tears in her eyes, Scarlet told them she did not.

"We need to keep our posts as surveillance Mam, but we have two more officers on their way. Their names are Detective Adams and Detective Clark."

"Okay," Scarlet said in a feeble voice.

Less than fifteen minutes later came another, less urgent, knock on the door.

Holding identification badges up for Scarlet's inspection, a man, who looked close to retirement age and a woman who looked not much older than Scarlet, entered the house.

After sitting in Scarlet's living room, the female detective spoke first. "Sargent Harraway reported seeing your bedroom light flash on and off repeatedly. Taking this as a sign of distress, he knocked on your door and received intelligence you were unharmed."

Leaning in towards Scarlet, the older detective said, "We can assure you Ms. Oaks, your home is secure. Are you able to tell us why you flashed your bedroom light in that manner?"

Holding her right hand out, palm upwards, Scarlet mumbled, "The phone." Staring at her empty hand, the detectives patiently waited for her to elaborate.

At length, Detective Clark asked, "Did you receive a disturbing phone call this evening?"

Remembrance increasing her heart rate, Scarlet nodded her head slowly.

"Do you remember where your phone is, Ms. Oaks?" the man continued in a soothing tone.

Scarlet rubbed a hand across her forehead. "I think so."

Smiling kindly, the detective asked, "Would you be so kind as to lead Detective Clark to where you believe your phone is located?"

The female detective stood and pocketed her notebook.

Receiving an instruction seemed to jolt Scarlet out of shock. Walking the short distance to her bedroom, she pointed to the floor where the phone lay, atop a thick patchwork quilt.

Returning to the living room, the two women found Detective Adams on his phone. Seconds later he hung up, suggesting brightly, "Despite the fact, it's almost two in the morning, may I propose we all have a coffee or something of that nature."

Reminding Scarlet of her Grandpa Herb, she smiled at the man before agreeing to his idea.

"Do we have your permission to view recent calls?" Detective Clark asked as Scarlet began walking into the kitchen.

"Yes, of course," Scarlet replied over her shoulder.

Reentering the room five minutes later, she found the detectives, heads together, examining her phone.

Scarlet set the tray down and received an appreciative nod from the male detective. While his partner looked through her notepad, he enquired, "Do you mind if this greedy old man has a few of those Oreos?"

Scarlet chuckled, "Please, help yourself."

Reaching over and taking a couple, Detective Adams gave his partner a playful scowl. "I know, I know," he began, "these are horribly bad for me, some kind of syrup."

Smiling, despite her attempt to look disapproving, Detective Clark responded, "High fructose corn syrup."

Polishing off his first cookie, Detective Adams explained, "Detective Clark is a bit of a health nut, Ms. Oaks. Always encouraging me to eat things I can't even pronounce."

Raising her eyebrows and shaking her head, the detective asked Scarlet, "Did you receive any other calls, after the one that alarmed you?"

Thinking for a moment, Scarlet replied, "Not that I'm aware of. I used my main light switch to alert the surveillance guys. Then when they knocked on the door, it gave me such a start, I dropped the phone."

"Very smart move with the flashing light, by the way," Detective Adams said through a mouthful of cookie.

Nodding in agreement, Detective Clark continued, "The last call to your cell phone is, hardly surprisingly, an unlisted number. It came in at five minutes after one this morning and lasted two minutes and four seconds. Does that sound accurate to you, Ms. Oaks?"

Thinking it seemed so much longer, but knowing it couldn't have been, Scarlet replied, "Yes, that sounds right. I don't remember hanging up, so I presume he did. I think I dropped the phone mid-call and ran to the front door."

Detective Clark placed the phone on the end table to her right. "Do you remember what the caller said to you?"

Scarlet's breathing instantly became short and shallow. "He was thanking me again. He'd done that on my show once, thanked me for helping him. He said something about women liking flowers."

Wiping the underside of slim fingers against his mouth, Detective Adams asked, "You believe it was the same man who called into your show?"

Paling at this reality, Scarlet said, "There is no question, it was Stewart. He said something I'd forgotten to mention to the other Detectives. He does this weird thing where after each statement he kind of adds self-confirmation, as if you've doubted his honesty."

Detective Clark gave her older counterpart a furtive glance. "Did he actually say he gave you flowers?"

Seeing the worried look on Scarlet's face, Detective Adams added, "Don't worry if you can't remember."

Scarlet rubbed at her increasingly tired eyes. "I think he did. He said something about it being a way of thanking me. Then he talked about women liking flowers."

Standing up, the male detective declared, "You're exhausted Ms. Oaks. It's time Detective Clark, and I let you get some rest."

Returning her cup to the tray, the younger detective informed Scarlet she and Detective Adams would be conferring with the lead detectives on the case.

Walking to the front door, they offered assurances of Scarlet's safety. Reaching down and petting Prudence, Detective Adams concluded, "But, purely for your own peace of mind, Ms. Oaks, it might be a good idea to stay with family or friends for a little while."

Closing the door on the detectives, Scarlet mused over who would fuss less, her Gran and Dad or Niles and Tom. Feeling grateful to have them, she and Prudence fell back into bed and attempted to assume their original sleeping position.

26

Waking up to the patter, patter of little hooves heading to their litter box, Scarlet groped around the bed looking for her phone.

Falling back onto her pillow, she remembered it was on a side table in her living room. Detective Clark had placed it there and with that recollection came the memory of all that had transpired.

How on earth did Stew find her number? Or maybe it wasn't even that hard. Was this call a sign Stew wanted to harm her?

Wrapping a blanket around her shoulders, Scarlet promised her pig she'd turn up the heat, then, inadvertently, dragged some undergarments with the length of the blanket, into the living room.

Thermostat adjusted and toast procured, Scarlet plugged her phone in to charge and scrolled through the list of missed calls. Deciding her mother's voicemail sounded most needy, Scarlet hit the callback button, then sunk back into her couch while an apparently still tired Prudence dozed on her lap.

Marilyn professed she was beyond distraught. What was it about her that made the entire family recoil? First Violet, then her husband and now Trent.

Focusing on the positive, Scarlet gave her mother the good news. Violet barely featured in the movie and was certainly never naked. Tentatively, Scarlet enquired after her brother. As she suspected, it was more Lisa than Trent. But, heaven forbid her brother could grow a backbone and stand up to the woman. Through tears, Marilyn said Trent and Lisa had decided to spend Christmas with Lisa's family. Apparently, Lisa's parents had joined the same church as them, and Lisa felt it was beneficial for the children to see family members follow the same path. After Marilyn imparted, more than once, how she'd be totally and completely alone at Christmas, Scarlet, agreed to forgo feeding the homeless at St. Christopher's. She would, instead, spend Christmas with her Mother in Aptos.

Pushing uncharitable thoughts about Lisa from her head, Scarlet readied to call Niles and Tom. Their message had voiced concern at not getting their nightly, I'm home safe, report. If they didn't hear soon, they'd stop by to check on her. Taking a moment to construct an explanation of last night's drama that wouldn't panic them too much, Scarlet was distracted by the doorbell.

"That'll be Niles," Scarlet informed Prudence, gently moving the pig's head from her lap. With the blanket still draped around her, Scarlet opened the front door.

In retrospect, Scarlet couldn't decide who looked more alarmed, the David Bowie look alike or the detective. Although to be fair, the detective should be getting used to the disheveled look by now. Mortifyingly aware she'd just opened her front door wearing a long t-shirt and a blanket, Scarlet muttered something about expecting Niles and a late night. Noticing the men pull their eyes from her legs to her face, Scarlet frantically pulled at the, maddeningly longer than it was wide, blanket.

Deciding her only option was to turn her back on them, Scarlet began walking towards her bedroom. "Do come in," she said looking over her shoulder. "Have a seat, and I'll be right with you."

Cursing under her breath, she ran into her bathroom and, for the first time that day, looked at her reflection. "Just perfect," she muttered to herself, "I even have bits of Oreo cookies stuck in my teeth."

Seeing the humor in it, Scarlet remembered how she'd looked the night of Niles and Tom's party. Her unfortunate date must imagine he'd come to the wrong house. Ten minutes later, in jeans and a cable knit sweater, Scarlet entered the living room looking presentable, if not date ready.

The detective spoke first, "I was apologizing to your boyfriend for the necessary grilling needed before we'd allow him close to your home."

Blushing at the term 'boyfriend' and being unable to fathom what the *boyfriend* must be thinking about the situation, Scarlet said, "David, I'm so sorry about all this."

Her date replied, "No apology necessary." Smiling, he added, "I'm James."

Wishing there was a hole she could crawl into, Scarlet became aware the Detective's cough had a decidedly pantomime quality to it. Smyth, after getting Scarlet's attention, raised his eyebrows before lowering his chin towards the ground a couple of times.

Turning in the direction of the chin point, Scarlet became newly mortified by the sight of two pieces of underwear strewn across the living room floor. James politely chose that moment to be enthralled with the view of the bay from her living room window. Hastily stuffing the embarrassing garments under a couch cushion, Scarlet asked,

"Would anyone like a cup of tea?"

Barely disguising a chuckle, Detective Smyth said he had questions regarding the previous evening but would stop by at a more convenient time.

Seeing Smyth out the door, Scarlet turned to face James. Whether it was the kind look in his eyes or the warm and understanding smile, she couldn't be sure. But, with no warning, her lower lip began to tremble, and tears filled her tired eyes. James, be it somewhat self-consciously, opened his arms to hug her. Scarlet, effortlessly cocooned herself within their strength, and unashamedly, cried into his shoulder.

"What must you think of me?" she asked him, pulling away minutes later.

"I think you're incredible," he replied in a low voice.

Laughing as she looked around for a tissue, Scarlet said, "I forget about our date; I call you David and have police surrounding my home."

Narrowed eyes coupled with a mischievous grin, James replied, "The first two are pretty surprising."

Scarlet simultaneously giggled and sniffed. "I have to find a tissue."

James looked at his watch. "I'm afraid I have to go. I brought ... well ... I need to get going because .... Can we, when you're ...

Squeezing the bridge of her nose with thumb and forefinger, Scarlet interjected, "Less pathetic, not surrounded by drama?"

Motioning towards the door with his right hand, James replied, "I have to leave, but I'll be in touch."

Scarlet forced a smile. "I understand and thank you for the much-needed hug." Waving her arms in the air, she added, "I'm so sorry about all this."

Pushing back a wavy blond tendril that had escaped from behind his ear, James, again, motioned towards her drive but appeared unable to vocalize the urgency. "Please, don't apologize. I'll call you," he added, walking out the door.

Closing the door behind him, Scarlet muttered, "I won't hold my breath."

27

When the doorbell rang, Scarlet became aware she'd been immobile on the couch since saying goodbye, no doubt forever, to James. The only part of her that had moved was her right arm, lifting Oreos, far too frequently, into her mouth.

"Oh dear," Tom said, as Scarlet opened the door to him and Niles. "Did I not mention one should wear makeup on a first date?"

Scarlet curled her lip. "If you think I look bad now, you should have seen me when the poor man arrived."

Following Scarlet into the kitchen, Niles enquired, "You forgot about the date?"

Filling the kettle with water, Scarlet sighed, "Yes, but I have a really good reason. The guy the police suspect of killing those two women. He called me last night."

"Oh my goodness," Tom said with both hands over his heart. Niles, wide-eyed stopped petting Prudence and asked,

"Why didn't you call us? We'd have come right over."

Sipping their favorite beverage, Scarlet told her friends how she'd answered the phone, believing it to be them checking in on her. At this, they all started apologizing at the same time. Scarlet saying it was her job to call them, the men saying they should have called her.

"That's it, Scar," Niles stated, authoritatively, "you are not going to be alone again until they catch this creep."

Nodding his head, Tom contributed, "Well done with the light thing."

Scarlet smiled. "Thanks, guys, but I was never in any actual danger. I'm being watched around the clock, remember."

Pouring more tea, Niles said, "Scar, I know it's in your nature to be calm and getting all panicked never helped anyone, but ... I can't help feeling you're taking all this a little *too* much in stride."

Using both hands to tighten her ponytail, Scarlet replied, "I can tell you I wasn't calm last night. The detectives were here super fast, so that helped. I feel like the San Francisco Police Department has a revolving door into my home these days."

Tom, with a sympathetic smile, asked, "So when Bowie arrived, you were exhausted and naturally still traumatized?"

Scarlet giggled. "We have to stop with the Bowie names. I called him David today!"

Niles roared with laughter as Tom closed his eyes and put his head back. After shooting a stern look at Niles, Tom, who was clearly taking this dating thing more seriously, said, "Dare I ask how the date went?"

Scarlet shook her head slowly. "There wasn't one."

Both men looking at her expectantly, Scarlet explained, "He arrived at the same time as Detective Smyth, which wasn't exactly a good start."

"True, he's a good-looking guy," Tom said gravely.

Scarlet frowned. "I don't think the detective's looks were the issue, more that he was a detective."

Nodding, Tom enquired, "Did you tell James what's been going on?"

"How could she not?" Niles interjected.

Scarlet placed a hand over her eyes, "It was so embarrassing, I looked like nothing on earth. I even managed to drag underwear in here on a blanket."

Not understanding what this meant but deciding he may be better off not knowing, Niles declared,

"Well, if he can't handle the fact you've got some stuff going on through no fault of your own, then good riddance to him."

"Here, here," Tom joined in. "Plenty more where he came from."

Scarlet stared into her empty teacup. "The thing is I kind of liked this one. I know nothing about him; he was here maybe fifteen minutes tops. I can't really explain why, but I just felt comfortable with him."

Tom and Niles glanced at each other.

Detecting their bemusement, Scarlet retorted, "I know he left when he could have toughed it out and stayed. Obviously, what I felt from him wasn't real, and he's not interested in me or my predicament."

Lifting Prudence off his lap and moving to sit next to Scarlet, Niles volunteered, "You said it, you don't know him, and he doesn't know you." Putting his arm around Scarlet's shoulders, Niles continued, "Maybe after this is all over, you could give it another go."

Tom coughed loudly. "I don't think so. If the man, and I don't care how much he looks like Bowie, can't hang while the hanging's rough, then he doesn't get to hang in smooth waters either."

Frowning, Niles enquired, "Did you just make up that bit, about hanging in smooth waters?"

Tom smiled sheepishly. "Yeah, it doesn't really make sense, does it?"

Niles and Scarlet shook their heads. Suddenly becoming serious, Niles said, "Scar, we need to talk about the upcoming week."

Scarlet, eyes wide, declared, "Oh my word, Christmas is in five days' time."

Niles gently squeezed her knee. "Tom and I are flying to Boston tomorrow. We're not going to be able to help at St. Christopher's this year."

Scarlet leaned back into the couch. "Me neither. Mom called yesterday, she'll be all alone if I don't join her in Aptos."

Tom walked towards the kitchen. "We'll contact the church and let them know, you have enough on your plate."

"Why Boston?" Scarlet asked. "You typically go to your Great Aunt Beatrice's for Christmas."

Tom came back in to retrieve the teapot. "My Uncle Victor's on his last legs. Dad asked my sibs and me to come spend one last Christmas with him."

"Oh, I'm so sorry, Tom," Scarlet said as she stood to hug him.

Putting the teapot back on the table to embrace her, Tom replied, "It's fine. Uncle Victor's had a good long life, and besides, he's really just been treading water since my Aunt Grace died." Walking back to the kitchen, teapot in hand Tom asked, "What is it with me and water analogies today?"

"We need to know your plans, Scar," Niles said determinedly.

Pausing before she poured milk into three cups, Scarlet said, "I'm at the station for the next three days."

At the men's look of horror, she went on, "It's fine. I have Christmas Eve and Christmas Day off."

"Barely enough time to get anywhere and relax," Niles said with a scowl. "Can't you just prerecord stuff and play repeat shows?"

Nodding her head, Scarlet replied, "Yeah, but Brian likes, at least, one DJ and the P.I.B. in the building. He has to be satisfied with just the P.I.B. on Christmas Eve and …"

Trailing off, she remembered Sylvia was spending Christmas in Hawaii. Typically, Scarlet would have enlisted the weekend P.I.B., but according to Sylvia, Brian had just fired him for doing his medical transcriber job during P.I.B hours. Scarlet had hoped Niles and Tom would be able to hang for a few hours on Monday and Tuesday, but now they would be out of town too.

Tom broke the silence. "Okay, so you're at the station on Monday and Tuesday, then on Wednesday, you and Prudence are driving to Aptos."

Thankful for the clarification, Scarlet replied, "Yes. Then we'll drive back here on the twenty-sixth, and I'm back at work that evening."

Heading to the front door, Tom said, "Any chance we can persuade you to stay at your Grans until you head to Aptos?"

Grinning, Scarlet said, "I'll give it serious thought. Where are you going?"

Halfway out the door, Tom shouted, "We have gifts!"

"Oh no," Scarlet whined, "I haven't done any shopping yet."

"Would you stop?" Niles admonished, "you know we love to spoil you and you also know we have the means to do it."

Squeals of delight, from Scarlet and Prudence, were heard into the evening, as box after box revealed clothes, some even matching, for them both. The last box contained shortbread cookies, mince pies, plum pudding and other ancestral favorites.

Laughing as Scarlet's eyes rolled back upon smelling a hastily opened jar of brandy butter, Niles looked towards the window. "So, where you go, they go?"

"I presume so," Scarlet replied, gleefully examining a large tin of Quality Street candies. "I feel terrible for the guys who have to follow me to Aptos over Christmas."

"I'm sure they're used to it," Tom said while wrestling Prudence into one of her new outfits.

With a heavy heart and some nagging apprehension, Scarlet said goodbye to her friends, thanked them again and wished them a very Merry Christmas.

28

The early morning fog had gradually burned off revealing the Golden Gate Bridge, looming high in all its splendor. The sight filled Scarlet with awe, despite the countless times she'd viewed it.

The man bobbing in the bay was awe-inspiring too. When his face came into view, she realized, awe-inspiring as he might be, he wasn't her father. Panicking for a moment, as she'd seen her dad's Honda Accord in the parking lot, Scarlet scanned the white caps.

Seconds later, his handsome head shot out from under a large cream and turquoise ripple. With a deep sigh of relief, Scarlet waved, then prepared the blanket and drinks for his arrival.

"Dan, this is my girl," Scarlet's father shouted over his shoulder as he walked towards her. The only other man in the bay waved his two arms in the air. Scarlet smiled and waved back.

"Nice guy," Joe said as he reached for his towel. "He's selling me on the Dolphin club; they swim and row in the bay."

"You should join, Dad."

Lifting his sweats out of a plastic bag and holding them up, Joe smiled, "I keep these bayside in anticipation of my beautiful daughter's visits."

"I love coming here," Scarlet admitted. "But be warned, I may never join you in that fifty-degree water."

Joe laughed, "It takes some getting used to, but boy is it exhilarating. Dan there," he added, nodding towards the water, "has been in the Dolphin Club for twenty years. He has some stories about what he's seen in these waters."

Scarlet shuddered when, unbidden, she visualized two murdered women, their bodies pale and bloated.

Sensing her morose, Joe declared, "Can you believe it's almost Christmas, are you feeding the masses again?"

Two mugs of hot chocolate later, Scarlet had shared Lisa's decision to spend the holidays away from Marilyn. Joe expressed his disappointment in Trent's apparent inability to stand up to his wife and understood the need for Scarlet to be with her Mother for Christmas.

"Your Gran will understand too of course. She's doing a smaller bird due to the fact we were eating Turducken sandwiches for a week after thanksgiving."

Chuckling, Scarlet said, "And that's after you gave me two-thirds of the leftovers."

Joe blew in his cupped hands. "Mom enjoyed the indulgence, but informed me last night we have an organic, free range chicken, humanely raised on a family run farm."

Scarlet pulled a funny face. "Did they play Mozart in this pasture?"

Slapping her leg gently, Joe responded, "It seems to be making your Gran quite happy, so I don't question the dead bird's upbringing."

Accepting a half-cup, as Scarlet drained the last of her huge thermos, Joe asked, "You're done with work until after the holidays?"

Shaking her head as she placed the thermos in her basket, Scarlet replied, "No, I'm working tomorrow and Tuesday."

Joe frowned. "Well, I'm glad you and that young girl are close now. I don't want you being alone. Did I tell you, I've got a work party tomorrow night?"

Having been about to ask for his assistance, Scarlet hid her disappointment. "Your Christmas parties are pretty fancy from what I remember."

Sighing, Joe replied, "Black tie and dancing. I was going to ask you to come with, but thought that might be considered cruel and unusual punishment."

Putting her hand on her father's, Scarlet said, "You skipped the last one. This is your first year going solo."

Lifting his other hand over hers and squeezing it gently, Joe replied, "To be honest, it's quite a relief. Your Mom always made such a fuss about her outfit. What if someone else had the same dress as her? Remember the ear bashing that sweet Vietnamese girl at the hair salon received? However she coifed your mother's hair, it wasn't right. Every year, I'd visit the Salon after Christmas armed with a conciliatory gift. What was the girl's name? I remember she loved almond cookies."

Scarlet scrunched up her features. "Veda or Vida. Mom still sees her once a month for a weave."

Joe nodded. "I'll make an appearance at this party, talk to the few people who are responsible for my paycheck, then make a sneaky retreat. I'll be back in time to trail my daughter, unseen, from the radio station at midnight."

Laughing, Scarlet said, "I do have a favor to ask you…"

Shaking his head, Joe interrupted, "Mom and I love doing it. You wouldn't take that away from us, would you? Your Gran says it gives her day real purpose."

Smiling at her father's beseeching gaze, Scarlet clarified, "I'm fine with the two sleuths in the parking lot, I have an added favor to ask you."

"Anything," Joe responded with a more serious expression.

Uneasy with the lie, Scarlet began, "The young girl you mentioned is going to Hawaii and won't be with me on Tuesday night. Would you mind hanging with me at the station? Gran too, if she's interested."

Patting her knee, Joe said, "Consider it done. I assure you, your Gran will be interested. We'll meet you on Tuesday, in the parking lot, at say six forty-five?"

"Perfect," Scarlet said happily.

Some forty minutes later, after dissecting the year almost past, Scarlet kissed her father's cold check and said goodbye.

During the drive between China Beach and her home, Scarlet decided she wasn't ready to give up on reentering the dating scene.

Full of determination, Scarlet kissed Prudence, complimented the little pig on the new outfit from Niles and Tom, then headed to her computer.

Following five drafted attempts to simply let Gary know she too enjoyed their date and would like to see him again, Scarlet finally decided it didn't sound needy, too interested, too cold or just plain loopy and hit the send button.

Christmas was looming, but Scarlet knew Union Square would be a zoo on the last weekend before the holidays. Vowing to get there on Monday and begin and end her gift shopping, she spent the rest of the day tidying and preparing for her trip to Aptos.

29

Hanging up the phone, Scarlet made a deduction - Gary did not work until midnight. Prudence, with a decidedly wrinkled expression, mirrored Scarlet's displeasure at being woken early.

Gary had said he was so happy to receive her email and was available for another date anytime. The conversation had taken a strange little turn from then on. Scarlet had enquired as to his plans for Christmas, expecting them to be fixed at this point. Her stomach dropped at learning he was free as a bird. She inwardly scolded herself for contacting him before the holidays. But didn't he know Christmas was for family and people you were in a serious relationship with?

He said all his family lived on the East Coast, but he had divorced himself from them many years ago. When Scarlet had attempted to lighten the mood by saying didn't everyone want to do that on occasion, Gary had elaborated. At fifteen years old, he'd taken court action to divorce himself from his parents. His two sisters had tried to stay in touch but, years later after moving to the West Coast, he'd managed to lose them too.

Experiencing a mixture of horror and pity, Scarlet decided the conversation was too deep and too sad for the early hour. Steering it onto lighter topics, she then felt guilty for skirting an issue he may *need* to talk about. Self-reproach at exclusively *mending men* from seven until midnight may have influenced her agreement to meet by the Christmas tree in Union Square that afternoon.

Scarlet looked at the phone, sitting on her nightstand as if it held some answers to her recently ended conversation with Gary. She visualized him sitting opposite her in the restaurant. If memory served, he was a very attractive man. Why would a handsome, successful lawyer be all alone over the holidays? Scarlet didn't flatter herself with the notion others were kept at bay in the hope of seeing her again. James had practically sprinted away after twenty minutes, and it was hard to forget how easily Max walked out of her life. Deciding she was overanalyzing poor Gary, Scarlet directed her thoughts to gift buying and fell back to sleep within minutes.

Ninety minutes later, impressed by how much fun it was to start the day in a tidy room with clean clothes hung in her closet, Scarlet danced to *Fun*'s, *Some Nights* in between each stage of getting date ready. Unsure whether it was the loud, fast music spurring her on, or the fact she wore less makeup during a day date, Scarlet found she had a good two hours to spare before meeting Gary. The plan had been to Christmas shop together. Upon reflection, that was a ludicrous idea. They barely knew each other. Did she want him there while she chose the perfect eyeshadow for her Mother? Was she ready to admit to him, gifts for her nephews could not be black or red because, per her sister-in-law, those colors represented the devil? Of course not. She'd leave now, get her shopping done, and then maybe save one non-personal gift to purchase in Gary's company.

Following the typical struggle to find a parking spot, Scarlet slowly made her way to Union Square. Aware it was high time she acknowledged the joyful season, Scarlet savored the crispness in the air and chose not to be fazed by the crowds drawn to the eighty-three foot Christmas tree. Standing amongst a group of French tourists, Scarlet stood a while and shared their admiration. Almost impossible to see the artificial limbs for the countless balls, Scarlet took a few paces back and managed to take a selfie that captured the star topper and all. Subsequently captivated by a young couple propping each other up on the outdoor ice rink, she smiled at their regular stops for laughter and kisses before continuing around the small oval. Snapping herself out of the pointless exercise of imagining how lovely this holiday would be if she were madly in love, Scarlet crossed the street to Macy's. Christmas wreaths adorning every window, the store beckoned her with perceived warmth.

The Bobbi Brown counter was in clear sight, but Scarlet's focus was diverted upon hearing a woman's raised voice. Stealing a curious glance at the source, she almost fell over a small child. Apologizing to the child's mother, Scarlet kept her head down, taking brisk steps to her destination. Hiding behind a large display of elaborately wrapped boxes, Scarlet studied the couple at the nearby counter. There was no question; the man with the angry woman was Gary.

30

In hushed tones, Scarlet answered the girl behind the counter, "I'm looking for an eyeshadow, brown and gold tones, I think."

Leaning over the counter towards Scarlet, the Bobbi Brown makeup artist enquired, "Are your eyes blue or green?"

Staring right past the girl towards the other counter, Scarlet distractedly nodded while the Bobbi Brown artist chatted about new and exciting colors for the season.

The woman with Gary appeared to be complaining about not getting a gift with her purchase. A taller, older woman had now come to the aid of the red-faced assistant. In a clear and precise manner, she reiterated what the flustered assistant had already explained, their promotion ended yesterday.

"So, you'll lose a valued customer over one lousy day, is that what you're telling me?" The woman retorted, her voice increasing with each word.

The employee, Scarlet guessed to be a supervisor, apologized for the strict start and end dates associated with giveaways. She explained that sadly, they were unable to make exceptions. Clearly, this customer had no interest in rules and explanations. She continued her tirade using various insults and curses. Not a moment too soon, two burly security guards walked up to the counter.

Thankfully, the young girl helping Scarlet had also chosen to watch this scene unfold.

After the uniformed men firmly offered to escort the angry woman from the store, she, while pushing their hands from her arm, turned to

Gary, and spat, "As usual, you have nothing to say, you're just going to stand back and let these people mistreat me."

Head down, Gary expressed in a barely audible voice, "You just keep talking, you don't know when to shut up."

Scarlet turned away, a shiver running up her spine and tingling momentarily on the back of her neck.

Opening a small black box, the Bobbi Brown artist said, "The holidays sure do bring out the worst in some people."

Nodding her head as she watched the couple disappear in the distance, Scarlet replied, "Yes, they do."

Presenting the small case of eyeshadows, as if she were a Sommelier in a fancy restaurant, the girl said, "These colors will look stunning on you."

Scarlet smiled politely. "They're actually a Christmas gift for my Mother."

"Wonderful," the girl exclaimed, "I'll gift wrap it for you."

Ten minutes later, instead of heading to the toy department as planned, Scarlet made her way to Starbucks on the fourth floor. Acknowledging there were benefits to being alone, Scarlet nabbed the one remaining stool seat overlooking Union Square.

Sipping on her latte, Scarlet struggled to process what she'd just seen. Surely that couldn't have been Gary. But if it was him, who on earth was the woman? Scarlet thought back to their one and only date in Italian town. The lighting had been low, and it was dark when they'd walked to her car. With an aha moment, Scarlet dug through a typically cluttered purse and retrieved her cell phone. Pulling up the dating site, she carefully studied Gary's headshot. The photo was a little fuzzy, but no, that was not the same man she'd just seen at the cosmetic counter. Scarlet smiled as she imagined what Niles would say, *Gosh, Scar, Gary must be the only tall blond man in the state of California!*

Relaxed enough to actually taste the latte, Scarlet people watched until the last bit of foam was consumed, then forged ahead to the toy store.

31

Mesmerized by glittering lights on the Christmas tree, Scarlet stood in Union Square once again. Her eyes were focused upward while her thoughts were full of contemplation. Did her sister-in-law, Lisa, truly care what colors represented the devil? Perhaps she just enjoyed knowing how hard it was for family members to find children's toys without any red on them. Contemplation morphed into resentment when she remembered Lisa was excluding Scarlet's mother and presumably all the Oaks family from seeing the boys at Christmas.

Feeling a hand on her shoulder, Scarlet turned to face… Gary.

"Are you okay?" he enquired. "You look like you just saw a ghost."

Attempting to regulate her breathing, Scarlet replied, "I'm fine, just a little chilly I guess."

Smiling broadly, Gary suggested, "Well, let's get you inside then. I thought we'd have a bite before starting our shopping. How does the Rotunda at Neiman Marcus sound?"

Unable to look him in the eye, Scarlet found an urgent need to close the clasp on her purse. "Lovely."

Thankful for the crowds making it almost impossible to hold a conversation while walking, Scarlet used the time to plan a quick getaway. She'd say her grandmother was unwell and she needed to go see her before work. No, she wouldn't say that. It always felt like tempting fate to lie about a loved one's health. Her car was being serviced before heading out of town for the holidays. But she'd have known that before agreeing to this meeting. She needed to get a grip.

Yes, this was the man she saw in Macy's, but there could be a perfectly reasonable explanation for it.

"Fourth floor, I believe," Gary said as they entered the upscale department store.

Wanting to interject, *liar liar*, Scarlet listened as Gary told her he'd come straight from the office and was worried he'd made her wait. As they alighted from the escalator, Scarlet said, "I wouldn't have minded, but I'm afraid I can't stay as long as I'd hoped. My car was acting up a little on the way here. I'd like to get it checked out before everything closes for the holidays."

Gary, unfortunately, asked for details about the car's problems. Scarlet circumvented the topic by alluding she didn't know the trunk from the hood.

Mercifully, they were both distracted by the arrival of the maître d'.

With a practiced smile and an outstretched arm, the maître d' exclaimed, "You're in luck. I have a window table."

Scarlet thought cynically, *of course, you do, but when I'm here with someone I like, you'll be all out of exceptional views.*

Forcing an attitude adjustment, Scarlet enjoyed her bird's eye view of Union Square. Aiding this shift was the maître d's suggestion of a high tea.

Scarlet kept her eyes heavenward longer than necessary while Gary educated her on the twenty-five hundred pieces of colored glass in the dome above their heads. When her neck began to protest, she diverted Gary's attention to the busy ice rink outside. It took just a couple more minutes of small talk until an eye-catching two-tier tower, laden with sandwiches, scones, cakes, and cookies arrived at their table. Scarlet, silently vowing to bring Niles and Tom here as a late Christmas gift, oohed and aahed over the miniature opera cakes. Wishing she'd ordered a tall over her Grande Latte, Scarlet thanked Gary for the suggestion to come to the Rotunda, before plucking an open-faced cucumber sandwich from the lower tier.

Able to catch every fourth or fifth word as Gary talked about a particularly challenging case he was working on, Scarlet resumed her musings on the identity of Gary's earlier companion. She certainly wasn't old enough to be his mother. Besides, he'd just said on the phone this morning he didn't see his parents or his sisters. But, he'd also said he'd come straight from the office, and she knew that wasn't true. It had to have been a woman who felt comfortable with him, although Gary would probably use a different adjective.

Realizing more than five words had passed, and Gary had stopped talking, Scarlet was forced to say,

"Sorry, Gary, I was miles away for a minute there."

Chuckling, Gary replied, "The Christmas season can do that to a person. I was just asking whether you have any spare time for a lonely guy over Christmas. Even an hour would be enough to share a hot chocolate together."

Her jam and cream laden scone poised in the air, Scarlet replied, "Gosh Gary, I'm afraid it's unlikely because I have to see so many family members in different parts of the state." Smiling, she added sarcastically, "We're all celebrating separately, like a real American family."

"I understand," he replied, looking like a small child whose favorite toy had just been confiscated.

Scarlet gave Gary a sympathetic smile and grabbed the check from the approaching waiter before her date had a fighting chance.

"Oh no, you don't," Gary argued.

Unzipping her black leather wallet, Scarlet replied, "You bought that delicious meal in Baldovinos. It's my turn to treat."

Ignoring his protests, Scarlet handed her credit card to the attentive waiter.

Minutes later the receipt arrived and with it, a couple of pink boxes.

At Gary's insistence she take all the leftovers, Scarlet said, "A single man could use some tasty treats over the holidays, are you sure you won't take a couple of these cute little cakes?"

Gary patted his stomach. "Got to watch the carbs." Frowning he added, "How do you manage to stay so beautifully slim?"

She wasn't about to tell him she could barely afford to keep food in her fridge, so instead, she chose to say, "Just a good metabolism, I guess."

Ten minutes later, almost giddy with relief, Scarlet headed for her car. The Christmas shopping wasn't complete, but Scarlet didn't want to bump into Gary after feigning an urgent visit to her mechanic. Plus, after spending seventy dollars on a high tea, there weren't sufficient funds for more gifts. That expense was not part of the planned budget, but Scarlet was determined not to feel beholden to the man. Granted, their Italian meal had cost a lot more than afternoon tea, but Scarlet hoped this relieved any further obligation.

Returning home in a perfectly working MINI Cooper, Scarlet and her pig snuggled together on the couch. After nodding off for an hour, Scarlet groggily made her way to the kitchen. Mid preparation of two hot chocolate filled thermoses, a sudden and dramatic realization flowed through her. Only one thermos was needed tonight.

32

Determined to keep her spirits up, Scarlet walked into the radio station with a backpack full of necessities. Her staple thermos, leftover goodies from the high tea, a framed photograph of Niles and Tom holding a significantly smaller Prudence, a flashlight, a bar of soap, and a man's thick gray sock.

It had been a couple of weeks since she'd packed the flashlight and soap in a sock. They were heavy, and besides, she was under twenty-four-hour surveillance now. But, something, probably just the fact Sylvia was lying on a far-off beach, made Scarlet grab them on her way out the door.

Forced by the weight of her backpack to take the stairs a little slower, Scarlet considered the words spoken between Gary and his disgruntled lady friend. *You just keep talking and never shut up.* Scarlet couldn't seem to shake from her consciousness, the fact she'd very recently heard this same complaint.

Reaching the sanctity of her studio, Scarlet placed her framed photo just behind the mic and then debated whether to eat something now or pace herself to keep the comfort food coming.

Nervous and jittery, she almost fell off the high stool when her cell phone rang.

"How's my favorite girl?" came Niles' soothing inquiry.

Bemused by the feeling of tears stinging her eyes, Scarlet took a breath. "She's just fine. How are my favorite boys?"

"We've got you on speaker," Niles and Tom returned in chorus.

Tom, who sounded as if he were munching on something, began, "Scarlet, you've never seen so much snow. And cold, I don't know why anyone ever leaves the house."

Laughing, Niles added, "Boston is so beautiful, though, Scar. We're bringing you next time."

Maddeningly, Scarlet's tears reappeared. "I'd love that. How's Uncle Victor doing?"

Still chewing, Tom replied, "He's got years to him yet; we were duped, the guy's healthier than me."

"That may be a slight exaggeration," Niles interrupted, "but he is a hoot, that old man can entertain a room like nobody's business."

Scarlet reached for a little princess cake. "I'm glad you two are having fun."

Tom's tone became serious. "We hate being so far away from you with, with ... well, we just miss you, Scarlet."

Determined not to let the tears win, Scarlet voiced, "I miss you too, but I'm fine. I even went on a date this afternoon."

"With James?" Tom enquired.

"No. With Gary. You remember we met for a meal in Italian town."

Sounding as if he'd just moved closer to the phone, Niles said, "Of course, we remember. He was a little too keen, though, wasn't he? Asking you to go away with him scuba diving or something."

Hoping the following statement was true, Scarlet said, "I think my rather hurried departure today may have curbed his enthusiasm."

"Oh, do tell," Tom said with mischief in his voice.

Taking a minute to remember the correct sequence of events, Scarlet began,

"He called really early this morning ..."

"Scar, are you okay?" Niles asked when Scarlet's voice faded off into the abyss.

Heart racing and beads of sweat forming on her top lip, Scarlet replied, "I never gave Gary my phone number. That's the good thing about a dating site. You just communicate through it, so it's easier if things don't work out."

In a soft voice, Tom volunteered, "Maybe you did, but forgot you did."

Shaking her head slowly and thinking hard, Scarlet said, "The first time was a voice mail, and I didn't even think about it because I had a ton around the same time. I remember giving my number to James at your house. I was so distracted by the news of Max; I'd have probably handed him my house keys if he'd asked."

Laughing, be it a little nervously, Niles said, "Tell us about the date."

"His voicemail said how much he'd enjoyed our first date and would love another. I left him a message on the site saying I'd like another date too. Then when he called again, this morning, we agreed to meet in Union Square to do some shopping."

A pause followed and Scarlet could only imagine the looks Niles and Tom were exchanging.

Forcing enthusiasm, Niles said, "That all sounds just fine. What went wrong?"

"I decided, and I know you two were thinking it, Christmas shopping is a little too personal for a second date. So, I got to the square early, took in some of the sights, and then went to buy Mom an eyeshadow pallet in Macy's."

Receiving neither denial nor confirmation of the *too personal for a second date theory,* Scarlet continued, "As I'm walking to the Bobbi Brown counter, my attention is caught by a woman's raised voice at the adjoining desk. With her, I mean clearly with her, is Gary."

Tom, a slightly higher pitch to his voice than normal, said, "Standing there, bold as brass with another woman? I cannot even believe this."

"Okay, let's think about this for a moment," Niles interjected. "Isn't there a very good chance it was his mother or sister. The pair of them could have been shopping for another family member."

Relieved to be sharing her muddled thoughts with such close friends, Scarlet contributed,

"I would have presumed exactly that, except on the phone this morning, he told me he was estranged from all his family."

Sounding as if he'd just said no thank you to someone offering him a drink, Niles went on, "Family is a vague term though Scar. Does it include every aunt and cousin and niece?"

Feeling her body relax somewhat, Scarlet responded, "Okay, this is why the two of you really can't ever leave town. I need your sound judgment. I'm sure you're right. I bet it was some highly-strung cousin."

Barely hidden excitement in his voice, Tom enquired, "So what happened after that?"

"We met at the agreed time and then went to the Rotunda and had a high tea."

"Oh my gosh, that place is fabulous," Tom enthused.

Smiling, Scarlet said, "I agree, and I'm taking the two of you there as a late Christmas treat when you get back."

Finishing the conversation with talk of how much fun the three of them would have there, Scarlet hung up feeling relaxed enough to start her show.

With no time for sports research, she adjusted her mic and pressed the button to hear her first caller.

"Hi, this is Barry," the now familiar voice began. "Do you remember the great advice I gave your listeners last time I called?"

Wincing, and wishing she could somehow reign him in, Scarlet said, "I'm not sure I agree it was great advice, Barry. Wasn't it something about tricking women into thinking you have a lot of money?"

Equipped with a slight slur - it was the season – Barry replied, "Tricking is a harsh word, I call it leveling the playing field."

Ignoring Scarlet's protests, Barry went on, "Listen up guys ... If getting laid is on your Christmas wish list, just call me Santa."

Seeing there were no other callers on hold, Scarlet decided to just sit back. Why fight it? Truth be told, he probably amused a significant percentage of her audience.

Sounding as if he'd just taken a large swig of something, Barry elaborated, "ATM receipts. If you have a decent amount of cash sitting in your bank, I don't care if it's all spoken for with damn bills, get some money out of your ATM and hold onto that receipt. Then, when you're at the bar, and you see a hot chick, write your phone number on the back of that receipt. Sure as Kaepernick can run, she'll call you."

In a very slow voice, as if he were talking to people as drunk as himself, he concluded, "She'll turn the paper over and see your bank balance. It don't matter if the money's already gone. *She* thinks you've got some serious cash and she'll be hot to trot."

Caught somewhere between total horror and the urge to laugh hysterically, Scarlet said, "Thanks, Barry. Merry Christmas to you."

Hanging up on him before he could dispense more advice, Scarlet began her nine in a row with, *All cried out* by Alison Moyet.

Thankful Gary had eaten so little at the Rotunda, Scarlet reached into her lunch bag and selected a raisin scone. Pairing it with a cup of hot chocolate, she sat back and looked around her studio. What had she been so worried about? She could manage one night alone. Niles was very likely correct about the woman with Gary being an aunt or cousin or something. It couldn't possibly be his wife. He'd asked Scarlet on a trip to go snorkeling with some sort of shark. He'd said he was completely open over Christmas. What would she do without Niles and his cool thinking? She'd forgotten to tell him what Gary had said to the woman. She certainly wouldn't have mentioned, not until they got back from Boston anyway, how it unnerved her. Digging into her memory bank, she tried once again, to remember who she'd heard say the exact thing Gary voiced to the angry woman.

Then, like an ice-cold blade, piercing her heart ... she remembered.

33

With trembling fingers, Scarlet pulled a black leather wallet from the bottom of her purse.

Retrieving a small card from an inner pocket, she held it in one hand while dialing with the other.

A familiar, be it rather groggy, voice said, "Detective Smyth."

Attempting, but failing, to not sound hysterical, Scarlet began, "You've got the wrong man. You're looking for the wrong man."

"Ms. Oaks?" the male voice enquired.

"I think I know who the killer is and it's not Stew."

The grogginess gone, Detective Smyth responded, "Where are you right now, Ms. Oaks, do you feel in danger?"

Looking out into the dim and deserted hall beyond her studio, Scarlet replied, "I'm at work and no … at least, I don't think I'm in danger right now."

"Remember Ms. Oaks, you are always under surveillance. No one, who isn't known to you, can get close to you."

Aware her point wasn't getting across, Scarlet elaborated, "That's just it. I think the killer is a man I've been on two dates with."

In what sounded suspiciously like a patronizing tone, Detective Smyth said he'd send over two on-duty detectives to get an updated statement. "Rest assured, Ms. Oaks, only persons cleared to enter your workplace can get past the surveillance team. Why don't you tell me the reasons you suspect this man you've dated?"

Trying to swallow over the massive lump now occupying her throat, Scarlet explained,

"I heard him say something that gave me chills, but at the time I couldn't really figure out why. It was before our date, in a department store, and he didn't know I was there. He was with this angry woman who was shouting at a sales assistant. When they walked away from the counter, he said something like, *you're always talking, and you never shut up.* I knew I'd just heard another man say the exact same thing, but I couldn't think where. Just now, it came to me. It was Stewart."

Scarlet paused to try and regulate her breathing.

Detective Smyth cleared his throat. "It's an ugly thing to say, I can see why it might stick with you. But do you not think perhaps the woman was his wife? Dare I say, there are a few men who would speak that way to their wives or girlfriends."

Hysteria creeping back into her voice, Scarlet said, "I think he did say it to his wife and his girlfriend, but then he murdered them. The wildflowers on my car, that happened right around the time of our first date. He told me himself he can change his voice to sound like he's from all these different places. He called my cell phone, and I'd never given him the number. Just like Stew called me. He lied to me today about having just come from work. He says he's a lawyer, but I doubt that to be true now. I was late for our first date, but he was even later. I think he watched me park, put the flowers on my car, and then came to the restaurant to meet me. I think the woman I saw him with today, will be his next victim."

Scarlet took a moment to exhale, and Detective Smyth seized his chance to talk. "Ms. Oaks, I understand how all these actions add up to one suspicious looking guy, but SFPD is pretty sure we're searching for the right man."

Scarlet voiced with frustration, "You've got the right person, but the wrong photo. The man you showed me is not the killer. The real guy goes by the name Gary. He's tall and blond and twenty years younger."

Smyth enquired, "What information can you give me on Gary?"

Closing her eyes, Scarlet tried to visualize the information on the dating site. "His name, or the name he used, is Gary Sterling. I met him on a site called, *Meet and maybe*, about six weeks ago. He's called my cell phone twice. The first time he left a message and the second time he called so early I was too sleepy to look at the incoming number. I've only ever contacted him through the message system on the site."

"That's great intel," Smyth responded. "These sights keep personal information private but not when the PD comes knocking. You've given me enough to find out exactly who this guy is."

Feeling some relief, Scarlet said, "Thank you, and I'm sorry if I woke you."

Smyth gave a low chuckle. "You didn't wake me. My job is not only to find this creep but to keep you safe and *feeling* safe Ms. Oaks."

Minutes after hanging up with Smyth, Scarlet felt part guilt, part relief about detectives being en route. Certainly, she was safe with constant surveillance, but at least she could enforce her belief of who the real killer was to them. Taking a couple of deep breaths, she poured another cup of hot chocolate, then felt somewhat capable of talking.

The first caller was visiting the Bay Area for the holidays. He'd come to the city to surprise his girlfriend for Christmas. They'd been dating for the last three years at Oregon University. The reception his surprise got was less than warm. Why did Scarlet suppose that was? Feeling so ill-equipped to answer this question on tonight of all nights, Scarlet fobbed him off with the suggestion his girlfriend was just a little shocked. How sometimes surprise can be misread as coldness. She proposed he sit down and have an honest chat with his girlfriend, then call Mending Men again to let Scarlet and the other listeners in on his progress. There was only one more caller on hold, and Scarlet prayed it was Rod from Modesto. Tonight, she would welcome the man who never required Scarlet to say a word.

In a quieter voice than normal, Scarlet said, "Thank you for calling Mending Men, this is Scarlet, how can I help?"

With no preamble, a gravelly voice asked, "How many other people are with you at the station right now?"

34

Instantaneously smothered in a thick blanket of fear, Scarlet held a shaking finger over the disconnect button. "Who is this?"

The voice responded, "This is someone who knows you're all alone right now."

Scarlet wanted to scream she wasn't alone, she was surrounded by beefy security guys and detectives would be with her any moment, but no words would come. Her jittery finger still hovered above the disconnect button. The lump in her throat had returned. Only this time, it appeared to have effectively restricted her vocal cords.

The gravelly tone morphed into a sneer, "Don't panic, Miss, how can I help. You're not really alone."

Scarlet removed her right hand from the console and clasped it together with a slightly less shaky left hand. "You're right, I'm not alone, and I'd appreciate you not …"

Cutting her off in midsentence, the caller said, "You're not alone because I'm here with you, Scarlet."

Certain all the blood from her body now lay solely in her feet, Scarlet looked out her studio window and silently prayed for the detective's speedy arrival.

Mumbling something about that not being possible, Scarlet reached towards the disconnect button but not before she heard the mystery caller say, "You're wearing jeans and a black sweater."

Briefly glancing towards the hallway again, Scarlet, be it weakly voiced into the mic, "I know it's you, Gary."

The sinister voice began again but was abruptly silenced when Scarlet cut him off.

She didn't need the confirmation, but the detectives might, Gary was the only person to have seen her today. Nobody else, save the surveillance guys, would know what she was wearing.

Seemingly brighter than it had ever been, the call button flashed madly, reminding Scarlet she had dead air. With what could only come from years of conditioning, she found the will to hit the button starting the next nine songs in a row.

Gary couldn't possibly be in the building but was determined to scare her to death from wherever he was. The detectives were on their way, and Smyth was investigating him. Surveillance had her covered, and she'd stay put until the detectives were mere feet away.

Feeling as if these facts might just keep her upright and breathing for a few more minutes, Scarlet sat and stared into the hall.

Eerily in sync, Queen began singing about their desire to ride a bicycle as the lights in the corridor flashed on and off. Telling herself the bulbs were just old and acting up, Scarlet continued to stare out her studio into the corridor, almost paralyzed with fear. Following moments of flashing, akin to a discotheque, the lights normalized. Forcing herself to breathe in and out, Scarlet reached over for her cell phone. What was taking those detectives? She'll have died from a heart attack before they got her statement.

About to redial Detective Smyth, Scarlet's studio was plunged into complete darkness.

Hearing a loud scream and then realizing it was coming from her, Scarlet's shaking hands scrambled into her purse and fingered the cold width of Tom's flashlight. The hall now in darkness too, Scarlet may as well have been underground, it was so black. Removing the familiar circular thickness from her purse, she felt around its trunk for the frustratingly elusive on button. Bang! The window, separating her studio from the hallway creaked in protest, as someone or something, thumped hard on the glass.

Scarlet's body lurched backward. The flashlight fell with a loud thud. Amid low, soft whimpering sounds escaping her constricted windpipe, Scarlet lowered her unsteady body beneath the desk.

The thumping on the glass came again, this time with more force.

Scarlet spread her hands across the old matted carpet until she located the flashlight. Feeling as if she were screaming but knowing the reality continued to be an animalistic type cry, she pushed the wide flat button upwards, the powerful light springing to life.

Remembering her phone was atop the desk, she was currently crouched under, Scarlet struggled with the dilemma of psychologically perceived safety where she was, over retrieval of her phone and outside contact.

Adrenaline now pumping forcefully through her veins, Scarlet could hear every beat of her heart, could smell the damp mustiness from the carpet mixed with the sweet vanilla from the half-eaten opera cake.

Repeating a short prayer over and over, Scarlet's almost chant-like plea was interrupted by a man's voice, shouting, "Scarlet, are you helping people in there? See, no need to worry, you're not alone."

Amid gasping sobs, Scarlet pulled shaking knees up under her chin, before wrapping arms tightly around them.

Rocking her trembling body back and forth, she thought about her father. She pictured him in his tux, chatting to the people he needed to talk to before making a hasty retreat from the Christmas party. She visualized her Gran sitting in the library, reading a treasured George Elliot novel. About an hour from now, the two of them would be driving to the station to escort Scarlet home. What would they find? A parking lot full of Police cars and Scarlet drowned in …

Feeling the flashlight against her hip, Scarlet picked it up, stood, and shone it into her purse. Retrieving the large sock covered soap, she then transferred the flashlight to her left hand and began swinging the sock with her right.

Continuing this exercise as she exited her studio, Scarlet practiced a little motivational self-talking. "Swing and whack, swing and whack."

Walking towards the reception area with newfound fortitude, Scarlet held the powerful flashlight a good foot in front and never stopped swinging.

35

Halfway down the long corridor, Scarlet voiced a warning, "There are police surrounding this building, Gary. We know who you are."

Breathing heavily and still wielding her sock weapon, Scarlet sensed she was getting close to the stairs. She'd be outside and safe in mere seconds. Gingerly placing one foot forward, she transferred the flashlight to join the sock in her right hand and felt for the stair rail.

A stream of light illuminating the stairs but not the banister, she fumbled mid-air for a solid object. Silently and seemingly out of nowhere, Scarlet felt a vice like grip on her left ankle. Emitting a blood-curdling scream, she stumbled forward but miraculously grasped what felt to be the railing. Twisting her entire body to the left, Scarlet swung her right arm towards the attacker. She felt the sock and flashlight hit something or someone.

Guttural curses and moans ensued. These continued, be it fainter, as Scarlet's ankle was released. Her center of balance compromised, Scarlet's right leg lost its footing. A long, slow squeak proceeded as her left hand failed to maintain its grip on the banister. Tumbling sideways, Scarlet's small frame thumped and bounced down the steep staircase.

Landing in a crumpled heap on the floor, Scarlet heard someone call her name. Lifting her head towards the voice, she winced from the stabbing pain behind her eyes. Returning her head to its original position, Scarlet knew, whoever it was, she was in no shape to defend herself.

Her eyes closed, because it felt so much better, Scarlet heard the voice come again. It kept calling her name and appeared to be getting closer as if traveling through a tunnel.

At length, her eyelids flickered open to half-mast. Leaning over her, with a worried expression on his face, was her Grandpa Herb.

Sounds of sirens filled the darkness. Countless flashlights illuminated the reception area while stomping feet ran past her and up the staircase. After being gently placed on a gurney, Scarlet realized the man's face did resemble her late Grandfather's, but he was in fact, Detective Adams.

****

The following morning, in a routinely sterile but bright hospital room, Joe and Rose helped fill in the details of Scarlet's ordeal.

"Your Gran and I were taking our normal sedate drive to escort you home when we were practically mowed down by an ambulance leaving the parking lot. I hadn't even put the car in park before your Gran jumped out and started running towards the station doors. I caught up with her just as two uniformed Policemen asked who we were and what business we had at Bay Radio."

Brushing some hair out of Scarlet's eyes, Rose added, "Your father was more than a little agitated, he demanded to know where you were. At that point, a tall black man came up to us and introduced himself as...."

"Detective Smyth," Scarlet suggested.

Smiling, Rose said, "That was him and rather handsome I think."

Frowning at her grandmother, Scarlet asked, "Did they catch Gary?"

Looking over at her son for confirmation and seeing him nod, Rose said, "Yes, I believe they did. The detective told me you gave him what for with that sock soap."

They all laughed, and Scarlet became aware her head wasn't quite ready for the exertion.

Detective Smyth entered the hospital room.

"Glad to see you're feeling better," he voiced, approaching the bed. "Do you feel well enough for a couple of questions?"

Scarlet nodded. Joe and Rose said they'd return shortly armed with a strawberry milkshake.

"You caught Gary slash Stewart," Scarlet said with a small smile.

Smyth sat on the chair Rose had vacated. "We caught the guy, but it wasn't Gary or Stewart."

36

Certain she must have misheard the detective, Scarlet stared at him until he said something that made sense.

"The man who attacked you is Andree White. He's got a pretty decent rap sheet. Mostly petty theft, but in the last few years, he's progressed to domestic abuse and indecent exposure."

Scarlet immediately had a headful of questions, but all she could manage was, "So Andree *is* his real name."

With a bemused expression, Detective Smyth asked, "Had you met this man before?"

Trying to focus, while her mind raced, Scarlet said, "Not exactly. He was seeing a girl who works for the station. Sylvia, her Uncle's the manager of Bay Radio."

Smyth retrieved the trusted notebook from his breast pocket. "That would explain why he was driving Miss Danico's car and used her keys to enter the building."

Shaking her head and discovering that hurt more than laughing, Scarlet said, "No that can't be. They're not together anymore. He moved to San Diego."

Seeing the look of discomfort on Scarlet's face, Detective Smyth suggested, "This is too much for you right now. How about I let you rest and come back later?"

Closing her eyes for a moment, Scarlet replied, "I'm fine, really. The doctor said I have a slight concussion is all."

Smyth raised his eyebrows. "And your fair share of bruises from a speedy decent down those stairs."

Scarlet forced a small smile. "Sylvia's in Hawaii for the holidays. He must have stolen her car somehow. She knew he'd used her to get into Bay Radio. He made a harassing call to me once before. It spooked me, but I figured the weasel was just rotten and showing off for Sylvia."

Detective Smyth looked up from his notes. "We have him in custody. He claims his girlfriend asked him to come by the station and see her. Our surveillance guys, who needless to say, are on leave pending an investigation, thought it was Miss Sylvia Danico coming to work. Mr. White arrived minutes after you and parked his, her, car very close to the building, next to yours. He used a key to enter the station. Surveillance assumed it was Sylvia who, of course, had clearance to be there."

Scarlet asked in a small, weak voice, "Was he trying to kill me?"

"No, I don't believe he was. However, he will be doing some serious time."

Scarlet's eyes widened with terrified remembrance. "Gary's still out there."

Clearing his throat, the Detective, eyes slightly downcast, said, "Gary Sterling is actually Gary Myers. His wife's father owns a law firm here in the city, but Gary never passed the bar. He met his wife in college, she became pregnant, and they married two months before the baby was born. I believe the marriage was strongly encouraged by the girl's parents."

Feeling as if she'd fallen down the rabbit hole, Scarlet said, "You must have the wrong Gary. I met Gary Sterling on a singles' site. He was always available. I mean really available ... for Christmas and even overnight trips."

Smyth frowned. "A sad truth I've discovered during my years with the force is married men *are* very available. They're, for lack of a better word, quite skillful at it. Many will force an argument so they can storm out of the house. Things like a friend going through a tough time and desperately needing them. If the wife can't understand, then it's her problem. You wouldn't believe how creative these men are when it comes to cheating on their spouses."

Feeling like a naïve fool, Scarlet said, "So the woman I saw him with in Macy's, *was* his wife?"

The detective pulled a face. "I don't know for sure, but I would guess so."

Scarlet scowled. "And he's not a civil rights lawyer."

Smyth shook his head. "He's a courier for his father-in-law's law firm."

Scarlet forced a smile. "He does sort of work in the legal field."

Narrowing his dark eyes, the detective returned, "The good news is, Gary, is not a physical threat to anyone. You won't be hearing from him again. He asked us to apologize on his behalf, for lying to you and wasting your time."

Feeling her face color with embarrassment, Scarlet asked the question hanging heavily in the air,

"So, Stew is the killer, and he's still out there?"

37

During the drive from the hospital to Rose's house, all three passengers agreed not telling Marilyn, Niles or Tom, until after the holidays, was the right decision.

Scarlet might, but probably wouldn't fill her mom in on the whole story later. Niles and Tom would certainly get a blow-by-blow account, but not until they were sitting in her living room. Scarlet didn't want to risk them returning home early or worrying when they should be enjoying Christmas.

Joe unlocked the large front door to reveal a newly bathed pig. Prudence greeted Scarlet with a distinct sense of nonchalance.

"Yeah, she's pretty at home," Scarlet's father gave in explanation while heading up the staircase with Scarlet's bags.

"She was slightly taken aback," Rose said, "to see us walk into your home without you last night. But the minute we got her here, she started marching about like she owned the place."

Scarlet and Rose stood transfixed as the little pig followed Joe up the stairs.

Rose put a slender hand to her throat. "I'm glad to see she *can* get to the second floor under her own steam. She made me carry her last night."

Resisting the urge to giggle at the image forming in her mind, Scarlet said, "Gran, I'm so sorry. She's getting heavy."

Rose waved a hand in dismissal. "I confess, with your Dad staying the night with you at the hospital, I was thankful for Prudence's company."

Joe returned to the foyer. "I hope I grabbed everything you'll need for your trip to Aptos, my love."

Scarlet expressed her thanks and assured him, whatever he had brought from her house, was just fine.

Rose rubbed Scarlet's shoulder. "I think some food might be in order."

"I suspect hospitals and schools share the same chefs," Scarlet proclaimed, upon entering the kitchen. "But I did get a kick out of the teeny weenie box of Rice Krispies this morning."

Joe, head halfway in the refrigerator, shook his head. "You and your sister would wear me down until I bought you those packs of miniature cereals. Then, you'd fight over the Rice Krispies and Frosted Flakes and leave the rest."

Laughing, Scarlet looked past her father into the large open fridge. "Is that more than one so-happy-before-I-died chicken, I spy in there?"

Joe stood aside, allowing his daughter a clearer view. "You spy correctly. We've got the whole carefree family of chickens now."

Gently pushing her son from the fridge, Rose retrieved a large ceramic bowl filled with, what looked to Scarlet, like pasta. "Your Dad and I decided we couldn't exclude the rest of the family from Christmas, as tempting as the thought of a peaceful and relaxing holiday was."

Cutting generous slices of French bread, Joe contributed, "Anna told us her parents didn't even attempt to celebrate Thanksgiving. It was treated like any other day, with she and your Aunt Elsa eating leftover pizza while your Uncle Cecil watched football at some friend's house."

Sighing heavily, Scarlet confessed she was concerned about how merry Christmas would be for her mom, with just one daughter for company.

Swallowing a large chunk of French bread, Scarlet continued, "It's always a little stressful with Lisa's rules about the boys, but I know Mom still loves having them around."

Handing Joe a large tray laden with three, now steaming, bowls of pasta and meatballs, Rose led the way to the family room.

"I know you don't want to worry your Mom with all that's been going on here," Joe began, "but how will you explain the surveillance guys?"

Mixing her spaghetti sauce evenly over a generous helping of bowtie pasta, Scarlet responded,

"I'm not sure I'll need to. They're pretty much invisible."

The room fell silent with only the occasional sound of forks hitting porcelain.

Joe effectively changed the subject with his Christmas party anecdotes.

"So, there I am in my monkey suit, feeling awkward."

"Your father looked very handsome," Rose interrupted.

Joe patted his stomach. "My swims in the bay have helped get me into shape." Running a hand through salt and pepper wavy hair, he struggled to regain his train of thought.

"Why did you feel awkward?" Scarlet asked.

Narrowing, large brown eyes, Joe replied, "I think for the plain fact I was alone. It's odd when you're with a spouse or a date, I don't think you notice if people around you are alone or not. But last night, I was so acutely aware of all the couples. I swear I didn't see one other person who'd come solo."

Wiping spaghetti sauce from her chin, Scarlet volunteered, "I'm sorry Dad, that must have been uncomfortable."

Joe shook his head. "Don't you dare feel sorry for me after the night you …"

Trailing off, Joe redirected, "So what did you get your nephews for Christmas? You mentioned, whether Lisa likes it or not, you're dropping off gifts at their place."

Smiling gently at her father and noting the concerned look on Rose's face, Scarlet said,

"I'm okay talking about what happened last night, and the reality of the killer still being at large. I appreciate you two wanting to take my mind off it, but actually, I think we should discuss it."

Experiencing an equal mixture of apprehension and relief, Rose asked, "You're not going back to the radio station until this guy is caught, right?"

Scarlet swallowed her last bite of pasta. "Brian, the station manager, called my hospital room this morning. They're going to stream some sports show from Spokane for the next week. He says past ratings for this time slot indicate listening is down over the holidays anyway. Seven days is plenty of time for me to recover and be rearing to go." Scarlet avoided meeting her Gran's eyes. "But whether they catch him in that time or not, I will go back to work."

Rose gave a small smile. "I know you too well to pretend not to understand. Besides, I'm sure they'll catch him within the next couple of days."

Scarlet inhaled a deep breath. "I agree, and if they don't, I still have surveillance and Sylvia with me the entire time I'm at work. Plus, if Abbot and Costello can stand it, I have an escort home every night."

Laughing as he put empty bowls on the tray, Joe said, "Pretty certain those two are still in business."

Over chocolate mousse and whipped cream, the story of Gary drew more laughter than tears.

By the time they'd progressed to coffee, Andree's name came up again.

Scarlet shook her head. "I should have taken his first harassment of me more seriously. Why was I so quick to dismiss him as just a young punk showing off to his girlfriend?"

Hands clasped around her coffee mug, Rose suggested, "Maybe *because* of the girlfriend."

Scarlet thought for a moment. "You think I made light of it because I didn't want to upset Sylvia?"

Joe waved his biscotti in the air. "You've mentioned how fond you are of Sylvia. I'm sure she felt bad enough about having brought that monster into the station. If you'd been completely traumatized by his initial actions, she'd probably have felt a hundred times worse."

Scarlet narrowed her green eyes. "I'm not convinced you two aren't just trying to justify my poor decision making. But, nonetheless, I'm totally on board with your rationale."

Three generations stayed up until the wee hours, predicting what joys and drama the Christmas holiday would bring.

Awaking to the welcoming sound of Rose placing a cup of tea on the bedside table, Scarlet felt as if she'd slept the day away.

"It's only ten," Rose soothed, watching Scarlet make a mad grab for her phone. An hour later, sitting in the sunroom with Prudence curled up beside her, Scarlet's motivation to start the trip to Aptos was sadly lacking.

Joe, presents stacked precariously in his arms, reentered the warmest room in the house. "Gifts from your Gran and me. Just some tokens for you, your Mom, Trent, Lisa, and the little rascals."

Scarlet jumped up to help her overburdened father. "That's lovely, and above and beyond, considering."

Joe sat on the padded sofa opposite Scarlet. "I won't lie and say I'm not a little bitter about your Mother's determination to keep me in a job I'm hating, but I do understand how upset and lost she's feeling."

Smiling up at Rose, as she joined them with a plate full of freshly baked blueberry scones, Scarlet volunteered, "I've come to a conclusion, after many hours of Mending Men, there is no right time to leave a marriage. Some may argue, if a couple splits while the children are young then the children are less affected because it's all they know. But, when I think about you and Mom doing that, I realize all the time us kids would have missed with you. Yes, we were aware you weren't crazy in love, but you both managed to make our home a safe and loving one."

Joe stood and placed a kiss on Scarlet's cheek. "Thank you for that. I can't tell you how good it feels to hear those words. The guilt I have for leaving is ridiculous and I truly never wanted to hurt your mother."

Scarlet squeezed her father's hand. "I think Mom is just feeling unsure of herself and her ability to find someone. She's hurt and sadly, I believe she needs you to be hurting too."

Pouring more hot water from a carafe into the teapot, Rose said, "My darling Scarlet, are you aware of how perfect your new job is?"

Almost choking on her first bite of scone, Scarlet enquired, "Mending Men?"

"Yes, your top forty show was fun and glamorous, but what you're doing now has much more meat to it."

Laughing at his daughter's bemused expression, Joe added, "We do listen you know."

Blushing, Scarlet asked, "You listen to Mending Men?"

Grinning widely, Joe said, "Of course we do, we're very proud of you."

"You're helping these men," Rose volunteered. "They're getting an intelligent, unbiased, female perspective on their relationship problems."

Giggling, Scarlet interjected, "But you must have heard that awful guy who gives his own sleazy advice. And what about the one who wants to replay every game and I can't get a word in."

Joe attempted to keep a straight face. "I tried the ATM receipt ploy at the Christmas party. Worked like a charm."

Throwing a napkin at her father, Scarlet said, "I really struggle with the sports metaphors. It's so hard to find ones that apply or heaven forbid, help these guys."

Rose leaned back in her chair. "Who says you have to use them. I've heard you omit the sports theme a couple of times lately. I don't recall hearing the guys complain."

Scarlet bit her lower lip. "You do know my misuse of said metaphors is the reason surveillance guys are surrounding your house right now."

Joe's eyes softened. "I know deep down you know this, your words didn't make that man kill anybody. He was a psychopath before he called into your show."

Scarlet gave a half-smile. "Just bad luck to have a serial killer call in on my first day."

38

Scarlet's mind was so preoccupied, the drive to Aptos was completed with no real knowledge of how she got there.

Marilyn excitedly ushered her daughter into the living room. "Voila!"

Scarlet lowered her pig to the floor. "The place looks amazing Mom. You went to a lot of trouble."

Marilyn drew in a deep breath. "I decided no matter how the rest of the family wanted to behave this year, you Prudence and I would have a wonderful festive holiday."

Scarlet smiled broadly before walking towards the tall Christmas tree. Gently touching a shiny green needle, she asked, "Is it real?"

Marilyn chuckled. "Looks it, doesn't it? It's an expensive fake. It even came with a pine scent spritz thingy. I saved the star for you. Do you remember how you kids would argue over who placed it on top of the tree?"

Scarlet pulled a face. "Oh yes. Trent would run off and hide it. By the time it resurfaced, Violet and I had lost interest. Clever logic, now I think about it."

With unmistakable resolve in her voice, Marilyn said, "Well, Trent won't be doing it this year, will he?"

Scarlet chose the moment to exclaim delight at a Christmas village adorning eighty percent of the large coffee table.

Marilyn's determination to be in the festive mood proved infectious. Scarlet suggested a serious amount of baking while listening to their favorite Christmas songs.

****

Having slept soundly in her childhood room, Scarlet awoke the following day to find her mother gone. A note on the kitchen counter explained Marilyn had nipped into Aptos for a few last-minute items. Scarlet used the time to wrap her gifts and place them around the tree.

Just as Scarlet tied the last bow, Marilyn swept into the house, arms piled high with bags and boxes.

Eyebrows raised, Scarlet enquired, "A *few* last-minute items?"

Marilyn placed the packages on the sofa. "I had the best time picking out some new clothes for my rather shabbily dressed daughter. Why you hide that figure of yours is beyond me."

Scarlet looked at the mountain of bags and boxes. "Mom, that's way too generous. I don't need a ton of clothes. I'm on the radio, nobody sees me."

Picking up Prudence before the little pig knocked over the contents of a large silver bag, Marilyn retorted, "Nonsense. You're a celebrity; I had confirmation of it today, in Aptos."

Before Scarlet had a chance to enquire how that was possible, they heard a loud rap on the front door.

Plumping her hair in the mirror above the mantle, Marilyn exclaimed, "Who on earth could that be?"

There, on the doorstep, looking suitably remorseful, stood Trent.

Marilyn, sporting a wide-eyed expression, returned to the living room, Trent following closely behind.

Glancing at the parcel covered sofa, Trent, with all the drama of a Shakespearean thespian, fell into the one empty chair.

Running hands through light brown hair in need of a wash, Trent began, "I know you struggle with her, Mom." Looking over at Scarlet who remained standing by the tree, Trent added, "And you have no time for her at all."

Scarlet opened her mouth to protest, but Trent hurried on, "She's different to us. Lisa doesn't go with the popular notion that everything's okay. We grew up believing if it feels right, then do it. Lisa doesn't follow that way of thinking, and I respect her for it. Look at Violet. We're all responsible for her living in a hippie sex camp. We should have reined her in, but we just stood by and let her run wild."

When Trent finally paused to take a breath, Marilyn argued, "Now that's not fair, Trent."

Scarlet, not usually at a loss for words, continued to stand with her mouth open.

Nodding his head slowly at his mother, Trent continued, "I couldn't let Christmas go by without coming to see you. I wanted to tell you in person how sorry I am we won't be celebrating together."

He turned to Scarlet. "I'm glad you're here, and Mom won't be alone."

Scarlet gave her brother a smile she saved for people she didn't know. "I have some gifts for you, I'll be right back."

Returning from her room, Scarlet found Trent pacing back and forth in front of the fireplace. Marilyn, parcels all around her, sat perched rigidly on the edge of the couch.

"It's so important to Lisa… and to me," Trent added as an afterthought, "our children be raised knowing right from wrong, with real structure and purpose to their lives."

Finding her voice, Scarlet said, "We get that Trent. You and Lisa have made it clear. What is it you want us to do, that we aren't already doing?"

Evidently irritated, Trent scratched at his stubbly chin. "Be more on board with her values and ideas. Don't defend Violet all the time. How many times does our sister need to leave this family before we leave her?"

Rubbing her hands across a taupe suede skirt, Marilyn said, "I don't know how more on board we could be. I remove all the mirrors. I remove my African art, my *Vogue* and *Cosmo* magazines. I'm mindful of the food I serve and of every damn thing I say."

Holding a shiny purple parcel in the air, Scarlett said, "Do you know how hard it is to find Christmas wrapping paper without the color red? I went to four toy stores before I found the right color toys. Where does it end, Trent? New rules are put in place all the time; we don't know whether we're coming or going."

About to defend Violet, Scarlet stopped when she saw her brother put his head in his hands and gently sob.

Biting her lip, Scarlet looked over at Marilyn, who in turn shrugged her shoulders. After a few uncomfortable moments, Marilyn gently escorted Trent back to the chair. Scarlet, still holding an armful of gifts, walked into the foyer and placed them on the table next to the door.

"I'm making tea," Scarlet voiced toward the living room as she headed for the kitchen.

Realizing it was past lunchtime and she hadn't had breakfast, Scarlet reappeared with not only tea but also a tray full of cheese, pate, and crackers.

Hands circling a china mug, Trent confessed, "I think she might need psychological help. Every time I say something she doesn't approve of, she writes it down in a little book to discuss later with her pastor. She's got me so nervous, I've pretty much stopped talking at all. Then, she says my silence shows a lack of interest in our relationship and how can we grow as a couple if we don't communicate. When I show any enthusiasm for a movie or a television show, she evaluates my interest and then picks it apart. Did I like it because I have hidden violent urges? Do I enjoy seeing women demean themselves? It was a rerun of *Cheers* for goodness sake!"

Repressing a smile, Scarlet said, "Oh Trent, I'm so sorry. What can we do to help?"

Roughly wiping a hand across his eyes, Trent replied, "There's nothing you can do. It's my problem, and I should fix it. I appreciate you both listening. Thanks for this," he added nodding at the tray of half-eaten food.

Marilyn chuckled, "It's not exactly Christmas Eve fare, but it hit the spot. Scarlet and I baked yesterday; you must take some goodies back with you."

Pulling a face, Trent replied, "Lisa thinks I'm out Christmas shopping. She'd be displeased if she knew I'd come here."

Closing her eyes to stop a scream from forming, Scarlet suggested, "Then stay for one more cup and have some pecan pie with it."

Marilyn enthusiastically contributed, "I have gifts for the boys that aren't wrapped yet. You could produce them as fruits of your labor."

Looking relaxed for the first time since he arrived, Trent leaned back in his chair. "I like the way you two think."

The next hour was spent talking about lighter subjects. Rodney and Hayden's progress at school, Marilyn's house hunting, and Prudence's expanding girth.

A reluctant Trent began his exit while apologizing for the necessary request that Scarlet, on her way out of town, drop the gifts on his doorstep.

When a large pinky orange sun began it's decent, Marilyn and Scarlet collapsed onto the sofa, both agreeing they felt emotionally drained.

Over a glass of spiced eggnog, a short discussion was had about Trent's predicament. No conclusions were reached, but mother and daughter decided attending midnight mass was just what they needed.

"We'll put Trent's problem in God's hands," Marilyn said before draining her glass.

Scarlet frowned, "Wow, Mom, I didn't know you had such faith."

Marilyn elevated her chin. "Let's get dressed up. I want the old biddies of Aptos to see the Oaks women still have it going on."

Concealing a cringe with a smile, Scarlet said, "Now, there's the mother I recognize."

Scarlet's version of 'dressed up' was taming her wavy hair, applying makeup, and wearing clothes that were the correct size.

Marilyn's version appeared to be sporting tight designer jeans, high-heeled boots, and every piece of jewelry she owned.

Sitting on a hard wooden pew, Scarlet cleared her mind and absorbed pleasant current surroundings. Despite being a little more modern than some of Scarlet's favorite churches in the city, the candles illuminating the young choir singing *Silent Night* made Christmas magically present for her.

An hour and a half later, Scarlet struggled to stay in the festive mood, despite the roaring fire and a mug of hot chocolate in hand.

Marilyn, stroking Prudence a little harder than the pig liked, insisted on filling Scarlet in on the looks she'd received from seemingly every woman at midnight mass.

Scarlet then suffered through reports of said women's apparent dirty laundry and cosmetic surgeries. "The nerve," was intermittently repeated with increased volume.

Rescuing Prudence, while the pig still had some hair on her body, Scarlet stated it was almost two in the morning, wished her mom a Merry Christmas and begged off to bed.

39

Waking to the smell of freshly brewed coffee and cinnamon, Scarlet savored it for a few minutes, before taking a quick shower.

She found her mother in the kitchen, singing, *I'm dreaming of a white Christmas.*

Scarlet chuckled, "Probably not going to happen in Aptos."

Abandoning the song, Marilyn said, "That's okay. I think the dream is better than the reality."

Over coffee and its namesake cake, Marilyn recounted her childhood in Colorado and having more than her fair share of snow.

Placing a ginger-marinated leg of lamb in the oven, the party of two adjourned to the living room armed with eggnog.

Following a friendly debate of which was more iconic, *White Christmas* or *It's a Wonderful Life*, Scarlet enjoyed a face time chat with Niles and Tom. Having walked into the kitchen to allow Marilyn uninterrupted viewing of Bing Crosby and Danny Kaye, Scarlet seized the opportunity to call her dad and gran. Making it brief, she wished them a wonderful day, assured them she was safe and happy and said she was looking forward to their own celebration in a couple of days.

Marilyn and Scarlet's ability to recite about every other line in the movie allowed them the luxury of opening gifts while watching. The eyeshadow palette was just what Marilyn had wanted. Opening a present from Joe, the latest novel by her favorite author, Marilyn said,

"I hope he doesn't think a token gift will change my mind about the alimony."

Biting her lip, because today wasn't the right day for that discussion, Scarlet held up a gold-colored rayon sundress. "This is beautiful, thank you so much."

Still holding the paperback, Marilyn replied, "I think you underestimate your popularity. You should always dress like a beautiful celebrity."

Scarlet's smile faded before it was fully formed. "Mom, what did you mean about my celebrity being confirmed yesterday in Aptos?"

Having walked over to look in the mirror above the mantle, Marilyn, with pallet in one hand and a brush in the other, asked, "Didn't I tell you about that friendly man who said you'd solved his relationship problems?"

Scarlet felt a tightening in her chest. "No, I think you were about to when Trent arrived."

Mouth open as she applied eyeshadow, Marilyn said, "Where was it? Oh, yes, I was in that darling new boutique on Liberty drive. That's where I got your … oh, you haven't opened it yet. What are you waiting for? Tear into the one with the gold and red ribbon."

Forcing herself to stay calm, aided by the rationale she probably had no reason not to be, Scarlet, unwrapped the soft package.

"Wow, it's lovely," Scarlett exclaimed holding up a white cotton embroidered shirt.

Marilyn turned from the mirror. "The sales girl said Cameron Diaz wears the exact same shirt."

Smiling, Scarlet enquired, "So how did you get talking to this guy?"

Marilyn turned back to see her reflection. "I had just asked the sales girl if Cameron wore it with skinny jeans and boots when up he walked and introduced himself."

Folding the shirt to fit back in the wrapping paper, Scarlet asked, "What was his name?"

Opening and closing her eyes to admire the new shadow, Marilyn said, "Gosh, I couldn't tell you. About ten minutes after our chat I was so irritated to see that awful Marjorie from the women's guild. Do you know what she said to me when your father and I divorced?"

Scarlet leaned back into the couch. "No, what did she say?"

Clasping the eyeshadow pallet to her chest, Marilyn whispered, "That Joe hadn't seemed happy for a very long time."

Before Scarlet had a chance to respond, Marilyn continued in a much louder vocal, "How dare she? How dare some stupid old biddy, who barely even knows our family, say something so vile to me in my time of need?"

"It's unforgivable," Scarlet said. Giving what she hoped was a long enough pause, she asked, "Do you remember what this guy looked like?"

Picking up the still unopened gift Rose had sent her, Marilyn sighed, "I don't think he's right for you. He wasn't very stylishly dressed. When are you going to find a cute guy to date?"

Feeling her patience wearing thin, Scarlet replied, "I wasn't thinking of any romance with whomever this guy was you met, Mom. I've been on a few dates. The timing's just not right at the moment. I'm working on getting my teeth into this new job. After that, I think things will improve in my social life."

Scarlet watched as her mother slowly unwrapped the gift from Rose. Despite being confident Marilyn was rapidly losing interest in this conversation, Scarlet continued, "I'm only curious about this guy because I didn't think Bay Radio had a receiver in Aptos. I guess he streams the show on his computer."

Marilyn pulled a face as she held up a silk scarf and what looked to be a gold locket. "Do you think she's trying to glam me up, so I'll remarry, and then her son won't have to pay alimony?"

"No, Mom. I think she cares about you and wanted to get the mother of her grandchildren a nice Christmas gift."

At her mother's sheepish expression, Scarlet added, "That scarf will really set off your eyes. Does the locket open?"

Setting the scarf on her lap, Marilyn inserted one long, red fingernail into the locket's opening.

Hastily wiping at an escapee tear, Marilyn responded, "Baby photos of you, Trent, and Violet."

Palm outstretched, Scarlet asked, "May I see?"

As Scarlet turned over the three inner circles of the locket, she heard her mother say,

"I guess this means I'll have to send something back for them."

Scarlet handed the locket back to her mother. "I'm sure Dad and Gran aren't expecting anything." With a determined intake of breath, she added, "Just one more question about that guy in Aptos yesterday."

"Of course," Marilyn replied. "And then we must eat."

Needing to know, but terrified of the answer, Scarlet enquired, "Did he have thinning reddish blond hair and light blue eyes?"

Marilyn raised her chin and looked towards the ceiling, "No. He had lots of thick dark hair. I couldn't say on the eyes; he was wearing sunglasses. Don't you hate it when people wear sunglasses indoors?"

Scarlet felt her body relax, "Yes, I do."

Not long after eating leg of lamb with all the trimmings, drinking too much red wine and crying at the end of White Christmas, Scarlet's curiosity resurfaced. "This guy you met in the boutique, did he say how I helped him?"

Marilyn moved a tray table to the side of her chair. "Oh, he was very complimentary. He said he called into your Meddling Men show and got first rate advice."

Laughing, Scarlet corrected her mother, "It's Mending Men, Mom."

Giggling, Marilyn volunteered, "He said he was having such trouble with his wife and thanks to you, they're both in a good place now."

Over a full yawn, Scarlet said, "That's nice. But how…"

Taking a moment to try and regain her focus after too much food and wine, Scarlet continued, "How did he know you and I were related?"

Marilyn waved a hand in the air. "We do look alike. You remember one of your Math teachers in high school said we looked like sisters."

Scarlet didn't remember that. Looking at her mother's straight blond, red and brown streaked hair and collagen filled lips, she wondered how a stranger could see any resemblance at all.

Marilyn watched Scarlet tap a thumbnail against her bottom lip. "Just take the compliment and don't worry about the how's or why's."

Exhaling, Scarlet admitted, "Mom, there's something I haven't told you because I didn't want you to worry."

Eyes wide, Marilyn said, "Oh!"

"My first day on the Mending Men show, this guy named Stewart called. Let me back up a bit first, though. The DJ I succeeded was a real sports guy. He doled out metaphors pertaining to, I guess mostly football and baseball. Supposedly this was, is, advice the callers can relate to. As you know, I support our Bay Area teams, but I'm not exactly a sports nut."

Pausing and looking around, Scarlet enquired, "Where did we leave those chocolates?"

Smiling, Marilyn pointed to the table right in front of her daughter.

Raising her eyebrows, Scarlet picked up the box and selected a strawberry crème. Offering the beautifully displayed selection to Marilyn, Scarlet continued, "So I was struggling with trying to find a sports analogy to fit this man's issue of his wife belittling him. I had all these websites open on my computer but I was so nervous, I managed to close the one I needed. Instead of saying send her to the showers, I said bath."

Marilyn reached for the chocolate filled box. Squinting at the little index of candies, she suggested, "Well honestly, what difference does shower or bath make anyway. If your Boss has a problem with a simple little mistake like that, then he's an idiot."

"It's a bit more serious than that, Mom. The guy I gave that advice to, murdered his wife and another woman by drowning them in the bay."

Marilyn hastily chewed her caramel. "The guy I read about in the paper. The suspected serial killer?"

Closing her eyes for a second, Scarlet replied, "That's the one."

Absent-mindedly reaching for another chocolate, Marilyn enquired, "You don't think this killer will come after you because you said bath instead of shower, do you?"

Thinking they should have had this conversation before consuming a bottle of red wine, Scarlet replied, "I think he might have taken the advice literally. He called in again and thanked me for helping him. I was feeling all happy with the kudos until the police told me he's murdered, two women."

Marilyn shook her head. "He called into a radio station full of lots of people. He doesn't know your home address or have any idea who you are or what you look like."

"The problem is…" Scarlet interrupted, "he's left flowers on my car and seems to want to sort of stay in contact."

Pausing to gauge Marilyn's level of concern, Scarlet deduced saying nothing of the call to her cell phone and additional flowers was the right thing to do.

Her face drained of color, Marilyn asked, "He wouldn't want to hurt you, would he? Why would he want to hurt you, it doesn't make any sense?"

Holding Prudence tightly, Scarlet replied, "None of this makes any sense, Mom. I'm sure he doesn't want to hurt me, but I have constant surveillance just to be safe."

Looking around her living room, Marilyn enquired, "You do? Are we being watched right now?"

Scarlet pulled a face. "Yep. But they're good at staying hidden."

Straightening her skirt, as if she were about to go outside and greet them, Marilyn asked, "How many are there? I wish you'd said something earlier. We could have given them a nice Christmas dinner, goodness knows we have enough food."

Laughing, Scarlet replied, "I don't think we're supposed to socialize with them. I have no idea how many there are, but they like to stay in the shadows, not meet in groups for a picnic."

Marilyn narrowed her eyes. "All the same, those poor young men out there are away from their families for Christmas."

Smiling mischievously, Scarlet asked her mother, "Who said they were young?"

Giggling, Marilyn avoided the question, "I don't think there would be any harm in leaving some baked goods on the doorstep tomorrow morning."

Relieved the thought of having her house surrounded by strong young men appeared to be distracting Marilyn from the worry of a serial killer, Scarlet volunteered, "They're not pigeons mother. How will they know it's for them unless you start breaking bits off and throwing it towards the trees?"

Throwing a chocolate wrapper at her daughter, Marilyn said, "You are an awful girl." Clasping her hands together she added, "No need to worry about your Aptos fan. I'm sure he just likes you is all. Definitely not your type, though. My goodness, he spoke so slowly, I think he'd drive a person crazy!"

40

Feeling as if she might possibly faint, Scarlet looked around frantically for her cell phone.

"The last I saw, it was on the kitchen counter," Marilyn responded to her daughter's panicked inquiry. "Who on earth are you calling at this time of night?"

Running to the kitchen, Scarlet called out, "When you say slowly, was it painfully slow?"

Struggling to comprehend the situation, Marilyn answered, "His speech was pretty slow, but lots of people speak slowly. Are you telling me this is the guy? Just because I said, he spoke slowly?"

Coming back into the living room with cell phone in hand, Scarlet enquired, "The hair, could it have been a wig?"

Nervously rubbing her hands together, Marilyn murmured, "I guess it could have been. There was a lot of it and men his age don't tend to have that much hair."

"His age!" Scarlet almost shouted, "you didn't mention his age."

With an edge of irritation, Marilyn said, "You didn't ask, and I didn't know it was important. I couldn't see his eyes, but he had loose skin around his chin which made me think he was in his late fifties maybe."

Having the foresight to enlist Siri's help as her fingers were trembling, Scarlet pressed the talk button on her phone,

"Call Detective Smyth."

When the automated voice affirmed it was making the call, Scarlet looked at her mother, "It's him, I'm sure of it. He must have followed me here and then followed you into Aptos."

Breathing hard, Marilyn asked, "But, the surveillance guys?"

Scarlet was about to respond when a voice from her phone said, "This is Detective Smyth."

Once she'd hastily apologized for calling late and on Christmas day, Scarlet told the detective she believed Stewart was in Aptos and had approached her mother the previous morning. After a brief recount of her mother's information on the meeting, Scarlet listened for a few minutes, thanked the detective, and hung up the phone.

Sitting on the edge of the couch, close to the chair her mother seemed unable to move from, Scarlet began, "In answer to your question, I think Stewart must know this house is secure and that's why he chose to follow you into town."

Eyes wide, Marilyn slowly nodded her head.

Reaching out and gently holding her mother's hand, Scarlet continued, "Detective Smyth assured me we are perfectly safe in this house. He and his partner will travel down here first thing tomorrow morning. In the meantime, he's put out an all-points bulletin on Stewart. I won't be at all surprised if they catch him tonight."

In a voice, barely louder than a whisper, Marilyn said, "But I saw him yesterday. He could be anywhere by now. This is all my fault. You asked me questions about him, and I didn't give you enough answers."

Scarlet shook her head. "That was my fault for not telling you about the seriousness of the situation. You thought I was just mildly curious about this guy and that's because I hadn't shared the facts."

Marilyn forced a smile. "We have a French apple tart in the fridge. How about I heat it up while you and Prudence make some tea?"

Laughing, Scarlet replied, "Great idea."

Following comic relief from three episodes of *Frasier*, two helpings of apple tart and no mention of a serial killer, mother, daughter, and pig finally let another Christmas go.

Scarlet awoke early the next morning to the sound of vacuuming. Finding her mother had also cleaned the kitchen and made fresh coffee, Scarlet, feeling suitably guilty, nudged her mother's hand off the handle and finished the job.

Returning the vacuum to the cupboard under the stairs, Scarlet heard her mother ask,

"Would you mind giving the guest bathroom a quick wipe down? I'm making some pancakes in case they're hungry."

Aware that cleaning and cooking at eight in the morning must be necessary for her mother's mental well-being, Scarlet cheerfully obliged.

An hour later, Detectives Smyth and Williams were devouring pancakes in Marilyn's immaculate home.

Admiring her mother's composure, Scarlet listened as Marilyn recounted the meeting with the man, who by all accounts and purposes was the killer Scarlet knew as Stewart.

Cheerfully allowing his partner procurement of the last pancake, Detective Smyth assured Marilyn she was in no danger. Nevertheless, they would have a surveillance team assigned to her.

"Do you think any of my other family members here in Aptos are in any danger?" Scarlet enquired as her mother cleared the table.

Wiping his mouth with a linen napkin, the fair-haired detective replied, "We don't understand that to be the case, Miss Oaks. Our team of psychiatrists believes Stewart Steele feels the need to converse with you and only you."

"That said," Detective Smyth interjected, "the fact he approached your mother is concerning. It shows a level of frustration at not being able to reach you. A frustrated killer is not a good thing."

As if that were a perfectly reasonable statement to make over breakfast, Smyth continued,

"Ms. Oaks, those were the most delicious pancakes, thank you."

The recipient of the compliment blushed. "Please, call me Marilyn."

Answering as many questions as they could, regarding the progress of the San Francisco police department, the detectives admitted they were a little stumped over Stewart's ability to elude them. But they could assure Scarlet and Marilyn, he was no longer in Aptos.

Ten minutes later, as the detective's car drove out of sight, Scarlet asked her mother, "Have you seen Prudence?"

Looking behind her, Marilyn said, "That's odd, she loves an opportunity to run around this front yard."

Feeling panic rise in her throat, Scarlet said, "I haven't seen her in hours. She hates the vacuum, so I assumed she was steering clear while we cleaned this morning." Taking the stairs two at a time, Scarlet added, "We were so distracted by the detective's visit, I didn't even think to go and find her."

"You look up, I'll look down," Marilyn suggested before she started calling the little pig's name.

Twenty minutes later, Marilyn in tears and Scarlet on the verge of throwing up, someone knocked on their front door.

41

Covered in mud and looking at Scarlet from under long eyelashes was Prudence. The man holding her was also covered in mud, but instead of looking remorseful like the pig, sported a wide, amused grin.

"I believe you two are acquainted," the man stated.

Scarlet, seemingly at a loss for words, welcomed her mother's inquiry, "Where on earth was she?"

Handing the filthy, but still cute, pig to Scarlet, the man volunteered, "I was on leaf and dirt duty." Seemingly to prove his point, he turned a hand in towards his mud-encrusted jumpsuit. "To my surprise and delight, up trots a little vision in pink."

Pausing for a moment while Scarlet and Marilyn laughed, he continued, "In no time, she proved to my colleagues and me, she has a solid future in surveillance. I apologize I didn't bring her back sooner, but I had to wait for shift change."

Scarlet, finding her voice, confessed of her panic and thanked the man profusely.

Marilyn, running towards the kitchen, returned moments later with three plastic containers. "Some home baked goodies for you and your incredible team."

Accepting the gifts with thanks, Prudence's savior returned to the unseen depths of Marilyn's yard.

For the next half hour, Scarlet listened graciously as Marilyn informed her how correct she'd been about the surveillance guys. Not only were they young, strong and handsome, but also grateful to have delicious home baked goods.

Marilyn concluded with a satisfied smile, she felt sure the SFPD would leave this surveillance team in place as they were already settled.

Scarlet seized her moment. "I really should be heading back to the city."

"Already?" Marilyn enquired, the smile gone.

Scarlet gave an apologetic nod.

"Just a couple more hours?" Marilyn asked in a pleading tone.

Scarlet smiled, "Why not."

Lunch was filled with endless surveillance questions from her mother. Would they be outside the salon when she had her hair done? Would they follow her through the grocery store? When it got to the question of would they be watching Marilyn as she sunbathed in the backyard, Scarlet decided it was time to start packing the car.

Despite a brief detour to drop off Christmas gifts on Trent's doorstep, Scarlet made good time, and she and Prudence were soon relaxing in Rose's sunroom for four o'clock tea. Scarlet's great grandmother was English, and Rose had grown up with tea being served daily at eleven in the morning and four in the afternoon. It was prompt and always accompanied by something delicious to eat.

Rose and Joe sat transfixed, as Scarlet, illuminated by the afternoon sun, recounted the events in Aptos.

An impartial observer may have had trouble gauging which was more shocking – Marilyn being approached by a psychotic murderer or Trent's current feelings about his wife.

Scarlet didn't put up too much of a fight when her father and grandmother insisted she stay with them. Knowing her mother had held a face-to-face conversation with Stewart was unnerving her more than she cared to admit.

Father and daughter decided to make a trip to Scarlet's home, before the sun went down, for added clothes and necessities. Said sun had recently disappeared behind thick gray clouds. Five minutes from Upper Terrace, slanting rain began to bombard their windshield.

Limited visibility and the urgency to escape the rain, almost prevented Scarlet and Joe from seeing a basket of flowers floating in a water-filled tub, on her front doorstep.

42

Cursing under his breath, Joe looked to his daughter, "Don't touch it. I'm calling the police."

With no desire to, or even the ability at that moment to touch anything, Scarlet stared and nodded.

Returning to Joe's Honda, they sat huddled together listening to the melodic sound of rain on the car's roof.

In no time, Detective Smyth's unmarked car pulled in behind them. Lifting a black jacket collar up to shield his neck, Smyth asked, "You haven't been inside?"

Waiting until they'd reached the cover of her porch, Scarlet replied, "No and we didn't touch the flowers."

Detective Williams, having stayed a little longer in the car, now joined them. "Unit One," he voiced into a walkie talkie. The rain and wind gathering momentum around them, all four eyed the wildflowers, bobbing unrhythmically, in a small plastic basket, atop browning water.

Lowering the walkie talkie, Detective Williams said, "Unit one followed you here from your grandmother's house. They'll check to make sure your home is secure."

Receiving the all clear, Scarlet, Joe by her side, frantically stuffed clothes and toiletries into a duffle bag. Rejoining Smyth and Williams on the doorstep, they watched as uniformed men, with gloved hands, placed the flowers into a police van.

"When will this end?" Rose asked hypothetically from her recliner, an hour later. Warmed by a roaring fire and cartons of Chinese food covering the coffee table, Scarlet felt relatively relaxed and safe. But, she had to agree with the question Rose sent out to the universe. How was this man able to elude the police? Was he much smarter than he sounded? Was it possible, he wasn't working alone?

The next morning, Scarlet found her grandmother raking leaves in the backyard.

"Let me do that for you," Scarlet said walking towards Rose.

Smiling, Rose said, "It's good exercise for me." When Scarlet scowled, Rose added, "You're as bad as your father. The best way for us old folks to stay fit and healthy is to keep moving."

Taking in the mature fruit trees and countless bushes, Scarlet replied, "No argument there, but raking is heavy going."

Sighing good-heartedly, Rose handed the tool to Scarlet. "Go on then, you finish this area, and I'll make us one of those frothy lattes, coffee houses charge a fortune for."

Half an hour later, Scarlet returned to the house, out of breath enough to remind her she needed to get back into a running routine.

"Yard de-leafed, rake returned to shed, and leaves awaiting removal by green waste dudes," Scarlet in mock military fashion, informed Rose.

Rose chuckled and handed Scarlet a tall, dark blue mug.

Looking from her place in the kitchen out towards the entrance hall, Scarlet enquired, "Is Dad still at the beach?"

"No, he's at work. He was a little anxious when he left; some bigwig is visiting from Denver today. Joe's anticipating she'll have a lot of questions for your dad and his team."

"I should have known that and wished him good luck this morning," Scarlet responded with a scowl. "All our energy is zapped up because of this lunatic."

"Your dad will be just fine, and none of this energy zapping is your fault. We're just happy to be here for you until it's all over." Rose glanced at the oven clock. "Aren't you lunching with your friend Mia today?"

Jumping off the high kitchen stool, Scarlet exclaimed, "Oh, yes I am. Thanks, Gran. I'm going to go take a shower."

****

Mia had said she was in the mood for Indian food, so the friends decided on a Haight St. eatery famous for its naan bread.

"Hope you're jiggy with this place," Mia said as they were led to a small table in the rear of the restaurant. "You know how I love to mop up curry sauce with my naan."

Ordering and agreeing it had been far too long since they'd seen each other, Scarlet filled Mia in on the drama recently befallen her.

Thick copper bangles jangling, Mia raised her right palm. "This is not good, Scarlet. This is not good at all. Do you know how hard it is to catch a serial killer? You must remember how long the zodiac dude was at large."

Scarlet pulled a face. "That was over forty years ago. I'm pretty sure police procedures, and technology has come a long way since then."

As if Scarlet had said nothing at all, Mia carried on, "Ted Bundy! How many years did it take them to find him?"

"Also in the seventies," Scarlet pointed out.

Mia absentmindedly rearranged all the condiments on the table. "We can't rely on the police. The consensus is, this man wants to talk to you, right?"

"Yes," Scarlet said in a small voice.

Mia narrowed her eyes. "Then we allow him to do just that and figure out a way of entrapping him."

Inwardly sighing with relief as their food arrived, Scarlet waited for her friend to take a few bites before asking, "So tell me what's been happening in your world. Are you still seeing Bruce?"

"Bruce," Mia repeated, "is ancient history, my dear friend. Can you believe the man doesn't vote?"

Scarlet's eyes widened with feigned horror.

Pulling apart her naan bread with unneeded force, Mia continued, "He doesn't recycle, and he thinks hybrid cars are a fad."

The remainder of the lunch was spent with Mia animatedly reporting on the disappointing men who had, as she put it, stolen hours from her she'd never get back. The only man now capable of enticing her, she concluded, would be able to quote Karl Marx, list five life lessons from the Dalai Lama, and figure out a tip without the use of a calculator.

"Quite right," Scarlet said, suspecting her friend may be single for some time to come.

Imagining she'd successfully diverted Mia's thoughts from the serial killer, Scarlet doubted this to be true when her friend suggested a short walk after leaving the restaurant.

Linking her arm through Scarlet's, Mia began, "He'll call into your show again, I'm sure of that. You must be ready to ask him some pertinent questions."

Feeling sick to her stomach at the thought of talking with him, Scarlet enquired, "Such as where he lives or what he does?"

Stepping out of a jogger's path, Mia responded, "Yes, exactly. But of course, it can't appear as if you're trying to help catch the jerk. Just come across as caring and interested."

Scarlet lifted the collar of her pea coat as the wind picked up. "I've thought a lot about what I'd say to him if he calls again, and I agree with you, I think he will call."

"I know it's not easy," Mia sympathized, tightening her grip on Scarlet's arm.

Scarlet shivered. "That's for sure, but, if I can, I really want to stop him from killing again."

"That's my girl!" Mia said with a broad smile.

43

"Let me get this straight," Niles asked, his voice raising, "Mia believes the police aren't doing enough and it's your job to catch this violent murderer?"

Tom and Niles had, just two hours earlier, arrived back in the city. After being all but housebound, due to the cold weather in Boston, they were ready to enjoy the sun, and mid-fifties temps the city afforded them.

"That's not what I said," Scarlet responded patiently.

Breathing in the crisp, clear air of the Golden Gate Park, Niles said, "We never should have left town. I can't believe this killer approached your mom in Aptos. He's getting way too bold, Scar. I don't think you should go back to the station at all, let alone engage him in conversation."

Scarlet released some frustration by kicking a pine cone into nearby bushes.

"You may have just assaulted one of your surveillance guys," Tom said with a laugh, then rearranged his dark curls in case they were indeed mere feet away.

Niles reached out and touched Scarlet's arm. "I'm sorry. I'm just worried, and you know I get bossy when I'm worried."

Scarlet gave a half-smile. "I know that. Plus, you've never been a huge fan of Mia's. I shouldn't have irritated you by relaying her thoughts on the subject."

Clearly, in a mischievous mood, Tom suggested, "I think he's jealous of her because you've been friends since you were in knee socks."

Niles stopped walking and glared at Tom. When Scarlet and the target of his anger looked back, Niles' sullen expression morphed into a smile. "Scar still wears knee socks."

Jogging to reclaim his space alongside them, he added, "Didn't you mention something about Mia trying to start a rebellion in your Brownie group?"

Giggling, Scarlet explained, "We were eight years old and working on our patches. I think Mia and I had about four each. We weren't the most conscientious brownies in the group. They were for things like Hiker, Dancer, Inventor, and Home Scientist. One evening, Mia walks into the hall with a new badge. But, it's a badge she made herself. Our brownie leader asks to take a closer look at it, and Mia proudly shows her."

Having slowed their pace, Tom and Niles, eyebrows raised, hung on Scarlet's words as she continued,

"Written in black marker on thick pink card, cut to the exact measurements of our other badges, Miss Coolidge read aloud, *Drug buster*."

"Are you kidding me?" Tom asked with a wide grin.

Shaking her head, Scarlet went on, "After Miss Coolidge sends the rest of us over to the craft table, she tells Mia to remove the badge. Mia refuses and her mother's called. Poor Mrs. Sumner arrives twenty minutes later, looking miserable. She explains to Miss Coolidge; her daughter was responsible for alerting the police to a meth lab in their garage. Mrs. Sumner's husband, Mia's dad, had subsequently been arrested."

Mouth open, Tom stared as Niles asked, "Mia knew it was a meth lab and told the police on her own dad?"

Nodding her head slowly, Scarlet said, "Yep. While our brownie leader was talking with Mrs. Sumner, Mia walked up to the craft table and solemnly informed us it was time to earn real badges that made a difference. Twelve confused little girls looked down at their badge-covered vests, and Mia was asked to leave. A week later, Mia's mother received a letter in the mail stating, despite the fact its organization was founded in nineteen fourteen, they strived to keep up with the times, but had to draw the line at drug busting becoming an earned achievement."

"Okay," Niles conceded, "I like her a little more now." Smiling, he added, "Despite the short skirts and hooker earrings."

Rubbing Niles' arm, Scarlet said, "She's had a hard life. The short skirts were just a phase; she's more into tie die and bangles now."

Three friends picked up their walking pace before Tom asked, "Did you tell her about Gary?"

Scarlet pulled a face. "No. Mostly because I want to forget about him myself."

Turning a corner and coming across the conservatory of flowers, Niles said, "James is still interested, he called me early in the day on Christmas Eve."

Frowning, Scarlet enquired, "David Bowie?"

"Yes, but remember we need to stop referring to him as Bowie. James told me you called him David and I managed to feign surprise."

Momentarily reliving that embarrassment, Scarlet said, "There is no way he's interested. He practically ran out of my house."

"Only because the police made him," Niles replied matter-of-factly.

Scarlet felt an unexpected rush of excitement. "What do you mean?"

"He had two horses in your driveway," Niles explained. "The police said they had to be moved right away; it was against city ordinance or something."

Tom gave a wistful sigh. "How romantic. He wanted to surprise you with a ride on the beach."

"Did he say that?" Scarlet asked, blushing.

"Yes," Niles replied. "He had a picnic and everything. You were headed to Fort Funston for the day. But, when he saw what turmoil you were in, he felt bad for getting in the way. Plus, the order to remove the horses, post haste, didn't help."

Tom, equipped with a playful scowl, said, "Niles and I have a theory, the handsome black detective wanted James out of the way so he could have you all to himself."

Blushing, for the second time in five minutes, Scarlet stared at her sneakers. "What absolute nonsense!"

44

Feeling content, despite the irony, Scarlet smiled as the maître d' led Niles, Tom, and herself to a table in the corner of the rotunda. As she'd pessimistically predicted, there were no tables affording views of Union Square available.

A discussion commenced on the history and splendor of the restaurant. Enthusiastic appreciation followed with the arrival of elaborately displayed sandwiches and cakes. Suddenly becoming serious, Tom cautioned, "If you think this, in any way, shape or form, makes up for your deception young lady, I assure you it does not."

Raising his eyes upwards, Niles looked at Tom and asked, "Is that Ivy League speak for, we're still not over it?"

Returning her cup to its saucer, Scarlet attempted to explain, "You were on the other side of the country. Impossible for you to help at the time and needless for me to worry you afterward."

His face crumpling, Tom enquired, "What do you think he would have done to you?"

Glaring at his partner, Niles said, "Impossible for her to know and sick of you to ask."

Looking affronted, Tom selected a miniature cake. "This is the most wonderful Christmas gift, thank you, Scarlet."

Niles added his sincere thanks. Scarlet dismissed it as nothing before volunteering, "Fortunately, he had priors, so will do serious time. Detective Smyth said rapists often start with verbal assaults and it keeps escalating from there."

Tom gave a dramatic shiver. "And poor old Gary was just looking for that long-lost excitement of his youth."

Setting a sandwich down that had been halfway to his mouth, Niles asked, "What is wrong with you today? Could we attach some kind of filter to your mouth?"

Coming to Tom's defense, Scarlet said, "To be fair, the Gary story is hilarious. I've given him a full pardon, only because I'm so relieved he didn't want to murder me."

Niles refilled three teacups. "Healthy attitude Scar, but Tom and I aren't leaving town again until they catch this guy."

Tom, a smile tugging at the corners of his mouth, leaned in, conspiratorially. "Tell us again, how well the soap and sock worked."

Laughing, Scarlet thanked Tom for the hundredth time, as he appeared to never tire of it.

"I had gained such momentum, walking down the corridor with the swing and whack motion, when he grabbed my ankle, my arm continued on its own volition."

Grinning excitedly, Tom suggested, "We should get a shadow box for the sock and soap. We can have it engraved: *Here lie the weapons that saved Scarlet Oaks.*"

Niles arched his eyebrows. "I'm surprised, Tom. I would have thought you'd want your name mentioned."

Leaning closer towards Scarlet, Tom, through barely parted lips, said, "My name and involvement would be on the back."

A fun filled hour later, Scarlet signaled the waiter for their check.

The beckoned young man placed two hands on his white, starched apron. "Your friend took care of the bill. He said he hoped you enjoyed it."

"Niles," Scarlet reproached with a scowl.

Raising arms in the air, Niles said, "Don't look at me."

Scarlet and Niles both eyed Tom.

Shaking his head, Tom asked, "Why would I steal Scarlet's Christmas gift thunder?"

The waiter smiled when three faces turned expectantly to him. "It was the gentleman over there."

Following the direction of his hand, all they saw was an empty table.

"Oh, he must have just left," the waiter said apologetically. Focusing on the remaining sandwiches and cakes, he asked, "May I get you a box for these?"

Tom and Niles looked at Scarlet, who, with her face drained of color, stared at the empty table, a short distance from theirs.

Standing, Tom said, "We're not done here; more tea would be nice." As the waiter nodded, Tom placed a hand on his shoulder and motioned towards the restaurant's entrance. "A word if I may."

Scarlet transferred her gaze from the empty table to Niles but still appeared incapable of speech.

Opening his wallet, Niles retrieved a card, then, placing a hand over Scarlet's, dialed Detective Smyth's number.

"Detective Smyth, this is Niles Remmy. Where the hell are your surveillance guys?"

In a slightly less accusatory tone, he explained the situation and gave the detective their location.

Before Niles had a chance to relay the conversation to Scarlet, Tom returned to the table. "Our waiter's on shift for another two hours. I informed him, somewhat, of our situation. He'll be over in ten minutes to give us a full description of the guy."

Niles squeezed Scarlet's trembling fingers. "Perfect. Smyth said he's only five minutes away, so the waiter will only have to describe him once."

Finding her voice, Scarlet asked, "How is this happening? How does he always know exactly where I am? Why aren't the surveillance guys spotting him?"

Niles clenched his teeth. "The police are going to answer all those questions. This is ridiculous. Their job is to keep you safe. I'm seriously losing my sense of humor now."

The gentle hum of chatter, from neighboring tables, filled the room as three friends sat in relative silence. Newfound alertness had them spotting Detective Smyth the second he strode purposefully into the restaurant.

Moments later their, now nervous looking, waiter approached the table accompanied by Detective Smyth.

"Miss Oaks," the detective said by way of a greeting. Nodding at Niles and Tom, he continued, "Mr. Remmy, Mr. Blythe, this is Carl Winters."

At the detective's instruction, Carl, sat down.

"I'm so sorry. People are usually happy when someone else picks up their tab."

Pen poised, Smyth said, "Please tell us exactly what the man said to you."

Wiping hands down the length of his apron covered thighs, the young waiter began,

"He said he wanted to take care of the table with the young woman. It sorta confused me for a moment, 'cos he didn't mention the two guys with her. I was looking for a table with just a lady, and there wasn't one."

Looking up from his pad, Detective Smyth enquired, "But he definitely meant this table?"

Carl nodded, "Yeah, 'cos I made him be more specific. I said, *the lady with long dark hair sitting next to the dude with blondish hair?* He confirmed this was the table and said the lady had helped him with a problem."

Wanting to scream, *what did he look like?* Scarlet forced patience while the Detective asked, "Do you remember if he came in before or after my friends here?"

"It was after," Carl replied with certainty. "I know because Todd begged me to take him. It's Todd's section, but he'd cleared his other tables and was just about to take off when in walks this guy. I agreed 'cos it was only one cover and Todd's girlfriend's leaving for New Zealand tomorrow."

"That was very nice of you," the detective said soothingly. "How would you describe this man, Carl? Take a minute to picture him sitting at that table and then outline his features for me."

"His features," Carl repeated. Narrowing his eyes, he asked, "Like how big his nose was?"

Scarlet, imagining Smyth suspected the man had been wearing the same wig he'd worn in Aptos, listened intently as Carl said, "It was a regular nose, not big and not small. He kinda reminded me of a Viking."

"A Viking?" the detective echoed in question. "Why was that?"

Carl's right hand made a circular motion around his chin. "He had a big red beard. It almost looked too big for his face, and by the time he paid, half his scone was stuck in it."

"Could it have been a fake beard?" the detective asked.

Carl shrugged, "I guess it coulda been, but it sort of matched his hair."

Smyth wrote something on his pad. "Did he have a lot of hair?"

The waiter shook his head. "Nah, it was pretty thin on top."

Nodding, Smyth asked, "Do you remember the color of his eyes, Carl?"

"Yeah, like I said, he looked like a Viking. Didn't they kinda have reddish hair and light blue eyes?"

Smyth responded, "Yes, I believe they did."

Once it was confirmed that, as suspected, the Viking look-alike had paid with cash, Carl, receiving sincere thanks, resumed waiting tables.

Preempting Niles' wrath, Smyth volunteered, "Mr. Remmy, I think I can imagine what you want to say to me right now and you have every right. But, please allow me to firstly apologize on behalf of my team."

Looking over at Scarlet and then back to Smyth, Niles enquired, "How many strikes should your team be afforded, Detective? Scarlet is attacked in her place of work; her mother is approached in broad daylight in Aptos. More flowers on Scarlet's doorstep just three days ago. Are you keeping count? 'cos damn sure, I am."

Lowering his head and closing his eyes momentarily, the detective responded,

"I understand how worried you are, how worried you all are," he added looking at Scarlet and Tom. "The incident at the station was unforgivable, and the team on duty that night has been suspended pending an investigation. But, I'm sure you can appreciate how hard it is to stop a man, who appears apt at disguise, from walking around this large city. It may at present not seem much of a consolation, but he will never be able to get within ten feet of Miss Oaks. Unfortunately, our department does not have the resources to question every person who enters a restaurant."

"So, what's the answer?" Tom asked in flat tones.

Mouth downturned, Detective Smyth replied, "Having Miss Oaks frequent only her home and workplace until he's caught. By eliminating all public places, we can offer her more security."

Seeing the look of horror this statement brought to Scarlet's eyes, the detective gave a half-smile. "Again, please accept my apologies and rest assured I will do my utmost to ensure your safety." Pushing his chair in towards the table, he concluded with, "I'll be in touch."

Focused on the retreating detective, Scarlet said, "No, Niles. I can't do it. It could be years for goodness sake. Mia reminded me how long it took them to find the zodiac killer."

"I wasn't about to suggest it," Niles returned. "I couldn't just go from work to home with no end in sight. I certainly don't expect you to."

Clearing some plates aside and then tapping his hands on the table, Tom asked with a grin,

"What was the name of that game where you had to remember stuff?"

With nothing but blank stares from Niles and Scarlet, Tom frowned, "It was before our time but hugely popular. You had to match things hidden under the squares."

"Concentration?" Scarlet enquired.

"Yes, that's it," Tom replied excitedly.

Scarlet explained to a confused looking Niles, "It was a huge game show. Gran still finds old reruns. You have to remember the prizes behind the numbers on this board and then when you get a matching pair you win the prize."

"Okay," Niles said slowly, his eyes wide.

"We need to be paying more attention to our surroundings," Tom declared, palms outstretched. In an exaggerated whisper, he added, "Psycho Stewart was right over there."

Scarlet bit her lip. "Tom's right. We just got a pretty good description from Carl."

"Minus the beard, I guess," Niles conceded.

"When he approached Mom," Scarlet informed her friends, "he was wearing a dark brown wig and sunglasses. This time, it appears, just the beard."

Tom narrowed his dark eyes. "Every time we go anywhere, we're going to be acutely aware of who is around us. I bet I could find one of those concentration board games on eBay. We can sharpen our senses and be primed and ready next time we're out."

Niles gave a sarcastic smile. "Well, that's it all sorted then. Who needs the police?"

45

It had taken some persuading, but Scarlet finally agreed to an evening of 'Concentration' and cocktails with Niles, Tom, and James.

Seeing James for the first time since their last awkward meeting evoked the embarrassment, Scarlet predicted she'd feel. To cover, she became fascinated by decorations adorning the interior of Tom and Niles' Tudor style home. "These are incredible," Scarlet gushed, taking in the gleaming silver balls of varying sizes hanging from the ceiling.

She was forced, however, to acknowledge her date when James approached with a glass of wine.

"Tom tells me you're a red girl," he said with a disarming smile. "Cocktails to follow, some issue with locating the maraschino cherries."

Relaxing somewhat, Scarlet accepted the balloon style glass with thanks. She then began apologizing for their last meeting and the drama he'd unwittingly walked in on.

"Scarlet," James interrupted, "none of it was your fault, and I'm sorry I couldn't have been more helpful. The police told me I had twenty minutes to get the horse trailer out of there. Once I returned the horses, I wanted to come back and check on you. But, then I worried you might feel like you needed to entertain me and I'd inevitably add to your stressful day."

Scarlet pondered on Niles and Tom's theory of Detective Smyth wanting James out of the way. Her musing ended abruptly when Tom voiced a loud, "Ta da!" Sporting a playful smile, he held a

Concentration board game up in the air. "eBay, vintage nineteen sixty."

James professed his enthusiasm to play the game. Not knowing him well enough, Scarlet found it impossible to tell whether there was any sarcasm in this declaration.

An hour later, sitting at a table in front of a roaring fire, Scarlet determined James had a great sense of humor and an impressive memory too. She and the Bowie look-alike had been teamed up together and managed to accumulate the lion's share of prizes.

Only upon the game being returned to its box, did the laughing stop and the conversation become a little more serious.

Moving across the room to adjust cream roses in a silver vase, Tom stated with gravity,

"Everywhere we go, we must take in all that our surroundings hold."

Leaning in towards Niles, Scarlet whispered, "How much longer until his next assignment?"

Talking out the corner of his mouth, Niles replied, "I'm hoping, I mean, thinking, it's got to be sometime in January."

Pacing up and down in front of the large antique fireplace, Tom continued, "Every person we pass in the park, must be observed. Never again will we sit around a table without looking at our fellow diners."

Niles scowled, "The neighboring tables I can handle, but I don't see how it's possible in the Golden Gate. You expect us to take in the appearance of the hundred-odd people jogging past?"

Scarlet, cringing with what she imagined James must be thinking, was surprised to hear him say, "We could go to a spy shop and buy one of those camera hats. It will record everything, so you can relax more and observe later."

"A spy shop!" Tom repeated, eyes wide.

As Scarlet studied James' profile, Niles said, "That's a great idea, James. Scar, when do you go back to work?"

Feeling caught and blushing slightly, she turned her attention to Niles. "Back tomorrow, but then I'm off on New Year's Eve."

"Well, I should hope so," Tom retorted. "We'll be throwing another unforgettable party. Did we tell you it's masquerade?"

"No," Scarlet replied, "but I'm pretty sure I have a mask or two." Tom waved an arm in the air. "I have a hat box full if you need one."

"What about you, James?" Niles enquired.

James wrinkled his nose. "I may need help with that."

"Wait right there!" Tom exclaimed excitedly, leaving the room.

Rolling his eyes, Niles volunteered, "I'm going to grab us some eats."

The hosts having left the room, Scarlet seized the opportunity to say, "James, please don't feel obligated to get involved with this whole, catch a killer thing."

Her 'Concentration' partner smiled warmly. "If you allow it, I'm all in. I realize we barely know each other, but I'd like to remedy that fact."

Trying to curtail a large smile she felt forming, Scarlet replied, "I'd like that too."

"I think you'll find something suitable amongst this lot," Tom breathlessly proclaimed, placing a large navy colored box in front of James.

Her spirits lighter than they'd been in some time, Scarlet giggled as James pulled varied faces with each mask he tried on.

Once an elaborate pirate mask was voted the winner, the four friends drank vodka Collins and nibbled on Bruschetta. The conversation went from silly to beyond silly, as they debated what other spy gadgets may be available to them.

At the evening's end, Scarlet looked up as James held her car door open. "I feel as if we're starting off on uneven footing."

James looked concerned, and Scarlet quickly explained, "You know a lot about me, or I should say, what's going on in my life right now, and I know very little about you."

"Would you permit me to bore you, I mean fill you in, on all those missing details, tomorrow at the radio station?" James asked brightly.

Thinking for a moment, Scarlet said, "I'll let Detective Smyth know you're stopping by. Would you mind texting me your car make and license number?"

"Consider it done," James replied with a grin.

Positioning herself behind the wheel, Scarlet enquired, "Do you like hot chocolate?"

46

"Oaks!" came a young, female voice from the top of the stairs.

Grateful and relieved to see Sylvia's smiling face, instead of a flashback from the last visit to this stairwell, Scarlet said, "Am I glad to see you."

Both women having arrived early were afforded plenty of time to share their news. Scarlet would have happily stuck with the Hawaiian Islands, but it wasn't long before Sylvia said, "I had a visit from some hot looking detective today."

Scarlet frowned, "Detective Smyth?"

Nodding her head, Sylvia confirmed, "That's him. Is it true Andree came back to the station and tried to hurt you?"

With an exaggerated turned down mouth, Scarlet nodded in response.

"Oaks, I'm so sorry," Sylvia said, staring into her empty cup. "If I hadn't been so stupid and fallen for such a loser, this never would have happened."

Reaching across the high console and touching Sylvia's hand, Scarlet replied, "There is only one person to blame for this happening, and that's Andree. I'm fine, he's in jail, and it's almost a new year, with endless possibilities for you and me."

Giggling, Sylvia said, "I told my brother, Sam, all about you, how you're always so positive with everything."

Scowling and smiling simultaneously, Scarlet said, "Tell me more about your Christmas in Hawaii."

Taking a deep breath, as if she were about to dive into water, Sylvia began, "The dufus was drinking heavily every day of course.

He'd flirt with all the waitresses and make stupid jokes over and over about the leis. He was a nightmare! Every female he saw, from our room attendant to the girls behind the bar, he'd ask about nude beaches. I guess there's one called the Donkey. You can imagine where he went with that. Sam and I got expert at ditching him, though. Then we felt so sorry for Mom, we took her with us. We'd return to the hotel at the end of the day, saying we'd looked everywhere for him and could never find him. He didn't have the nerve to say that he was right where we'd left him, propping up the lobby bar."

Barely hearing her cell phone over the laughter, Scarlet smiled at Sylvia and hit the talk button.

Blushing, as she ended the call, Scarlet, explained, "There's a guy on his way up here, who maybe, kind of, perhaps down the road, a boyfriend of sorts."

"Sounds serious, Oaks," Sylvia said with a sarcastic smile.

"How do I look?" Scarlet enquired.

Sylvia rolled her eyes. "Stunning as always."

Standing and squeezing the younger girl's shoulder, Scarlet glanced at the console. "Oh no, look at the time!"

Sylvia pushed her stool back. "You're live in two minutes."

Moving back to her place by the mic, Scarlet asked, "Would you mind chatting to him for a bit, until I get my bearings?"

Sylvia grabbed her purse. "Sure, no problem."

As the studio door began to close, Scarlet called out, "His name's James."

Watching Sylvia shake James' outstretched hand, Scarlet leaned in towards the mic. "Thank you for calling Mending Men. This is Scarlet, how can I help?"

Turning her gaze from the two people in the corridor, Scarlet focused on her computer, ready to open the appropriate window.

Once the caller announced himself as Barry, from Daly City, Scarlet knew assistance from the internet wasn't needed.

"I've got some advice for all the lonely, horny men out there," he began.

Despite a few sarcastic retorts on the tip of her tongue, Scarlet resisted the urge. "What's your advice, Barry?"

"It's now or never!" Barry replied dramatically.

Scarlet waited out the pause until he continued. "Women are desperate on New Year's Eve. The year didn't go how they planned, so they make one last ditch attempt at finding love. The booze is flowing, and that old land something song is playing. Guys if you don't score now, you never will, you know what I'm saying?"

Closing her eyes momentarily, Scarlet responded, "I'm sure the Bay Area appreciates your dating tips, Barry. Happy New Year to you."

Apparently sober enough this time to detect sarcasm in Scarlet's voice, Barry reiterated the need for a sympathetic male DJ. Cutting him off, Scarlet said, "Here's a song for you, Barry. *What becomes of the broken hearted?* by Jimmy Ruffin."

Sighing as she turned to see Sylvia open the door for James, Scarlet invited them to sit down. Declaring she had P.I.B. duties to take care of, Sylvia left, pulling the heavy door behind her.

James looked around the small studio. "This is so cool." Reading the messages on Scarlet's posters, he added, "I sit in a cubicle, in which I look eerily like every other man sitting within twenty feet of me. We all put our suit jackets over the back of our chairs. At ten a.m., we take a short stroll around the building, all going in the same direction of course, or it's like swimming upstream."

Giggling, Scarlet interjected, "At least, it's daylight. I should have a pet bat in here."

Laughing, as he slid onto the high stool opposite Scarlet, James said, "I enjoy this station's music."

"It's a little more our parents' genre," Scarlet said, "but I'm getting into it too. On my top forty show, I had to keep up with all the latest artists and all the gossip of said artists. With this new gig, I can just pick songs I think will appeal to my new market."

"What is that market?" James enquired.

Enjoying his interest, Scarlet replied, "Well, all men of course and the data from our last survey put the listeners between thirty and fifty-five."

Nodding, James eyed her colorful console. "That looks complicated."

Shaking her head, Scarlet turned her attention to the control board. "I agree the size is daunting, but in reality, I only use a third of these buttons."

Seeing the on-hold light flash, Scarlet continued, "Here's a couple I use often. This one turns the music bed on and off, and this one answers the call-in line."

James listened eagerly as Scarlet recited her signature welcome.

"All I want to do is thank you," the caller said.

Scarlet, while attempting to silence her gasp, turned to look at James. Eyes wide, he mouthed, "the guy?"

Nodding in the affirmative, Scarlet checked to make sure she was recording the call.

"Just wanted to show my appreciation, yes I did," the caller continued.

Still looking at James, Scarlet asked, "Is this Stewart?"

James gave an encouraging nod, and the caller slowly replied, "You can call me Stew."

Relatively calm, no doubt due to the fact James was feet away and Sylvia just down the hall, Scarlet said, "I did get some flowers. Were they from you, Stew?"

After a lengthy pause, Stew answered, "All women like flowers, yes they do."

Forcing her voice to sound light and casual, Scarlet volunteered, "I think you're right about that Stew. Are you and your wife still getting along well?"

In a significantly louder and minutely faster tone, Stew answered, "I already told you things were better. You didn't appreciate the flowers, no you didn't."

Looking from the mic over to James, Scarlet, desperately trying not to stammer, said, "That's right Stew, you called into the show and thanked me. I did like the flowers; they were very pretty."

The pause, this time, was so long, Scarlet wondered whether she'd lost connection. What must have been thirty seconds later, painfully slow words voiced, "When somebody wants to thank you, you should let them thank you, yes you should. I don't like it when women stop me from doing things I want to do, no I don't. My mom liked rabbits, but Dad wouldn't buy her one. I saw a really good rabbit in a field and brought it home for her. She said we couldn't afford to feed it and made me take it back, yes she did."

"I can see how that would be upsetting to you, Stew," Scarlet replied in soothing tones.

Without preamble, Stewart asked, "Then why didn't you put those flowers in a vase?"

47

Scarlet mumbled some sort of an excuse. Coming up beside her stool, James pointed towards the music bed button.

Nodding her head, Scarlet leaned into the mic. "Thank you for calling Mending Men, Stew. I'm going to play…" she struggled to locate the next song on cue, "*Absolute beginners* by David Bowie."

Scarlet looked up at James, now just inches from her side. "Thank you for keeping your cool and remembering the buttons."

James grinned, "It's all thanks to Tom and his Concentration game."

Both laughed, more for tension relief than from amusement, until Sylvia gently knocked on the studio door.

"I heard the call," Sylvia announced after Scarlet motioned for her to enter.

James did his best to answer some of Sylvia's questions, while Scarlet dialed Detective Smyth. Hanging up with the detective, Scarlet sat back and listened to the conversation James and Sylvia were having.

"Why don't I know about this Stewart creep?" Sylvia asked James.

"I know very little about him myself," James admitted.

Scratching her head, Sylvia said, "I thought Andree was her only nightmare. Now there's a second dude."

Smiling apologetically, James said, "I don't know anything about Andree."

Holding a thermos up in each hand, Scarlet asked, "Hot chocolate, anyone?"

Receiving eager nods, Scarlet talked while pouring.

"On my first day with Mending Men I got a call from Stewart. He was having marital issues, and I tried to give him sports minded advice. Only I messed up the analogy and said bath instead of shower. A couple of weeks later, the police inform me he's murdered his wife and another woman by drowning them in the bay."

Fiddling with the large skull and crossbones ring on her forefinger, Sylvia enquired, "Do the police think he wants to kill you?"

Scarlet forcefully shook her head. "They believe he just wants to communicate with me and because of that fact, I saw no reason to worry you."

Her face draining of color, Sylvia asked, "Does my piece of shit uncle know about this? He was too cheap to find a replacement for me when I was in Hawaii. Tell me he didn't know."

The room fell silent. James looked confused and concerned. Sylvia, just plain furious.

Skirting the question, Scarlet said, "The police are watching me constantly, I'm sure they assured your uncle I'd be fine."

Sylvia scowled, "If my uncle were halfway decent, you'd have had someone here, and Andree couldn't have scared the life out of you."

Giving Sylvia's hand a gentle squeeze, Scarlet looked at James. "A few days before Christmas I was here alone. It was just one of those situations where I thought I'd have friends and family around, but they were either out of town or needed elsewhere. Andree was a guy who weaseled his way into Sylvia's affections. He frightened me with a couple of harassing phone calls. The second one was while Sylvia was in Hawaii. He'd made copies of her keys and then knowing she was away, drove her car to the station. The car fooled the surveillance guys but I imagine Andree had no idea I was being watched. Must have got quite the surprise by how many police stormed in here that night."

"I'd ended it weeks before and we thought he was in San Diego," Sylvia interjected.

"He's in jail now, so it's over and done with," Scarlet responded.

Leaning back into the padding of the high stool, James ran hands through his blond hair. "I can't believe how much you've gone through."

Scarlet offered him a playful grimace. "Despite the fact, my life, right now, does seem like a made for TV movie, I promise you, it's not usually this way." Pausing to look around her studio, Scarlet added, "It all started with this new job."

Sylvia moved to a lighter topic, informing Scarlet and James of how poorly Candy was handling Scarlet's old top forty show.

Experiencing an equal mix of horror and amusement, Scarlet and James sat transfixed as Sylvia recounted a recent interview Candy had conducted with a well-known rock band. She'd apparently giggled continually and failed to ask a single question regarding their music. "She could have redeemed herself when she ended the interview by playing their latest single," Sylvia went on, "only it wasn't their song. Uncle Brian tried to apologize, but they told him there were plenty of other DJ's in this city who were worthy of the title and appreciated their music."

About to ask more, Scarlet stopped when Detective Smyth knocked on the studio door.

"Miss Danico," he said, shaking Sylvia's hand, "good to see you again." Hand still outstretched, he turned to James. "You're the guy who likes big four legged animals?"

James forced a smile. "That leaves some serious room for misinterpretation, Detective. I enjoy riding horses on occasion."

Undeterred, Smyth said, "Enough enjoyment to warrant ownership of the animals."

With a slight scowl, James responded, "The *horses* belong to my sister."

Detective Smyth now owned the fake smile. "And you thought they might make a unique sort of date for you and Miss Oaks."

A distinct edge to his voice, James replied, "Something like that, yes."

Exchanging glances with Sylvia, Scarlet volunteered, "It's all here." Holding up a CD she added, "The most alarming part, was him knowing I hadn't put the flowers in a vase."

Thanking her as he put the recorded material in his breast pocket, Detective Smyth said, "My guess is, he has no idea what you did with the flowers. Probably fishing to see if he gets a reaction from you."

Not feeling too comforted by this suggestion, Scarlet enquired, "Are you any closer to finding him?"

"Most certainly, we are," Smyth said with practiced ease. He patted his breast pocket. "Well done on this and I'm happy to see you have company. I'll be in touch."

All three watched the detective exit the studio. Sylvia was the first to speak. "Uh, that was awkward."

Standing, James said, "I don't think Detective Smyth likes me too much." He glanced at his watch. "I should get going and let you wrap up for the night. Niles mentioned you have an escort home."

"Yes, my Gran and Dad. I'm staying with them for the time being, so they drop and pick me up."

"Perfect. Could I do the same for the party?" James asked nervously.

Feeling relieved he still wanted to, Scarlet answered, "That would be lovely."

Revealing the smile, she'd so enjoyed during their game night, James volunteered, "I'll call you tomorrow and get directions to your Gran's house."

Nodding, smiling, and blushing all at the same time, Scarlet watched him walk out the door and down the corridor.

"What?" she asked Sylvia, after receiving a varied sequence of facial expressions.

"Someone's got it bad," Sylvia jeered mischievously.

Biting her thumbnail, Scarlet asked, "Do you like him?"

Sylvia sat and put her head to one side. "He kinda talks old fashioned like my Grandpa. But apart from that, he's super sexy."

Scarlet laughed. "He is very polite, but I like that in a man."

Sylvia narrowed her eyes. "I like mine a little rough around the edges."

Giving her friend the last of the hot chocolate, Scarlet said, "You'll get over that."

48

The severity of what transpired only truly hit Scarlet on the drive home. The combination of first day back and James being there had undoubtedly acted as a buffer.

Rose voiced her concern, "So, this comment, about you not putting the flowers in a vase, didn't seem to worry the detective?"

Shaking her head, Scarlet replied, "He believes Stewart's bluffing, maybe trying to unnerve me."

Joe interjected, "Like you're not sufficiently unnerved already."

Scarlet fell silent, prompting Rose to change the subject. "So, young lady, what are your plans for seeing in the New Year?"

The thought of James instantly brightened Scarlet's mood. "A very nice guy will be picking me up and taking me to Niles and Tom's masquerade party."

"But you'll come back to us straight after?" Joe asked with a hint of panic.

"Providing I don't have a curfew," Scarlet joked.

Joe chuckled. "I only ask, because I know Niles lives just up the road from you."

"True, and many a year I stumbled home on New Year's, but not this year. Tomorrow I plan on making a couple of drinks last and getting to know this new guy better."

"You mentioned he works with Niles," Rose said as Joe pulled the car into her steep driveway.

Sighing, Scarlet said, "I know; you'd think it was the only place of employment in San Francisco. But, Max left before James started there, so that saves some awkwardness."

"The simple fact you seem happy to see the New Year in with this young man, tells me he must be alright," Rose said as they entered her Victorian home.

Scarlet scooped an excited Prudence into her arms. "I know so little about him, Gran. I hope getting better acquainted won't leave us disappointed."

Scoffing as he stole Scarlet's pig from her arms, Joe volunteered, *"He* won't be disappointed." Kissing Prudence on the nose, he added, "Prudence and I have a late-night ritual of strolling the yard together before bed."

Rose put an arm around her granddaughter. "We need to find someone for your father before he and Prudence start wearing matching outfits."

Seven hours later and, untypically, the first up, Scarlet started breakfast.

"Happy New Year's Eve!" Scarlet said in greeting when Rose and Joe entered the kitchen.

"Do I smell cinnamon rolls?" Joe asked with a grin.

"You do," Scarlet replied, checking the oven timer. "And there's O.J. and fresh coffee for you in the sunroom."

Scarlet, accompanied by a doughy, sweet cinnamon aroma, walked in on her father and gran discussing how relieved they were at her apparent happiness.

"Dad!" Scarlet scolded as Joe gave Prudence a piece of cinnamon roll. "My landlord will throw us out if that pig gets any larger."

Smiling at Prudence, who sat contently next to Joe on the padded wicker sofa, Rose said, "I think we may have to embrace the reality of Prudence not being a micro pig."

Joe playfully covered Prudence's ears, and Scarlet asked, "How big do you think she's going to get?"

Joe removed his hands from the pig's ears. "I've researched it a little. She's not even a year old yet, and they don't reach their full size until they're three. If she is indeed a micro pig, I think the only way we'd know her potential for growth would be to see the size of her parents."

"And if she's a regular farm girl?" Scarlet asked hesitantly.

Smiling, Joe responded, "Let's cross that bridge when we come to it."

49

Having brought only a couple of evening dresses to her current digs, the decision of what to wear was not a hard one. Gathering in Rose's bedroom, Scarlet asked,

"Suitable for a New Year's Eve bash?"

Taking in the strapless satin cocktail dress, with taffeta underlay, Joe said, "You get my vote."

"Stunning," Rose agreed, patting the padded stool in front of her French style vanity.

"I don't think I've ever enjoyed getting ready for a party more," Scarlet said as Rose coerced her granddaughter's thick dark hair into an elegant updo.

Carefully listening to his mother's instructions, Joe opened the third drawer down in a cherry wood jewelry armoire. "This one?"

Rose looked in the mirror at Joe's reflection from across the room. "That's it."

Prudence at his heels, Joe cautiously placed a diamond necklace around his daughter's neck.

Eyes wide, Scarlet said, "Gran, I couldn't possibly."

"Nonsense," Rose replied, retrieving a bobby pin from the vanity and securing one more curl in place.

Standing back to admire her work, she added, "Your Grandpa Herb is smiling down from heaven, to see this necklace being worn again."

Joe sat on the edge of his mother's ornate four-poster bed. "I remember the day Dad gave it to you."

"Do you really?" Rose asked with a smile. "You were very young."

"I was six," Joe confirmed. "He'd been overseas for weeks; we were all missing him horribly."

Looking at, but never focusing on, the mirror, Rose said, "That's right. Your sister, Elsa, was ten and going through a stage. I remember she was on me relentlessly about getting her ears pierced. Herb had been in Brazil, helping a new company with sand mining. They paid him a ridiculous amount of money for his mining know-how and the fact he spoke Portuguese."

Placing her hand over the exquisite necklace, Scarlet volunteered, "Grandpa's mom was from Lisbon."

Rose gave Scarlet's curls a quick burst of hairspray. "Benedita was quite a woman. Her father was killed in the First World War, making her childhood tough even by early nineteen hundred standards. Benedita learned to hold on to what was hers, very tightly." Momentarily closing her eyes and nodding her head, Rose continued, "It took your great grandmother a good few years before she fully welcomed me into the family. I believe she softened a little once I started making Queijadas though."

"Queja what?" Scarlet asked with a laugh.

Scowling, Rose replied, "Don't tell me I've never made you Queijadas!"

From his place on the bed, where Prudence had now joined him, Joe interjected, "I'm sure you did when the kids were little, but it's been a while."

"It's a basic batter," Rose said. "I'll remedy that tomorrow."

Admiring three rows of flower shaped diamonds, Scarlet enquired, "So Grandpa bought this for you in Brazil?"

"Yes. The company he was helping had been mining diamonds for some time. It was a family affair. A cousin made the jewelry and sold the pieces from a market stall if you can believe it. Herb picked the most expensive piece and insisted on paying full price for it. I can't remember the jewelry maker's name, but he told your Grandpa a lovely story about this necklace. He said, the strand nearest the throat would give the wearer ability to only speak kind words. The middle strand would make the soul as pure as a newborn child's. And the third strand, her heart capable of intimate love, for only the giver of the necklace, until the end of time."

Scarlet and her Gran simultaneously got misty eyed, but Joe was unmoved. "I'm sure he said that to every Tom, Dick, and Harry who bought his jewelry."

Rose, still marveling at the beauty of her late husband's gift, found Joe in the mirror. "You are a cynical boy, and Prudence is the only girl who'll have you if you can't buy into a little romance."

Dramatically placing a hand on his heart, Joe retorted, "I can be as romantic as the next guy, but you know what these market stall traders are like. They'll say anything to get the sale."

Placing a decorative diamond pin in Scarlet's hair, Rose said, "Your father had already agreed to the piece and the price before he heard the story."

Pulling a face, Joe conceded, "Prudence and I will dress alike, starting tomorrow." Over Rose and Scarlet's laughter, he added, "I remember how happy you were to see Dad after that trip and I remember how excited he was to give you the necklace."

Smiling softly at her son, Rose reached into one of the vanity drawers and retrieved a salon-style hand mirror. Holding it up behind Scarlet's head, she asked, "What do you think?"

Taking in the tousled curls perfectly held in place, with just the right amount left loose to frame her face, Scarlet said, "It's perfect, thank you, I love it." Scarlet gently touched the shimmering diamonds adorning her throat. "And thank you for loaning me this incredible necklace."

Before Rose had the opportunity to respond, the doorbell rang, setting Prudence off into a series of squeals and snorts.

Immediately flooded with nervous excitement, Scarlet asked, "Will you two entertain James, while I finish my makeup?"

Ten minutes later, Scarlet found James being *entertained* in the library.

Confessing to Rose he only knew of the televised Elizabeth Gaskell novels, James, his back to the door, was unaware of Scarlet's entrance.

Rose, pausing to answer a question about *North and South,* smiled when she caught sight of her granddaughter. James turned slowly, his lips parting slightly as he gazed at Scarlet.

Blushing, Scarlet said, "A man who knows his Victorian literature."

James shrugged modestly, "I have two sisters, who've taught me well."

When his staring resumed, Rose said, "You young things should probably be on your way."

Taking in a short deep breath, Scarlet replied, "Yes, I just need my mask."

James walked towards her. "Mine's in the car."

Joking that it sounded as if the pair were about to rob a bank, Joe added in undertones, "You will be very careful while having a great time?"

Helping Scarlet into her coat, James assured Joe he would not let her out of his sight.

Twenty minutes later, James pulled his Lexus into a, hidden from view, garage at the rear of Niles and Tom's home.

Niles, looking handsome in a navy-blue suit and lilac shirt, helped Scarlet from the car. "Tom's grilling the door monitors for I think the third time in fifteen minutes." At Scarlet's quizzical expression, Niles explained, "We had a visit from Detective Smyth earlier today. He asked us to be diligent about assuring we have no gate crashers."

Scarlet sighed, "Oh Niles, I'm so sorry."

Shaking James' hand, Niles replied, "Nonsense, we'd do it whether the detective asked or not. With the mask theme, it's very necessary. Once the bulk of our guests arrive, we'll have someone posted at every entrance to check for stragglers."

Scarlet bit her lower lip and Niles elaborated, "Tom went overboard this year with the number of catering staff he hired, we can easily spare a few of them to man the doors."

James and Scarlet slowly made their way through crowded reception rooms, James proudly introducing his date to work colleagues along the way. Tom, dashing in a silver colored slim fit suit and purple paisley vest, found them in the billiards room. With a flushed face and wide grin, he exclaimed, "I can't believe how many people showed up. Are there no other parties in this city?" he added with a laugh.

Scarlet began to thank him for his diligence with security, but Tom waved her off. "Before I forget, I have a favor to ask you."

"Anything," Scarlet said.

"Did Niles tell you, I've received my next assignment?"

Scarlet shook her head.

"January fifth, I'm off to Haiti. Cholera has been out of control since the earthquake in two thousand ten, so we're going to see what we can do."

Pausing briefly to greet an attractive blond haired woman in a long velvet gown, Tom continued, "So, I'm on the phone with my boss, Larry. He'd filled me in on the shots I'll need, the expected length of our assignment and so forth. Then on the off chance, I asked him if he'd like to come to our New Year's Eve party. I don't know what possessed me to ask when he's never socialized with coworkers before. But, lo and behold he says, yes."

In an exaggerated whisper, Tom divulged, "Poor guy would have been all alone for New Years. His daughter is moving to the east coast, I guess her husband's military and overseas. Larry's wife is helping their daughter move, then spending a month there to get her settled.

Larry couldn't go because he's getting me and twenty-five other guys organized for Haiti."

Scarlet and James' heads nodded in sync and Tom went on, "He's pretty upset about his daughter moving to the east coast. She's their only child. I can't remember her name; it's something like Serena or Sienna. Larry has a good size wedding photo of her on his desk." Tom looked over his shoulder conspiratorially. "She's not as beautiful as you, Scarlet, but there is a definite resemblance. I know it's a lot to ask, but I thought it might be nice if you spent a little time chatting to Larry this evening. Maybe make him miss his daughter a little less."

Scarlet, while inwardly doubting her likeness to his daughter would be a comfort, said, "I'd be happy to."

Clasping his hands together, Tom exclaimed, "Thank you so much. I'm lending him my gold jester mask."

Scarlet raised dark eyebrows. "He's honored, that's your favorite from New Orleans."

Smiling mischievously, Tom replied, "What can I say? The man signs my checks."

Sipping her champagne, Scarlet admitted, "I'm glad you told me about the mask, that thing covers your entire face."

Tom accepted a spring roll from a passing waiter. "I doubt he'll wear it for long, it's pretty heavy. Besides, I'll personally introduce you to him, so you don't need to worry about spotting him in this crowd. Although," he added pushing his lips together, "no one else has a mask like my golden jester."

As if, just now, seeing them for the first time, Tom gushed about how incredible Scarlet and James looked. "You're like a Hollywood couple," he concluded, before leaving to play host.

Gently touching Scarlet's arm, James asked, "Before you meet Tom's boss, would you mind if we attempted to find somewhere quiet to chat?"

"I'd love that," Scarlet replied, "and I know just the place. But, there's a condition. First, we acquire a nice little selection from these wonderful men and women with trays in their hands."

James chuckled and professed his agreement.

Looking around, eagerly, Scarlet instructed, "How about you take the front reception rooms and I'll take the rear. Meet back here in five."

Raising her eyebrows as James shook his head, Scarlet asked, "You don't think we'll manage it that quickly?"

"I told your father, I wouldn't take my eyes off you," James responded. "Could we tray shop together?"

Looking into his thick-lashed, almond-shaped eyes, Scarlet replied, "Deal!"

Masks secured and focused on the prize, Scarlet and James had full plates in no time.

"This way," Scarlet whispered.

James, equipped with an appreciative smile, followed her up a narrow staircase.

At the top of the steep, blue-carpeted stairs, they were confronted by a small, wooden, arched door.

Taking in James' look of amazement, Scarlet explained, "This house was built in the nineteen-fifties. It stayed in the family for three generations, before it was placed on the market and Niles bought it. The Polish lady who had it built was quite famous. Niles could tell you more about her, but I believe she saved over a hundred Jews during the Second World War."

Turning the heavy iron door handle, Scarlet led James into a small, windowless room with rose-patterned wallpaper. Silver gray carpet lay thick beneath their feet. Scarlet kicked her shoes off before turning on three antique floor lamps. Setting champagne glasses and plates on the round mosaic tiled table, James suggested Scarlet sit on the small couch, and he take the floor cushions.

Positioned to face his date, James said, "This is fascinating. Tell me more."

Scarlet happily obliged. "The base of the stairs was originally concealed with wooden paneling. The door, apparently so well crafted, was impossible to see."

Reluctant to interrupt, but having a pressing question, James asked, "Was it just for sentiment, being that it was the fifties and America?"

Scarlet scrunched up her pretty features. "Sentiment, habit ... a basic need perhaps?"

Shaking his head, James mused, "Over a hundred people, what an incredible woman."

Nodding and leaning in towards James, Scarlet elaborated, "Apparently, she became fixated with priest holes. When her granddaughter sold this place to Niles, she told him she believed there were, at least, three in this house."

"Priest holes in this house!" James repeated, eyes wide.

Scarlet placed her palms outward. "They've never been found."

Standing to hand Scarlet her champagne and retrieving his own glass, James volunteered, "Weren't they an English thing; way back?"

Scarlet crinkled her brow in concentration. "I think sixteenth century."

James leaned back into oversized cushions. "That would be right. The persecution of Catholics during Queen Elizabeth's reign."

Enjoying their historical discussion, Scarlet said, "Catholics had to have Mass said in secret. I read priest hunters would take a full week searching a house and usually never found them."

Looking around the room, James enquired, "Do you think the granddaughter was correct? Undiscovered Priest holes are in fact hidden in the walls of this great home."

Scarlet bit her lip. "Exciting, isn't it? The story was, this brave woman carried an overwhelming sadness and regret. She believed she could have saved many more innocent people if her Polish home had been equipped with priest holes."

James, seemingly speechless, gazed at Scarlet intently. With enough time spent on this exercise to make Scarlet blush, she said, "I still know so little about you."

Returning his glass to the small table, James clasped his hands together. "Where would you like me to start?"

"Your earliest memory," Scarlet said, relaxing into the gold and bronze striped couch.

James frowned. "Gosh. Let me think."

Scarlet contentedly reached for her plate of appetizers. "Take all the time you need."

Halfway through her crab salad canapé, James began, "My father getting a tattoo."

Scarlet nodded with encouragement, and James continued. "It was my mom's name on his right forearm. 'Isabella' tattooed in large italics went from wrist to elbow. My sisters and I thought it was the coolest thing."

"How old were you?" Scarlet enquired.

James looked up towards the ceiling. "I want to say five."

"Was your Mom pleased?"

Returning his focus to Scarlet, James responded, "She didn't say a word. Just looked at it and left the room. I remember we were in the yellow and green kitchen on Sixth Street. Dad watched Mom leave before taking camel cigarettes out of his denim jacket and systematically smoking the entire pack. My sisters and I stayed with him in that kitchen for hours. Then, Dad returned the empty package to his pocket, kissed my sisters, and then lifted me up to sit on the table. His breath smelled so bad, I had a hard time not gagging as he spoke to me."

Motionless, and not taking her eyes off James' face, Scarlet asked, "What did he say?"

Looking at the busy wallpaper, James answered, "I don't know if I truly remember this, or if my oldest sister, who was ten at the time, told me. He said, don't let life beat you down and never ever stop dreaming."

Desperately wanting to know more, but sensing the recollection had been somewhat draining for James, Scarlet said, "That's quite a first memory. I hope you'll forgive me for not asking your star sign instead."

Laughing, James assured her he appreciated the depth of her question and hoped he hadn't been too morose.

Reluctantly, Scarlet suggested they show their faces for a while downstairs, before returning to their secret hideaway.

"You must help me find the ever important, Larry," Scarlet instructed with a chuckle as they made their way down the steep staircase.

Conspicuous among all the other masks, in a corner of the library, stood the gold jester, Larry.

After spending a fruitless fifteen minutes looking for Tom, Scarlet proposed,

"Why don't I just go and introduce myself. Strike up a conversation by complimenting him on his choice of mask."

Having thoroughly scanned all the bustling rooms, James agreed there'd be no harm in approaching the man, who was clearly not engaged at present.

Accepting her second glass of champagne from a passing waiter, Scarlet touched James' arm. "If Larry and I are still chatting in twenty minutes, please come rescue me."

"Can we make it ten?" James countered with a boyish grin.

Scarlet gave a cheerful consent before crossing the library to greet Larry.

"That's the best-looking mask here," she said brightly. "I hope you don't mind me coming over for a chat. Tom has talked about you often; I believe you're off to Haiti in a few days."

Nodding his head, Larry said something, but with all the other voices and the thickness of the mask, it was hard to make sense of it.

Putting an open hand up to where his ear would be under the mask, Larry pointed to the foyer. Although skeptical as to any rooms being much quieter, Scarlet nodded her agreement. Briefly stopping to let James know her new location, Scarlet and Larry walked the short distance before resuming a somewhat one-sided conversation aside Tom's neo-classical Greek bust.

James' six foot four frame gave him the advantage of seeing over many people's heads. This enabled him to keep his promise to Scarlet's father, even as groups of people walked through the foyer.

Looking at his watch and selfishly hoping ten minutes had passed, James was startled by Tom's voice behind him.

"Thanks, I'm having a wonderful time," James gave in answer to Tom's question.

Tom took in the bustling room. "It's one for the books this year. Everyone loves the mask theme, and I think I've set up a couple of my friends with some of the lovely ladies from Trade Elite."

"Well done," James said with a smile.

Looking around the library, Tom asked, "Where's Scarlet? I want to introduce her to Larry."

"Already done, my friend," James said confidently. "We spotted him here in the library, Scarlet's talking to him now."

"Are you sure?" Tom asked quizzically. "I just left Larry in the billiards room."

Frowning, James responded, "They're right over there, by your Greek bust."

Standing in that exact spot was a plump blond woman talking animatedly to a bemused looking member of the catering staff. Scarlet and the Jester were nowhere to be seen.

Eyes trained on the foyer, Tom said, "I don't know who Scarlet was chatting with, but it wasn't Larry."

50

Tom's statement hung in the air for a few seconds, before its meaning had his complexion paling dramatically.

James forced his way into the foyer. "We need to call the police."

Tom, already on the phone with Niles, nodded as he abruptly instructed Niles to meet them by the bust.

Ending the call, Tom looked down at his phone. "Call her. We can call her."

James shook his head. "We both left our coats and cell phones in the car." Trying to control his breathing, he added, "We need to search the house."

Tom began biting his thumbnail. "We'll take sections, as soon as Niles gets here."

Right on cue, Niles briskly walked towards them, reddish blond eyebrows questioningly raised.

Without taking a breath, Tom gushed, "I just left Larry in the billiards room. He's not wearing a mask. I told him about Scarlet's resemblance to his daughter, and he said he'd be honored to meet her. The mask was too hot and cumbersome for Larry. He tried it on, then set it down on a table in the great room. I asked one of the waiting staff to give it to the housekeeper before it walked away. Scarlet was talking to someone wearing that mask, and now she's disappeared."

"How long has she been missing?" Niles asked as soon as he got the opportunity.

Looking at his watch, James said, "Five minutes."

Nodding, Niles volunteered, "Okay, let's just take a moment to think. Every single person in this room is an invited guest. I've had all the doors covered. Some drunk guy picked up that mask. A beautiful woman comes up and starts chatting to him. Of course, he's not going to tell her she's got the wrong man."

"Guys," James began, looking from one to the other, "I honestly believe she wouldn't have moved from the foyer without telling me."

Niles placed a hand on James' upper arm. "I agree. You two have been thick as thieves since you arrived tonight. I'm calling the police."

Snapping into action, Tom said, "James you take the great room, billiard, study, and library."

Waiting until Niles had explained the situation to Detective Smyth, Tom continued, "You take kitchen, pantry, dining, and sunroom. I'll cover the game room, cozy, gym, office, and breakfast room."

Over James nervously repeating his list of rooms, Niles volunteered, "Smyth is on his way with a group of cops to help us look. Let's meet here after our searches. Quick but thorough," he said to the men's departing backs.

Returning to the foyer within seconds of each other, the trio gave their reports. Unable to hide their disappointment at none returning with Scarlet in tow, Tom was the first to speak, "We've only covered the first floor. There are two more stories."

No one wanting to mention the fact that anything innocent would not have taken Scarlet above stairs, James struggled with his nagging thoughts. "What about a basement?" he asked, unable to look Niles and Tom in the eyes.

Coughing, to clear an uneasy tightness in his throat, Niles said, "No basement, just a wine cellar."

"Can you check it out while I grab Scarlet's and my cell phones from the car? James asked. "She may be somewhere where there's a phone and tried to call."

Three men agreed, once again, to meet back in the foyer.

Gutted, but unsurprised by no calls to either of their phones, James took the opportunity to search the four-car garage. On his way back to the kitchen entrance, he found Detective Smyth chatting with the door monitor.

"Just him, Sir," the young man reported, pointing at James.

Detective Smyth looked over his shoulder as the young man added, "And he's been approved by Mr. Remmy."

Turning and shaking James' hand, Smyth began, "I'm going to have five of my men interview every single person here. Someone has to have seen something."

James concurred with the Detective's logic. Smyth introduced the arrival of a second man as his partner, Detective Williams.

Looking through the door, into the kitchen, Smyth said, "This is James Attwood. A friend of Miss Oaks."

Allowing the fair-haired detective a moment to shake James' hand, Smyth continued, "Jeff, I need you to organize questioning of all the guests and the entire catering staff. In fact, start with the catering staff. They haven't been drinking or engrossed in conversation, so are more likely to have noticed goings on."

Williams gave an affirmative and Smyth said, "I need to talk with the owners of this," he stood back to take in the full height of the Tudor-style house, "enormous home."

Looking over at James, Detective Smyth enquired, "Do you know where I might find Mr. Remmy and Mr. Blythe?"

"In the foyer," James replied, leading the way.

Tom and Niles answered questions regarding background checks of the catering staff. Leaving them scratching their heads when asked if any guests had criminal records, James climbed the steep blue-carpeted stairs.

James' breath caught in his throat. The aroma of Scarlet's perfume still hung in the air. Less than an hour ago, he'd been happier than he'd been in a very long time. Now, because he'd taken his eyes off her, she was missing and possibly in great danger. Remembering their conversation, James, heart pounding, ran back down the stairs and almost fell into the foyer.

Smyth, Niles, and Tom all turned to stare at him. "Scarlet was telling me about the history of this house," James panted. "How it belonged to a Polish woman who'd hidden Jews during the Second World War."

Somewhat bemused, Niles confirmed, "Yes, her name was Irena Lazinski. The woman was a saint, but sadly went a little batty in her old age."

Impatient for the three men to understand his meaning, James blurted, "Scarlet and I were in that windowless room at the top of the blue stairs. She said this Polish lady was kind of obsessed with still having secret places to hide people. She had always wished for Priest holes, correct?"

Niles narrowed his eyes. "If they exist, they've never been found. There used to be a tunnel beneath the house, but it was boarded up long before I bought the place."

"The previous owners of the home closed it up?" Detective Smyth enquired.

"Yes. The only living relative is a granddaughter. I purchased this home from her three years ago. She relocated to Amsterdam directly after the sale, I believe."

Scratching his chin, the Detective asked, "This woman would know of the tunnel's location?"

"I don't understand it," Niles responded shakily. "We checked every single person who entered this house. She has to be here." His voice raising an octave, Niles added, "The bathrooms, maybe she got sick and is cradling a toilet somewhere."

Tom, eyes downcast, reported, "I checked them."

"We need to locate this tunnel, Mr. Remmy," Detective Smyth imparted, gravely.

His legs, suddenly weak, James said, "I think we should alert Scarlet's Dad."

Detective Smyth reached into his inner jacket pocket. "I'll do that right now."

Smyth walked away from the group, talking into his phone in hushed tones. Moments later his partner approached at speed. "One of the catering staff reported another member of staff asking questions about the dynamics of this home. Places he could go and not be interrupted."

"The description?" Detective Smyth enquired.

Tapping the notebook in his hand, Detective Williams replied, "Possible."

Glancing at the three men who'd followed them into the room, Smyth asked, "Can you bring him in here, Jeff?"

Returning moments later, Detective Williams introduced a broad-shouldered man, seemingly to be in his mid-thirties, as Dave Wainright.

"Have a seat, Dave," Detective Smyth said casually.

Taking in the proximity of Niles, Tom, and James, the man did as instructed.

Trusted pad and pen poised, Smyth said, "Please recount, to the best of your ability, every detail of the conversation you had regarding the dynamics of this home."

Running his hand along the edge of the table, Dave began, "He asked if I knew of any secluded areas where he wouldn't be discovered."

"Why didn't we hear about this?" Tom demanded.

Throwing Tom, a warning look, Detective Smyth continued, "Did it seem an odd question for this man to ask?"

Red-faced, Dave said, "It's a very common question to be asked at these events, Sir."

Trying, but failing, to sound non-accusatory, Niles enquired, "It's a common question for catering staff, who we pay top dollar, to want to sneak off into private areas on our grounds?"

Palms placed flat on the dining table, Detective Smyth exhaled. "I understand how worried you are Mr. Remmy. We are all, I believe, tired and frustrated. But, please allow me to do my job, or I'll have to ask you to leave this room."

Muttering to himself, Niles took a couple of steps back from the table.

Looking directly at Dave, Detective Smyth asked, "Why is that a common question?"

"Because it's New Year's Eve," Dave replied with a shrug. Nodding towards a passing waiter, he elaborated, "Some of the staff are seeing each other. They want to grab a little personal time to... you know."

Smyth looked up from his notebook. "I see. You understood this to be the man's intention."

Dave pulled a face. "This guy, more likely he wanted to light up."

Unable to practice patience, James asked, "What did he look like?"

Receiving, you've done it now, looks from Niles and Tom, James hastily apologized for interrupting.

With a curt nod in James' direction, Detective Smyth continued to look at him as he said, "That was my next question."

Narrowing his eyes, Dave explained, "Lots of people working these gigs are models hoping to get their break in acting. They're a pretty tight-knit group. When time allows, they find secluded spots and cover for one another. This guy sure didn't fit that demographic. He was wearing a baseball cap, which I found a bit odd. I told him once the party began, he'd need to take it off."

"How old would you say he was?" Smyth asked, pen poised once again.

Rubbing a hand against his jaw, Dave replied, "Certainly older than me. I'd guess late forties or early fifties. Looked like he didn't take care of himself. Had that saggy, sallow skin thing going for him."

Exchanging glances with his partner, Detective Smyth asked, "Did you notice the color of his eyes or any hair that was visible?"

Dave shook his head. "I didn't see any hair, and I'm sorry, I don't remember the eyes at all."

Smyth tapped a pen against his lower lip. "You only saw him one time, early in the evening?"

"Yes, Sir," Dave replied with certainty. "He was one of the first to get here, told me he was new and wanted to get the lay of the land."

While Dave continued with his description of the clothes the man wore and the estimated time of the conversation, two uniformed police officers approached Detective Williams.

Completing his notes and allowing Dave to leave, Smyth looked up at the officers, "You found the tunnel?"

The younger, rosy-cheeked officer, replied, "No, Sir."

Smyth massaged his temples. "What have you got?"

The second, marginally older, officer spoke, "We interviewed a young woman named Susan Rider. She was asked by Mr. Tom Blythe to give a jester mask to Mrs. Elma Teague, the housekeeper. Ms. Rider was quite upset as she says she lost the mask. Per the young woman, directly after receiving this order from Mr. Blythe, she was asked by Mr. Niles Remmy to refill the punch bowl. Ms. Rider says she placed the mask on the butcher's block while she retrieved more punch from the butler's pantry. After refilling the punch bowl in the great room, she returned to the kitchen and found the mask was gone."

Just as James wanted to scream, *we all know the mystery man was wearing a mask,* a third uniformed officer ran up to Detective Williams. The officer relayed a message in rushed, low tones.

Detective Williams, with relative abruptness, addressed the two officers, "All officers outside now. Abort all other interviews and cover every inch of these grounds."

51

Concluding a brief discussion with his partner, Detective Williams, talking into his phone, hurriedly left the room.

Smyth turned to face, James, Niles, and Tom. The three men, struggling to remain calm, looked expectantly at the detective. "Six members of the catering staff have monitored activity in and out of the kitchen this evening," Smyth informed them. "The fifth shift was taken by a young man named Todd Silver. He remembers two staff members leaving together and not returning in what he considered the typical time frame. He presumed they were doing what Dave has alerted us to but said it was quite bizarre."

Niles, Tom, and James listened intently as Smyth continued, "Todd said it was a man and woman, both in the uniform black and white, but the female's clothes were way too big for her. He said the pant legs were dragging on the floor and the shirt cuffs hanging over her hands."

Pausing for a moment, the detective solemnly added, "Todd said they were walking very closely together. Unnaturally so. He said the woman looked extremely nervous, but Todd assumed it was… well because of the behavior Dave outlined."

Niles enquired whether all the door guards had confirmed there was no re-entry by this couple and Detective Smyth while answering his cell phone, nodded in the affirmative.

Sighing the detective said, "I need to go and speak with Joe and Rose Oaks."

"We're going to help with the search," James declared, speaking for his friends.

Placing a hand over the mouthpiece of his phone, Smyth said, "We'll need information on any exterior underground structures."

Frowning in thought as they walked outside, Niles said, "Pretty sure there are no wells or bunkers."

Spotting Detective Williams alongside the garages, Tom asked him, "You don't think they may have left already? Shouldn't we have helicopters and stuff?"

Williams replied in a soft, calm tone, "We have all available units searching the …" Lowering his head slightly, the detective finished, "The area of recent discoveries."

Observing the fact all three men looked as if they might pass out, Williams hastily added, "We have every reason to believe Ms. Oaks is still on this property."

Feeling a little air return to his lungs, James enquired, "Why do you believe that?"

"Our surveillance team, Sir."

"The surveillance team!" Niles repeated with a nervous laugh. "They would have seen her leave."

"Exactly, Sir," Williams said before excusing himself to answer his beeping walkie talkie.

Flashlights in hands, Niles, Tom, and James, began searching the orchard area.

"I can't get that little Polish lady out of my head," James admitted. "Could there be secret hiding places on these grounds?"

"The only real structure," Niles said, "is the old greenhouse. Our gardener uses it to store his tools."

"Wait!" Tom exclaimed, "what about the old stable?"

Niles pulled a face. "Let's check it out, but it's just a tiny enclosure." Walking past a rose garden, Niles explained, "Irena bought a miniature donkey for her grandchildren to ride."

Tom forged ahead, taking the lead. "But there's something else in there, Niles."

"There is?" Niles asked quizzically.

"I keep cans of beer in there," Tom supplied in answer.

"What are you talking ...?"

Before Niles could finish, James interrupted with, "Carry on, Tom."

Glancing over his shoulder at Niles, Tom said, "Niles is such a snob about his wine cellar. Nothing but wine can be stored in there. Unlike your fancy traders and brokers, no offense James, I work with tough guys who like to drink beer. Every party we have, I run out of room in our fridges. Then I came across this sort of pulley thing, kind of like our dumb waiter, in the old stable."

"Is it a type of storage area?" James enquired.

Tom crinkled his nose. "I guess. It has a little shelf-like elevator."

"So, it goes up and down?" James asked.

"I think so," Tom replied with uncertainty. "I just stack my beer crates on it 'cos it's off the ground and in a cool place. I'm sure there is a little crank thing, though whether it still works is doubtful."

"Guys, hold your flashlights up higher," Niles demanded coming to a standstill.

As they did so, a small wooden structure came into view.

"Watch your footing around here," Tom volunteered. "The gardener doesn't venture this way, and there's a fair few tree roots."

Upon reaching the stable door, Tom peered in, stating, "There's my beer. It was all about the champagne tonight."

Boards creaking beneath his dress shoes, James illuminated the unusual contraption.

"There's the turn thingy!" Niles exclaimed excitedly, as James' flashlight revealed a rusting, old-fashioned crank handle.

Handing his light to Niles, James removed two cases of beer before attempting to turn the handle.

"This should go down," James said, viewing the shelf like box structure. "But the handle's useless."

Positioned on his haunches, James continued to examine the contraption, while the other two men did their best to follow his hands with light.

Suddenly, falling backward, James squinted up into the brightness. "Did you hear that?"

Lowering their lights, Tom and Niles confessed they'd heard nothing.

Pushing himself onto his knees, James leaned over the structure and shouted, "Scarlet!"

52

What came next had Tom intermittently thanking God and screaming with delight.

Niles, showing great composure, called Detective Smyth.

"Yes, it's me," James voiced down through a crack revealing nothing but darkness. "And Tom and Niles," he added, grinning.

Tom knelt next to James. "Dearest girl. Are you okay?"

A very faint, "Yes," traveled back up the shaft.

Turning to Niles, allowing him his turn to talk, Tom realized his friend was too choked with emotion for speech.

"We're going to get you out of there, Scarlet," James assured her.

"He cut the cords for the pulley," came the echoed response.

"How did you get down?" Tom asked, hoping there was another entrance.

Straining to hear the reply, they learned there was another handle at the base of the underground enclosure. This allowed elevation to the surface, but Stewart had cut the cords, preventing Scarlet from getting up or anyone else, down.

"You're definitely not hurt?" James, needing reassurance, asked.

"I'm fine," Scarlet replied shakily.

Tom, attempting conversation, was thwarted by the sounds of sirens filling the air. Not wanting to be outdone, fireworks began exploding above the Golden Gate Bridge.

Finally finding his voice, Niles called down, "Happy New Year, Scar."

Tom and James followed, to which Scarlet responded with a small sob, "Happy New Year, guys. I love you."

Tom and Niles hastily professed their love for her, as James stayed silent, fighting back tears. He knew it was forbidden to say those words on a second date, however unusual that date may be.

Illuminated by a backdrop of multi-colored fountains and Catherine wheels, San Francisco firefighters ran towards the small stable.

Scrambling to get out of their way, James quickly shouted of their arrival to Scarlet, as he, Tom, and Niles exited the enclosure.

Using skill and precision, San Francisco's finest cut away the tray-like top. Three muscular men then shouldered a heavy rope, allowing a fourth, limber man to shimmy down. Within the blink of an eye, the agile man was pulled back to the surface. A filthy, but smiling, Scarlet, holding on to him like a baby koala bear.

The cheering that followed almost drowned out the booming, whooshing, and whistling sounds from fireworks over the bay.

A casual observer would have seen three men fervently hugging each other. In reality, a petite dark haired woman stood tightly encased within their strong arms.

Releasing the firm squeeze he had around Scarlet, Niles turned towards the house, enquiring,

"What was that?"

Detective Williams, taking large, determined strides in their direction, informed them, "I believe it was your guests, celebrating the New Year, Mr. Remmy."

Tom laughed, as Niles, with an exaggerated turned down mouth, exclaimed, "That's right, we had a party."

Niles, Tom, and James reluctantly allowed Scarlet to be whisked away for medical attention.

Motioning towards the house, Detective Williams said, "I took the liberty of returning your catering staff to their duties once the interview process was complete. No one has been allowed to leave the premises, so I felt more refreshments were in order."

Thanking the officer for his intuitiveness, Tom and Niles joined James, rocking anxiously from toe to heel, a few yards from the ambulance.

Stepping up into the vehicle, Detective Smyth spoke a few words to the EMT, who, in turn, helped Scarlet sit up from her horizontal position on the gurney.

"There are a couple of people desperate to see you," Detective Smyth informed Scarlet with a smile.

Turning her head to look out of the ambulance's open doors, Scarlet saw her father, one arm around his mom, the other holding onto a small pig, walking towards her.

Having patiently waited, Joe and Rose, pale and shaking, enveloped Scarlet between them while Prudence ran in circles squealing hysterically. No words were spoken, except an apology from Rose for soaking Scarlet's hair with her tears.

Detective Smyth placed his hand on Joe's upper arm. "Would you mind if I had just a few minutes with your daughter? I promise not to overdo it."

Joe nodded, and Rose, kissing Scarlet said, "Your father and I stumbled across a lovely old bench just over there. That's where we'll be until you're ready to go home."

Joe, giving her one last squeeze, added, "How does a bubble bath and hot chocolate sound?"

"Like heaven," Scarlet said, before giving her attention to Detective Smyth.

"Mr. Oaks," James voiced tentatively.

Picking up Prudence, now pawing at his shoes, Joe handed the pig to Rose and watched as the two returned to a rustic, curved back bench.

James took a deep breath. "I am so very sorry."

Able to look him clearly in the eye, due to all the lights from fire trucks and police cars, Joe responded,

"I don't want to hear it."

His breath halting somewhere between heart and mouth, James managed, "I understand …"

Joe cut him off, "I don't want to hear an apology from the man, who by all accounts and purposes took exceptional care of my daughter this evening."

Not knowing him well, James could have believed Joe was being facetious. But the look of warmth on the man's face assured James this was not the case.

"I promised you I wouldn't take my eyes off her," James volunteered, the words catching in his dry throat.

Joe placed his hand on the younger man's shoulder. "Surveillance teams and police detectives have been continually outsmarted by this guy. Detective Smyth, all but told us, if Scarlet wasn't at home or work, he could not guarantee her safety. From everything I've heard, you were incredibly diligent tonight, and I'm indebted to you."

Smiling with relief and fighting back persistently threatening tears, James said, "Thank you, Mr. Oaks. It's only our second date but I …"

Smiling kindly as James struggled for words, Joe acknowledged, "Some second date, hey."

James shook his head, and Joe said, "How about you drive Scarlet home, as planned? The car following closely behind will be her Gran and me."

Thanking him again, James watched as Joe joined Rose and Prudence.

Hearing commotion by the stable, James joined Tom and Niles who, excitedly, informed him a backpack had been retrieved from the place of captivity.

Still not wanting to have Scarlet out of his sight, James glanced back towards the ambulance to see her talking, as Detective Smyth, simultaneously nodded and wrote.

"Do we know what's in it?" James enquired.

"Not yet," Niles said. "Here comes Detective Williams now."

Without hesitation, the Detective answered their question. "Just some broken flower stems."

Niles, experiencing a sudden and terrifying realization, said, "Steele is still on our property."

Looking around, as if Niles had said something he'd rather others didn't hear, Detective Williams admitted, "That is probable."

"More than probable," Tom argued. "You just told us no one could leave without being spotted by your surveillance guys."

Detective Williams ran a hand roughly across his mouth. "Typically, a perpetrator will want to get away from the crime scene as soon as possible. From the timeline we've put together, it's feasible Steele could have done that before Miss Oaks' disappearance was reported."

"Presuming," Niles began, while shooting dagger eyes in Williams' direction, "your surveillance was notified the second I called the police, I don't see how he'd have had enough time."

His neck reddening, Williams replied, "When you're panicked and distraught, time can stretch out to distorted proportions. Steele, on the other hand, had a seemingly clear and organized plan. As I said, the timeline put together with intelligence from Ms. Oaks and the distance they traveled, suggest it's possible he left before we arrived."

"What did surveillance say?" Tom almost screamed. "Did they observe a guy wearing a banquet uniform leaving our property or not?"

Suddenly fascinated by his shiny black shoes, Detective Williams replied, "They did not."

Seeing Scarlet return her blanket to the paramedics, the three men, muttering and cursing under their breath, left Detective Williams standing alone and still staring at his shoes.

James, hastily removing his jacket, placed it over Scarlet's shoulders.

Smyth thanked Scarlet for her valuable information, leaving her to be, once again, affectionately squished between Niles and Tom.

Joe and Rose joined James, who stood close by, smiling.

Rose said, "I'm going to be the bossy grandma and insist Scarlet get some sleep now."

Tom, Niles, and James offered no argument. Joe, who had been talking softly in his daughter's ear, nodded towards Rose, who then continued, "How about a late brunch tomorrow, I mean today, at my place?"

The invite was eagerly accepted before Tom and Niles said their goodbyes and returned to their all-but-forgotten guests.

Five minutes later, Scarlet and James sat in his idling car, waiting for Joe and Rose to pull up behind them.

"It was much bigger than your Mom not caring for tattoos, wasn't it?" Scarlet enquired softly.

Looking from his rearview mirror to the beautiful woman next to him, James marveled, "You've just had a near death experience, and you want to discuss my first childhood memory?"

"It's very important. Plus," Scarlet added with a tilt of her head, "It was a great distraction while I was down that shaft. I formed a mental list of the questions I was going to ask you."

Smiling warmly at Scarlet, James caught sight of flashing headlights behind him. Waving a hand of recognition in his rear-view mirror, he pulled out of Niles and Tom's drive, Joe and Rose close behind.

"Dad was such a dreamer," James began. "I was too young to remember the specifics, but my sisters have given me a faithful account. Apparently, a friend would give him a couple hundred cans of paint at a great price. *Your father is now the proud owner of a house painting business*; he'd inform us over dinner. A month later, as the paint sat unopened on the garage shelves, Dad would announce, *No one wants to clean their own gutters anymore. Your old Dad's decided to hire a couple of young lads to do the job and make us rich.*"

Relaxing into the leather headrest, Scarlet turned her neck towards James. "How did you survive financially?"

Sadness crept into James' voice. "Mom took a second job. She worked as a school secretary during the day, and a hotel housekeeping supervisor at night."

Scarlet stayed silent, leaving James to state brightly, "I believe a warm bed awaits you."

Smiling, as she took in her Gran's steep driveway, Scarlet declared, "We'll finish this conversation later."

Shaking his head, James said, "If you insist."

Concerned, Scarlet asked, "As long as it doesn't cause you pain?"

"Not at all. I'm very flattered by your interest," James replied honestly.

"I'll see you for brunch at noon then," Scarlet confirmed cheerily.

Opening the passenger side door, James said, "I'm looking forward to it."

Instinctively, they wrapped arms tightly around one another. Breathing in the scent of him and hearing the pounding of his heart, Scarlet felt a new, and at present, undeterminable emotion flood her exhausted body.

Faintly aware of the existence of something other than this embrace, Scarlet slowly lifted her head.

Smiling, James stood back, allowing Joe, with Prudence, tucked under one arm, to escort his daughter towards the large Victorian home.

As Rose unlocked the solid cherry front door, Scarlet turned to see James standing by his car.

Smiling at each other, neither one appeared willing to break the gaze. Only when Prudence started squirming and squealing her desire to be released from Joe's arms, did the enchantment fracture.

Joe and Rose, amid furtive glances, declared their desire to run Scarlet a bath.

Accepting the proposal with gratitude, Scarlet, in somewhat of a haze, followed Prudence as she excitedly reconnected with her current home.

Finally, leading Scarlet to her bedroom, Prudence collapsed on a pink princess cushion, apparently worn out by the evening's endeavors. Walking into the adjoining bathroom, Scarlet found Rose filling the light blue pedestal tub.

"Gran, I can do this," she protested. "You and Dad must be exhausted too."

Nodding as she turned the faucet off and straightened her back, Rose said, "Tired, but so happy and so grateful."

"Me too," Scarlet said. Then pushing a hand into the pocket of her baggy black pants, proclaimed, "I almost forgot!"

Holding up the exquisite three-string diamond necklace, she elaborated, "Stewart asked me, quite politely, if I'd take it off. He said it looked a little rich for a banquet server."

Rose asked, "He didn't want to take it?"

Before Scarlet could answer, Rose continued, "No, don't tell me. Your father and I agreed, no talking until you've had a good long rest."

Rose took the shining gems from Scarlet's outstretched hand. "There would have been no tears if the necklace hadn't made it back."

"I know you well enough, to believe that," Scarlet responded.

"Knock, knock," came a voice from outside the open bathroom door.

Turning to face Joe, both women invited him in.

"Hot chocolate for my brave girl," Joe declared, placing a large mug on the blue and yellow tile table.

"We'll leave you to relax now," Rose said, linking an arm through her son's.

"Whenever you wake is the right time," Joe said determinedly. "Your Gran and I are perfectly capable of entertaining your friends until you're good and ready to join us."

"Thank you both, so much," Scarlet said as Rose and Joe left the bathroom.

"And I'm taking Prudence," Joe voiced over his shoulder. "I don't want her waking you too early."

Scarlet laughed as she heard Rose sarcastically say, "That'll be why he's taking her."

53

Following the sounds of laughter, Scarlet located her father, Niles, Tom, and James, sitting in the sunroom.

Evidently, the cause of this joviality was Prudence, standing on her hind feet, looking lovingly at Joe.

"Scar!" Niles declared, "you didn't tell us Prudence knew how to shake hands."

Blushing, as James stood to acknowledge her entrance, Scarlet admitted, "*I* didn't know."

Grinning, Tom said, "There's no hard scientific proof, but we do believe she just snorted, *I love you*, to your father."

Patting the vacant sofa cushion next to him, Joe enquired, "How do you feel? Did you sleep well?"

Scarlet accepted the seat. "I slept very well. What about you guys?"

Tom and Niles informed the room of heavy overnight police presence, still in force at their house. Standing to achieve the best result, Tom, statue still, imparted, "Please inform us if you hear or see any unusual activities around the home, Sir."

Niles said, "I wanted to ask him to define unusual. The motley crew cleaning our home this morning certainly fits *my* description."

Sitting down, Tom explained, "Mrs. Teague, our housekeeper, enlists her grandchildren for cleaning duty after big parties."

"We pay them, of course," Niles interjected seriously.

"Three, even two years ago," Tom continued, "they looked like ordinary, pimply youths. Now, they have those massive holes in their ears and bars through their lips."

"Poor Mrs. Teague," Niles contributed. "She won't let us leave the house without combing our hair, I can't imagine how mortifying their fashion sense is to her."

Chuckling, Scarlet turned slightly to find James' steel blue eyes gazing at her intently. Having been caught, he smiled self-consciously.

Momentarily tongue-tied by the sight of him, Scarlet took a few seconds to clear her throat. "Where's Gran?"

"On the phone with your Mom," Joe replied. "We didn't want to alarm her last night, but also didn't want to wait too long if that makes sense."

Scarlet nodded, and the room fell silent.

Almost hidden under a large wooden tray, Rose, exclaiming her delight at seeing Scarlet looking rested, entered the room.

Eagerly and full of thanks, the guests helped themselves to the selection of juices and hot drinks.

At the invitation to sit, Rose said, "I've got crepes, queijadas, banana streusel muffins, Irish soda bread, and all other kinds of naughtiness for us to celebrate with."

James stood. "Let me help you, Mrs. Oaks."

Taking his arm and insisting he call her Rose, the two made their way to the kitchen.

Wasting no time, Tom enquired with an exaggerated whisper, "What do you think, Scarlet? Could he be a serious contender?"

Delivering a swift slap to Tom's shoulder, Niles asked, "What is this, a boxing match?"

Deflated, Tom sat back on the wicker sofa.

Scarlet gave him a reassuring smile. "I like him a lot, Tom. He's incredibly easy and fun to talk with. And... he makes me feel safe."

Ignoring Tom's dagger eyes, Niles said, "Safe is really good right now."

Seriously appetizing smells wafted in with the return of Rose and James.

Plates fervently filled, Niles, having decided his good friend was as steady and strong as ever, said, "Okay, Scar, I can't wait any longer. How did he manage to make you vanish before our very eyes?"

The room fell silent. Everyone shifted forward on floral, cushioned seats, in curious anticipation of Scarlet's response.

Scarlet swallowed a piece of butter laden soda bread. "The library was pretty noisy, and I couldn't hear Larry, who I thought he was at the time, from behind his mask. I did think it odd that he wouldn't help the communication problem and just take it off. But, some people do take a masquerade theme very seriously."

Her audience nodded their agreement, and Scarlet took a small sip of grapefruit juice. "He cupped a hand around one of his partially visible ears and then motioned towards the foyer. Our perceived improved location was next to Tom's Greek bust, but he never said another word. It was beyond awkward, and I was just about to give up and return to James when I felt something jab into my ribs."

Following a collective gasp, Scarlet explained, "This person, whom I now assumed wasn't Larry, handed me a note. It confirmed the hard object pushing into my side was indeed a gun. Listed in numerical order were my instructions. First, I had to walk a few steps to the cupboard under the spiral staircase, stand with my back to it, and then push back and release."

"It's a concealed door," Niles said. "Just one gentle push and it springs open."

Tom shook his head. "Smyth said they checked every closet and cupboard, but of course you were long gone from the foyer by the time they arrived."

Nodding, Scarlet went on, "Secondly, I had to change into the banquet style clothes I would find in a backpack on the cupboard floor. My third instruction was to return to him promptly, or he would come in and retrieve me. Fourth, was to walk calmly beside him to the kitchen. Fifth and final was to say nothing to anyone, including the kitchen door monitor."

Scarlet looked at James. "I knew it wouldn't be long until you noticed I was missing. I contemplated taking my sweet time in the cupboard, but the thought of him coming in after me was too scary."

Running hands through his hair, James said, "He must have had you out of the house in little over five minutes. Of course, the kitchen may have been one of the last rooms we searched."

Giving him an understanding smile, Scarlet continued to the group, "To be honest, I was relieved to be leaving the party. I knew at this point, it was Stewart. Being painfully aware of what the man's capable of, I didn't want him loose in the house with a weapon. He kept a tight hold of my arm, the gun ever present against my ribs. We walked slowly towards, well you know where. The tears came, and I pleaded with him to let me go. He never said a word. Finally, we reached that little barn. His flashlight was pretty pathetic so I couldn't tell where he was putting me. He lowered me down on this little shelf thing. I don't know how far underground I was, but with each inch, it got darker and colder. Then I heard him slowly crank the shelf up to the surface. Minutes later, it came back down with something on it. He tells me it's a backpack and I'll find a vase and flowers inside. I'm then instructed to put the flowers in the vase and place them in front of me. Once I did this, the shelf went back up. Then he calmly asks me to describe the flowers to him. It was the first time he sounded like the Stewart I recognized from Mending Men. That slow voice and bizarre self-confirmation thing he does. The light he was shining down was so weak, I could only see an outline. I had to assume they were the same wildflowers he'd placed on my car and faked it. Minutes later, his demeanor changed drastically. It was like he was suddenly in a rush. *Was I thankful?* he asked me. *Did I love the flowers and appreciate the thought behind them?* Then I heard the shelf come back down and from the creaking and straining it sounded like he was on it."

"Oh no, he was down there with you!" Tom breathed.

Scarlet frowned. "I honestly don't know for sure, but I think he may have been. But then, minutes later, I heard a loud ping which was unmistakably the pully cable being cut."

Breaking for a gulp of tea, Scarlet let her body relax into the seat, allowing her grandmother to say, "You were incredibly brave and composed, my darling."

Scarlet smiled as the others concurred. "I never heard another word from him, but was afraid to shout for help, in case he was still there. It didn't seem long at all until I heard James' voice. Only when the firefighter came down with a powerful flashlight could I tell for sure Stewart wasn't down there."

For the next half hour, Scarlet listened to the information from her rescuers' point of view. The lion's share was delivered by Tom, with occasional contradictions from Niles.

James' contribution was that he planned never to send Scarlet flowers. After much-needed laughter, Joe proposed,

"I think it's time we let Scarlet call her mom." Looking at his daughter, Joe added, "I promised her you'd be in touch within a couple of hours."

Scarlet nodded her agreement and James, Niles, and Tom began returning empty plates and cups to the kitchen.

Stealing a moment, while Niles and Tom thanked Rose for the delicious brunch, James asked Scarlet if she'd mind him stopping by the following day.

Wondering when she'd stop blushing at the sound of his voice, Scarlet said, "I'd like that. I want you to finish that first memory."

Promising her he would do anything she asked of him, James thanked Rose and Joe for their hospitality, before following Niles and Tom out the door.

54

An hour later, Scarlet was fifty minutes into a call with her mom.

"Why...." her mother's voice filled the bedroom, "do some families have all the bad luck, while others just sail through life?"

Rubbing her hands across a lavender and cream silk bedspread, Scarlet said, "I'm actually feeling really lucky right now, Mom. Some families do have more than their share of tragedies; we've been fort..."

"Look at the Babcocks, for example," Marilyn interrupted. "Three daughters married and their son just started his residency."

"Peter's going to be a doctor?" Scarlet enquired, pushing off her bed and walking towards the bay window.

"Oh yes," Marilyn said. "He's such a sensible, well-adjusted, young man."

Smiling in remembrance of a drunken Peter making lewd advances to her one summer evening, Scarlet said, "Isn't he, though."

Marilyn began to cry softly. Scarlet moved closer to where she'd left her phone by the bed. "Mom, it's okay. Everything will work out well for our family, too."

"You could have been killed," Marilyn sobbed.

Scarlet picked up the phone and moved over to the window seat. "I honestly don't believe he would have hurt me. I'll come down to Aptos soon, and you can see for yourself how well and happy I am."

Her voice cracking, Marilyn said, "There's something else."

"Oh?" Scarlet replied, then paused for her mother to continue.

"Trent's gone."

When Marilyn left it at that, Scarlet enquired, "What do you mean, gone?"

Sounding exasperated, Marilyn explained, "Lisa called me this morning. Apparently, they had an argument last night. Trent took off and hasn't returned."

Slowly exhaling, Scarlet said, "Well, it's only been one night. He's probably still asleep on some friend's couch."

In a small voice, Marilyn said, "Lisa told me, they have an understanding. If Trent is ever gone overnight for anything other than work, he knows he'll never be able to return."

Scarlet rubbed her temples. "Why am I not surprised? So, Lisa was letting you know, even if he does come back, it's over as far as she's concerned because he broke one of her rules."

Marilyn's reply came amid short, sharp breaths. "She was so rude to me, Scarlet. All but told me I'd never see my grandsons again."

"Don't worry, Mom," Scarlet soothed. "We'll sort it all out, I promise."

"Thank you, my sweet girl," Marilyn sniffed. "You will come see me very soon?"

"Just as soon as the police say it's safe to do so, I'll be there," Scarlet confirmed.

"And you'll stay for more than one night?"

A beep signaling another call interrupted Scarlet's response.

Taken aback by the number showing Niles and Tom's landline, Scarlet distractedly said,

"For sure, Mom. I'll call you soon."

Accepting the incoming call, Scarlet voiced, "I thought you only kept this phone, so your gardener could covertly call Mexico?"

"You didn't take the flowers with you, no you didn't," came the, now unmistakable, voice of Stewart Steele.

Paralyzed with fear, Scarlet stared out the window. A middle-aged woman strolled down the street, her sweater-clad dachshund trotting by her side. The woman looked so calm, so normal. Didn't she know Niles and Tom were in danger?

Trying, but failing, to regulate her breathing, Scarlet slowly walked towards an antique writing desk.

"I couldn't," she stammered, "a firefighter lifted me up. I didn't have time ..."

"You're lying," the eerie voice interrupted.

With a shaking hand, Scarlet wrote, *Steele is at Niles' home. Call Police.*

"I'm not lying, Stewart," Scarlet professed while exiting her bedroom.

Finding her father first, Scarlet put a finger to her mouth before Joe had a chance to speak.

Confused, Joe accepted the paper from Scarlet.

Color draining from his face, Joe reached into his pocket. Retrieving his cell phone, he turned and made his way to the library. Scarlet, standing between the kitchen and dining area, continued, "It all happened so quickly. I had been admiring them for a long time, then a man on a rope ..."

Again, not allowing her to finish, Stewart Steele said, "You knew they were coming, yes you did. Your boyfriend told you they were on their way. It would have taken two seconds to grab the flowers. Why aren't you grateful?"

Walking towards her, Joe nodded. Then, hand on heart, stood listening.

"I am very grateful," Scarlet reiterated. "They were beautiful flowers."

Hearing movement from the kitchen, Joe rushed off to warn his mother.

"I want to believe you, yes I do," Stewart said. "I don't want you to be like the others, no I don't."

Feeling as if she might faint, Scarlet, backed up to the winding staircase. Grabbing onto the wooden rail, she gingerly eased down onto a partially carpeted step.

Words refusing to come, Scarlet waited, painfully aware how loud her breathing was.

"Willy Wonka wasn't a bad man," Stewart said slowly. "But he knew those kids had to be taught a lesson, yes he did. It wasn't like they weren't warned. They just took and took. Wonka put a swift end to that."

"Willy Wonka," Scarlet heard herself say, knowing she was losing her ability to focus.

Rose and Joe now both stood in front of her. Scarlet imagined their looks of horror mirrored hers.

Stewart asked, "May I still call your show for help?"

"Yes of course," came Scarlet's shaky reply. Gaining strength from her father and grandmother's presence, she added, "I could thank you on the air for the beautiful flowers you gave me."

Hearing his tone change, to what Scarlet guessed might be as happy as he was capable of sounding, Stewart said, "That would be very good, yes it would. Then everyone would know, yes they would."

Again, a lengthy pause before Stewart concluded, "East Coast cops know how to think like a mole person."

And with that, he hung up.

55

Brown Trader Joe's bags looked out of place atop a highly polished burgundy leather inlaid desk. Tom sat perched on the very edge of a button tufted leather sofa, while Niles paced in front of the fire.

Joe and Rose stood back a few feet while Scarlet hugged her friends.

"We're fine," Niles responded to Scarlet's panicked expression. "If he was here, which I highly doubt, he's not now."

Turning from a small huddle of dark-suited men, Detective Smyth said, "I'm afraid he was here, Mr. Remmy."

Niles staring open-mouthed, left Tom to ask, "How is that possible? He would have been seen."

Scarlet turned to see Niles and Tom's housekeeper, Mrs. Teague, allowing James entry to the library.

Displaying half his usual breadth of a smile, James walked up to Scarlet and discreetly squeezed her hand.

All attention was on Detective Smyth as he reached into the inner breast pocket of his navy suit. Instead of his signature notepad, he produced what looked to be a hand-written note.

"He's playing with us now," Smyth said. "Let me know if anything written here makes sense to you."

With only the sound of cracking wood from the fireplace, Smyth unfolded the note and read aloud, "Dad always said kids should be seen and not heard. Mom said they shouldn't be seen either."

Looking up at his audience and receiving the blank stares he'd anticipated, Smyth continued reading, "If you keep quiet, you don't need much air. Mom said I was an oxygen thief."

Not bothering to look up as he turned the piece of paper over, Smyth finished, "As they said in the days of the Roman Empire, Molus Iracus."

"What a bunch of mumbo jumbo," Tom proclaimed, watching Smyth return the note to his pocket.

Eyes focused on his phone, James reported, "Molus Iracus is Latin for Mole."

"He mentioned Mole," Scarlet said. "Something about a mole and East Coast Police."

Smyth looked at Niles. "You believe there is a tunnel beneath this home, but it's boarded up. Have you ever located the entrance?"

Shaking his head, Niles responded, "The grandmother of the woman I purchased this home from was big into secret, concealed areas. I was never told where they were and suffering from claustrophobia, never had the desire to look."

Having joined Smyth, while additional policemen searched the grounds, Detective Williams asked, "But in the two-plus years you've lived here, you've never come across anything inside, or on the grounds, resembling an entrance?"

Frowning in concentration, Niles at length replied, "Nothing."

Giving floor to ceiling bookcases more scrutiny than she ever had before, Scarlet enquired, "Did these books all come with the house?"

Looking at the objects of interest, Niles said, "Yes. They're all classics. Too deep for me. I only read books that advise me how to make more money."

Scarlet gave him a friendly scowl before turning to Joe. "Dad, remember that movie we loved with all the secret doors?"

"Clue," Joe returned. "I think they designed the movie set around the game."

With mutual understanding, father and daughter approached the bookcases for a closer inspection.

All eyes watched as Scarlet, and Joe gently pushed and pulled at various leather bound novels.

"The candles!" Tom exclaimed excitedly. Moving his mouth to one side, he added in a muffled voice, "Put the candle back."

Detectives Williams and Smyth looked on in bewilderment. Raising blond eyebrows, Niles explained, "Young Frankenstein. One of *our* favorite movies." Turning to Tom, he lowered his eyelids to half-mast. "We got those candlesticks at Pottery Barn. How could they possibly reveal a secret room?"

Grinning and agreeing Niles had a good point, Tom joined Joe and Scarlet in their pushing and pulling of books.

The room now encasing too much silliness for him, Detective Smyth said, "In the event, the movies, Clue and Young Frankenstein don't lead us to our killer, we have specialists en route to search your house and grounds."

Niles and Joe, looking suitably sheepish, walked the detectives out, leaving James to join Rose, Scarlet, Joe, and Tom with their sleuthing.

Turning to face Tom, Rose asked, "Are you and Niles able to contact the woman who sold you this home?"

Tom bit his lower lip. "She left really suddenly, and Niles said she gave no forwarding address. All he knows is she moved to Amsterdam."

Rose sighed, "You and Niles are moving in with me until this madman is captured."

"Where are we moving?" Niles, returning to the library, enquired.

"Into my home, until it's safe to return to yours," Rose replied matter-of-factly.

Before Niles had a chance to reply, Rose looked to James, "And that goes for you too."

Smiling, James admitted, "I don't think I have any tunnels under my ultra-modern apartment."

Enjoying her moment of authority, Rose retorted, "That's beside the point. More the merrier and safety in numbers."

Clapping James on the shoulder, Tom pronounced, "It'll be like an extended grown-up sleepover. We'll have a blast."

Looking to Scarlet and receiving a nod and a smile, James said, "Thank you so much, Rose, I'd love to."

James addressed Niles and Tom, "I'd like to spend a bit more time here. Would you mind if I did a little searching of my own?"

Wide-eyed, Tom said, "If you're searching, we're searching."

Nodding, Niles said, "I recorded Smyth on my phone as he read that note. We need to dissect what Steele said and see if we can learn anything from it."

Smiling as the room's occupants looked at him admiringly, Niles added, "I'm done with this dude. Time to catch our mole."

56

The following morning, Niles, clearly exasperated, joined James, Tom, and Scarlet in his library. "How many times do I need to tell these guys?" he asked the room in general, "no, I don't have plans to the house. And no, I don't know how to find said plans." Running hands through his hair in frustration, he fell back into an oversized leather chair.

Scarlet, clasping a gold embossed red leather bound book, soothed, "I'm so sorry Niles. This is all my fault."

Niles pulled a face.

"It certainly is not." Sitting up straight he added, "It's my fault. You do know I spent less time pondering the purchase of this home than I spend on deciding what tie I'm wearing to work."

Mouth, barely open, Tom mumbled, "That's shocking when you consider his clothes never even match, let alone flow."

Casting Tom a look of mock indignation, Niles said, "Guys I think we've exhausted our efforts in this room. Let's try the great room."

"But Steele left the note in here," Tom argued as they all filed out the library.

Niles waved his arms in the air. "Clearly the guy has cojones enough to move from room to room."

Wasting no time upon entering the great room, James knelt to lift rugs and examine hardwood panels beneath them. Looking up, he asked Niles, "Can you play that recording one more time? I'm wondering if there's a reason he said Mole in Latin."

Niles reached into the pocket of his jeans. Walking out the door, he voiced over his shoulder, "I left my phone in the library. Be right back."

Less than a minute later, "Shit!" reverberated through the large house.

Running to find the owner of this exclamation, Tom, Scarlet and James found Niles standing by the library's fireplace, a note held in his shaking hand.

Not daring to say what they imagined it was, three friends stared and waited.

His breathing hard and sharp, Niles informed them, "It's from him. He was here. He was right here just now."

Scarlet and Tom, rooted to the spot, watched James as he called Detective Smyth. Hanging up, he reported, "He'll be here in ten minutes. Williams is on the grounds and will be right in."

Tom, now composed enough for speech, asked, "What does it say?"

Not needing to look at the note, Niles replied, "You were so close."

In a strangled whisper, Scarlet asked, "Does he want us to catch him?"

Niles shrugged his shoulders, dispiritedly.

"I would guess not," James said. "I imagine he thinks he's way smarter than us, which gives him the belief he's uncatchable."

Shuddering, Scarlet looked around the luxurious room. "Could he be watching us right now?"

James and Tom moved closer to her. Watching Niles as he studied the fireplace, Scarlet said, "I just remembered something else he said on the phone." All eyes on her, she explained, "He was on this rant about me not being grateful enough for the flowers. He wanted to know why I didn't take the ones he'd left in the shaft with me. I told him I didn't have time. He called me out, said he knew I'd had time. I don't know how, but I think he was able to see me."

Nerves on edge, Tom almost shouted, "Niles why are you staring into that fire? This isn't the Gryffindor common room. Sirius Black isn't going to appear in the flames."

At this, Niles turned and exited the room. Bewildered, the other three followed.

Ending in the enclosed patio, Niles picked up a remote and when Adele's beautiful voice filled the room, said, "The entrance has to be in the library. We were barely in the great room two minutes when Steele deposited that note. He may be able to hear every word we say or like Scar said, see us."

"You're right," James agreed. "How else would he know we'd left the room."

Looking at each other with a collective sense of panic, all jumped upon hearing,

"Mr. Remmy, Miss Oaks."

"Williams," Niles voiced, walking out towards the foyer.

Now on the phone, Detective Williams accepted the note from Niles with a nod of thanks.

When the detective walked away, still talking with, they guessed Smyth, James looked to Scarlet.

"Can you tell us anything more about that phone call?"

Exhaling, Scarlet began, "He knew I was lying. He said I had been told by my boyfriend the firefighters were on their way. Giving me enough time to grab those awful flowers."

Paling, James stared at Scarlet.

Saying what they were all thinking, Tom, voiced, "He had to have been right there."

Taking both her hands in his, James asked, "You said he lowered you down into the shaft."

Scarlet nodded. "Yes, then it came back twice before he cut the pulley rope thing."

Looking over to Niles, James suggested, "The tunnel must lead to that shaft."

Suddenly cold, Scarlet whispered, "He was there with me the whole time?"

Shaking his head, James replied, "Not necessarily, but I think the shaft and the tunnel may be connected."

Narrowing green eyes, Niles said, "It explains how he's managed to elude the police. He was never seen leaving these grounds because he never left."

57

After they'd all but told Detective Smyth what they'd eaten for breakfast that morning, James, Niles, Tom, and Scarlet decided to call it a day.

Relieved to be back in the comfort and safety of a beautiful Victorian home, they recounted the morning's events for Joe and Rose.

"So, they're going to check out the shaft?" Joe asked, pouring tea for the group.

"They were waiting for some specialists and the fire department when we left," Niles replied.

"And you checked every book on those shelves?" Rose asked, placing a large plate of finger sandwiches in the center of the table.

Scarlet groaned, "Yes and looked behind every painting."

Eyes trained on a large tree limb swaying in a strong afternoon wind, Tom mused, "He's let us know he knows we're close to finding him. Surely he'll move on at this point."

Gratefully accepting a cucumber sandwich, Niles said, "I think James' theory is right. Steele thinks he's invincible."

"The man's insane," Joe declared. "I feel sick imagining him being so close by. No way are you four going back into that house until he's caught."

Scarlet gently voiced, "Dad, you can't forbid Niles and Tom from going into their own home."

Smiling, Joe said, "You're right." Looking at Niles and Tom, he continued, "But please don't and if you do, don't take my daughter with you."

Laughing, Niles replied, "We figured we'd be fine. The four of us together and Williams joined by countless uniforms right on property."

"Sounds logical," Rose said after insisting Tom have a third egg and cress sandwich.

"What's scary," Tom said, waving triangular shaped bread in the air, "Is that this monster knows our home's layout better than we do."

"How can that be?" James asked, leaning his head back into the padded wicker chair.

Door chimes diverted attention from this impossible-seeming question. Joe followed an excited pig into the foyer.

Returning with Detective Smyth in tow, Joe offered the man refreshments. Politely declining, Smyth sat on the edge of his chair. "We found no tunnel leading off the shaft. It's eight feet by fourteen with a steel wall on all four sides."

The recipients of this information appeared to visibly deflate, and silence filled the room.

The first to compose himself, Joe asked, "What do we know about this man?"

Rubbing the underside of his fingers across a strong jaw line, Smyth said, "A split personality. He barely knew his Dad. The mother was abusive. Stewart ran away from home as a young teen before being bounced around a fair few foster homes. He was eventually adopted by a socialite couple who sent him to the right schools and colleges. All appeared well until they divorced and then it seems Stewart began having social interaction problems and the like. Three female college students filed restraining orders against him, and he was fired from two jobs for misconduct."

Marveling at how Smyth could list these facts off, akin to reading a shopping list, Scarlet asked, "Can I assume he's not done with me?"

Avoiding the question, Smyth replied, "Rest assured we'll catch him Ms. Oaks. We're getting very close now. Just don't go anywhere alone. I recommend you continue staying here with your father and grandmother."

At this, he stood, straightened his jacket, and gave the familiar parting words, "I'll be in touch."

Afternoon became evening while watching the movie, Young Frankenstein. Laughter turned into pure hysterics when both Gene Wilder and Teri Garr said, "Put the candle back."

Despite a long day and comic relief, sleep alluded Scarlet. Upon hearing a faint tap on her bedroom door, she was alert enough to say, "Come in."

To her surprise and amusement, three men gingerly walked across the very-likely-to-creak, wooden floor.

Smiling, Scarlet asked, "Can't sleep either?"

James pulled the velvet covered vanity stool closer to Scarlet's bed. "Remember how I wanted to hear the recording of the note one more time."

Scarlet nodded while simultaneously giggling at the sight of Tom, unashamedly getting under the covers next to her.

Niles, perched on the end of the bed, raised his eyes to heaven.

"These old houses are cold," Tom said by way of explanation.

Everyone comfortable, their attention returned to James as he posed the question, "Why the need to use Latin? Why not just say mole?"

Scarlet scrunched up her nose. "Just to be clever?"

"Perhaps," James replied. "Or maybe it's a cryptic clue."

"Have we examined every single masterpiece on that bookshelf?" Niles asked.

Scarlet shook her head. "We pulled each one out slightly to see if it opened a hidden door. But no, we didn't look closely at the books."

"In googling molus iracus," James shared, "we came across links to the Vatican City and how there's a tunnel leading from it to an ancient building in Rome." Running a forefinger across his phone a couple of times, James added, "Castel Sant' Angelo."

"It's beautiful," came the muffled voice of Tom, who'd slid down into the bed with only his nose and eyes visible above the silk bedspread. "It means castle of the holy angel."

Niles, seemingly about to say something to Tom, instead focused on Scarlet. "We think maybe this is Steele's way of letting us know he's found the tunnel."

Pushing himself up against the lilac satin headboard, Tom pronounced, "You never finished telling us what you'd remembered about the mole stuff."

Scarlet frowned in concentration. "He only mentioned mole at the very end. I think he called himself a mole person. He was kind of erratic, talking about Charlie and the Chocolate Factory and disobedient kids."

James shifted uneasily on his vanity stool. "We have a hunch, but it's a crazy one. We're heading over to Niles and Tom's place right now. You try and get some sleep, and we'll give you a full report in the morning."

Scowling at James, Scarlet asked, "Are you out of your mind?"

James looked apologetic. "I know it's two in the morning, but we have to eliminate this hunch and move on."

"I mean," Scarlet continued, her jaw clenched, "you really think you can bestow your speculation and then just trot off without me?"

"I told you," Tom delivered, before disappearing beneath the covers again.

"Scar," Niles reasoned, "your Dad will kill us if we take you back to that house, let alone in the middle of the night."

Looking at each man, in turn, Scarlet asked, "Who are you more worried about upsetting, Dad or me?"

James stammered something incoherent while Niles hung his head.

Swinging his legs out from under the bed covers, Tom proclaimed, "We make sure Joe and Rose never find out."

Ignoring the dubious looks from Niles, James, and even Scarlet, Tom continued, "No shoes until we reach the kitchen door. We put the car in neutral and coast down the driveway. Wear sweats, and if we're seen on our return, we'll say we went for an early run."

Nodding with eyes wide and a turned down mouth, James returned the vanity stool to its original position.

Staring at Tom, Niles said, "Kind of scary how effortlessly you can fabricate."

Rearranging his dark curls in Scarlet's full-length mirror, Tom retorted, "What some would label fabrication, others would call a creative mind."

"Whatever you want to call it, it's genius," Scarlet declared. "Now get out of here and let me get dressed."

"Let's all go down separately to minimize the chance of noise," James suggested.

"Perfect," Niles agreed. "We'll meet by the kitchen door in five minutes."

Ten minutes later, James' Lexus, with Scarlet behind the wheel and Tom by its side, eased silently down her grandmother's steep drive. James and Niles were positioned at the drive's end to ensure the car stopped before meeting the road.

"We're certifiable," Niles stated as they pulled into his driveway. "The fact there are four of us will do no good at all if he's got a gun."

"He did have a gun," Tom pointed out.

Receiving a look that could kill from Niles, Tom added, "We all know he had a gun. I'm just saying what we already know."

"Please tell me you left these lights on?" Scarlet asked, exiting the car.

Nodding, Niles replied, "We have at least six that come on automatically."

"We're going to be fine, guys," James said soothingly. "We're just going to look for a book about Ancient Rome or Roman ruins."

Opening his front door but feeling as if he were entering a house he'd never seen before, Niles said,

"I'll get some strong coffee going while you three get started."

Scarlet and James scanned the bookshelf on one side of the fireplace and Tom the other side.

"A Modest Proposal," Tom read aloud, holding a black leather book in front of him. "Jonathan Swift," he continued wistfully. "Didn't he write, Gulliver's Travels?"

James began to concur but was interrupted by Scarlet grabbing his arm with one hand and pointing with her other.

Three pairs of eyes stared at the bronze colored book as if were a ticking bomb. James finally pulled it from the shelf and carefully lifted the thick leather cover. With a collective gasp, they took in the deep square, cut into gold edged yellowing pages.

Tom, a hand held to his heart, exclaimed, "You have got to be kidding me!"

"Shall I press it?" James asked, referring to the small black button located in the center of the cut-out pages.

Shaking with nerves, Scarlet turned towards the library door. "Shouldn't we wait for Niles?"

Tom shook his head. "He'll be here any second. I say press it."

Taking Scarlet's hand, James eased her away from the fireplace and surrounding bookshelves. Waiting for Tom to do the same, he then firmly pressed the button.

Nothing happened. Almost owl-like, heads swiveled to take in the entire room. James was prevented from pressing it again by an ear-piercing crash.

"Niles!" Tom gasped, running from the room.

Seconds behind him, James and Scarlet found Tom in the kitchen standing inches from Niles. Pale and shaking, Niles appeared to be staring right through them. In his hands was a large wooden tray held at an angle unsuitable for carrying objects. On the floor lay shattered ceramic cups in a lake of dark coffee.

Seemingly rooted to the spot, Niles nudged his head in the direction of the pantry. Careful not to slip on the spilled liquid, James, Tom, and Scarlet walked towards the pantry's entrance.

There, beneath shelves holding large glass containers of oatmeal, Rice Krispies, sugar, and flour, was a narrow opening revealing steep wooden stairs.

The tray still clasped in his trembling hands, Niles stammered, "I was on my way to you guys when I heard this weird, creaking sound."

James gently eased the tray from Niles' grasp. Scarlet put her arm around his shoulders and Tom warily peeked into the mysterious opening.

"Where do you think it leads to?" he asked, still eyeing the puzzling space.

"How about you let us find that out?" came a deep voice from behind them.

James jumped, and Scarlet screamed. Tom almost lost his footing and fell down the stairs, while poor Niles remained incapable of movement.

"Dear God, Detective," Tom panted, stepping out of the pantry, "you almost gave us a heart attack."

"This is your home, why so jumpy?" Detective Smyth asked with a smirk. "Could it be because this is a crime scene and you shouldn't be here?"

Finding his voice and a little irritation to go along with it, Niles retorted, "You never said we couldn't be here. We're staying with Rose of our own cognition."

Looking directly at Niles, Smyth said, "May I make the request now then, Mr. Remmy? There is every reason to believe a serial killer is on your property. It is unsafe for you to be here until this man is caught."

Smyth walked up to the entrance of the pantry. "I presume this is a new discovery?"

"We found a hollowed-out book containing a button," James explained. "I think in pressing it, we inadvertently opened this door."

"How did you know we were here?" Scarlet asked, grabbing a towel to mop up the spilled coffee.

Looking up from the mysterious wooden stairs, Smyth replied, "Surveillance called me."

Scarlet bit her lower lip. "Would you mind not mentioning this to my dad and Gran?"

Smiling at Scarlet, the detective replied, "Never saw you here."

Pulling out his phone, he added, "On the condition, you leave us to it."

An hour later, watching the sunrise from an otherwise deserted China Beach, Tom asked, "Is it possible Steele had time to run from the pantry to the library while we were in the great room?"

Both hands wrapped around her coffee filled cardboard cup, Scarlet responded, "I don't think so. I still believe there's a secret room or tunnel leading from the library."

"Honestly," Niles said, "I don't think I can go back there. Seeing a floor suddenly open that I've stood on countless times seriously freaked me out."

Taking his sweatshirt jacket off and placing it around Scarlet's shivering shoulders, James said,

"I'm sorry guys, I shouldn't have suggested it."

Tom grinned. "Finding a button hidden in a book. So worth it."

Chuckling, Scarlet agreed.

"I can't feel my extremities," Niles pronounced. "How about we head to China Town for Dim Sum?"

Despite returning to Rose's house with calories gained versus lost, the four friends looked disheveled enough to have been on a run.

Later that day, still drowsy after a much-needed afternoon nap, Scarlet welcomed Detectives Smyth and Williams into her grandmother's home.

Tom and Joe abandoned the obstacle course they were constructing for Prudence in the sunroom. James and Rose left historical city maps on the ornate library desk. Niles, having just lost his assistant, Scarlet, washed sticky scone dough off his hands and walked into the living room.

Clearly not a good poker player, Smyth looked at Scarlet before stating, "We got a lucky break this morning."

Rose and Joe looked as intrigued as Scarlet, James, Tom, and Niles looked guilty.

Detective Williams said, "A hidden entrance in the pantry of Mr. Remmy and Mr. Blythe's home led us down to a small room."

Gasping, Rose reached over and held Scarlet's hand.

Sighing, Scarlet whispered, "Dad, Gran. We were there. We shouldn't have gone, but I had a hunch, and we did."

Smyth and Williams looked down at their notepads as Joe, wide-eyed, appeared at a loss for words.

"It was my hunch," James volunteered. "I was the one who suggested we go back there."

Preventing Joe from responding, Tom said, "I couldn't sleep until we figured out how that creep got into the library right under our noses."

"It was all my idea really," Niles declared. "I thought geez this is my house; I'm getting to the bottom of it."

Spotting a little grin forming on her grandmother's face, Scarlet squeezed Rose's hand, saying,

"Bottom line is these three were adamant about leaving me here safe and sound."

Finding his voice, Joe said, "But you weren't having any of it."

Scarlet gave her father a smile that had worked countless times as a child, and she sincerely hoped still did.

"What's that saying?" Rose asked brightly, "No harm, no foul."

Taking his cue, Smyth reported, "Initially, we thought we'd found a similar enclosure to the one at the base of the outdoor shaft."

Looking over to Detective Williams, Smyth added, "Thankfully my colleague had the foresight to check under the stairs."

Smiling at Niles, Detective Williams explained, "The lady who built your home was one creative individual. There was a button located under the third to last stair. When pressed, one of four steel walls lifted. A short tunnel led to your library."

Allowing for gasps and exclamations of wonder to pass, Williams continued, "The opening in the library is located under your desk."

Jaw dropping, Niles asked, "Was that the only tunnel? From the pantry to the library?"

Detective Williams looked pointedly at Detective Smyth.

"Are you ready for this?" Smyth asked his anxious audience.

Receiving solemn nods, Smyth said, "Six." Nodding at the looks of astonishment, Smyth explained, "Just one leads off from the exterior shaft into the pantry. From there, three tunnels lead to the great room, dining room, and library."

Shaking his head, Williams contributed, "We found two more tunnels leading from the enclosure beneath your desk in the library." Grimacing at Niles' look of horror, Williams concluded, "They lead to the cupboard under the second-floor stairs and your home office."

Niles, his freckles appearing to turn white asked, "How on earth did he find them? How did he know?"

Before Smyth or Williams had the chance to respond, Scarlet in a small voice said, "He made me change into banquet clothes in that cupboard. Why didn't he use the tunnel?"

Raising thick brows, Smyth replied, "He wasn't aware of its existence at that time."

Scooting to the edge of his chair, Joe asked, "Are you saying… how do you...?"

Smyth laughed. "I wondered when you were going to ask."

A barrage of excited chatter and questions followed. Smyth chose not to wait for Prudence to stop snorting. "Mr. Stewart Steele was apprehended at fourteen hundred hours today. It appears he'd been living in the tunnel leading from the shaft since New Year's Eve."

Looking directly at Scarlet, Williams reported, "In Steele's words, he wanted somewhere private for you to appreciate the flowers he'd given you. After locating the shaft, he stumbled across and subsequently obliterated, a small lever that opened the steel wall. He was hiding on the other side of that wall when you were rescued."

With an involuntary shudder, Scarlet said, "It's over. It's finally over."

58

Tom and Niles, a little groggy after the cocktails consumed in celebration, left early the following morning. James, with a business meeting scheduled, reluctantly, left soon after.

Scarlet was savoring peace and tranquility found when surrounded by her grandmother's leather bound masterpieces. This was halted, however, by the old-style ring of Rose's front door bell.

"Who on earth could that be?" Joe asked, looking up from his newspaper.

To Scarlet's surprise, Brian, the station manager followed Rose into the room.

Accepting the offer of a seat from Joe and a cup of coffee from Rose, Brian looked over to Scarlet. "I owe you an apology. You made a success of the top forty show, and now Candy has systematically run it into the ground."

Backing into an antique French throne chair, Scarlet stared at Brian, mindful to keep her mouth from dropping open.

Struggling to get his large finger out of the cup handle, Brian placed the delicate china on a side table. "I hope you can forgive my poor judgment and pick up where you left off with Scarlet's top forty."

Taking in the wide-eyed looks from her father and grandmother, Scarlet focused her attention back to the station manager. "I really appreciate the offer Brian, but I'd like to stay with Mending Men."

To Rose and Joe's credit, they stayed silent, although their shocked expressions replaced words quite sufficiently.

Brian squinted already heavy-lidded eyes. "But it's middle-aged men, talking sports."

Scarlet smiled. "Remember when I took over the top forty show from Crystal Clear?"

Nodding as he looked at Joe, Brian raised bushy black eyebrows, "Got to love the names these DJs choose!"

Joe returned Brian's incredulous look before Scarlet continued, "She never deviated from the top forty, for five years that's all she played. No requests, no giveaways. I wanted to take a concept and make it better, more varied, and more interesting."

Brian pulled a face. "Yeah, and I think I gave you a hard time about it."

Chuckling, Scarlet graciously said, "I don't remember that part."

Allowing Brian to accept a piece of coffee cake from Rose, Scarlet continued, "I've been giving Mending Men's format a lot of thought lately. I believe I can add some changes that will double our ratings."

Brian brushed cake crumbs from his pant leg to the rug beneath him. "I believe you'll do it." Looking over at Rose and Joe, he proclaimed, "This girl of yours. She's something, hey?"

Scarlet's father and grandmother offered their agreement before Brian stood. "You'll be getting a twenty percent pay raise, as of today."

Standing to shake his hand, Scarlet thanked him.

"My niece thinks very highly of you," Brian directed at Scarlet, as Joe opened the front door.

"The feeling's mutual," Scarlet called out, watching her boss struggle into his large, black land rover.

Back in the library, Rose picked up Brian's almost untouched cup of coffee. "Isn't he the one you call brainless Brian?"

Scarlet picked up the tea tray. "Yes, but I think he'll have to be renamed, bestie Brian since he's giving me a raise."

"What a way to start the New Year!" Rose said.

Scarlet suddenly felt a lump form in her throat. "What's wrong with me?" she exclaimed, tears beginning to flow down her cheeks.

"It's over. Steele's been caught, and I can go back to living a normal life. No more flowers, no more looking over my shoulder."

Rose gently took the tray from Scarlet's shaking hands and guided her to the couch. Sitting next to her, she wrapped a slender arm around her granddaughter's shoulders.

Moving to sit opposite them, Joe said, "And in due time, that will sink in and truly make you happy. But right now it's simply all too much. Remember, just two days ago you told us about your New Year's Eve ordeal."

Scarlet sniffed and nodded.

Joe continued, "Then you received the news from your Mom, about Trent and Lisa. Beautiful Brian, is he now? Shows up..."

Laughing, Scarlet interrupted, "Bestie Brian, Dad. You saw him; he could never be beautiful Brian."

Encouraged by the laughter, Joe went on to suggest, with an eyelift and tummy tuck he could perhaps be known as beautiful Brian.

59

Early the next day, Scarlet found Rose talking on her Downton Abbey style phone. Joe, with an occasional nod of his head, stood watching her.

Once observed, Scarlet was met with a smile from her father and a hand gesture towards the writing desk, from her grandmother.

Smiling her thanks for the indicated location of freshly baked banana and walnut bread, Scarlet sat in the window seat and listened.

"He's fine with that Marilyn, dear."

Watching Joe lift his shoulders, palms outstretched, Rose added, "He's just not sure it will do any good."

Giving Scarlet a warm smile, Rose continued into the phone, "No, he's absolutely willing to try, Marilyn. Joe's simply not spent much time with Lisa and wonders if she'll hear him out."

Playfully, scowling at her son, Rose agreed, "Yes, that is absolutely his fault."

Stifling a giggle, as Joe dramatically let his head fall forward, Scarlet called out, "Gran, I'm so sorry, Prudence just disgraced herself on your foyer floor."

Rose continued into the old-fashioned handset, "Yes, it was. She must have just now got up. I'll be sure to do that. Take care dear. Chat soon."

Placing the ear piece back in its cradle, Rose turned to her granddaughter. "That was naughty and clever and so appreciated." Placing her hand on her heart and breathing deeply, Rose added, "She'd love you to call her today."

Pulling a face, Joe said, "Mom, I'm so sorry. I should have talked to her. It's not right you having to play go-between."

Rose waved her hand dismissively. "I do it more for Marilyn than for you. She seems comfortable telling me how she feels and I'm okay with that."

"It's very good of you, Gran," Scarlet said.

Nodding, Joe said, "I'm going to grab the coffee pot. When I come back, please tell me what I've agreed to."

Chuckling as her son left the room, Rose turned to Scarlet. "I hope you don't mind, I told your Mom the good news."

"About the capture or my raise?" Scarlet enquired.

Rose placed her palms together. "I'd forgotten about the raise. This year's starting off very nicely."

Joe re-entered the library, coffee carafe in hand. "Did Marilyn actually say she expects me to talk with Lisa?"

Biting her bottom lip, Rose replied, "I'm afraid so."

Pacing up and down in front of the arched stone fireplace, Joe argued, "I've barely said two words to Lisa since Hayden was born."

Rose gave him a motherly smile. "I think Marilyn wants you to be more involved, shoulder some of the drama."

Sighing, Scarlet said, "I think Gran's right, Dad. I know Mom misses having you around to fix this sort of thing."

Joe shook his head. "I'm not sure I ever fixed much. If I had, Violet would have spent Christmas with family and Trent would talk to me."

Scarlet helped herself to coffee. "I think you fixed, or, at least, eased, burdens in Mom's mind. She tries so hard with Lisa and then it all crashes and burns despite her efforts."

Sinking into a soft, green leather chair, Joe put his head in his hands. "I did run away. For all intents and purposes, I did." Looking around the ornate study, he added, "Here in the comfort of this incredible home, I can refer to my grandsons as Rodney the rotten and Hayden the horrible. I choose to dismiss my son's attitude towards me as childish and unfounded. I justify Violet's absence as occurring long before I left, and then I live this free, peaceful life."

Rose leaned forward in her chair. "Do you call a highly stressful job, you're forced to stay in, peaceful?"

Placing a cup on the antique trunk next to her father's chair, Scarlet said, "Trent was in his twenties when you left, Dad. A grown man with a wife and child. We all know you did your very best and stayed as long as you could. Sometimes I wonder if Trent regrets marrying so young and secretly envies you."

Mouth turned down, Joe said, "With this latest development, that doesn't seem too unlikely, does it?"

Rubbing the fingers of her right hand across her lower lip, Rose reminisced, "Violet has always been a free spirit. I'll never forget that summer your job took you to Switzerland. I believe you were consulting on a new airport there."

Joe nodded in confirmation, and Rose elaborated, "Marilyn wanted to join you, so Herb and I took care of our grandchildren for a few weeks." Smiling at Scarlet, Rose explained, "We moved into your home in Aptos because Marilyn felt the less your routine was disrupted, the better."

Scarlet lifted her second piece of banana bread in the air. "Very good of you and Grandpa."

"It was such a pleasure," Rose said. "One of your grandfather's favorite duties was taking you three to and from school. It must have been around the fourth day of doing this, when he walked back into the house, red in the face from laughter. He confessed he'd laughed all the way home. Violet's teacher had requested a brief conference with him. Miss Fine was the teacher's name. She informed your grandfather, Violet's behavior was becoming more and more disruptive in class. Now keep in mind, Violet was seven years old. So, picture your six-foot grandpa sitting on one of those little chairs as Miss Fine, in a solemn manner, tells him about Violet's proclamations before each class activity. When it was time to draw and color, Violet would state, she and the other children were not in the right mood to produce good art. She suggested Miss Fine allow them to play outside first, then they would be more inspired to create. Counting, Miss Fine informed your Grandfather, followed recess. *How could children count,* Violet would ask out loud *when their heads were full of recent play time's imaginary castles and unicorns.* Your grandfather was trying so hard not to laugh at this point and would have almost managed it, but alas the reading, threw him over the edge. Miss Fine recounted Violet saying, she and many others in class could only read a book when leaning up against a big tree with a summer breeze gently blowing by. Certainly, not sitting in a plastic chair with harsh overhead lighting."

Scarlet almost choked on her coffee from laughter, and Joe shook his head, a wide grin spreading across his face.

"So, you see," Rose concluded, "Violet has always danced to her own beat. Who's to say where she is and what she's doing, is not the better way to live."

Looking from his mother to his daughter, Joe said, "Thank you both for making me feel better." Lost in thought for a moment, he asked, "Do you think Lisa will give me the time of day?"

Scarlet narrowed her eyes. "I'm not letting you do this alone. I'll come with you."

Joe crinkled his brow. "I confess I was hoping you would."

60

Relishing her newfound freedom, and wanting to share the news in person, Scarlet arranged to meet Niles and Tom in the Golden Gate Park. Concluding enough hugging to draw attention, they began their usual walk towards the Japanese Tea Gardens.

Unlike Joe and Rose, Scarlet's good friends chose not to practice composure when Scarlet informed them of her choice to stay with Mending Men.

"Are you crazy?" Tom asked dramatically. "You've been stalked and kidnapped and ... forced to wear ill-fitting clothes."

Giggling, Scarlet said, "Who's to say that couldn't have happened with the top forty show?"

Smiling, as a passing girl struggled to keep from being hogtied by her four dogs, Niles volunteered,

"Scar has a valid point there."

Managing to pull all his facial features into one central location, Tom reasoned, "But the whole sports thing and the sleazy guys with their disgusting dating advice?"

Rubbing Tom's shoulder, Scarlet said, "I can reel them in a little, but they are amusing. Why do people listen to the radio? To be entertained, right?"

Niles and Tom nodded, and Scarlet continued, "I believe there's an audience out there who want to hear great music and relate to or laugh at, other people's problems. Look at all these daytime television shows, where people lay out their train wreck of a life for all to see."

Three friends moved collectively to their right, allowing a family of cyclists' ease of passage.

"You're right," Niles agreed. "They're hugely popular, but I think they get paid to be on those shows."

Scarlet pulled a face. "I have no desire to emulate that kind of dysfunction. I certainly don't want Mending Men to be a circus. But if people like Barry bring a little comic relief, so be it. Primarily, I'd like to help these men if they're genuinely seeking advice. I want to steer away from the sports metaphors and give them a female perspective on their problems. In time, I'd like to add a men's health section with a visiting expert. Perhaps a legal section for men facing divorce with custody and alimony issues."

Coming to a halt, Tom declared, "Damn, Scarlet. That sounds really good."

When Tom started walking again, Niles enquired, "Do you think you'll lose your true sports guys, though?"

Scarlet frowned before asking, "What do you think about having a time allocated sports section, where my die-hards can still call in and talk about the Niners, giants, warriors, etc.?"

Niles lifted his chin. "Perfect. You'll just contain it, so it doesn't consume the whole show."

"Exactly," Scarlet said cheerily. "I'll study up on the results of the games, and then a certain caller can dissect the play, or inform other listeners of how it should have gone down."

Following a brief discussion about James, Scarlet had little to tell them, as they'd barely had any alone time since the New Year's Eve party, the conversation turned serious.

"Tomorrow?" Scarlet repeated with dismay.

"Yep," Tom confirmed, "got my shots yesterday."

Sensing a tension between Niles and Tom, Scarlet, in as happy a tone as she could muster, said, "Well, I'm sure you'll do your magic and be home in no time."

"That's the plan," Tom replied.

Niles gave a halfhearted smile. "His flight leaves early. SF to Miami and then from there to Port-au-Prince."

Hugging Tom as they walked, Scarlet confessed how much she'd miss him while making a mental note to check on Niles the following day.

Standing by their cars in the underground parking lot, Scarlet and Tom held each other and cried. Niles, all the while, informing them how ridiculous they were being.

Returning to Pacific Heights, Scarlet discovered her grandmother nonchalantly sweeping the steep front stairs and her father staring out of a third-floor window beneath a cone-shaped turret.

Reaching the top stair, Scarlet only needed to raise her eyebrows before Rose caved. "It's your first time out alone since, well since New Years. Your father and I were just ..."

"Being foolish," Joe finished for Rose, having arrived at the open front door.

Rose pulled a face. "We even calculated how long the drive was to and from the park. Then allowed for the walk and perhaps a stop at a café. Around the time we imagined you'd be back, Abbot and Costello couldn't help but start looking for your little car."

Giving them each a hug, Scarlet said, "You could have called me."

Kissing his daughter on the cheek, Joe responded, "Then you'd have known we were worried. The staring and sweeping made much more sense."

Scarlet laughed. "And so clandestine."

Over a chicken salad lunch, three generations discussed how the New Year would begin its future normalcy the following day. Joe would return to his job with the airport authority and Scarlet with Mending Men.

Upon declaring her need for an afternoon nap, Scarlet enquired, "Gran, do you mind if James and I steal some of your four o'clock tea today?"

Smiling fondly at her granddaughter, Rose replied, "I'd be delighted to share. Where would you like it?"

Scarlet raised her chin. "Seeing Dad up there today, reminded me it's been forever since I went up to the third floor. Would you be okay with me taking a tray to our old den?"

"I think that's an excellent idea," Rose replied. "Apologies for the dust you may encounter."

Clearing the plates from the dining room table, Joe tried to conceal a grin. "Remember the rules. If there's a boy in there, the door stays open."

Scarlet's eyes widened with indignation. "I had one boyfriend that summer and always kept the door open. It was Violet who closed and LOCKED it!"

Returning condiments to the fridge, Scarlet continued, "Oh sure, go ahead and laugh. Do you know what it was like having a sister who pushed the limits so far, she ruined any chance of freedom this teenager," Scarlet added while comically pointing to herself, "ever had."

Trying to curtail her laughing, Rose said, "To this day, I don't know how she found that old key." Looking to her son, Rose asked, "We never shared the story with Marilyn, did we?"

Joe shook his head. "Goodness no. You and Dad had offered to take the children for a good chunk of the summer vacation because Marilyn was feeling overwrought. The Den adventure may have thrown her over the edge."

Closing the dishwasher door and leaning against it, Scarlet reminisced, "Violet and I met these cute brothers at your company picnic, Dad. They were nice boys, and I saw Violet happily hanging with the red-haired brother one time. Then in the blink of an eye, he was replaced by at least four other boys. When I asked her where she met them, she looked at me as if I were a simpleton and said, *through the red-haired geek we met at Dad's picnic.* When I stared at her blankly, and no doubt more simpleton like, she said, *you didn't really think I was interested in him, did you? He was just my ticket to meet other, cooler boys."*

Determined to be sympathetic to Scarlet's remembered teenage pain, Rose and Joe refrained from additional laughter.

Leaving her father and grandmother to solve the mystery of how Violet found the key, Scarlet let all thoughts of teenage angst leave her body as she sank into her soft bed. Having left the lavender colored drapes open, she watched dark foreboding clouds float in from the bay, darkening the room as if someone was dimming the lights.

What felt to be minutes later, Scarlet was awoken by her cell phone.

"Hello," Scarlet mumbled groggily.

"OMG," came a young girl's voice.

Lifting her head from the pillow and blinking her eyes, Scarlet said,

"Who ...?"

"Unbelievable, Oaks," the girl's voice continued.

"Sylvia," Scarlet declared with a smile.

As if her identity had never been in question, her friend continued, "Friggin' unbelievable."

Scarlet swung her legs out of bed. "What's unbelievable?"

"Don't tell me you haven't seen the news or the front page of every single paper in the city, Oaks?"

Beginning to understand, Scarlet asked, "Stewart Steele?"

"Uh yeah," Sylvia said, "and you and Mending Men and Bay Radio and even me."

While Scarlet's, still foggy brain, processed this information, Sylvia chatted on about this and that, only catching Scarlet's attention again when she finished with, "You and me, tomorrow girl. According to the paper, there's an adventure every day at Bay Radio."

Finding this declaration a lot less appealing than her young friend, Scarlet told Sylvia how much she was looking forward to seeing her and hung up the phone.

Not too thrilled with her reflection in the mirror, Scarlet decided a shower was required before James' arrival.

An hour later, Scarlet observed James, wearing relaxed fit, faded jeans, paired with a blue and white striped rugby shirt, to look casually perfect.

Tray in hand, James followed Scarlet up two flights of stairs. Opening the arched wooden door, Scarlet inhaled familiar musty scent and was instantly fourteen years old again.

Not having this powerful memory trigger, James' focus was carefully placing the tray on a little oval table, while admiring the slanted ceiling and round windows. "This is an incredible room. Since meeting you, I've been in the most beautiful homes with endless character and history. The Tudor Niles and Tom share is off the charts, but this house is right up there too."

Chuckling as she poured their tea, Scarlet conceded, "Niles and Tom's home is amazing, but … this house survived the earthquake and fire of nineteen hundred and six."

James gave an appreciative whistle. "When was it built?"

Handing him a mug of tea, Scarlet replied, "Eighteen eighty-nine. It's been in the family for five generations."

James looked around the room again. "Wow!"

Gesturing for him to sit on the cream colored, linen sofa, Scarlet joined him and continued, "The story is, my great, great, great, great, grandfather came from somewhere on the east coast in a covered wagon."

Eyes wide, James enquired, "For the Gold Rush?"

"Yes. He was one of the original forty-niners," Scarlet replied proudly.

As James shook his head, smiling, Scarlet said, "Now, back to your first childhood memory. What happened after the tattoo incident?"

James put his cup down and stretched his long legs in front of him. "Ironically, my first childhood memory was also my last memory of Dad. He left that day and never came back. Every time I asked my sisters where he was, they'd tell me he'd gone to get more cigarettes."

Eyes softening, Scarlet touched James' knee. "I'm so sorry. I shouldn't be asking you about this stuff."

Placing his own hand gently atop Scarlet's, James responded, "It actually feels good to talk about it. My family members are experts at suppressing difficult or uncomfortable emotions." Looking down at their hands, he continued, "Mom remarried about a year later. He was an army officer, and we moved around a lot. My sisters and I got used to continually being the new kid in class."

Nodding, as she swallowed her last gulp of tea, Scarlet asked, "And they're still together and happy?"

A sadness clouded James' eyes. "Mom died of ovarian cancer two years ago."

Scarlet placed her empty mug on the threadbare rug and slid towards James. Instinctively, he wrapped his arms around her narrow waist and laid his head on her shoulder. Scarlet gently stroked his blond wavy hair. When the embrace loosened, his eyes found hers.

Neither one daring to blink, James placed his hand on the right side of Scarlet's face. Breathing heavily, as his thumb traced the outline of her full lips, Scarlet jumped when a voice called out,

"Do you two need some hot water?"

Giggling as James, with a mischievous grin, mumbled, "Cold may be needed more." Scarlet called out towards the stairs,

"We're good, thanks, Gran."

"The kettle just boiled, if you do run out," the voice returned. "Your dad and I are off to the grocery store. Prudence is taking a nap."

Standing up and coming to the top of the third-floor stairs, Scarlet, still unable to see her grandmother, said, "Good to know, thanks, Gran. See you in a bit."

Pouring James and herself a second cup of tea, Scarlet enquired, "What about your sisters, tell me about them."

James leaned back into the well-stuffed sofa. "Charlotte lives this side of Napa. She and her husband, Greg, own a small winery. They have two beautiful little girls. My other sister, Amy, lives in Oregon. She's in a, well, I guess the correct term, is facility."

Scarlet's brow furrowed. "She's not well?"

James sighed. "Amy always felt things deeply. Apparently too deeply to function peacefully in this world. Don, our stepfather, was routinely posted in Central American countries. We were in Guatemala for the last two years of their civil war. Then a year in Venezuela. I don't believe she saw fighting or violence as such, but human suffering did feel a little too close, too real. We finally returned to the states in my final year of high school. Amy would have been twenty-one. But even at that age and here in San Fran, I remember how incidents, seemingly minor to us, would upset her terribly. For example, a young child being shouted at by a parent in a store. Amy would panic about how that child was treated in their home. If the Dad was prepared to shout so horribly in front of strangers, how would he treat the little boy behind closed doors? There was a news article in the paper about a high school student committing suicide after relentless bullying. Amy cried for days on end, then she began walking the perimeter of the high school, hoping to prevent another young person from such a fate."

James took a much-needed gulp from his refilled teacup.

"Your sister is a sensitive, caring, wonderful woman," Scarlet responded with feeling.

James smiled. "I agree, but sadly that level of sensitivity cripples her emotionally. She's unable to cope with life's harsh realities."

Scarlet tentatively enquired, "So this place in Oregon, is it, I mean … do they take good care of her?"

Tilting his handsome head slightly to one side, James replied, "Most definitely. It's a big country estate on acres of lush land. They don't dose Amy up on countless pills, but more shield her from the outside world."

Eyebrows raised, Scarlet enquired, "Forgive me for asking, but does it cost a small fortune?"

James frowned. "It's funny you mention it because something odd occurred just days ago. Amy has been at Cedar Acres for three years now. Charlotte and I divide the cost between us and yes, it's a pretty penny. On New Year's Eve, I received a very large check in the mail. It was from Cedar Acres and the letter attached stated they were returning my thirty-six months of payments. They also informed me Amy's costs are now being taken care of by an anonymous donor. This mystery person will continue to do so, for as long as he or she is able. My sister, Charlotte, also received a check and the same letter."

Scarlet sat a little straighter. "That *is* odd. Your stepdad perhaps? Or your Dad, sorry, I should have asked, is your real dad still alive?"

"As far as I know," James replied. "Charlotte's almost certain she spotted him at Mom's funeral. As kids, Don would never allow us to talk about our Dad. The years went by, and we got used to not mentioning him and then in time, we stopped thinking about him. I and I believe my sisters too, have no animosity, just indifference. As to your question of who this mysterious donor is, Charlotte and I are quite perplexed."

Pulling her feet up onto the couch, Scarlet eagerly enquired, "You don't believe it's Don or your Dad?"

James placed a hand on one of Scarlet's socked feet. "If it were Dad, I think he'd want us to know. Want us to be aware he cared and was, for all intents and purposes, back. Don remarried within a year of Mom's death. A lady from Russia, three years younger than me. The last we heard, he was none too happy about her large family eating into his retirement account. Him parting with thousands a month for Amy, no I just can't see it."

Blushing as James started massaging her foot, Scarlet said, "I hope you don't think I strategically placed my foot here with this in mind." Giggling, she added, "That being said, please don't stop."

James laughed. "The thought never occurred to me. But, if in five minutes, it's replaced by the other foot, I may need to rethink your motives."

Exhaling as James expertly manipulated the ball of her foot, Scarlet asked, "So no wealthy grandparents or long-lost uncles?"

Gently squeezing her toes, James replied, "Nope, none that I know of."

"No other relatives at all?" Scarlet pushed.

James grinned patiently. "We do have some aunts and uncles, but none with the means to help and plus they wouldn't require anonymity. We have a step brother too, but we haven't seen him for a decade at least."

"Oh, what's the story there?"

Working her foot with both hands now, James said, "More oddness I'm afraid. For the longest time, we didn't even know of Ian's existence. Then, out of the blue, a teenage Ian appears on our doorstep. Apparently, he'd been living with Don's ex-wife. The tension between him and his Dad was palpable. Ian was only with us about two months before Don shipped him off to boarding school. Never saw him again, not even during the holidays. A few months before Mom died, my sisters and I asked her to tell us more about him. All she would say is he'd done something unforgivable. As I mentioned, my family routinely avoid talking about anything difficult."

Hearing Prudence squeal from two floors below, Scarlet said, "Gran and Dad probably just got back."

James glanced at his watch.

"I should get going. This has been," he added lifting a pink woolen covered foot to his mouth and gently kissing it, "so wonderful."

Closing her eyes, unable to move, Scarlet with a lazy grin echoed, "Wonderful."

Relieving Rose of her grocery filled bag, James thanked her for the delicious tea and professed his joy at discovering the third floor of her beautiful home.

Placing a slim hand on his arm, Rose suggested, "How about I give you a full informative tour next time you're over?"

With thankful acceptance of the offer, James turned to shake Joe's hand, then followed Scarlet through the side kitchen door.

"I'm going to stay here for a few more days," Scarlet informed him. "Just until I'm settled back at work. When I move back to my own place, I'd like to cook you something. What kind of food do you like?"

Watching as more and more white teeth appeared in his mouth, Scarlet realized she was becoming addicted to his smile.

"Anything and everything," James replied. "But how many days are we talking?"

Returning his smile, Scarlet replied, "Didn't Gran just ask you to come back for a tour? You don't want to keep her waiting."

Still grinning, James said, "That would be terribly rude."

Scarlet stated formally, "Tomorrow then."

"Would you allow me the pleasure of driving you to work after the tour?" James enquired.

Scarlet playfully lifted her chin. "I would."

Placing a soft kiss on her cheek, James turned towards his car.

Trying, but failing, to remove the massive grin from her face, Scarlet floated back into the kitchen.

Finding Joe and Rose, both standing in the kitchen with their noses in a newspaper, Scarlet put the all but forgotten, groceries away.

"Are we all famous?" she asked.

Joe, eyes still glued to the black and white print, said, "We're certainly getting our fifteen minutes."

"Oh, I like this," Rose exclaimed brightly.

Head in the fridge, rearranging bottles of juice to make way for Greek yogurt, Scarlet gave the tub a gentle shove, then turned back to face her grandmother.

"I'm in my early seventies," Rose, patting her curls, informed her son and granddaughter.

Scarlet smiled. "No one would ever believe you're in your mid-eighties, even if the paper had got it right."

Thumbing through a third of the newspaper, Joe, amid crinkling noises, turned it towards Scarlet.

"That's a good photo of you, my love," he said, revealing a large black and white headshot.

Scarlet observed the familiar portrait. "It's from the Bay Radio website."

Reading about her life and seemingly everyone's she'd ever met, Scarlet concluded the hastily typed summary could have been worse.

61

Marveling, how it was possible for one small pig to make so much noise, Scarlet left her bedroom a little earlier in the morning than usual, to find the source of the commotion.

Lottie, Rose's housekeeper, was standing at the open front door, repeating to a man in a crumpled gray shirt, that no one entered the home without an appointment.

Rose was in the kitchen, voicing into one of her more modern phones, that yes, her house had survived two earthquakes and one fire. Shrugging her shoulders, as Scarlet gave her a quizzical look, Rose successfully terminated the conversation with, "That would be fine, we'll see you then."

Replacing the phone on its cradle, Rose explained, "That was a lady named Eleanor. She's a freelance writer for Homes with a History magazine." A hand placed on either side of her head, Rose divulged, "They want to write an article on this old place."

Helping herself from the pot of freshly brewed coffee, Scarlet enquired, "You're okay with that, Gran?"

Running a hand along the marble-topped kitchen island, Rose responded, "Oh yes dear, I think it'll be fun. I told Eleanor I've modernized the kitchen and bathrooms a fair bit, but otherwise, it's pretty much as it was. They're coming next week to take photos."

Lottie, looking exasperated, entered the kitchen, exclaiming, "Finally!"

Taking in Scarlet's look of bemusement, Lottie explained, "Three television crews in what...?" Looking at the oven clock, Lottie calculated, "twenty minutes. Everyone wanting the same thing, an interview with Miss Oaks inside this home."

Scarlet shook her head. "I guess after that lengthy newspaper article, we shouldn't be too surprised. I am sorry, Lottie. What did you tell them?"

Assuring Scarlet she didn't mind and accepting the offer of coffee, Lottie replied, "The first bunch, channel seven, I think it was, got here just as your father was leaving for work. He gave them an email address and instructed them to request an interview in writing. I did the same thing for the other two, but your dad was better at sending them on their way than I proved to be."

"Not true," Scarlet declared. "I heard you being quite bossy with that last guy."

Lottie raised brows above wide-set hazel eyes. "These young hot shots, give them a camera and they think it's a free pass to wherever they want to go."

Thirty minutes later, Scarlet, accessing Bluetooth through her steering wheel, listened to message after message during the drive to Niles' home. The calls were from friends and colleagues wanting to hear more details than the newspaper had provided.

Scarlet pulled up to the large Tudor mansion, just as, fortuitously, a news crew van pulled away.

Spotting Niles, watering catmint by his front door, Scarlet, with her nose wrinkled, gestured towards the van descending the hill. "Sorry about them."

Dismissing the apology with a wave of his hand, Niles replied, "Tom would have enjoyed it. I sent him copies of the newspaper articles."

Their friendship strong enough to get right to the point, Scarlet asked, "You're not okay with this latest assignment, are you?"

Ushering her inside and then taking an immediate left into the great room, Niles fell back into one of his leather couches. "There's unrest in Haiti, but then there has been in most of the countries Tom works in. I'm just having trouble with my usual mindset of nothing bad will happen. Tragedy strikes other people; all the people I care about will be all right." Niles shrugged. "Maybe it's just my age. I'm finally mature enough to realize how precious and fragile life is."

Scarlet sat perched on the edge of the recliner closest to Niles. "Maybe it's the fact Stewart Steele was in this house. It's my fault the darker side of life feels closer to home. Excuse the pun!"

Niles forced a smile. "None of what happened was your fault. Plus, me being more aware, more appreciative, those are good things."

Catching Scarlet's look of skepticism, Niles added, "Besides, Tom was driving me crazy. Do you know what came in the mail today?"

Not expecting an answer, Niles continued, "Citizenship applications for our gardener's entire family. He decided Mario needed help with the process. Now I have twenty blank application forms on my desk and where's, Tom? Like I have the time to help them fill out those things."

"I'll help you," Scarlet soothed.

The corners of Niles' mouth turned down. "You'll be too busy, hanging with James."

Scarlet narrowed her eyes. "Do you really believe that to be true?"

Pushing his lips over to one side, Niles replied, "No. I'm just feeling sorry for myself. Tom keeps my pessimistic side at bay. When he's not around, I'm just a boring, grouchy, workaholic."

Scarlet shook her head. "Nonsense. You and I will spend loads of time together. Didn't I hear Tom instruct you to take care of me?"

Niles released a dramatic sigh. "You have James to do that now."

Laughing as she got up and sat next to him, Scarlet placed a hand on her friend's cheek. "He could never do it as well as you."

"Does he know your love for Oreos?" Niles enquired.

Removing her hand, Scarlet said gravely, "Nope."

A smile forming, Niles asked, "Does he know your very favorite thing to do in the city?"

"No clue," Scarlet confirmed.

Close to laughter, Niles went on, "Does he know how much you hate horror movies?"

Scarlet sucked in a deep breath. "Probably out buying one, as we speak."

Niles' spirits now lifted, the two friends continued with the nonsensical, until it was time for Scarlet to leave and Niles to sell some stocks.

Armed with a healthy mixture of nerves and excitement, Scarlet prepared for her first day back at Bay Radio. She'd only taken a few extra days off after the incident, but it felt much longer.

Having changed clothes three times, strangely something she'd never done pre-James, Scarlet settled on black leggings with calf-length brown boots and a loose-fitting cream crochet sweater.

Due to his genuine interest in her grandmother's Victorian home, Scarlet enjoyed ample viewpoints of James as he walked from room to room. Happily, led and educated by Rose, he'd turn his head and smile as Scarlet, a few feet back, followed the tour.

James held his own, as he and Rose discussed San Francisco's rich history.

Later in the sunroom, Scarlet relaxed by his side, breathing in the scent of him. One minute the aroma was reminiscent of an ocean wave, the next, it transported her back to a walk she and Prudence took through the Redwood Shores Bay Trail.

"Gran, how about you show James some old photos of this place next time?" Scarlet suggested.

Smiling, as James volunteered his enthusiasm for the idea, Rose said, "My grandfather had an old Kodak box camera. It would come preloaded with one hundred exposures. He'd finish that roll in no time. As soon as the factory sent back the photos and more film, he'd be at it again. My dad bought him an Aeroscope movie camera, but it never thrilled him the way that old box camera did."

Half an hour later, James, expertly maneuvering his way through city traffic, confessed how enamored he was with Scarlet's grandmother.

Unashamedly telling him he had great taste in women, Scarlet turned the conversation to her earlier visit with Niles.

When she'd concluded her recount of the meeting, James said gravely, "I'm the newcomer and so grateful to him for allowing me to meet you. Not that you need permission from me, but of course I'm happy to include him in everything we do."

Seeing Scarlet's dark eyebrows raise, he clarified, "Well, maybe not everything. On that note," he added blushing, "would you be interested in meeting my sister?"

"Of course," Scarlet replied without hesitation. "Which one?"

Smiling as he pulled into Bay Radio's parking lot, James said, "Charlotte, the one in Napa."

Scarlet reached for her purse, "I'd love to."

"Wonderful. They're launching a new wine with a tasting party. Charlotte would like us to stay for the weekend."

Walking up to the double glass doors of Bay Radio, James announced, "I'll be back at midnight to pick you up."

With a soft but lingering kiss on her cheek, James turned and with long, athletic strides, returned to his Lexus.

"Oaks!" Sylvia shouted from the top of the stairs, "I've got loads to tell you."

Easily settling back into their routine, Sylvia poured hot chocolate, while Scarlet checked levels, opened sports related websites on the computer and adjusted her mic.

Moving, now cherry red, hair to one side of her neck, Sylvia said, "I've met a guy, and he's my new bae."

"Bae?" Scarlet asked, with a slight scowl.

"Before anyone else," Sylvia said dismissively. "We met at Dolores Park. He liked my dog, and no one likes my dog, not even me."

"What's wrong with your dog?"

Sylvia curled her lip. "She's super standoffish. Totally disinterested in everything and everybody."

Chuckling, Scarlet asked, "What breed is she?"

"Tibetan Mastiff. I think Mom thought she'd be all Zen and stuff."

The chuckle morphed into a laugh as Scarlet pictured a dog, legs crossed and front paws placed on knees.

Despite the dog, visualized in her head, now wearing a saffron robe, Scarlet managed to say, "But this guy liked her?"

With an exaggerated turned down mouth, Sylvia said, "Yeah, he walked right up to us and started talking to Pema."

"Pema's your dog?" Scarlet asked.

"Yeah," Sylvia replied, waving her chap stick in the air. "Pema didn't like him any more than she likes anyone else. But I did. He has, *let it be* tattooed on the inside of his right forearm."

"Nice," Scarlet said before taking a sip of her hot chocolate.

Chin down and eyebrows up, Sylvia enquired, "Are you still seeing your very polite gentleman?"

"I am," Scarlet said with a playful scowl. "He was raised by a military man. You know how they are about manners. Besides, I like it."

"I'm just teasing you," Sylvia confessed. "Like I said before, polite or not, he's super sexy."

Scarlet pressed her lips together. "I think it's going to be a good year for you and me."

Nodding, eyes wide, Sylvia rushed, "Uncle Brian's going to call you tomorrow to arrange a meeting. Everyone and I mean everyone, wants to advertise on Mending Men."

Continuing, before Scarlet had a chance to talk, Sylvia said, "I think you need to demand a huge pay raise. He'll give it to you, I'm sure of it. The whole city's talking about this killer and how it all started when he called into your show."

Wincing with the reminder, Scarlet informed her friend, "Brian already gave me a twenty percent hike."

"Not enough!" Sylvia, draining her cup, voiced authoritatively.

Scarlet chuckled. "How about this, instead. I've got some ideas on ways to improve and expand the show, but I can't do it alone."

Clearly interested, Sylvia listened, empty cup in hand.

"How would you feel about being my assistant?"

"Me?" Sylvia asked incredulously.

"Yes, you. We'll need to do lots of research for the segments I'm planning, and from what you've heard about advertisers, that'll involve remotes all over the city."

Staring, open mouthed, for a few moments, Sylvia enquired, "Do you mean it, Oaks? I don't have to be a P.I.B. forever?"

Scarlet smiled warmly at her young friend. "You were never going to be a P.I.B. forever, and yes, I mean it."

Smiling broadly, Sylvia asked, "You're telling me, the only haggling you'll do with my tight-fisted uncle, is on my behalf?"

Scarlet smiled mischievously. "Well, I may suggest we're on the air a little earlier. This midnight finish is going to mess with our love lives."

Sylvia reached for more hot chocolate. "I like the way you think, Oaks."

Nodding, Scarlet elaborated, "We won't use that argument as a bargaining tool, however. We'll say, and it's the truth, more men will be listening on the commute home. It's mainly kooks who call after ten pm."

Amid Sylvia's enthusiastic agreement, Scarlet said, "One minute and I'm live."

Sylvia, practically skipping out of the studio, left Scarlet alone to say, "Thank you for calling Mending Men, this is Scarlet, how can I help?"

Ready for the next Scarlet Oaks adventure?
SCARLET OAKS AND THE EXPOSED PHOTOGRAPHER
Find it at MichaelaJames.net

Michaela James lives in northern Nevada with her husband and two sons. Originally from England, she drinks lots of tea, enjoys playing tennis and watching great films.

For the last decade, Michaela has been an on-air personality for a local radio station, 93.7 BOB FM in Reno, Nevada. She also does voice work, including the narration of twenty audio books available at Audible.com.

Books by Michaela James
Love Me Or Die
The Healing Room

Scarlet Oaks series
Scarlet Oaks and the Serial Caller
Scarlet Oaks and the Exposed Photographer

Lambsy La La Stories, a series for young children
Who is Lambsy La La?
Rosie The Perfectly Dressed Penguin
Sebastian The Superfast Seahorse
Ella The Daring Dog
Monty The Magic Mouse
Henry The Helpful Hedgehog

El Arbol Magico (co-authored with Carrol Guzman)

Follow Michaela James
MichaelaJames.net
MichaelaJames.co.uk
facebook.com/AuthorMichaelaJames
twitter.com/AuthorMichaela

Printed in Great Britain
by Amazon